MW01128863

BOSTON BOLTS HOCKEY:
TROUBLE

BRITTANÉE NICOLE

This is a work of fiction. Names, characters, places, and incidents either are the product of the author's imagination or are used fictitiously. Any resemblance to actual persons, living or dead, events, or locales is entirely coincidental.

Trouble © 2024 by Brittanée Nicole

All rights reserved. No part of this book may be reproduced or used in any manner without written permission to the copyright owner except for the use of quotations in a book review.

First Edition October 2024

Model Cover Design by Sara of Sara's PA Services

Trope Cover Design by Sara of Sara's PA Services

Illustrated Cover Design by Cindy Ras of cindyras_draws

Formatting by Sara of Sara PA's Services

Editing by Beth at VB Edits

Dedication

Sometimes the most empowering thing you can do is...
Let them.
Let them judge.
Let them misunderstand.
Let them be wrong.
The only thing you can control is how you live your life, not how others
view it.

Anonymous

Foreword

Dear Reader,

With each book I write, the world I build becomes more connected and complex. While Trouble can absolutely be read as a standalone, you will see some character overlap and since I know many of you enjoy the easter eggs I hide and prefer to read in order, here is a suggested reading order as it comes to this world:

Revenge Era: Ford Hall and Lake Paige
Mother Faker: Beckett Langfield and Olivia Maxwell
Pucking Revenge: Brooks Langfield and Sara Case
A Major Puck Up: Gavin Langfield and Millie Hall
Hockey Boy: Aiden Langfield and Lennox Kennedy

And since this book contains not two but *three* love interests, you will find the firefighters that Declan works with in A Very Merry Margarita Mix Up and can meet more of the characters from Bristol in the Bristol Bay Series.

I hope you enjoy this world as much as I enjoy writing it.

XO,

Brittanée

Content Warning

THIS BOOK CONTAINS ADULT THEMES THAT MAY BE TRIGGERING FOR SOME INCLUDING DISCUSSIONS OF SEXAUL ASSAULT/ABUSE, ON PAGE VIOLENCE AND PSYCHOLOGICAL ABUSE.

Our Story

Lose You To Love Me
Bad Liar
Same Old Love
Fun
Naturally
The Heart Wants What it Wants
Come & Get It
Fetish
Who Says
Good For You
Hands To Myself
Look At Her Now
Baila Conmigo
Round & Round
Back To You
Vulnerable
A Year Without Rain
Love On
Magic

Performed by: Selena Gomez

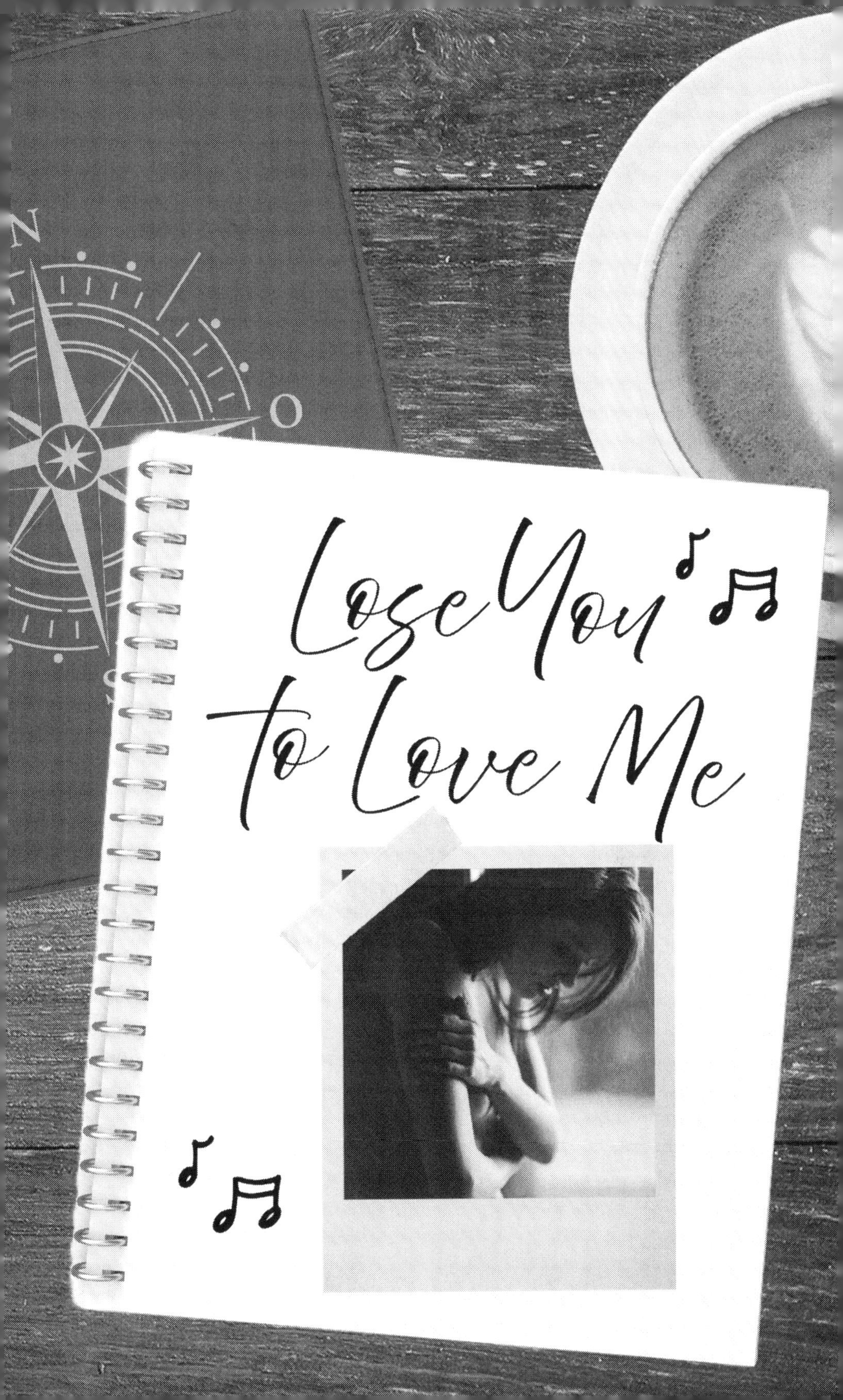
N
O
Lose You to Love Me

CHAPTER 1

Melina

> Worst Human Alive: You really can't do anything right, can you? The first track was due to the label last week. Now you've up and disappeared for the holidays? What the hell are you thinking?

> Worst Human Alive: You can't really believe you can hide from me.

> Worst Human Alive: You're breaking your mother's heart. It's CHRISTMAS.

> Worst Human Alive: Please, baby. I'm sorry. I promise things will be different. But you need to tell me where you are. Come home. We can fix this.

I STARE at the new round of texts in an almost steady stream that hasn't stopped over the last two weeks. They've been coming in at regular intervals since I ran out of my apartment, leaving behind everything I owned, foolishly believing that I could just break up with him, and this would all end.

> Worst Human Alive: I'm your fucking agent.
> I'm legally entitled to know where you are.

A scoff full of rage bursts from me. The heat in my lungs makes me want to roar at the insanity of this situation.

He is my agent. He's also the person I loved for nearly a decade. My brother's best friend. The man my mother considers a second son. And my abuser.

God, why did it take me so long to figure out who he really was?

The tougher question is: If he hadn't done what he did the last time I saw him, would I have ever left? I don't want to even think about my answer. It'll only show how truly weak I am.

Melina Rodriguez: International Pop star. Three-time Grammy winner. Coward.

I power my phone off so that I don't have to be taunted by his constant musings tonight. Should I block him? Probably. But that will only make him more desperate. More dangerous. He's already more unhinged now that he doesn't know where I am.

I shake my head. "I shouldn't be here." Pushing my chair back from the counter, I clasp my hands in front of me and prepare to tell my best friend that I'm going to find a hotel in a city where no one will find me and lie low there.

"Of course you should be," Lake replies with a flip of her hand. As if she can magically change my mind.

Normally, she could. Lake gets her way with just about everyone. To the rest of the world, she's Lake Paige, the greatest female musician of our time. People are too enamored with my beautiful bestie to tell her no.

But to me, she's the girl who stayed up late after our shifts at the Bluebird to write music together. Who dreamed about sold-out bar shows while we ate ice cream on our worn brown couch in our tiny apartment in Nashville. The woman who made me her opening act when she headlined her first tour, where we sang to sold-out stadiums.

She's my ride or die. My soul sister. And yet, even now, I'm lying by omission. Because I haven't told her just how bad things are with the man I'll continue to call the Worst Human Alive.

Swamped by a wave of guilt, I open my mouth to tell her the truth. But I snap it shut again at the sound of creaking floorboards in the other room. We spin at the tap of footsteps at the entry to the kitchen and find her husband Ford Hall—who also happens to own the label I owe music too—holding their five-month-old son Nash against his chest. "You ready to go?"

"Yes," Lake says.

At the same time, I mutter, "I think I should leave."

My best friend turns her blue eyes on me, mouth turned down in a frown. "You aren't leaving."

Her husband shifts a squirming Nash in his arms and studies me. I've known Ford for years. I signed with him before Lake did, in fact. In a strange turn of events, when she did sign with Hall records, she went on to date his son Paul. Oddly, the father and son could not be any more different. While Paul was an unmotivated man child who didn't believe in fidelity—though he's come around recently, I've heard—Ford Hall is one of the most devoted people I've ever met. That extends to his clients and his wife.

Which is good. If not, I'd have to hurt him. Even if he is like a dad to me. Kind of weird considering my best friend now calls him Daddy, but it's fun to tease her about it.

"I agree with Lake."

I snort, even as my heart sinks. "Of course you do."

Lake bites her famous red lips and smiles.

Shit. It's pointless to argue with the two of them. Ford will do whatever makes Lake happy. Happy wife, happy life and all that jazz.

"It's the holidays. You should be with family for the holidays," Lake starts, stepping up beside me and squeezing my hand.

Just the thought of my family has me taking a step back.

Ford is on my other side now, gently cupping my elbow. "And you're family. Right Nash?" he adds in that higher tone people only reserve for babies.

"Of course he's right," Lake replies in a similar tone as she pulls me into a hug.

"Oh my gosh, you're squeezing me so tight I can hardly breathe," I whine, though I snuggle into my best friend's chest.

With a chuckle, Ford presses a kiss to my forehead, then steps back. "We'll always be here for you, Mel. I know you don't want to stay here—"

I shake my head. While Lake doesn't know the extent of what's going on, I couldn't hide it as easily from Ford. Since the Worst Human Alive is my agent, I had to inform Ford that I'd fired him, so he found out pretty quickly that things had gone south. If only the jerk would listen to a word I said and accept that he's been relieved of his position.

"I appreciate you reaching out to your friend. Staying at his house will be just fine."

"I really wish you'd just stay here." Lake pushes her bottom lip out in a dramatic pout.

"Nah, I heard my roomie is a hottie," I say with a shake of my head, trying to lighten the mood. I've always been the wiseass of the two of us. The tease. The girl with a smile. I refuse to allow my ex to steal that too.

Ford snorts. "Who told you that?"

I point to Lake, who merely shrugs. "What? Obviously, I like older men."

Her husband, who is the definition of a silver fox, pulls her into his side and nuzzles her neck. "You're going to pay for calling me old, Red."

She winks at me, then turns a haughty eye at him, mindlessly grasping Nash's wrist gently when he tugs on her hair. "Who said I was talking about you? I was referring to our fire chief, broody Declan Everhart."

Just the sound of his name stirs a sensation to life inside me. Maybe it's the promise of a new beginning, or the thrill of letting go. All I know is that, in this moment, I decide I'm not going to live in the past anymore.

"Okay, family," I tease. "Tell me more about this chief."

CHAPTER 2

Declan

> Beckett: We'll be there within the hour. Is everything set for Melina to stay with you?

I NOD at the text and flip my phone over on the bar top.

"You realize the person who's texting you can't see your nod, right?" my best friend Cade says from the stool beside me.

With a grunt, I study the menu.

"Why bother looking?" he teases. "We both know you'll order the same thing you always get."

My phone vibrates, so I turn it over. Naturally, it's my pain-in-the-ass brother-in-law again.

> Beckett: She's coming to the event with Ford and Lake, but her stuff will be in the car. Can you have one of the guys grab it and bring it into the station?

With another nod, I set it face down again.

"Seriously, Dec, they can't see your response. Why the fuck can't you just reply when people text?"

I arch a brow, amused that this bothers him so much.

I'm saved from having to respond when Hailey, the bartender who also happens to own the place, turns her attention to us, ready for our order. "Hey, Chief, how are you?"

"Good." I glance around the bar, taking in the crowd. The place is filling up quickly. This is my favorite hangout, but only after the summer rush. I can't stand crowds, and not many people other than the locals are interested in sitting around a small-town bar on the water in the middle of winter.

Clearly, I underestimated how many people the event today would bring into our town.

Stupid mistake.

"You have enough staff working to handle the crowd? Fire code—"

Cade places his hand on my arm, the contact stealing the words from my mouth. "What he means is that we're here if you need help. Not that he'll shut you down if you're unprepared."

I pull away, ignoring the niggle of guilt that hits me when he grimaces. "I was getting to that. Do you want me to call Shawn?"

Shawn works for me at the station, and he's engaged to Hailey's twin sister. A twin she didn't know existed until not too long ago. But that's a story for a different day.

Hailey's responding smile is bright. She likes the crowd just as much as I hate it. I suppose that makes sense. Where I see bar fights, people being trampled, and fire hazards, she sees dollar signs.

"We're all set. Amelia is working tonight, and Nate and Jack will be here to help after the festivities." She turns her warm gaze on Cade, her voice going sugary sweet. "We really appreciate the Bolts doing this. It's going to help the town out more than you know."

Cade leans his forearms on the bar and slides his barstool in closer. The wood dragging against the floor is almost as grating as his shameless flirting. With a bat of his eyes, he smiles, allowing the dimple on his left cheek to pop. The one on his right cheek only appears when he's laughing. When he's truly happy. It's never aimed in my direction, because I don't make people laugh.

"The guys are happy to do it." He winks. "Got them out of practice this weekend." Cade is the goalie coach for the Boston Bolts hockey team. The hockey team that is, unfortunately, owned by my pain-in-the-ass brother-in-law's family. I honestly can't get away from the man. Beckett seems to be everywhere I turn.

Scowling, I nudge him with my elbow. "Can we order? I need to get downtown shortly."

Hailey straightens. "Of course, Chief. The regular?"

Cade snorts. "Bacon cheeseburger, medium rare, with onion rings *and* fries."

Hailey's eyes dance, and a smile creeps up her face. "Exactly. You forgot the Coke, though."

Tutting, Cade shakes his head. "If I ate like that, I'd be huge." He lifts the hem of his shirt, flashing his washboard abs, then offers her another flirtatious wink. "I'll take the salmon, steamed, with brown rice and broccoli. And a vodka tonic on the rocks with a lime."

With a nod, she disappears to put in our order.

My phone buzzes again. I turn it over, this time pulling it closer to read it.

> Liv: You know Beckett hates it when you don't respond. He's been going on about it for the last fifteen minutes. Please promise me you'll try to have a personality when we get there. And text him back!

I get a perverse joy out of knowing I've annoyed Beckett Langfield. He's like a forty-year-old toddler. A billionaire who's always meddling in the lives of the people around him. He married my sister in Vegas two years ago, and while I assumed he'd taken advantage of her and I thought I'd have to kill him, my sister is happy, and he's turned out to be an amazing stepfather to my nieces and nephew. That's all that matters to me.

> Me: Tell him to park at the station. Tell Ford to do the same. I'll have the guys put Melina's stuff in my office. Of course I'm set for her to stay. I told you she could. Excited to see you and the kids.

"Holy fuck, he texts," Cade deadpans.

I glare at him as I put the phone down again.

"You never reply to my texts," he prods, ducking down and turning my way.

Jaw clenched, I tamp down my annoyance. "I don't like to text. You know this."

"So who's the chick who finally got you to reply?" he asks, waggling his brows. He's such an idiot.

"Liv."

He grins. "The hot younger sister."

"I'm not even going to growl at you for that one. I'll just relay your comment to Beckett."

"Don't you fucking dare. The man is a psychopath when it comes to his wife, and I like my job."

"I'd be more concerned about your eyes than your job. If he thinks you looked at his wife in any sort of way, he'll gouge them out."

Cade barks out a laugh. "It's hilarious how Liv married a man just like her brother."

My jaw locks.

He nudges his elbow against mine. "Come on, if you won't reply to my texts, the least you can do is smile at my jokes."

"Why are you so obsessed with how I communicate?"

He leans back, hand to his chin, assessing me. "It'd make it easier for us to catch up. We barely talk unless I come to Bristol."

Hailey sets our drinks in front of us, and Cade immediately sips his, staring at her ass as she walks away.

"Don't," I warn.

He doesn't take his eyes off her. "Why?"

"She proposes to everyone who sits down at the bar."

He pulls back like I've just waved a fire stick in his face. Exactly as I expected. The man is as averse to relationships as I am to texting. "The fuck?"

"Something to do with needing to be married to inherit the bar. I don't know," I grumble. "Point is, you don't do relationships, and she doesn't do one-night stands."

Cade smirks, and I can't help but zero in on that right side, waiting for the damn dimple to pop. It doesn't.

"I don't do one-night stands either," he says. "Not unless it's against the wall, or in the shower. Hm, have you tried out the fire pole?"

With a roll of my eyes, I push away the visions that hit me.

"I much prefer the use of a bed," he admits. "Not that I'd turn down a woman on her knees."

Before I can tamp it down, an image flashes through my mind. Cade gripping a ponytail, our hands linked as he guides her onto my cock.

When I don't reply, he gives my shoulder a squeeze. I flinch beneath his touch. I *always* flinch at his touch.

"None of that shit with Melina in the house this weekend," I grit out, silently berating myself for my reaction to a simple touch. "She's going through enough. She doesn't need you bringing home a random woman and keeping the rest of us up all night."

Cade pulls back, scowling. "Give me some fucking credit. I'm not twenty anymore."

"*I* know that, but I wasn't sure you were aware."

He rests his elbows on the bar and drops his head. "Fuck, you're in a mood tonight."

Internally, I wince. I don't want to be an ass to my best friend. We rarely see each other, and he's one of the very few people I like.

I roll my neck and angle my barstool so I'm facing him. "Sorry, I'm stressed and not handling it well. These damn fires keep popping up everywhere, and with the event tonight, there will be even more people to worry about. On top of that, Melina Fucking Rodriguez will be staying at my place for who knows how long. I haven't lived with a woman since Liv was in high school. And I'm pretty sure eighteen-year-old Liv was nothing like a world-famous pop star."

Cade's eyes widen. "I think that's the most words you've ever strung together at once."

Huffing, I turn back to facing the bar. I don't know why I try. Everything is a joke to this guy. Nothing is serious. He'd say I'm too serious, but becoming chief because the guy before me died in a fire makes it hard not to take fire safety seriously.

With a laugh, Cade pulls on my arm.

I go rigid as he squeezes, completely unaware of the effect he has on me.

"I'm teasing," he says, lowering his voice. "I know you've got a lot on your plate. And I promise I'll help keep Mel safe."

"*Not* in your bed," I growl, my neck heating.

He laughs like I'm joking. "She's twenty-eight years old, Chief. She can make that decision for herself. Besides, she's a pop star. If anyone's going to be calling the shots, it's her."

"She's got a stalker," I remind him. "That's why she's staying with me rather than with her best friend. She wants to spend the holidays with Lake and her family. Instead, she gets to put up with the town's fire chief as her babysitter. Don't complicate it."

Cade sighs. "You're always ruining my fun."

Fun? I don't even know what that means anymore. It's been years since I've even considered having fun. Honestly, the last time Cade and I had fun...

No, I shake my head to rid myself of the memory. Thankfully, Hailey appears, snagging my attention as she sets our food in front of us. I'm not thinking of that night ever again.

CHAPTER 3

Melina

A CUTER TOWN in America does not exist. The streets are decked out in red, white, and blue—a patriotic tribute with the perfect amount of charm. Antique streetlamps decorated with holly light up the winter evening. Townspeople sporting Charles Dickens–style dresses stroll the cobblestone in front of the fire station, singing Christmas carols.

Don't even get me started on the firefighters standing outside the firehouse, suspenders holding up black pants that no doubt hide beautifully thick thighs. And holy arm porn. Muscles upon muscles strain under white T-shirts with a simple BFD printed on the sleeve.

Yes, a girl could get used to a town like Bristol. It seems like the perfect place to start over. And maybe, just maybe, I'll find my voice again here. Find my music.

I grip Lake's arm as I suck in an exaggerated breath. "Holy shit, who are those hotties?"

Lake is laughing at me as two of the most beautiful men I've ever seen walk toward us, their swagger making my girlie bits flutter. Hmm... Instantly, I'm running through ways I can get one of them to play with me.

The dark-haired man tilts closer to the other guy—the one wearing a backward blue Bolts hat. *Hello, new kink unlocked.* In response, hat guy grips his friend's forearm and throws his head back and laughs.

That simple touch ignites a small fire in my belly. "Can you imagine being lucky enough to have boyfriends who were boyfriends? Talk about hot."

Lake's next comment throws a whole batch of kindling on my fire. "That's your new roommate, the fire chief, Declan Everhart."

Ford leans across her and whispers, "And that's his best friend, Cade Fitzgerald, goalie coach of the Boston Bolts."

"Damn, you weren't kidding when you said the chief was sexy." I fan my face. "Hello, hotties," I mumble under my breath. "My name is Mel, and I'll be your sexy catnip for the night."

"Hate to break it to you, Mel," Lake replies, her lips barely moving, "but the chief doesn't seem like that kind of guy." As the duo gets close, she breaks into a bright smile. "Chief, Coach," she says. "It's so good to see you both."

As happens when people see my best friend, both men blink like cartoon characters.

The grumpier one swallows audibly and nods. "Lake, Ford, good to see you."

When he turns to me, his gaze is like the snick of a lighter against my skin. It burns, the way I instantly and irrationally want this man. He's not pretty. Not even a little. But the ruggedness is what draws me in. His chin is covered in a layer of scruff that looks like an afterthought. Like some days, he shaves and others, he's too busy to worry about it. If I had to guess, it's been a few since he bothered. It's grown wild. Like it would burn between my thighs.

I'd relish every second.

While his jawline is hard and his cheekbones defined, his eyes hold a warmth I'm not expecting. They're the color of milk chocolate, and they ooze empathy.

The moment that emotion registers, the fire that's started to rage in my core is extinguished. This man is looking at me with pity. Like I'm an obligation. A woman he has to watch out for—because my stupid past is coming back to bite me in the ass.

As if his friend can sense the shift in my mood, he grins. "You must be Mel." A flirtatious wink and a dimple pop round out the boyish charm that has me instantly forgetting why I was sad. "I'm Cade Fitzgerald, but everyone calls me Fitz."

"The hockey coach," I say with pizzazz in my tone.

He waggles his brows, making his ball cap shift slightly. "You been stalking me?"

Huffing, the chief nudges him in the side. "Maybe don't mention stalkers," he grumbles so quietly he probably thinks no one but his friend can hear him.

What he doesn't know is that I grew up with a grandmother who constantly corrected my behavior in Portuguese, but she'd do it under her breath, so I have exceptionally good hearing.

"Bossman! Look, I found Uncle Dec," a child shouts nearby. The ear-piercing noise is accompanied by a bundle of energy running straight for the chief. "Uncle Dec!"

Without missing a beat, Declan holds his arms out and lifts the boy into the air. Then he pulls him against his chest for a hearty hug. "You found me, Finn."

I don't know much about kids, but if I had to guess, this one is about seven or eight, with wild brown hair and a big, blue puffy jacket.

"Holy shit, he smiles," Fitz says, his eyes going wide as he watches Declan and the little boy.

With a grimace at his friend, Declan gently sets the kid on his feet.

Finn taps his left foot and peers over his shoulder at the family walking up behind him. Beckett Langfield is part of the pack. I've met him several times, since he's Ford's best friend, but even if I hadn't, I would have recognized him. He's routinely seen in magazines and on television, since his family owns pretty much all of Boston sports. Beside him is his wife, Liv, and a parade of children.

The oldest of the four girls is almost as tall as her mother. Another is smaller than Finn. Maybe five? And in the double stroller Beckett is pushing are two babies. Twins, if memory serves.

"Bossman, Fitz owes me a thousand dollars."

"Watch your language in front of the kids," he says to the hockey coach, scowling. Then he lowers his focus to the kid. "Swear jar is only for the family, Huck. You can't go collecting money from every person you meet."

Finn—Huck? I'm thoroughly confused about what the kid's name is—twists his lips in thought and then sighs. "Fine. But if he does it again, I'm telling Uncle Gav to take it out of his salary."

"What is happening here?" I mutter, leaning into Lake.

Her smile is warm. "Uncle Gav is Gavin Langfield, the head coach of the Bolts and Fitz's boss."

Fitz grins at me. "Guilty." Then he kneels in front of the kid. "Sorry, Finn. I'll watch my words."

"The twins say that only people who are intellectually lacking use bad words."

I glance over at the babies in the stroller. "Those twins said that?"

Liv giggles. "No. He's referring to my friend's twins. They're ten."

"Bossman calls them the Shining Twins because they're wicked smart," Finn tells me, his chin tipped up with pride.

"Something like that," Beckett mutters, holding out his hand to Declan. "Thanks for helping us out. I gave Mel's stuff to one of your guys. They said they'd put it up in your office."

With the reminder of my situation, my giddy mood evaporates. I just want to focus on the hot firefighters and the hot coach who keeps eyeing me like he's going to have lots of fun making me forget tonight.

And you know what? I think I'll let him. I can worry tomorrow.

CHAPTER 4

Cade

"NEED anything from your luggage before the event starts? I'm happy to bring you up to Dec's office to grab it." I can't help but drink in the beautiful woman in front of me. She's far too pretty to be wearing the frown that tugs at her lips every time Declan speaks. The man is about as subtle as an elephant walking through a mouse's birthday party, stomping around and making a mess of things.

I love the guy, but sometimes I'd like to smack him around a bit and force him to lighten up.

She shakes her head and hits me with a genuine smile. "I'm good. Thanks. Though I would love a tour of the fire station at some point." She eyes my best friend, her gaze sweeping across the wide planes of his chest before she fixes her focus on me again.

"I can make that happen. Dec will probably have to stay here late, so when the event is over, you and I can swing back in and pick up your stuff. I'll show you around then."

Declan merely shakes his head at me. He thinks I'm hitting on his new roommate, and he's not wrong. She's fucking stunning, with long dark hair flowing past her shoulders like the soft waves of the bay at the end of the street and green eyes full of a playfulness I'm eager to bring out. But more than that, I'm drawn to the nervousness that buzzes beneath the surface. The way she bites her lip when she thinks we're not looking makes me want to lean in and sink my teeth into it too. Ease her worries. I could give her a few orgasms, help her relax so she can focus on the beauty of this town rather than what's clearly worrying her.

Declan mentioned a stalker, but is that a serious issue? I just assumed all pop stars had stalkers. It's par for the course, isn't it? Though the way she's acting is very *un*-par for the course.

"You gonna take her down the pole too, Fitz?" Daniel Hall asks with a smack on my shoulder.

"Smart-ass," I mutter to our star right winger, though there's no hiding my smile.

Beckett glares at me, but fortunately, his kid has already run into the station and is chattering with some of the guys on shift in the bay.

"Now that's an offer I wouldn't turn down," Mel whispers.

Fuck. I can practically feel the caress of her breathy voice against my cheek.

With a wink, I press my teeth into my bottom lip. Yeah, I'm going to make this woman forget all her problems tonight.

"Everyone else here?" I ask Daniel, craning my neck and searching for the rest of my guys. Beckett rounded up a good chunk of players from both the baseball and hockey teams so that he could help raise money for Declan's department. As much as Dec complains about his brother-in-law, he's gotta be grateful that the man cares so deeply.

Daniel points to Brooks, Aiden, and Gavin Langfield—Beckett's brothers—who are standing with their significant others and laughing as one of our other wingers, Camden Snow, gestures wildly. "The rookies are in Jorgenson's car, and Parker should be here shortly with his wife. He's riding with Cortney Miller."

I nod. "Good. Let's all meet up at Thames after. You staying at your dad's tonight or driving back to Boston?"

His dad is Ford Hall, the lucky bastard who married Lake.

Daniel grins. "Heading back to Boston. Although..." He eyes Mel, who is currently talking to Lake. "If she were staying at my dad's, I could make an exception."

An irrational flare of possessiveness hits me as he gives her a once-over. I have to flex my fingers to keep from grabbing her hip and pulling her toward me.

She's younger than me—as well as much closer in age to Daniel, who is only twenty-four—and I don't do possessive, so the sensation baffles me.

Declan steps closer, and the scent of him—clean, masculine soap mixed with the hint of fire—infiltrates my senses. "I gotta go. I'll see you after." He nods at me, then at Daniel.

Before he can disappear, I grab his shoulder and lean in close. "I'll bring Mel down to the bar after so you don't have to worry about rushing. Meet us there when you're done?"

Declan glances at my hand on his shoulder, his brows furrowed, and the smallest hint of dread works its way through me, so I release him. Shit. He's weird about being touched.

His expression clears, and he nods. "Sure. I'll see you there."

I give him a playful smile. "I'd say text me when you're on your way, but I know you won't, so..."

He huffs, his expression darkening. "You're never going to stop with that, are you?"

Without waiting for me to respond, he disappears into the crowd.

When I turn back, Daniel is watching me with a curious frown. "What?"

"You two ever...?" His eyes widen, but he doesn't finish the question.

I have to laugh. My extracurricular activities are no secret. His aren't either. Hell, the guys on the team call him Playboy. It's common knowledge that I bring men or women back to my hotel room after games to unwind. Sometimes both. But Declan? Yeah, no. He hasn't known how to have fun since college. And he's definitely not comfortable with a man's touch, let alone sex with a man.

"Nah. Just friends." Family, really. Our friendship is the most meaningful and longest lasting connection I've ever had. And likely ever will. With a playful grin to hide the bitterness I sometimes feel when I think of him as only a friend, I add, "The man can't even bother to text me back."

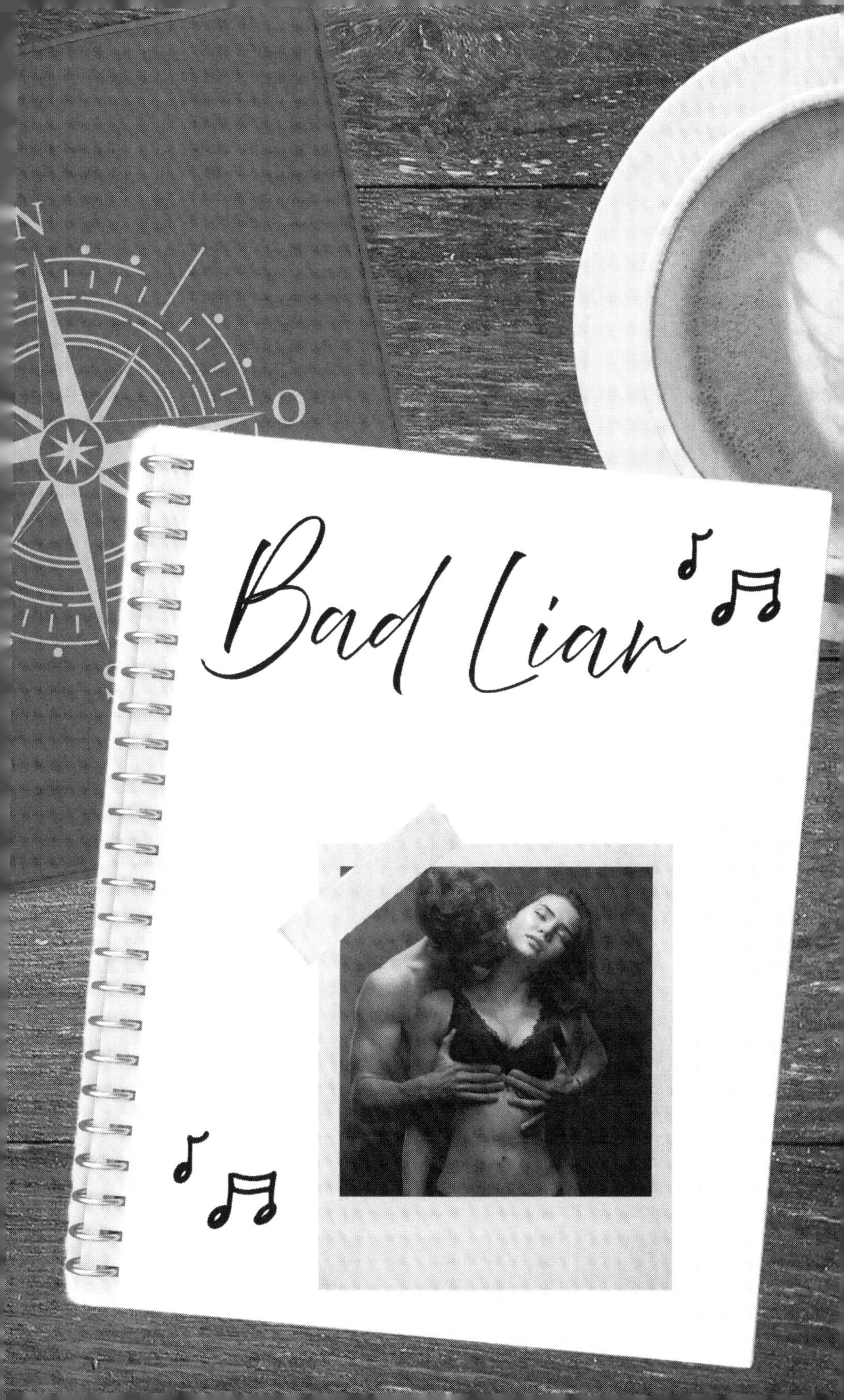

Bad Liar
N
O
S

CHAPTER 5

Declan

"DID you see how many reporters were here?" Shawn asks as we finish tidying up the station. The event raised an insane amount of money. Thank fuck. Already, the constant heartburn that plagues me has eased up a bit. Multiple massive fires over the last year have wiped out just about all of our resources, and we've been running on fumes. If the loss of our chief in a fire weren't heartbreaking enough, add to it the dent it put in the number of applications we've received. People are scared, and I can't blame them. Then, to make matters worse, even if we had applicants, we haven't had the money to hire any. We need recruits. Volunteers aren't going to cut it any longer. Our town is over thirty miles wide, and the buildings downtown date back to the Civil War. Grandfathered electrical, lead paint, and empty warehouses make fires not only more likely but also much more likely to spread when they get going.

We need properly trained people and updated equipment.

After tonight, I'll rest a little easier. Not only did Beckett's event bring in hundreds of thousands of dollars, but Shawn was right about the media coverage being huge. With any luck, we'll receive more donations once our charming town is featured on the news.

"Not your scene?" I joke.

Shawn laughs as he leans against the fire engine. "Even less so yours."

He isn't wrong. Interacting with anyone, let alone the media, all but makes me break out in hives. But Shawn was an All-Star pitcher for LA for years until his career ended after a car crash, so it's hard to wrap my head around how little he likes the media.

"You coming to Thames?" I ask, flipping off the overhead lights in the bay.

He shakes his head. "Jules needs help getting ready for the morning rush. It'll be a madhouse with so many visitors in town."

His girlfriend owns a bakery and makes the most incredible donuts. I should tell Melina about them. Or ask Shawn to set some aside. Shit. I should have thought of that beforehand. If I get called out tonight, there won't be much for her to eat in the morning. I grip the back of my neck to ease the tension there. Dammit. Maybe I should head to the grocery store now and stock up.

I blow out a breath, willing my anxiety to abate. "Think you could set aside a few tonight? I can send one of the rookies over to pick them up in the morning."

Shawn claps me on the back, his smile easy. "You got it."

Once he leaves and the place is quiet, I head out into the crisp winter night. Most of downtown is walkable, and the bar parking lot is likely a zoo, so I make my way on foot.

Due to our location near the water, we rarely get snow, but the scent of cold lingers in the air, signaling that we could get a dusting.

I dig my hands into my pockets, hunch my shoulders to protect myself from the cold, and nod to people as I pass. Most know who I am, and the faces are familiar to me since I've lived here my entire life, but I'm a man of few words, and people tire of trying to make conversation with a wall.

Most of the storefronts are dark this late. Only the bars on Hope Street create a buzz of noise. As soon as the harbor comes into view with the bar lit up against the dark water, I pick up my pace.

It's as if my body knows everyone inside is having fun. Everyone is laughing. Cade and Melina are laughing. And I'm missing it.

As I step inside, the music and loud chatter drown out all my thoughts. I search the bar for Cade, his hockey players, or my firefighters, but it's Melina who catches my attention. She's by the bar, surrounded by a group of men, her tongue poking out from one side of her mouth as she studies something with great effort.

She flicks what appears to be a quarter, and the crowd around her cheers. She squeals in delight, and her cheeks lift. I'm halfway to her when a set of hands circles her waist and lifts her up into the air. I'm about to reach for the guy, push him off, when I realize it's Cade. He's shed his Bolts sweatshirt, and now he's in nothing but a black T-shirt, jeans, and his signature backward Bolts hat.

Melina, who's now dangling over his shoulder, her legs flailing, smacks his ass repeatedly. "Put me down!"

"No can do, rock star," he yells with a slap to her ass. He spins in a circle, practically walking right into my chest.

I put my hands up to keep him from crashing into me.

His grin widens. "Dec," he yells, clearly already buzzed. It's not surprising. Cade is a fun guy, and he's charming as fuck. This is his MO. I'm not even a little surprised that he's got an international pop star in his arms after knowing her for only a few hours.

Melina peers around one side of him, still upside down, and grins at me. "Hi, Chief."

Maybe it's the way she says *Chief* or the slight flirtation to her tone. Maybe it's her position, draped over Cade's shoulder. Or maybe it's how Cade is gripping her thighs and wearing a big smile. Regardless, I can't help the way my lips twitch. "I see you're going to be trouble."

She pushes out her lower lip in a mock pout, but before she can reply, Cade walks away.

"Come on," he calls over his shoulder. "The guys have a table by the fireplace."

I follow him through the crowd, not at all surprised by the way it parts as we go. Melina peeks up at me and winks, then pinches Cade's ass. He swats her again, and I cough out a laugh. Like he's surprised by the sound, Cade eyes me over his shoulder, though he keeps moving.

He stops in front of an oversized booth where Brooks Langfield and his fiancée Sara sit on one side, and Aiden and his wife Lennox sit on the other. As soon as Lennox spots us, she's scooting over and patting the vinyl cushion. "Put her here."

In one quick move, Cade drags her down his body, then spins her as he drops into the seat. As he settles, she's sitting on his lap, his hand splayed across her stomach.

"You think you raised enough money?" Brooks asks as I drag a chair from a nearby table and situate it at the end of the booth. Brooks is the Bolts' goalie and so very unlike his oldest brother, Beckett. He's always smiling and chatty.

"If we didn't, I'm sure your brother will cover it," Cade answers for me, his thumb stroking along the skin just above Melina's waistband. Every time his finger moves up, her shirt shifts.

"The surprise performance by Mel and Lake didn't hurt. The holiday music was genius," Lennox says.

A blush creeps up Melina's chest at the mention of her name. She turns away from Lennox and into her own shoulder, her head on Cade's chest, and her green eyes catch mine.

With her lip caught between her teeth, she gives me a soft smile.

I shift in my chair, uncomfortable with her intense focus on me. I like watching her, even when she's sitting on his lap. Maybe because she's on his lap. But I don't like being watched.

"This town is awesome," Aiden says from his spot in the corner of the booth. He's got his arm around Lennox's shoulder. "I'm glad we had time to come out here before our game."

"Boston tomorrow, then Philly, right?" Lennox asks, nuzzling into his neck. "I can never remember where he'll be on any given week," she says to Melina. "Unlike this lucky bitch"—she points a pink-painted nail at Sara, who, like my sister did for so long, travels with the team as their head of PR—"I don't get to travel with my husband."

Aiden presses a kiss to her forehead. "You can travel with me anytime. But I get it. You don't want to be a trophy wife, no matter how much I beg."

Lennox shrugs her shoulders in an exaggerated manner, her pink hair fanning across her neck. "I would make an excellent trophy."

"That's what I'm telling ya," Aiden crows as the rest of the group laughs.

"What's your favorite city?" Melina asks Cade.

There I go, back to watching the two of them together.

He drops his head back against the bench seat, studying the ceiling.

"Hmm," he says, dragging the sound out. "I love renting a motorcycle in Vegas and disappearing into the mountains. And hiking before sunrise in Denver is unreal. Don't even get me started on the surfing in La Jolla."

Sara pushes forward, resting her forearms on the table. "You've done all those things? How?"

Cade grins. "While you two are off screwing around before away games," he says, pointing to his goalie, "I spend time exploring each city."

Brooks has the decency to blush, but Sara just shrugs. "We like public sex, so sue us."

I practically choke on my own spit at that flippant admission. I cough and gasp for air. When I can breathe again, I find Cade watching me in amusement.

"I like exploring," he says, his tone a little dark and full of hidden meaning. When he turns back to the group, his voice is casual again. "I used to go alone, but then Daniel discovered my routine, and now he joins me."

"Wait," Aiden says, leaning around Lennox. "You and Daniel hang out before games *without* me?"

With a groan, Cade roughs a hand down his face. "Fuck. I should have kept my mouth shut."

Melina shakes with laughter on top of him.

"You think this is funny?" he asks, tickling her sides. "This idiot is going to be following me around singing songs he makes up about every city we're in now."

Aiden shrugs, a lazy grin on his face. "Guilty."

The group falls into a fit of laughter.

I watch on, here but not really part of their banter. This is how I exist. At the station, the guys all talk around me, half the time probably forgetting I'm even there. Which is good. I don't want them to censor themselves around the boss. I like being in their presence, even though I rarely have anything to add.

Normally, when I speak, the mood grows serious. My tone often suggests action, not fun, I suppose.

Cade whispers in Melina's ear, and her cheeks turn a lovely shade of pink again. Fuck, would I love to see whether that color spreads to other parts of her body when she's aroused the way she is right now.

How could any woman not be aroused around Cade? He oozes sex. I know exactly what they'll be doing when we get back to my house.

I'm annoyed at the idea, but I'm more annoyed with myself.

Because it shouldn't be hot.

I shouldn't like the idea of his hands on her when I want my hands on her. But fuck, I'm half hard just watching her sit on his lap.

My perverse thoughts are interrupted by the flash of a camera. Without hesitating, I'm on my feet, immediately blocking Melina.

"What the fuck?" I growl at the man holding a camera and trying to shift around me for another shot. Guy's got balls, I'll give him that. I'm about to squeeze the life out of them, though.

To one side of me, Brooks puts up a hand, blocking the man's attempt.

"I'll say it again," I grit out. "What the fuck?"

Fingers reach for my belt and tug. "It's okay," Melina says. She leans forward and gives the man a small smile. "We're trying to have dinner. Ask next time, and I'll be happy to let you take a picture."

My jaw hardens, and my chest tightens. Fuck. She's used to this kind of intrusion. Is this how her life always is? She's been on for hours, singing for our town, taking pictures and signing autographs with Lake, answering the press's many questions. After all that, she's trying to relax with people she trusts. Can't they just let her have a drink in peace?

"Who's the guy?" the man says, unaware of how close to a fist in the face he's coming.

Melina's responding laugh isn't light like the ones she's let out all night. This one is rehearsed, tight. "You know the rules. We leave civilians alone."

With a glance at his phone, the guy breaks into a smarmy smile that tells me I won't like the next thing out of his mouth. "My source says he's Cade Fitzgerald, assistant coach of the Boston Bolts." One by one, he scans the people at the table, his eyes getting brighter as he goes. He's no doubt realized he's hit the jackpot. Not only is Melina here, but so are Aiden and Brooks, two of the NHL's most famous players. "He your boyfriend, or is he just keeping you company for the night?"

"Watch your mouth," I warn, my tone deadly now, my blood pressure spiking.

Cade presses a hand to my back. "I got this."

My every cell is telling me not to move, to protect my people. But the way he's touching me leaves me little choice. His touch burns my skin, even through my T-shirt. With a sigh, I step to the side, relinquishing control to my best friend.

Cade nods at the reporter. "Boyfriend."

It takes all my willpower not to whip around and shout out another *what the fuck?* Never in his life has Cade been anyone's boyfriend, and I know for a fact he's not hers.

Melina bites her lip shyly. "It's new, though. So if you could keep it quiet..." She winks at the reporter like he's in on this secret.

My blood boils. Reporters don't keep secrets. This is reckless. Stupid and reckless. The girl is supposed to be in hiding because she has a stalker. Instead, the two of them have been flirting and flaunting themselves. Now they've drawn a big-ass bull's-eye on my little town. Everyone will know where she's hiding. I should have shut down the press at the event earlier. I should have stopped her from singing. But, fuck, selfishly, I was focused on how much good this event could do for the town.

Now I realize how reckless that was.

Of course, it took seeing the two of them claim each other for me to feel that way.

Hypocrite.

Nothing I say right now will be helpful, so I stalk to the bar and order a drink.

As if they have no idea the storm they've likely just caused, the group falls back into easy banter and laughter.

I sit at the bar, sipping my whiskey, watching. Because that's all I ever do.

"They're hot together," Hailey says, leaning across the bar, following my line of sight.

I turn back to her and shrug noncommittally. "Who?"

She throws her head back and laughs. "Oh, Chief, you're a funny one."

Then she disappears to check on her other patrons.

She's wrong. I'm not the funny one. And there's nothing funny about the way I'm feeling right now. So instead of heading back to the table, I shoot a text to Cade, telling him I'll see them at home. Then I head back out into the cold winter night.

Alone.

CHAPTER 6

Melina

BESIDE ME, Cade scoffs, and on instinct, I lean back, almost making the mistake of looking at the screen of his phone.

You trying to hide something?

The memory of Jason's words—a.k.a. the worst human ever—echoes through my brain, bringing with it a wave of dread. Quickly, I shift out of Cade's lap and into the chair Declan vacated. Speaking of Declan, where did that broody man get off to? I scan the bar in search of him, but Cade's hand on my thigh stops me.

"He left."

"Hmm?" I force my attention to his face, keeping my eyes off the phone, which is, unfortunately, a trigger for me.

He chuckles, but it's an annoyed sound. "The man never texts, and the one time he does, I can't even enjoy it."

"I'm lost," I admit.

"Declan. He left. Said he'll meet us at home."

A strange disappointment sweeps through me. As much as I like Cade, I can't help but feel some sort of way about Declan. Maybe because he's opening up his house to me. Maybe because of how good it felt when his eyes were on me...which, I'll admit, is odd. I'm constantly in the spotlight, under the microscope. And lately, since the issue with

Jason, I can't help but squirm when I'm the center of attention. Yet he's different, and I don't have the slightest idea why.

"Should we go?"

Cade leans in, running his tongue over his bottom lip. The man has made it abundantly clear that he wants me, and I like that he doesn't play games.

And he's gorgeous.

Blue eyes, easy smile, broad shoulders, and thighs that bulge in all the right places against his jeans as he spreads his legs wider and pulls my chair between them. "Do you want to go?"

What I want to do is lick his lips. Get lost in his touch. Forget my name and my problems and Jason. I haven't allowed anyone close since him, and suddenly, I want to purge my body of his touch.

Is that a thing? It should be. Maybe Lake and I can dance around her bonfire, and I can burn all the clothes I wore when I dated Jason.

You'd be burning hundreds of outfits.

It'd be worth it, though, if it helped me shake this writer's block and I'd remember how to write a song again.

I shiver at the thought of never writing another song. Of having completely lost my talent.

Cade ghosts a finger up the slope of my neck, mistaking the reason for the cascade of goose bumps as desire rather than trepidation.

Though that single touch quickly sends all thoughts of my problems scattering. Now my body is buzzing for a completely different reason.

"I think we need privacy."

He lets out a light laugh, his breath ghosting over me. "Public sex not your kink like Sara?"

My pulse picks up as I scan the group. I'd all but forgotten that we aren't alone. Shit, I'm in my own little world with this man. He's intoxicating. "Not quite sure what my kinks are, but"—I suck in a breath, garnering my courage—"I think I'd like to find out."

Cade's blue eyes blaze as he shifts in his seat. "I've got to get Mel home. You guys going to be okay?"

Brooks nods. "We're staying at the hotel across the parking lot. We'll see you back in Boston for the game."

We say our goodbyes, and as the door to the bar swings shut behind us, muting the noise of the people inside, my thoughts are suddenly impossibly loud. Like that little voice in my head grew so it could be heard over the din of music, and now I'm adjusting to the quiet again.

"My car is here, but since I've had a few drinks, we should probably call for a driver." He pulls out his phone, narrating his thoughts. "Dec's house is only a few blocks from here, but it's cold out."

I can't help but smile at the way he processes out loud. "I don't mind the walk."

Cade looks up from his phone. "You sure?"

"Absolutely. It'll sober me a bit."

With a grin, he slides his phone back into his pocket. "Good, because now I can tease Declan about ditching us and forcing us to walk home."

I snort. "You two have an odd friendship."

Cade grasps my hand and links our fingers. The connection is oddly comforting. He's clearly comfortable with physical touch and doesn't overthink his actions. His personality couldn't be more different from that of the standoffish man I'll be living with through the holidays. The man who appears to do nothing *but* think.

Though he didn't take his time thinking about how to react when that reporter came at me. He acted on instinct alone, blocking the man's view of me. Though the move was a simple one, it instantly put me at ease. Made me feel safe.

I can't remember the last time I truly felt safe like that.

That's the worst part of a loved one's betrayal. The stolen sense of safety. Of control over oneself.

My heart pounds, the echo of it drowning out my thoughts. I take a long, slow breath. My anxiety is spiking, and if I don't get it under control, I'm liable to spin out.

Focus on something you can feel: Cade's hands. Something you can smell: The ocean. Something you can hear: His steady voice.

While he's been talking, I've been stuck in my head. Jason has held me captive emotionally for far longer than he ever did physically.

I press my tongue to the roof of my mouth, willing myself back to the present. We're walking on the boardwalk, the reflection of the moon on the water casting a gorgeous golden light over the bay.

"How long have you and Declan known one another?"

Cade chuckles. "I don't remember a time I didn't know him."

I hum and survey the water. Lake and I are like that. We came up together in Nashville, singing and working in bars, hoping to get our big break. Hers came far sooner than mine, when she was only sixteen. She stayed in Nashville with me, though our dynamic changed greatly. Suddenly, she was a star, and I was her sidekick. In certain ways, I still am. She's far more brave, more bold, than I am. She pushes the envelope, while I wait in the wings, watching to see how each scenario plays out for her. Often, that turns into yearning to follow her lead.

Her marrying an older man has me considering the man at my side and wondering how it will feel to be pressed down by his heavy weight tonight. Because we both know that's where we're heading.

Though I can't imagine a man like Cade settling down the way Ford did with Lake. He's got to be in his mid-forties, yet he acts like just another playboy in a bar.

I'm not judging whatsoever. That attitude is what makes me so comfortable with him. He knows what he's doing.

Makes me wonder what else he could teach me.

"Has Declan ever been married?"

I'm not sure why I keep asking about his friend. If Cade is concerned, he doesn't show it. He just laughs. "No. The only thing Dec is married to is stress."

"Like I said, you make an odd pair."

His shrug is casual. "He wasn't always like this. Life hasn't been easy for him."

"Is life easy for anyone?"

Though Cade's feet don't stop moving, he goes just the slightest bit rigid. "No, I don't suppose it is."

Not liking the serious tone that's so foreign coming from him, I shift the conversation back to Declan. "What was he like before life got hard?"

Cade rolls his tongue over his bottom lip, making it shine in the moonlight. "He was always stern, don't get me wrong. Control has always been his thing." He's quiet for a moment, like he's lost in thought. "He just knew how to let his guard down, I guess."

Before I can really consider what to ask next, he guides me off the boardwalk and down a dirt path.

"His house is around the back." Cade points to a large cape that, in the dark, appears to be a deep shade of blue.

With a hand at the small of my back, he urges me up the front steps. The simple wreath on the door makes warmth spread through my chest. I can almost hear Declan saying *look, I decorated* to anyone who dared call him a grinch.

When we enter the house, the smell of a dwindling fire hits me. Low flames dance behind the gate in the oversized brick hearth in the corner of the living area, as if Declan has just walked away from it. Disappointment settles heavy in my belly at the thought of him getting Cade's text and then feeling the need to disappear.

"Can I get you a drink?" Cade walks around the space comfortably, like he stays here often.

"Whatever you have is fine."

"Tequila?" He dangles a bottle from his fingers and hits me with a devilish smirk that makes my stomach swoop. For so long, the only emotions I've experienced have circled around fear and anxiety. But after just a few hours in this town, other feelings are bubbling to the surface. Though it has more to do with the people here than the town itself. Namely, two people.

I'm staring down the dark hallway when Cade settles beside me on the couch, two shot glasses in one hand, the bottle of tequila in the other. "Everything okay?"

I shift my attention to him. "I hate that he disappeared into his bedroom. Feels like we chased him in there."

Cade sets the glasses on the coffee table and opens the bottle. Once he's poured us each a shot, he hands one to me, meeting my gaze. "Declan doesn't do anything he doesn't want to do. I'm sure he's fine." He licks across his lip, his eyes dipping down to my shaking hand, then focusing on mine again. I feel the trail of his gaze like a flame, and another shiver of lust slithers through me. "What would you have done had he been here?"

His dark tone, the way he angles closer, make it feel like a naughty dare. Like he can see inside my head. Like he can read every dirty thought that has been taunting me since I saw Cade watch Declan while he held me on his lap. And how I caught Declan staring at the two of us when he thought no one was looking.

It's a hunger.

It takes effort to swallow past my trepidation and voice my true thought. "Have you ever shared someone?"

Cade's pupils dilate, sending a shiver down my spine.

I toss back the shot of tequila, hoping the burn will make me forget the ridiculous question I uttered. He watches me for a long moment, his scrutiny causing me to squirm. I'm afraid to meet his gaze, unsure of what I'll find. I'm not even sure what I want to find. But seconds bleed into a minute, and finally, I look at him.

"I can do one better," he says. I swear he's closer than he was only seconds ago. "I've shared with Declan."

The air in the room grows heavy, and the burn in my throat intensifies. "Really?"

"Do you like that idea?" He pours another shot into my glass, then zeroes in on my face. "Four hands on you." Smoothly, he shifts until his lips are so close, his warm breath skates over my neck. "Two mouths. Heat everywhere."

Drenched with a desire there's no fighting, I launch myself at him, fusing my lips to his. He sets the bottle of tequila on the table with a grunt. When both hands are free, he palms my hip, then my ass, kneading the flesh as he plunges his tongue into my mouth. The kiss tastes like tequila and bad decisions, like filth and desire and fun.

With his other hand, he fists my hair and pulls me back. His breaths are harsh as he licks my lips. "Tell me, are you trouble like Dec said?" He sinks his teeth into my neck.

Fuck. I writhe in his arms, needing so much more.

"Or are you a good girl who likes to do very bad things?"

Holy shit, I gush at that simple question, soaking my panties instantly. "What kind of bad things?"

"You want me to tell you how the two of us would have fucked you if he were out here when we got home? How he would have enjoyed watching me strip off all these clothes? How he would have poured the tequila over your tits and told me to clean you up? You see, Dec is a neat freak. Likes everything tidy. But me..." He bites my lip again, all sense of decency flying out the window. "I like to make a mess." He tugs on my hair again, the tension just short of painful. "He'd tell you to get on your knees and take out my cock." He nods to the floor.

I take the hint and slide off him. The wooden floor is hard, but I welcome the burn. It reminds me that I'm alive.

"Then he'd pull your hair back. He'd be gentle about it, because that's how he'd treat you—like you're special. Precious. *Rare*. You'd love the way his rough fingers felt sliding across your scalp as he made a delicate fist."

As Cade speaks, I help him out of his jeans and then his boxers, leaving both to pool at his feet. His cock is rock hard, long, and curving to the right. The thought of how perfectly he'd fill me sends a lick of fire up my spine. I press my hands against his thighs, waiting for further instruction.

"Then he'd tell you to lean forward."

Eagerly, I obey, still gripping my thighs.

"Circle that fat cock."

I wrap my fingers around his shaft and tug. The warm, smooth length of him makes my mouth water.

"And suck."

Licking my lips, I do as I'm told, opening my mouth and sliding down until he hits the back of my throat, causing me to gag.

He tugs on my hair and groans. "Good girl. Do it again."

So I do. I continue working him with my mouth, all the while getting wetter. The way he tastes makes me hungry for more. Insatiable. Circling his crown, sliding my tongue across the knot at the bottom, I relish the way he curses. When he tugs me back, I'm panting, and tears stream down my face from having taken him so deep.

"Get a condom from my wallet and sit on my cock, Trouble."

I tip my chin higher and smirk. "Thought I was your good girl."

With his lip caught between his teeth, he groans. "You're a filthy girl. A little slut who's thinking about my best friend fucking you while you've got *my cock* in your mouth."

Guilt mixed with desire courses through me. Is he upset? Or is he turned on?

He chuckles like he can read my mind. "Don't tell me you weren't thinking about what it would be like if he were telling you to do those things while you sucked me off."

Fuck, he's gorgeous. Those lips tipped up in a wicked smile, his blue eyes bright beneath that backward cap. Right now, I'm pretty sure I'd do anything he asked.

"I hope that's what you were thinking about. I know I was."

Scrambling, I dig through his pockets, then his wallet, for a condom. With a shaky hand, I hold it out to him. I don't dare even breathe as he rips it open and slides it down his length, tugging gently once.

"Strip," he orders.

One word. Five letters. And I'm ready to combust.

I don't make a show of it. I wouldn't be capable if I tried. I'm desperate to have him inside me. So I slide my jeans off quickly, barely keeping myself from stumbling, and toss my shirt, relishing the "fuck" that slips past his lips when I straighten, and he scans first my tits, then my stomach, then my bare pussy.

When I go to straddle him, he grips my hips and shakes his head. "*Face him.*"

All the air escapes me. Hell, I think it's all been sucked from the room.

Face him.

Fuck.

Dizzy, I spin, expecting to find Declan watching us. Instead, all I find is a painfully empty room. The disappointment doesn't have a chance to stick, though, because Cade is clutching my hips again and pulling me onto his lap, grounding me to the fantasy again. "Put my cock inside you."

With my fingers wrapped around his shaft, I line him up. Then, with a deep breath in, I lower myself slowly, reveling in the way he fills me as I slide down until I'm seated fully on his hips.

With a gentle hand, he sweeps my hair off my shoulder. "Ride me, Trouble," he murmurs, his lips ghosting my ear. "Make us both come."

I writhe against him, drowning in ecstasy. I'm completely naked, the warm fire crackling, and dim flames causing shadows to dance around us. With each thrust of his hips, I feel more and think less until I'm losing myself completely. My climb to the top stalls just as I'm on the edge of an orgasm. It's there, teasing yet evading me.

"I need—" I whimper.

With a hand splayed across my stomach, he taunts me. "What do you need, Trouble? You need his fingers to play with your clit. His mouth on your nipple?" He sits up, pressing his warm chest against my back, and loops his other arm around me. With one hand, he tweaks my nipple. He slips the other between my legs and weaves serendipitous circles against my clit.

Desire floods me, pushing me closer to the precipice, but it once again eludes me.

The clatter of a glass startles me. Heart leaping and eyes flying open, I zero in on the hall, where the sound came from. Squinting, I can just make out a shadow. A mere silhouette.

Declan.

He shifts then, and I can make out the way his hands are fisted.

Lust singes all my senses at the thought of him watching me writhe on his best friend.

How long has he been there? Did Cade know? Is that why he told me to *face him*?

That last question is what does it. The elusive orgasm I've been chasing suddenly barrels into me. As I crest the wave of ecstasy, Cade bites down on my shoulder. With a groan, he thickens, and then spills his own release.

Shutting my eyes, I pant. I'm still reeling, still coming down from the high, when Cade presses a kiss to my shoulder and then my cheek and whispers, "You were such a good girl for us."

CHAPTER 7

Declan

TROUBLE. She's so much fucking trouble. I barely make it to the bathroom before I'm pulling out my throbbing cock and tugging on it. Just a second to ease the pressure that built while I watched her strip and writhe, her heavy tits bouncing while she rode Cade.

The memory of her licking him sends a zap of electricity down my spine. How he talked her through it? Fuck. My cock bobs as I kick off my pants. I yank my shirt over my head and lean into the shower to start the water, then quickly fist myself again. My hand is no comparison to what her warm pussy must have felt like to him. Or her mouth.

Those swollen lips were like a beacon, luring me closer. And the way mascara streaked her cheeks after she took him all the way back in her throat? The way she gagged on his cock?

I'm a sick bastard for watching. For enjoying it so fucking much. The sight of him thrusting up into her, his muscles straining as he reached around and fondled her nipples and her clit. Pinching and prodding until she exploded. I wished I could hear the words he was muttering in her ear. The rasp in his tone. The sound he made when he came.

The mere idea of it has my cock swelling. It only takes one more tug before I explode, coating the shower wall. Panting, I fall against it, and as my heart rate slows, shame swamps me. I just jacked off to the vision of my best friend fucking the girl *I* want to fuck.

What is wrong with me?

And how the hell am I going to face them in the morning?

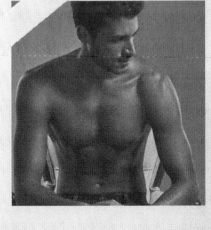

CHAPTER 8

Cade

FOR THE FIRST time in maybe ever, I woke up questioning my decision to sneak out of a woman's bed. I never do sleepovers, but we're staying in the same house, so there was a moment where I considered it last night. But when I looked over at her sleeping form, studying the way her chest rose and fell, how her lashes fluttered as she dreamt, I got lost for far too long.

That's all it took to have me hightailing it out of her room last night. I could get lost in a woman like her, and getting lost in people is a bad idea.

The grump I find sitting in the kitchen, a cup of coffee in hand and a spread of donuts on the table in front of him, is proof of that.

"Surprised you're still here," I grumble, moving through the kitchen. "Figured you'd have left early for work after last night."

"What are you talking about?"

Is that how he's going to play this? He's going to pretend he didn't stand in the shadows and watch as Mel gave me the best goddamn blowjob of my life? That he didn't eat up the way she bounced on my cock? That he didn't disappear to his bedroom so quickly I can only imagine what he did as soon as the door shut?

Fuck. The idea alone makes my dick swell.

"Nothing," I say, heading for the coffeepot. When I'm out of his line of sight, I discreetly adjust myself. If he doesn't want to talk about it, then we won't talk about it. He's a man of few words. It shouldn't surprise me, and it shouldn't piss me off.

Even so, it does.

"If you're talking about how you claimed her as your girlfriend last night, then yeah, we do need to talk about that. It was reckless and stupid."

Teeth gritted, I swallow back a curse. "It was just one reporter."

"One reporter who probably blasted it to every news outlet in the country, but only after he sold the photos to TMZ or some other cockroach entity that will now be staked out, waiting to catch a glimpse of *Calina.*"

My lip quirks, and then I can't hold it in. I laugh. "Did you just give Melina and me a celebrity couple name?"

Declan palms his face. "Fuck, I don't know." Dragging his hand down, he shakes his head, and for an instant, I swear he's smiling. "I think I did."

"Dude," I grumble.

He blinks, his face a stony mask once again. "This is serious. You fucked her. Now you're going to head back to Boston and what—be seen with another woman tonight?"

With a shrug, I snag the milk from the fridge. "Or a man."

He glares as I pour a splash into my coffee.

I set the jug down and hold up my hand. "I'm just kidding. No, I've got a game tonight. And I can keep it in my pants for a few days."

He grunts. "How chivalrous of you."

Sighing, I lean against the counter and cross one ankle over the other. As I sip from my mug, savoring the first hit of caffeine, I take him in. He's in a pair of gray sweats and a long-sleeve white T-shirt that says Bristol Fire Department in red. His BFD baseball cap makes him look more relaxed than I've seen him in years.

"I'm serious," I say. "I like the girl. Maybe I'll come back and fuck her again."

I bring my coffee cup to my lips, studying him over the rim.

He picks up his coffee, seemingly ignoring my comment. "Whatever you do, remember she's got a stalker. Real life problems. She doesn't need you bringing drama or attention here."

Chest tightening with a hint of hurt, I lift my chin. "Sounds like you don't want me to come back while she's here."

Declan shifts in his chair and angles toward me. "You know that's not what I'm saying."

"Then what *are* you saying?"

The question comes from the curvy brunette who walks in wearing nothing but an oversized T-shirt I found in a drawer in her room. Fuck. The sight of her in Declan's clothes is a bigger turn-on than I could have imagined. Especially when paired with her messy hair, makeup-free face, and bare legs covered in a smattering of freckles. Need instantly heats my blood. What I'd do to drop to my knees right now, push up her shirt, and explore just how high those freckles go.

At the table, Declan is gawking at her, his mouth ajar. I'd feel bad that he's so tongue-tied if he wasn't being such a judgmental ass right now.

He yanks his cap off his head and runs a hand through his hair. "I got donuts. Do you want a coffee?"

To Mel's credit, she doesn't back down. With her hand on her hip, she glares at him. "No, I'd rather you fill me in on your house rules. If you're uncomfortable with what happened last night, I can check into a hotel."

Declan glances at me, his eyes pleading for me to step in and help. But I won't give him the out he so desperately needs. Finally someone is calling him on his mixed signals.

And fuck, was he giving them last night. One minute, he's laser focused on the way I'm touching Mel, smiling even, and the next, he disappears from the bar. Then, as I was breaking out the tequila, he came out of his room. He could have joined us, but he made a choice to stand in the shadows. To watch. He knew I knew he was there. We made eye contact the moment she circled my cock with those perfect lips of hers. And he licked his.

He wanted to watch. Hell, I have a feeling he wanted more than that. Maybe he doesn't understand the desire or the reason behind it. And maybe he doesn't intend to ever act on it. That's fine. I made my peace with that years ago. But this? The way he's forcing us to try to figure out what he wants when his actions say one thing and his lips say another? It's a mind fuck. It'd be so much easier if he'd just come out and tell us his rules.

He gets up and pulls a mug from the cabinet. Silently, he fills it with coffee and sets it on the table. Once he's settled in his seat again, he motions to the empty spot where he set the mug. "You're welcome to stay here for as long as you wish. There are no rules. I just want you to be safe."

Mel crosses her arms over her chest, the move making the T-shirt ride higher on her thighs. "And I wasn't being safe last night because I had sex with your best friend?"

Damn, this girl is impressive. The way she holds her ground and stares him down is making me hard as steel.

Once again, Declan side-eyes me. I know the instant he sees how turned on I am, because for a beat, he lowers his focus, and his chest rises with a heavy breath. He forces his gaze back up to my face and holds eye contact as he says, "It's not about that. It's about what happens after. Cade isn't a relationship guy."

Smiling, I lean back against the fridge, ready to tell them that she may just be worth changing for, but before I can open my mouth, she once again steals the air from the room.

"Good thing I was just looking for some fun, then, huh?" With a sharp breath in, she clutches the back of the chair and eyes me. "Listen, I know this probably isn't ideal for you, but if you wouldn't mind keeping up with the relationship story for a little longer, I actually think it would be helpful. That way, people will assume I'm in Boston with you, and my ex—"

The pain etched on her face as she turns away has my heart sinking and my grip on my coffee cup tightening.

She clears her throat. "The person who's been stalking me won't think to look for me here."

Up until ten seconds ago, the armor she wore, the strength she showed, was so damn natural, so smooth. Now, though, her mask has slipped. Her knuckles are white from squeezing the chair so tight, and her eyes are swimming with fear. Whoever did this to her, whoever made her feel that she couldn't be comfortable in her own skin, will pay.

Determined to ease her worries, I stride toward her, grip her by the neck, and gently angle her so that she can only see me. "I'd be a lucky bastard to date you—real or fake. You've got me for as long as you need, hear me?"

Those green eyes mist over, and she swallows thickly beneath my thumb. "Thank you," she whispers.

I lean in close and press my lips against hers. Dammit, I wish I could swallow her pain.

When we pull apart, her lips tip up just a little. "I'm heading over to Lake's, and then we're going to grab lunch." She bites her lip, and that hint of a smile turns wicked. "I've gotta shower first, though."

With one more kiss to her lips, I release my hold on her neck and step back. "Okay."

Mel turns toward Declan, whose presence I completely tuned out during that exchange. "And for the record, you could have joined in last night."

My heart stutters, and I'm left blinking at her as she snatches a donut from the box on the table, shoots me a wink, and backs out of the kitchen. "So fucking good," she mumbles around her first bite. Laughing, she points her donut at me. "Shower sex. *Now.*"

At the table, Declan shakes his head, grumbling, "Not a word out of you."

With a shrug, I stride across the kitchen. At the doorway, I spin to face him. "I'm going to take a shower. You heard what she said; you could join."

With one hand, I pull off my shirt and grin. The bastard won't follow, but fuck if I didn't wish he would.

CHAPTER 9

Melina

AFTER SPECTACULAR SHOWER sex and then another loud round before we got dressed, Cade dropped me off at Lake's house with a promise to call me this week.

I don't expect him to follow through. This morning was fun—especially the part where I screamed his name so loud when I came that the entire house probably shook, knowing that Declan heard every second of it—but I'm not a fool. Declan's warning that Cade is a playboy was unnecessary. I knew that about him before we slept together.

I *like* that about him.

I'm not ready for a real relationship. But to feel wanted in the way Cade is so naturally good at? I couldn't have asked for more. And I wanted to remember what it felt to *want* to be touched again.

For so long, the idea of another person's hands on me made my skin crawl.

Damn Declan for making me feel dirty for enjoying it.

He's ruining my fun.

"So, Cade Fitzgerald?" Lake asks, her brow raised as she bounces Nash against her chest.

My best friend is never anything short of perfection, so it's not surprising that she's taken to motherhood so naturally. Though it's

45

endearing, how casual and comfortable she looks right now. She's got her hair up in a messy bun on the top of her head, and she's wearing one of Ford's old Led Zeppelin shirts and a pair of oversized black sweats. Ford disappeared when I walked in the door, saying he was going to listen to the tapes his assistant sent over.

The two of them—three now, I guess—have a pretty perfect life. Though the once pristine house is scattered with baby items, the scene before me makes tears prick my lids. Will I ever have this? Do I even want it?

Will anyone ever truly want me?

"It's nothing." I wave a dismissive hand, batting away the emotions threatening to surface. "Just got caught by a reporter. It made more sense to say he was my boyfriend than to tell the guy that I was just interested in banging him and my new roommate."

Lake squeaks, clutching the baby to her chest. "I—did you—" She blinks, speechless.

I laugh. "Don't act all innocent. You are currently rocking your ex-boyfriend's brother in your arms."

Lake covers Nash's ears. "Don't say things like that in front of him." Even as she scolds me, she giggles. "It really is ridiculous when you put it like that." Chin tucked, she smiles down at the five-month-old who is completely oblivious to the absurd circumstance into which he was born. "And yet, I wouldn't change a thing." Her soft smile turns sharp as she looks up at me. "Now tell me about how you ended up with not one, but two men last night."

With a shake of my head, I drop onto the couch and pull my legs up under me. "I didn't. Not that I would have minded if it had turned out that way."

"*Mel*," she laughs. "I've got to be honest, I can't imagine Chief Everhart sharing. He seems so broody."

I sigh, my mood sinking a little. She's not wrong. "Honestly, you're probably right."

She settles beside me. "But he's been kind?"

With a shrug, I swipe at the arm of the couch, avoiding her scrutiny. "He's fine."

"That isn't what I asked. You put up with fine for a long time with—"

I hold up my hand. "I don't want to talk about him."

Lake frowns. "Okay, but please tell me if he reaches out. You can't hide things like you did before."

Pulling my bottom lip between my teeth, I duck my head. "I know."

She brushes a hand down my arm. "I'm serious, Mel."

What she doesn't know is that I didn't hide it from everyone. I told two people. I told my brother, and I told my mother. But Jason is so much more than just my agent. He's my brother's best friend. Like a second son to my mom. Though I told them separately, their responses were the same. They told me that I must have misunderstood the situation. That fame had changed me. That I'd become arrogant, behaving like I was too good for everyone.

Telling people only to have them not believe me made it hurt more. And to add to the pain, they almost had me convinced that I was the problem.

And though I know Lake isn't like them—

"Mel," she says, softer now, her expression full of sympathy.

Dammit. I can't stand the pity, especially from my best friend. "Can we watch a movie?" I snag the remote from the coffee table and press the power button. "Or, oh—" I say, my tone a little too chipper, "have you watched *Bridgerton*? It's so steamy."

She's silent, watching me, worrying her lip, but I ignore the concern. Finally, as I select the first episode of season one, she settles back against the couch, her head falling to my shoulder, offering me the type of comfort that so few people could.

Hours later, we're still watching, take-out and candy laid out in front of us compliments of Ford, and I feel like I can finally breathe again.

This is why I came here for the holidays. I don't need the people who raised me. Family doesn't have to be blood. These days, family is the girl I met at sixteen. The girl who helped pull me out of some of my darkest moments. The woman who sits beside me, eating copious amounts of sugar, just letting me be. Who hasn't forced me to explain why I won't go home for the holidays. Who hasn't asked why I haven't turned over the first few songs of the album I promised to Hall Records...

Family is the woman who welcomed me into her home with a hug and a smile.

It eases my mind knowing that her husband loves her enough to make sure I have a safe place to stay while also ensuring that she isn't put at risk. If it were up to Lake, I'd be staying here, but Ford, who'd give her the moon if he could, put his foot down and worked with Beckett Langfield to make arrangements for me to stay with Declan instead.

Because Jason does make me a risk. I hate it, but it's true. He's unstable, and once he hears the rumor that I'm dating again, it will likely get worse. The only hope is that my plan will work. He'll assume I'm in Boston with Cade, and he'll never think to look for me at Declan's.

Which is why despite Declan's poor ass attitude this morning, I'm staying put. I can handle a grumpy roommate, and I can abide by his rules. Or maybe I can ignore my problems and have fun breaking each and every one of those rules.

Ford walks me to Declan's door, where the man himself greets us. As they shake hands, I have to hold back a giggle. I feel like a teenager whose friend's dad just returned her home to her own father.

Though I never knew my father, and I was in Nashville and living on my own at sixteen, so maybe I'm way off base.

Even so, I stick with the feeling, and the minute Ford is gone, I find myself acting like a brat.

"There's a plate in the oven for you if you're hungry," Declan says as he ambles inside behind me.

"You didn't have to wait around for me, you know. I'm not a child."

Though I'm certainly acting like one.

I wince, prepared for his anger. I'd deserve it. God, Jason was right. I am a spoiled brat, and I do act like I'm too good for everyone.

Declan steps closer, his brows pulled low.

I hold my breath, readying myself for a lecture.

"I didn't wait around," he says, his voice quiet, serious. "It's my night off. If I went into the station, the guys would accuse me of not trusting them and send me right back here anyway." He grips his neck and meets my gaze.

My heart thumps hard against my breastbone when he's this close to me, engulfing me in his masculine scent.

His eyes soften a fraction. "Okay, they did tell me that," he admits, cringing. "And I didn't make dinner; it's from the station. Mason made lasagna. It's his mother's recipe. So you should eat. It's good. Really. Okay, you're making me nervous, so I can't stop talking. I'll just be over there—" He points to the living room, where the television is turned down low.

When I don't reply, because I'm truly thrown off by his gentle demeanor, his nervousness, his shoulders slump, and he walks away.

Dammit.

"Thank you," I call after him.

Halfway across the living room, he looks over his shoulder, though he keeps his body turned away. "For what it's worth, I'm sorry about this morning. My sister tells me I'm shit at communicating, and well..." He shakes his head. "I'm sorry."

I nod, confused but also concerned that if he says anything else so strangely charming, I'll either burst into tears or throw myself at him. Since I can all but guarantee he wouldn't know how to handle either situation, I force myself to head to the oven and pull out the dinner he brought home for me. I'm full from all the junk Lake and I indulged in, but it seems important to accept this olive branch.

I return to the living room, plate in hand, and when Declan looks up, I pull up short. Shit. This was a bad idea. "Sorry," I say, taking a step back. "Cade mentioned you don't like messes. You probably don't eat in here."

"Was just surprised you were joining me. Figured you'd hide in the kitchen." The smirk he gives me is so shocking, I almost drop my plate. Didn't know the man had it in him. "Feel free to sit."

I settle on the opposite end of the couch, keeping my plate balanced on my lap rather than setting it on the coffee table. The piece is beautiful, and I'd hate to damage it. It looks like the interior of a tree trunk, with swirls and natural designs in the grain. I could study it for hours if I had the time. So that's where I focus, too intimidated by the stoic man beside me to meet his gaze again.

The Bolts game is playing on the TV, and the commentators are talking about how Aiden Langfield's game has turned around since he shared his struggle with depression. I find myself leaning forward, lips pressed together and holding my breath. I'd have never thought the man who sat at the bar with us last night suffered from depression. Then again, I've become a pro at putting on a mask in order to hide parts of me I don't want the world to see. Who's to say others don't do the same?

Though it sounds like Aiden Langfield went the opposite direction and shared his secrets.

I fight back a shudder at the idea. I can't imagine really opening up to the people I'm closest to, let alone the world.

"It's good, right?"

I glance at the fork I've just pulled from my mouth and realize I haven't tasted a single bite I've eaten. "Um, yeah," I stammer. "Delicious. Thank you."

With a nod, he returns his focus to the game.

Between plays, the camera pans to the sidelines, where Cade stands proudly in a suit.

I practically swallow my tongue at the sight. It's like his clothing is molded to his body, stretching to accommodate the broad shoulders and the muscles I was licking just this morning. "Holy shit, does that man clean up."

Declan snorts, then quickly covers his mouth like he didn't mean to be caught laughing. Clearly, he doesn't realize he's already smiled at me a handful of times since I walked through the door.

Maybe, since he's not working, he had a few drinks to loosen up. With the way the tension is filling this room I could really use something to take the edge off. Especially when Cade appears on the screen again. When Gavin leans in and speaks to him, and he laughs in response, then looks back toward the ice, in the direction of the camera, it feels as if he's looking right at us. His blue eyes heat, clearly over a play, which is where the camera pans to catch the action, breaking the spell. The puck is about to drop, but the guys on either side of center ice are chirping at one another. Then, before the ref can even move out of the way, they're lunging at each other.

"What do you think he said?" I turn to Declan, studying his expression.

Once again, his lip twitches like he's trying to keep from smiling. "It's not a high school locker room, I don't have the gossip."

I grin, my heart rate picking up at the tease. "I bet that tall guy said something about the other dude's girlfriend—" I suck in a breath, grinning, and practically drop my plate in my lap, my hands flapping. "Or maybe he slept with his mom?"

Declan levels me with another one of his stares.

My mood deflates, and I give him a sheepish shrug. "Or maybe he just told him he sucked. But I like my story better."

"It's some story," he mutters, turning back to the TV.

Both guys are heading for the penalty boxes now, while the rest of the players line up for the puck drop.

"That's what I'd do on Sundays while sitting through church, then afterward, when we'd inevitably end up at one of the parishioners' houses for what felt like an eternity."

"Watch hockey?" Declan asks without taking his eyes off the game.

"No," I say. "Make up stories about people. What was going on with the family three rows up. Why the father was there one week and gone the next." I stab another piece of lasagna. "Maybe he got a new job that kept him from coming to church. That kind of thing. Sometimes, my mom would catch me zoning out, and I'd tell her my stories. She'd reprimand me. Tell me to stop gossiping. Really, though, I was just passing the time."

"What happened to the father?"

Declan's attention is like a caress, urging me to turn his way. When I do, my stomach flips. A girl could get lost in those dark eyes of his. The depth of his stare. The knowledge he holds. Like he knows what I'll say before I say it. Like he knows what's on my mind, even as I'm doing my best to hide my thoughts. "He showed up three months later with a new family." I swallow and force a smile.

Declan's mouth drops open, and his eyes go wide.

Why the hell did I tell him that? If I'm not careful, I'll be like Aiden and spill all my secrets.

"I'm going to put this away," I say, lifting the plate. "Then get changed. Need anything?"

"No. I'm fine."

The commentator's voice gets louder, and he's speaking quickly now, going on about how Tyler Warren is on a breakaway. Declan's focus turns back to the television, and a moment later, the Bolts score. Once again, the camera pans from the ice to the sidelines, where the team is celebrating. I smile at the sight of Cade, and though I try to fight the urge, I peer over at Declan. He shifts on the couch, his focus completely on the screen, like he's just as entranced by Cade as I am.

Hmm, interesting.

Hours later, when the game is over, the Bolts having secured a win, I send a congratulatory text to Cade. When my phone buzzes with a Face-Time call from him, I can't help the squeal that escapes my lips.

Declan has just disappeared down the hall, likely holing up for the night. I can't imagine he'll come back out here for more awkward non-conversation with me, now that the game is over. As it was, we watched in silence—me keeping all my stories to myself—and afterward, he busied himself starting a fire in the hearth while we watched the after-game commentary, which was just more of the same thing, but with a bunch of men talking about how the guys on the ice could have done things differently.

God, I can't imagine what it would be like to finish a show, only to have a group of people sit around and critique my every move on live television. Though I guess there are plenty of people on social media who do exactly that.

Fortunately, I avoid that like the plague.

"Hey, you," I say when Cade's face appears on my screen.

"Hey, girlfriend," he says in a flirtatious tone. There's chatter and low music in the background. He's probably out with the team, though he's holding the phone really close, probably so he can hear, so I can't make out his surroundings.

"That was a great game, Coach."

He licks his lips and smiles again. "Fuck, you're pretty."

I laugh, my heart pinching. "Is that why you called? You missed me?"

His wide smile slips into something smaller, more intimate, and his eyes soften. "Yeah, I think I did."

For a long moment, we watch each other silently. What the hell is happening right now?

"That Cade?"

Declan's voice has me jumping so abruptly, I bobble the phone. "Yeah, you want to say hi?"

Cade chuckles, his image going blurry. "Yeah, right. The guy doesn't do phones."

With a shrug, Declan settles on the couch again.

I swallow back a flutter of nerves at his presence. I truly didn't get the impression that he had any intention of coming back out. As he sits back with a sigh, I can't help but take him in. The T-shirt he's changed into—emblazoned with a Bristol Fire Department logo, like most everything he wears—pulls tight across his broad chest. The mesh material of his gym shorts does the same over his thick thighs. As he puts his feet up on the coffee table, crossing one ankle over the other, I force myself to focus on Cade again rather than continue to study him.

"I wanted to introduce you to my friend Leo. Leo, this is my girlfriend, Mel." He taps his phone screen, flipping the camera.

The guy behind the bar gives me a shy wave, then he throws a towel over his shoulder and shakes his head at Cade.

"Isn't that the guy you told me gives great head?" I whisper.

Cade is an open book, and I didn't bat an eye when he told me about his casual hookups with the bartender at his regular hang out.

Cade throws his head back and roars with laughter. "Shh, his ego doesn't need any more stroking."

Declan is watching me. I can feel the attention, the anger, radiating off him. I ignore it as Cade continues talking.

"Trying to sell this relationship, Mel," Cade teases. "Keep it down over there."

Zaps of excitement course through me as he grins. He's at a bar, hanging out near a guy he could easily take home, yet he's calling me. What game is he playing?

I bite my lip. "It's fine. Maybe we're not monogamous. Who gets to say what we're good with?"

Cade's eyes flash with an emotion I can't name. "I kinda liked thinking that you'd be a little jealous."

"Oh, you find jealousy hot." I can't help but snort. If he's looking for a jealous partner, then he's looking in the wrong direction. The guy on the other end of the couch, though, has it in spades.

"Maybe," he admits.

"Then consider me very jealous." I let a sly smile tip up one side of my lips. "When will I see you again?"

He goes quiet for a long moment, and a wave of dread washes through me. I've overstepped. Obviously this is all just a joke. He doesn't *really* miss me. Maybe he started this banter in order to sell the relationship. Or maybe the bartender was getting too clingy, and he's using me as an out for the night.

"We're headed to Philly tomorrow, but we have a home game on Friday. Think you'd want to come up to watch, then stay at my place for the night?"

Lips pressed together, I side-eye my warden in the corner. "Sure."

In a heartbeat, Declan is out of his seat and leaning over the couch, staring Cade down from over my shoulder. "I don't think that's a good idea."

Anger floods me. How dare this man think he can call the shots for me? "Good thing it's not your call, then, huh?" I look back at Cade. "I'm going to get some rest. Just text me the info, and I'll make it work."

Cade nods, though his lips are twisted into an uncomfortable wince.

I force a smile. "Have a good night."

"Night, Trouble," he murmurs.

I don't bother saying good night to Declan.

CHAPTER 10

Cade

THE ENERGY after a game always makes it hard to sleep. For hours, my ears buzz from the loud arena and my blood pumps with adrenaline. This is exactly why I normally hit up a bar at the end of the night.

A few drinks, a little flirting, then a round of sex are the perfect combination to ensure a good night of sleep.

Tonight, though, rather than heading out, I'm sitting in my hotel room in Philly, twiddling my thumbs, racking my brain for an excuse to call Mel.

Sure, Saturday night was one thing. She and I had been up most of the night before, then we'd followed that up with two rounds that next morning, so by Saturday night, I was wiped.

When I saw Leo at the bar after the game, I had this heavy, uncomfortable feeling in my stomach. Like even engaging in innocent flirting with him would be wrong. Which made zero sense. She's not really my girlfriend. And even if she was, there's no rule that says I wouldn't be able to talk to people I've fucked before.

Did I call her hoping she'd stake a claim in front of him? Maybe. Did I want her to be jealous? No. Not really. But I also didn't expect her not to even bat an eye at the idea of me being with another person.

All night, I'd wondered whether she and Declan were together. Not because I was jealous of the idea, but because I missed her. *Them.*

Fuck.

Flat on my back, I stare at the ceiling. The guys are probably out celebrating after our win. I could easily go out, find someone to work out this frustration with. It's the logical thing to do. No feelings. No chance to get hurt.

Instead, I snatch my phone from the nightstand and shoot a text to Declan.

> Me: How's Mel been?

I don't expect a response. In fact, if he doesn't reply in the next five minutes, I'll force myself to get dressed and go out.

Fuck it, he's definitely not going to text. I drop the phone on the bed and haul myself up to sitting.

The familiar ding alerting me to a text makes my stomach flip in a way that's concerning. It's hope and excitement: something a forty-year-old man shouldn't feel.

> Declan: Fine.

I cough out a laugh. Why do four letters on a screen attached to his name make me fucking smile?

Absolutely fucking pathetic. Sinking my teeth into the pad of my thumb, I contemplate my next move.

> Me: Why don't you come up with Mel on Friday for the game? Stay in Boston for the night.

Dots dance on the screen just like the damn butterflies in my stomach. The guy never replies. When two full sentences appear, my jaw falls open.

> Declan: And where am I going to stay? You have one bed, Cade.

Even though the words are printed rather than spoken, I can hear his reprimanding tone. Can see his jaw clenching in annoyance. He hates texting. So why is he? Is it because of Mel? Something about her softens him. Makes him try a little harder. And for some godforsaken reason, I like that. I shouldn't want him to soften for someone else. But I like her, and I like that he likes her. It makes no fucking sense.

Neither does my response. But I'm feeling daring, I guess. Wondering just how much he'd do for her. How far he'd go to make her happy.

Me: You could share the bed with us.

My chest tightens as I wait for the dots to dance, and my mind races with thoughts of what could happen if he did.

I know he won't take me up on the offer, but the image of him in my bed, with her, both of them naked on either side of me...

"Fuck." With fumbling hands, I undo my belt and suit pants and pull my cock out. I'm so fucking hard it hurts.

In my mind, it's not my rough hand gripping my cock, it's Declan's. The way he strokes me instantly sends heat rushing through my veins. He tells Mel to spit on it in that gruff way of his. I whimper at the mere thought, closing my eyes and losing myself to the dream.

CHAPTER 11

Melina

DON T you dare let him see you cry...
All I ever do is sigh.
Just look me in the eye.

"Ugh," I growl. *Cry. Sigh. Eye. That's* the best I can come up with?

"Everything okay?" Declan asks as he waltzes into the kitchen wearing his standard uniform—black work pants and a long-sleeve T-shirt with the department's name stamped on it. Today's shirt is navy blue with red writing. Yesterday's was white.

No, I'm not memorizing what he wears, my life is just that freaking boring right now. The only thing that changes daily is the color of his shirt.

"I'm fine," I grumble.

Declan pours himself a cup of coffee and leans back against the counter, watching me. He's scruffier today. His dark hair is unruly, and even his eyebrows are unkempt. But the beard on this man? God, it looks softer, and I'm annoyed by how much I'd like to touch it.

I could probably write loads of sonnets about the way I want to feel it against my fingers—between my thighs—eh, who am I kidding? I can't write a single fucking song to save my career.

Seriously.

It's been a year since I released a new album, and anything I wrote before the Worst Human Alive destroyed my journal and my life is useless now.

He'd say it's because I need him. That he helped me get to where I am. I'm really hoping that's not true. We were one of those couples that broke up more than we stayed together. Always my fault, of course. He'd sleep around and gaslight me into believing I was in the wrong and that he only flaunted other women to remind me he was a catch.

The problem was my career was so tied to the man, my family too, that I truly believed I did need him.

God, I hope he was wrong.

As if he's been summoned, my damn phone dings with another text from him.

> Worst Human Alive: You're seriously dating that loser wannabe hockey player?

I fist my hands and fight the urge to respond. He's bating me. He wants my attention. He'll never know he has it.

"You sure you're fine?" Declan taunts.

> Worst Human Alive: I get it. You wanted my attention. You have it now. But you better get tested before we get back together. That guy is a slut.

I hate him. I despise him.

"I'm. Fine," I say slowly, working to keep my breathing even.

> Worst Human Alive: Ya know what? Fuck you. You're nothing without me. And when that guy is done with you, and he will be, because you're nothing but a second-rate whore who isn't even good in bed, don't come crawling back to me.

> Worst Human Alive: By the way, I fucked your assistant and mine. And Lake. She's always been better than you at everything.

"Ha!" I shout. He's such a fucking narcissistic asshole. I'm sure he cheated on me plenty. Probably with the assistant I fired after catching her flirting with him one too many times. But Lake hates Jason. With a passion. She wouldn't have touched him with a ten-foot pole.

It shouldn't make me happy to know that he's gaslighting me, but it does. It validates every instinct I've had when it comes to this man. And as a girl who stopped trusting her own instinct a long time ago, that feels like a fucking win.

And, god, do I need a win.

"Is that your stalker? Is he bothering you? You need to tell me if he's bothering you."

It's in that moment that I realize Declan is much closer than he was before. Standing over me, looking at my phone, reading my messages.

Humiliated, I lash out. "Could you back up and not read my personal messages?"

Declan's brown eyes swim with concern. "*Melina.*" The single word is soft but so damn patronizing.

"I'm fine." I push my chair back and grab my phone. "You aren't my father. Stop acting like it."

His nostrils flare in response. Why is it that even when I'm angry and hurt and humiliated, I can't help but push his buttons? Maybe because it makes me feel alive.

"Though I'd be happy to call you *daddy* if you'd like," I tease, my tone harsh rather than playful.

Declan lets out a hurricane-like sigh, the sound all growly and thundering. He stalks to the sink, sets his coffee down, and turns around.

But I don't want to hear what he'll say. I need the last word. So I head for the door, but not before meeting his angry eyes with an equally pissed off smile. "And by the way, I am *excellent* in bed."

My bratty comment does the trick. Declan is left speechless as I rush out of the house, determined to win this round.

CHAPTER 12

Declan

I'VE NEVER BEEN good with words. To be fair, I've never really tried to be good with words. I don't censor my thoughts, but I don't say much either way. Normally my face does all the talking.

But with Melina?

With Melina I *want* to be better. She's hurting. She's scared. She's embarrassed. But she's also pissing me the fuck off. And that makes it nearly impossible to follow through on my commitment. I walk into the kitchen set on making things right. To apologize—*again*—for telling her what she can and can't do. And again, I make it worse.

Can't she see that I'm trying, though? Can't she see that I care? I care so goddamn much. The woman is all I think about. It's absurd. Three days ago, I didn't know her. To me, she was just another pop star with songs that my nieces sing along to far too loudly and off key.

Now I find myself searching out her music when I'm driving to the station. Listening to her songs when I'm in my office. Decoding lyrics to decipher her innermost thoughts. What makes her tick, why she's so sarcastic and bratty, but most of all, why she's so scared.

Beckett gave me the broadest of details. That she needed a place to stay for a few weeks because she wanted to spend the holidays with Lake, but that she had an issue with a stalker that made Ford uneasy. I figured a stalker meant an overzealous fan. I'm beginning to think it's way more than that.

I wish she'd open up to me. Otherwise, how can I keep her safe?

These things keep me up at night, and when they're not doing the job, thoughts of another pain in my ass do it. Because Cade won't stop texting and asking about Melina. Since when does he care about anyone this much?

And why do I find the need to respond to his every question?

I can't leave him on *read*, knowing he cares like this.

I'm fucking happy he cares. Melina deserves to have people in her life who have her best interests in mind. And Cade deserves someone as amazing as Melina.

I just need to get out of their way and let them be happy. Stop fucking it up like I fuck up everything good in life.

So now I'm texting more than I ever wanted to, tapping my foot to pop songs I can't get out of my head, and pulling my hair so hard that I swear it's grown half an inch in just three days.

That last issue is why I'm currently walking into a hair salon for a trim when I'm not due for one for another week.

> Cade: Given any more thought to coming up to Boston?

As I wait for Lily to finish with her client, I glare down at the last message Cade sent me. Have I given any thought to it?

Ha. What an absurd question. It's all I've thought about. *Share the bed with them.* What the fuck does that even mean?

Why can't I get the image of what it could mean out of my head?

And why am I actually considering it?

"Hey, Dec. I'm ready for you."

I blink a few times, bringing myself back to the moment. Back to the woman standing before me.

Lily Reilly. The wife of one of my best friends. Or rather, his widow.

Kyle was so much more than just a friend. He was my chief. Lily never calls me chief, likely for that reason. Sometimes I wonder if it hurts her to see me like this. I come in every other week for a cut. I've

BOSTON BOLTS HOCKEY: TROUBLE

been doing it ever since we lost him. Before that, I always went to the barber downtown.

Guilt has a way of molding a person's every move, even the most mundane activities.

"Hey, Lil. How's Benji doing?"

Her son is one of the cutest kids around. The guys all make sure to spend ample time with him, and that includes bringing him to the station, so I see him often.

Her face lights up in the mirror as she gets me settled in, already pulling at my hair, likely realizing it's much more out of control than normal. "He's good. Spending time at Jules' Bakery today. Helping Jules and Shawn make donuts."

I dip my chin. "That's good."

"What's new with you? I hear you have a famous guest staying with you through the holidays."

She gets to work on my hair, and I find myself making conversation with her, because like I said, guilt forces a person to do things they wouldn't normally do. And for me, that includes talking.

"Seems like you really like her," Lily says as she stands in front of me, stopping to really study my reaction. With her scissors in one hand and her fingers holding the hair that hangs over my forehead, I find it hard to lie.

"She's a sweetheart. What's not to like?"

"Life is short, Dec," she says in the way only a woman who's lost her husband can. In a way that doesn't feel like lip service. A way that feels more like a punch to the gut. "You should enjoy the good things."

I don't smile, even though she's smiling at me, because her expression isn't a happy one. No, it's pained and brutal.

But it does make me think.

And when I get called into a fire right after my appointment, when I feel the lick of flames singeing my skin as I run into the building, I realize I never replied to Cade. And if I never come out of here, that last question will be left unanswered. Will he always wonder about how I would have responded?

Fun

CHAPTER 13

Melina

"WHY CAN'T you take a bodyguard? Or take Ford. He'd love to get out of the house and see a game in person," Lake says over the speaker as I finish up my makeup.

It's been a long, quiet week, and I'm itching to get out of the house.

There was a fire in an abandoned warehouse, and that kept Declan pretty busy. Not that he told me about it. I heard about it from Ford when I was over at their house.

While difficult to admit, it hurt not to hear about it from Declan. I crave his attention, even if all we seem to do is fight. It makes zero sense.

Even though I barely saw Declan, his control was still felt. I swear a patrol car drives by on an hourly basis. Each time I see it, my unease grows. It feels like I'm being watched. Like I'm the one who did something wrong, rather than the one who needs protection. Like rather being there to keep people out, the police are monitoring to ensure I remain in the house.

Even when Lake and I grabbed lunch in town, a gaggle of firefighters just so happened to be taking their lunch at the same place.

It's stifling.

Although focusing on my irritation with Declan has distracted me from stressing about how I can't write a lyric to save my life, so I guess that's a plus.

"You know as well as I do that your husband doesn't want to leave your side." One last swipe of mascara, and I'm ready.

The car service has already been arranged, compliments of Cade, my bag is packed, and Sara and Lennox made arrangements for me to sit with them. It's exactly the kind of night I need. A reminder that I'm not a prisoner.

That I'm a twenty-eight-year-old woman who's done nothing wrong. That I'm allowed to have fun.

Once the game is over, win or lose, I'm counting on Cade to take me back to his apartment so he can do filthy things to my body.

My legs tingle at the mere thought of it.

Since Saturday, I've been insatiable. Getting off in Declan's house, knowing he's on the other side of the wall, is strange.

Especially since every time I shut my eyes, I can't help but imagine his body, despite how annoyed with him I am.

I blame Cade. He painted this picture of the two of them touching me, and now I can't get it out of my head. I want them both. Badly.

But only one has made himself available to me.

Declan warned me that Cade was a playboy, yet Cade's the one who's not playing games. He tells me what he wants and follows through. With Declan, I constantly find myself questioning whether I'm misinterpreting his actions.

"Then we'll both go. We'll bring Nash. He'd love to watch his big brother play."

"Lake, he's an infant. Pretty sure he won't be watching the game," I say. Then, with a wicked smile, I throw in "It's twenty degrees out. Keep him warm at home with his mom and dad. He's got enough of an uphill battle, seeing as how his other brother is your ex."

"Shut it," she hisses, though the sound quickly turns into a laugh.

My chest feels lighter. My life has felt so serious this week. "I'm serious. Can you imagine the memoirs they're gonna write about that kid? You better start saving up for all the therapy he's going to need."

"I hate you."

"I love you too."

She sighs. "I just want you to be safe."

My heart clenches at her sincerity. God, she's a good friend. "I will be. I'll be at a hockey game with a million people. Jason hates hockey. And he lives in Jersey. Even if he somehow spotted me on TV, he couldn't get there quick enough to cause a problem. It's going to be fine."

Dina: We're going to the festival of lights tonight. Wish you were here.

I stare at my cousin's text for a long moment, hit with a confusing mix of emotions. Attending the festival of lights is a family tradition that's existed for as long as I've been alive. It's held at this beautiful church that has acres of private land. Every year, the space is decorated beautifully. The older Portuguese parishioners cook for days and serve the food family style on cafeteria tables covered in beautiful linens that have been passed down for generations. Every Friday night in December, they hold a candlelit vigil, and our family always attends the second one.

As a child, I'd sing in the chorus, and as an adult, I donate and kept my head down. Year after year, I'm reminded by my family that it's improper to boast, and apparently, they believe that if I continued to sing with the chorus, that's what I'd be doing.

I loved the event, even when I couldn't participate, and a part of me wishes I were there. Though a bigger part, the part that finally worked up the nerve to cut off everyone there but Dina, knows that I can't go back. That the tradition has been sullied. The magic that surrounded it and so many other special activities died when my family chose Jason over me.

Me: Miss you.

It hurts, how Jason is still stealing from me. How often I think that it would be so much easier to agree with my brother. To believe that my consent was implied because he was my boyfriend. Or that I obviously tripped the time I ended up with a broken ankle. But I do know better, and wishing for things to be different does no good.

As the car pulls into the arena parking lot, my phone buzzes again.

> Sara: Are you here yet? I'm stuck with the press right now, but Lennox is going to meet you at the players' entrance. That should allow you to stay under the radar.

"Excuse me," I say to the driver.

He glances at me in the rearview mirror, then quickly returns his focus to our surroundings. "Yes, ma'am."

"Could you take me to the players' entrance?"

He gives me a warm smile. "Yes, ma'am. Mr. Fitzgerald directed me to drop you there."

My belly does a swoop at the mention of Cade. For most of the day, I was focused on sneaking out without getting another lecture from Declan. Then Dina's text diverted my attention to my family. All of it put a damper on my excitement, but now that I'm here, so close to Cade, the giddiness returns.

As the car comes to a stop, Lennox steps up to the curb. She's dressed in a Bolts jersey and black pants, with her pink hair pulled back in a pretty braid. I love how confident she is in her own skin. While she's much taller than I am, we're both curvy, and she knows exactly how to accentuate all her assets.

"Ah, you're here!" she cheers as the driver comes to a stop.

The man can't even open his own door before she's yanking on mine. She clutches my arm and drags me out of the car, then pulls me in for a hearty hug. I swear her boobs swallow me. I laugh the entire time, already knowing this was the best decision I've made all week.

"Players' entrance, huh?" I say, unable to temper my wide smile.

She grins and holds out her arm. "Stick with me, Mel. I know all the good tricks."

I follow her inside, practically floating with giddiness. Normally, I'm flanked by security no matter where I go, but since Ford came up with the idea of hiding me in Bristol, where both the police department and fire department have taken on the task of keeping me safe, I've given my security detail time off. They deserve it after the last few months.

Cade spoke to Ford about tonight, promising that his driver would be my security to and from the arena, and that once I arrived, I'd be with Lennox and Sara. Everyone in Boston knows the Langfields are ridiculously overprotective about their women, so obviously I'm safe in their company.

So even though they've got their own security stationed everywhere, and even though there are eyes on us at all times, I feel a lighthearted freeness that I haven't experienced in years.

My phone buzzes, so I pull it out of my pocket. Dina again. I don't want to lose this feeling, but if she has sent me a picture from the festival, there's no way it won't bring me down. I just want to live within the sparkle for a little while, so I press the button on the side of my phone, powering it off, then tuck it away again.

"Looks like trouble has arrived," a voice says from up ahead in the private hallway.

Heart leaping, I take off at a run toward the hot man in a navy blue suit. Already, his dirty blond hair is swept back, as if he's been running his hands through it.

Cade opens his arms, and I launch myself at him. In one fluid motion, he grabs my ass, holding me tight against him while I wrap my legs around his waist.

"Hey, Coach."

His face splits in a smile so wide it's blinding. Tipping his chin up, he presses his lips to mine. "Fuck, I missed you," he says, his breath skating over my skin. With another kiss, he squeezes my ass. He says it like he's surprised he feels this way, and somehow, that makes me feel even lighter. I like surprising him. He's certainly surprised the hell out of me.

When he pulls me closer, his fingers digging into my ass, Lennox squeals. "Okay, there's press," she warns.

Cade is zeroed in on me, his blue eyes full of fire. "I don't care. I'm currently kissing the hottest woman I've ever seen. The woman I'm lucky enough to call my girlfriend."

My cheeks heat, and my heart thumps hard against my breastbone. "I don't care either."

"Good," he murmurs, dipping back in for a kiss.

"Great, you're obsessed with one another. But we've got a hockey game to coach," Gavin calls as he walks past us, waving his clipboard.

"Coming," Cade calls after him.

"Not till tonight," Lennox jokes behind me.

Cade sets me down, still laser-focused on my face. "So much trouble," he mutters. With a final peck to my lips, he strides away.

I don't take my eyes off his ass until he's completely disappeared from view. He's got the perfect bubble butt, and the way his suit pants mold to it allows me to see every flex as he moves.

Lennox links her arm with mine and tugs me toward the suite. "That was fun."

She's not wrong. Everything about Cade is fun.

I haven't been able to stand in line for my own beer or souvenir in years. Most people would gladly give it up if they could, but it's one of those normal activities I miss. When I'm touring, venues provide gift bags full of their team's merch, and when I'm out and about, I'm always assigned a server who takes care of my every need.

So between the first and second period, while Sara and Lennox are busy chatting with a donor, I sneak out the suite's door and head to the concession stand. My shoes stick to the floor as I walk, and the concourse smells like fried food, stale beer, and sugar, yet I can't help but smile like I'm meandering down the streets in Paris.

Bolts fans push past me, and not a single one stops to notice me. Because hello, why would anyone with celebrity status like mine willingly fight through a throng of people to fetch their own goodies?

Because they can.

Excitement courses through me, making my steps lighter. Like I'm getting away with a crime. It's absurd, I know, but truly, this simple act is renewing me, pouring life back into me.

When the concession stand comes into view, I've almost convinced myself that I've gotten away with it. I've almost completely bought the lie I've told myself—that I'm safe here—when a hand grasps my arm roughly, and I'm slammed against a wall. Before I can react, another hand covers my mouth, and the eyes of the one person I never wanted to see again look down at me.

"You've been a very bad girl."

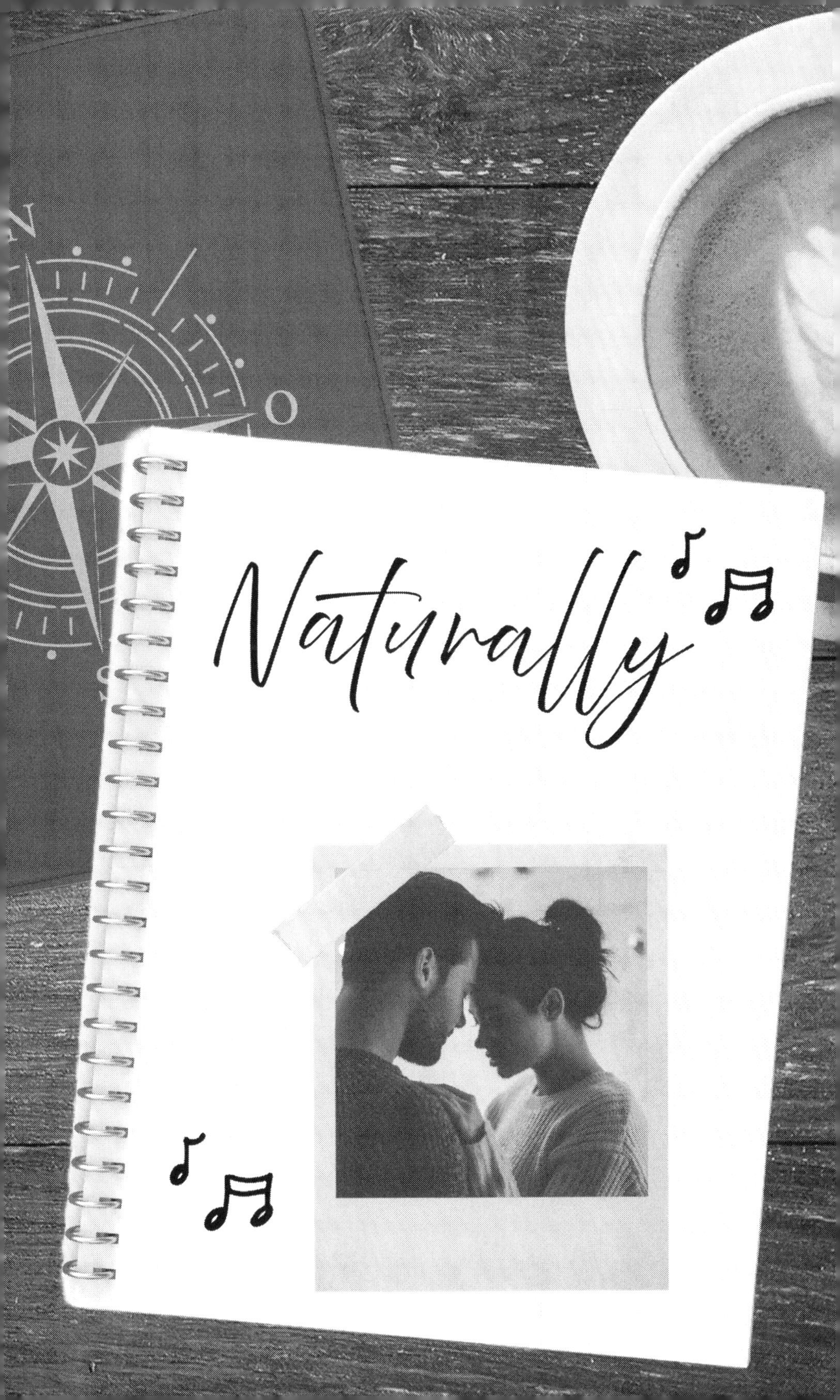
Naturally

CHAPTER 14

Declan

MY PHONE RINGS as I weave my way through the swarms of people in the concourse, ignoring the stench of sweat and fried food hanging in the air.

"Chief Everhart."

"Declan, it's Lake Hall."

"Hi, Lake. Everything okay?" I ask distractedly while I search the crowd for the short brunette I lost sight of a moment ago.

"Mel's cousin just called. She's been blowing up Mel's phone, but she can't get ahold of her."

The tension in Lake's tone leaves me uneasy. "What did she say?"

"She accidentally spilled to her mother, who told Mel's mother, who must have told Mel's brother—"

"Lake," I grit out.

"She thinks Mel's ex is in Boston at the game. Can you get ahold of Cade? Tell them to assign someone to stick with her at all times? Her ex is seriously deranged, and I can't reach her to warn her."

"I'm on it."

"*You're* on it? Oh my god, please tell me you're on your way there. I knew you weren't going to let her leave without following her."

I hang up the phone without responding.

No one needs to know the many reasons as to why I'm here in Boston. How the fire this week fucked with my head. How Lily's words affected me more than I'd like to admit. How Cade's taunt—or offer, however you want to look at it—has kept my brain working overtime.

No, the most obvious reason that I'm here is because I'm a control freak. Of course I wouldn't let Melina out of my sight. Regardless of how badly she doesn't want to believe she's in danger, she is, and because she's fucking trouble, she needs to believe she has at least a modicum of freedom.

Rather than locking Melina in her room like I was tempted to do, I followed her, and now here I am, walking through a fucking throng of people because I lost sight of her for half a damn second.

God, the woman drives me fucking crazy. She's not even mine, and yet I can't stand the thought of losing her. If anything happens to her...

Breathe, she's going to be okay. She's probably in the—

The sound of a slap rings out over the din, instantly putting me on alert. A sickening sense of dread twists in my gut as I pull up short and do a one-eighty, searching for the source of the noise.

"You think you can leave me?" a man hisses. "You think you can parade around like a little slut and leave *me*?"

Melina's there, only a few feet away, pushed up against the wall, her cheeks stained with tears, one an angry red. The man looming over her has her gripped by the neck.

Without hesitation, I'm charging at them. I'm not the first person to react—thank fuck for Bolts fans; this town is full of good people—but I'm the one who clutches at his shoulders and tears him away from her.

"I will fucking kill you." I slam him against the wall and grab him by the throat just like he did to Melina.

"We were just having a conversation. She's my girlfriend. You know how it is." He says it as if we're best friends. Like because I'm a man, I should understand why it was necessary for him to knock a woman around.

Filled with blind rage, I squeeze his throat tighter and slap my hand against the wall. "Here's what I know. I know that every camera in this vicinity will be wiped if I ask. I know that every person in the stadium will forget that you were even here. Forget that you even exist. I know that if I squeeze just a little tighter right here," I pinch down, and his face turns so purple I think he may actually pop, "I'll break your windpipe and air will escape into your neck and chest, which will cause you to have a heart attack and die in mere minutes."

"Declan, please," Melina cries. "He's not worth it."

Despite her pleading, the sound of her voice only makes me squeeze tighter. I hate the fear in it. Hate that only an hour ago, she walked into this arena and jumped into Cade's arms, wearing the brightest smile, yet now, this jackass has stolen that smile. I love that smile. I want to see it every day, even if it's only aimed at Cade.

"Dude, you're going to kill him," someone shouts.

Dammit. He's probably right.

My pulse is pounding so loud in my ears that I can barely hear the crowd around me, but I can feel her fear, and that guts me.

"Please," she whispers as I meet her tear-streaked face.

With a grunt, I release him. His body crumples to the ground, but I don't stop to watch. I march straight over to Melina and press my hand —the hand that almost took the life of another person—to her cheek. "I'm sorry."

She sobs. "No. You saved me," she whispers, covering my hand with hers. "Take me home. Please. Take me home."

Like it's second nature, I sweep her up into my arms. I don't put her down even once we get outside.

As I step out onto the sidewalk, her driver scrambles out of the car and darts over to us, brow furrowed in concern.

"Can you take us back to my house? I'll come back for my car later."

He leads us to the car and opens the door. I still don't put Melina down. It's a challenge, but I manage to get us both settled inside. Then I hold her in my arms the whole way home.

My phone rings nonstop the entire way. I know I'm an ass for not calling to let Lake know Melina is okay, but with the way she's shaking in my arms, I don't dare let her go for even a second. I stroke her arm with my thumb, molding my body around hers, wishing I could shield her from pain.

The driver helps me get her into the house, carrying her bag and unlocking the door once I've dug my keys out of my pocket. I head straight to her bedroom, but when I try to set her on the bed so I can lock up, she clings to my chest.

"Please don't go."

Pulling her tight to me again, I nod at the driver. "Thank you. I'll lock up later."

With tears streaming down her face, she whimpers. "I'm so sorry I'm a mess."

"Don't ever apologize for your emotions. I know I'm not good at this. I know I'm probably not who you want—"

She clutches at my shirt and buries her face in the crook of my neck. "You're who I need."

The desperation in her voice, the sadness, it's all overwhelming.

Just as I drop my cheek to the top of her head and soak in the feel of her pressed up against me, my phone chimes again. "That's probably Lake," I murmur.

Sucking in a hard breath, she peers up at me. The brokenness in her gaze damn near kills me. "Why would she be calling you and not me?"

"Your phone is off. It's why no one could reach you to warn you about—"

Melina flinches, so I snap my mouth shut and swallow his name.

"Shit," she whispers. She wriggles in my arms, so I ease her down and help her settle on the side of the bed. With her phone out, she powers it on, and when the screen lights up, one message after another pops up in rapid succession. She doesn't bother to read them; she just hits Lake's name and calls her.

My head is a jumbled mess as I listen to her tell Lake that she's okay, that she's home with me. I take a step back and thumb over my shoulder at the door, silently asking whether she wants privacy. She responds with a resolute shake of her head, so I pull out my phone and get to work dealing with the mess I made at the arena.

Without sorting through the text messages and missed call notifications, I navigate to the contact I need.

> **Me:** I need you to pull the security footage from the hallway outside of C 110 and probably the surrounding ones too.

> **Beckett:** It's already done. Is she okay?

> **Me:** No. But I've got her. Don't destroy the tapes. If she wants to press charges, I want her to have that choice.

> **Beckett:** If we turn over those tapes, that guy won't be the only one facing questions.

> **Me:** Don't care. It's her choice, and I'm not taking it away from her.

> **Beckett:** Done. Liv and Sara have a team dealing with witnesses.

> **Me:** Thank you.

I set my phone on her bedside table and turn it on silent. I never switch off the ringer. It's important for me to be available for the guys at the department. But for tonight, they can figure it out. The entire town could be on fire, and I wouldn't leave this room.

"I don't know what to do," she whispers, though I don't think she's talking to me.

Thank god I'm trained in trauma response. If I had to do this using only my own instinct, I'd fail. And failing her isn't an option.

"How about we focus on small things right now? Like getting changed and ready for bed?"

With her lip caught between her teeth and her eyes downcast, she gives me a small nod. From there, though, we're both still, quiet. She drags her focus up to my face, frowning, like she doesn't even know where to start.

I push off the mattress, but she grabs my leg, halting the movement. Dropping down again, I place my palm over her trembling hand. "I'm just going to grab something for you to sleep in."

She shakes her head. "Please don't leave me."

I squeeze her hand and duck closer. "I'm not leaving you."

She's dressed in a Bolts jersey and jeans. Neither would be anywhere close to comfortable enough to sleep in, so I slip off my sweater, then pull my white undershirt over my head.

I hold it out to her, my heart stuttering. "You can sleep in this if you want."

She nods but doesn't make a move to take it or to undress.

"Do you need help?"

Her eyes well with tears, and her breathing grows more ragged. "I-I —" She snaps her mouth shut, quieting a sob.

"I got you," I murmur, my heart aching for her. "Can you put your hands up for me?"

She does as she's told, and I undress her. Her chest is covered in red blotches, the sight enough to make my anger surge again. Despite the way her breasts spill out of her bra when she unhooks it, nothing about this is sexual.

Once I've tugged my white T-shirt over her head, she sighs, and the tension in her shoulders eases. She brings the collar of my shirt to her lips and rubs it against them. "Smells like you."

It probably smells awful. Fear and adrenaline combined inside me tonight, causing me to sweat buckets while I searched for her and as I pulled that asshole off her. But her expression has softened, like the scent brings her comfort, so I don't give it too much thought.

"Can I unbutton your jeans?" I ask.

She nods again, her breath finally beginning to even out, and lifts the T-shirt high enough that the underside of her breasts peek out. I focus on the task at hand, getting her comfortable, all the while ignoring the longing that hits me at the sight. The desire to hold her against my bare chest. I'm not sure either of us will be at rest until I do. Once I've undone her pants, she leans back, allowing me to pull them off, revealing a pair of black lace boy shorts.

She sits again, the shirt falling over her hips before I can study the way her panties mold to her curves. Thank god for that.

"You should have some water and an aspirin before bed. Do you want me to come with me to get them, or do you want to stay here?"

The fear that flashes in her eyes is the only response I need. Hovering in front of her, I grip her ass and guide her legs around my waist. Once she's settled and I've got a good hold on her, I carry her like a koala.

For the first time tonight, she smiles at me. "Thank you."

The ache to kiss her, to thank her for allowing me to take care of her, almost overtakes me.

But she's not mine, and even if she were, the last thing she needs right now is to be mauled by another man.

So I ignore the way her plump ass feels in my hands as I lumber down the hallway and toward the kitchen. I ignore the way she lays her head against my collarbone as I detour to the front door and turn the lock. And I ignore how her warm breath skates over my neck when she sighs and the shiver that runs down my spine as she curls her hand around the back of my neck and plays with my hair.

Bottle of water in hand, I take her to my bathroom, where I set her down on the counter and search the medicine cabinet for aspirin.

She looks around my space, eyes wide, as if she's memorizing it. "You have a nice shower," she says of the oversized tiled space with multiple shower heads, including a rain one.

I grunt my agreement. "Feel free to use it whenever you want."

She gives me a soft smile as I press two aspirin into her palm and then hold out the bottle of water.

Once she's recapped the water, I pick her up again and carry her back to her bed.

As I settle her beneath the covers, she lets out a heavy sigh. "Okay, you've done enough babysitting me. I'll be okay."

I study her, searching for a hint of what she really wants. If she's not comfortable with me here, I'll sit outside her door. But if she wants me close, nothing could pull me from her side.

"I can sit above the covers until you fall asleep. I don't want to make you uncomfortable," I offer.

She turns so she's on her side, her face smooshed adorably against the pillow, making her lips pout as she regards me. "I think I'd be pretty comfortable wrapped up in those big arms of yours."

This girl. Even after the night she's had, she's still got the flirty sarcasm going for her. Breathing easier knowing he hasn't destroyed her spirit, I tug back the covers. "Then that's what you'll get."

"You can't sleep in your jeans." Her voice is raspy, and fuck if I'm not cursing myself for what I'm about to do.

Head dropped back, staring up at the ceiling and deciding that I'll ask for forgiveness from Cade rather than seeking approval, I unbutton my pants and shuck them off. Then I slide beneath the sheets with his girl.

I have no idea what the fuck is really going on between them, but she cares for him, and he likes her too. And even though the two of us are in bed together, wearing very little, I'm here as her friend only. Or at least that's what I tell myself when she pulls my hand to her lips and kisses it and then doesn't let go.

I'm woken by a loud noise and then heavy footsteps.

Guilt mixes with adrenaline as I realize that Melina has wrapped her warm body around me, her thigh draped over my hips and my hard cock, her lips brushing against my bare chest.

The door swings open, startling me. Out of instinct, I roll on top of her, hovering over her body, shielding her.

"What the fuck?" Cade hisses.

I breathe a sigh of relief and look down at the sleeping woman beneath me. Sitting up, I nod at Cade, silently signaling him to move out into the hall. He's panting like he ran here, and his eyes are murderous.

Fuck.

Despite the dread that's working its way through me, I don't rush off the bed. I take my time so as not to wake her. The last thing she needs is to be woken in the middle of the night.

I slip out the door and press it closed before I turn to face my best friend.

"What the fuck?" He looks me up and down, teeth gritted, eyes blazing with anger.

It's then that I realize that I'm in only my boxers.

I adjust myself, because my cock is jutting out like I was just naked in bed with his girlfriend. Then I fold my arms across my chest. "It's not what it looks like."

"I don't care what it looks like. I've been calling you for three fucking hours. I was in the middle of a press conference when I heard, and when you didn't pick up any of my hundred fucking phone calls, I got in the car and drove here. Is she okay?"

His breathing is ragged, and he's shifting his weight from foot to foot like he's considering going through me to get to her.

I hold up my hand. "I'm sorry. I should have called, but she needed me, and I—" I pinch the bridge of my nose. "I'm sorry."

"Is she okay?" he grits out again.

I force myself to meet his gaze, and for the first time tonight, I really take him in. This is a side of Cade I didn't know existed. He's never emotional. Never out of control. But right now, I'm pretty sure he could tear me to pieces. It's in this moment that I understand just how much he cares about her.

"She's okay. And nothing happened between the two of us."

He frowns. Probably because he doesn't believe me after the way he found us tangled together in bed.

"You can trust me. She was in shock and didn't want to be alone."

With a heaving breath, Cade deflates a little. "Did he hurt her?"

Anger pummels me from the inside when I replay the moment I heard Jason's palm hitting Melina's cheek. The memory of the fear in her eyes as he squeezed the air from her lungs is like a knife to the heart. "It could have been worse," I say.

"Beckett says he was hospitalized."

Maybe I should feel bad. Maybe I should be concerned about what happened to him. Instead, I feel nothing.

"You did that?"

With a single nod, I say, "I told you, I've got her. You can trust me."

Dropping his head forward, he curses softly. "Can I see her?"

"She needs rest."

"Fine." He lifts his hat from his head and settles it again, a nervous tic of his. "I'll sleep in the guest room and check on her in the morning."

"Don't you have a game in California on Sunday?" I glance at the clock on the wall. "You have to be on the plane in what, five hours?"

Shoulders sagging, he roughs a hand down his face. "Four."

I frown. "Go home."

"No."

I stare at my best friend. What the fuck is his issue? Does he just want to know that she's okay? Or is it something else?

"Cade, I've got her. You've got a job to do, and this is my job. Let me take care of your girl until you get back. She's going to need a few days to recover anyway. Let her lick her wounds and get her bearings."

Hands clenched, he mutters something indistinguishable, his head still bowed. The man is clearly at war with himself.

Without overthinking it, I step forward until I'm chest to chest with him, then I grab him by both arms and force him to look at me. "She's okay. I've got her. I promise you. She's going to be okay."

Cade's blue eyes swim with so much emotion, so much conflict. "I care about her," he admits, like he needs me to hear that she's different. As if I didn't know. I've never seen him this way. Never knew he had it in him to break for someone else. This is a different side to Cade, and I'm not sure how I feel about it.

But outside of my family, he is my closest friend—the person who matters most to me in the world—and right now, he needs my help.

"I know you do. And you can trust me to take care of her. You know that, right?"

Cade blows out a breath, and I taste the acceptance against my lips. For a moment, I consider pulling him into my chest. He looks like he needs a hug, and dammit, so do I. I could fall apart so easily right now, if only I weren't the one who needed to hold it all together.

I'm still battling with myself when he steps back and claps me on the shoulder. "Thank you."

Swallowing back my disappointment, I dip my chin. "You need to get back to Boston. You okay to drive?"

It's after one a.m. By the time he gets home, he'll be lucky to get an hour or two of sleep before he has to head out again.

"I'm wired," he admits. "I'll be fine." He regards the door, roughing a hand over his mouth. "You gonna go back and sleep in there with her?"

I clench my fists at my sides. Fuck. I have no idea how I should handle this. Or maybe I do. Melina made it clear what she wants, and I can't say no to her. "She asked me to." My chest goes tight. There's no way he's okay with how he found me in bed with his girl.

To my utter shock, he nods simply. "Good. You should do that, then." He thumbs toward the door. "I'll lock up on my way out."

Even after he's dismissed me, he stands in the hall, watching me. Like he needs to see me go. Like he needs to know that I'll be there to protect her. So, despite the discomfort settling in my gut, I shuffle into the bedroom and climb into bed with Melina, ignoring his scrutiny. I can't handle looking at him right now. I don't want to see the hurt or jealousy or anger he's got to be feeling.

The moment I settle, it's like she subconsciously knows I'm back. Without waking, she scoots closer, wrapping her warm body around me.

The sharp hiss from the doorway snags my attention, and I finally force myself to look at Cade. I'm not sure what to make of the expression he wears as he watches us. Maybe it's my exhaustion, or maybe it's the dark, or maybe I know jack shit about feelings and reading people and I'm making it all up in my head, but to me, his expression looks a hell of a lot like love.

CHAPTER 15

Melina

FOR YEARS I dated a man who was never content with what he had.

More money, more attention, more sex. More, more, more was his mantra.

I can't count the number of mornings I woke up with a pounding head after he'd spent an evening shouting at me. Or with a bruise he explained away by blaming my sensitive skin.

"Someone just has to look at you, and you bruise."

So when I wake up to a cup of coffee by my bed and the strong arms of Declan Everhart wrapped around me as he gently rocks me awake, I burst into tears.

"Shh, I've got you, Melina. You're safe." The deep timbre of his voice is a calming melody that I wish I could write a song about.

"Because of you." I peer up into his warm brown eyes. As the sunlight streams in, they turn golden. "Did I dream that Cade was here?"

Declan shakes his head. "He was worried about you. Drove here like a bat out of hell. Woulda missed his flight if I hadn't sent him back, promising that I have you."

I smile, imagining that entire scenario. Waking up in Declan's arms may be the most comforting experience of my life, but butterflies flutter in my belly at the thought of Cade coming for me. And that he left knowing Declan would take care of me. Though I'm not sure what any of it means, the two of them settle me in completely different ways.

"Want your coffee?"

The butterflies settle, and the heavy weight on my chest presses a little more firmly. Coffee sounds incredible, but he'll have to let go of me in order to reach it, and the feel of his arms wrapped around me is a decadence I've never known. I'm not ready to give it up.

"Maybe in a minute."

With a soft grunt of agreement, he strokes the hair from my brow.

Pressing my face to the crook of his neck, I inhale deeply, then pull back to look him in the eye. "I have a question."

His lips curl up almost imperceptibly in response, like he's maybe enjoying this moment as much as I am.

"Why do you pretend to be grouchy when you're really a big, snuggly teddy bear?"

He shakes his head, but there's no hiding the way that hint of a smile grows just a fraction. "I'm not."

"You are with me."

Sighing, he looks away. "You're different."

Chest tightening, I search his expression for some kind of clue as to what he means. "Why?"

"Stop asking questions and drink your coffee."

I don't fight him. I'm too busy dissecting those simple words.

You're different.

How and why? And what does it mean that I'm asking these questions of him, the best friend of the man I'm sleeping with?

It's a bizarre conundrum. One I'd rather focus on than the very real disaster that happened last night. Though from what I know of Declan, he will only let me live in this land of denial for so long.

"Would you want to go into town with me?"

The question is so surprising, I actually sit up, escaping his hold.

He clearly takes my reaction as a negative one, splaying both hands in the air in front of him. "Or not. I could drop you off at Lake's while I run errands."

With a long exhale, I lean into him. "I was just surprised, is all. I'd love to go to town."

Declan blushes. The grown man who speaks almost exclusively in grunts *turns pink*. "It's nothing great. I told Shawn that I'd try to bring you by the bakery since Jules has been dying to meet you. Then I need to stop at the station to check in with the guys. Normally I'd be working tonight, but they can handle it without me."

With a mixture of gratitude and guilt swirling inside me, I squeeze his bicep. "It sounds perfect. But if you have to work, that's okay. I'm a big girl. I can hang out here alone."

Declan's no is immediate. "I know you can, but you shouldn't have to."

Heart lifting, I smile. "Thank you. Can I have my coffee now?"

As promised, our first stop is Jules' Bakery. If I wasn't already smitten with this town, this magical heaven would have sealed the deal. From the pink walls to the checkered floor to the adorable donut signs—my favorites being *Donut worry, be happy* and *Donut stop believing*—I adore every inch of this space.

And don't get me started on the actual donuts. Declan informed me that this is where he got the donuts the first morning after I came. Naturally, I giggled and asked if there was a plural version of the word *came*, because Cade made it happen multiple times. Declan blushed again, and I swear my damn heart floated in my chest.

After I discovered that Jules's blueberry donuts are what made her famous, there was no question about which kind I'd order. As I devour it—I can see why she's known for the recipe; it's incredible—I can't help but feel Declan's heavy stare.

"So," he hedges. "We need to talk about last night."

"Not supposed to talk with food in my mouth." With a grin, I take a giant bite.

The glower he directs at me is oddly comforting.

"There's video," he says evenly.

A phantom pain, the sensation of Jason's fingers digging into my arm, flashes in my mind. The way he slammed me against the wall grips me, and my heart drops when I remember the slap. From that moment on, the encounter is a blur. The marks I found on my body this morning when I got out of the shower are evidence enough of what happened, but video? I shudder at the thought of ever seeing it.

Cold dread seizes me then, at the memory of how Declan slammed Jason against the wall. How he held him up by his neck so his toes dangled off the floor and the color drained from his face.

"No," I say resolutely.

Frowning, Declan ducks down and catches my gaze. "No what?"

"If there's video of what he did, there's video of what you did," I whisper, scanning the small shop to make sure no one is watching us.

"Is this the first time he's hurt you?"

My stomach sinks at the question. At his knowing expression.

"You're hiding here for a reason. He's obviously part of it, but is there more?"

Lips pressed together tightly, I shake my head. I'm not doing this now. Not here. Maybe not ever.

How do I explain that I told people I thought would support me, help me? That I told my family, and they didn't believe me? That he was my agent, so it wasn't as easy as just walking away? It all seems absurd now. Excuses I made so that I didn't have to make a difficult decision. Though eventually I did when I turned to Ford and asked for help.

Declan covers my hand with his, his palm warm and rough. It's then I realize my hands are trembling. "There is video. He can't lie about what happened. There is no other version of the truth."

"But you—"

"I did what I did, and I'd do it again." He strokes my hand with his thumb. "I'm not worried about explaining my actions. Or answering for them. So you tell me what you want to do, and we'll make it happen."

His expression is softer than I thought possible, his brown eyes imploring me to do what I need. The comfort I find in a man I barely know is unexplainable, and yet...

"I want to file a report," I admit. I don't think I'd have been able to even utter those words if not for the strength he's giving me by holding my hand, by simply sitting quietly with me.

His eyes warm with affection. "Okay, let me make some calls."

Declan sits beside me in his office, a pillar of unwavering support, while the detective from Boston takes my statement. I have a feeling I have Beckett Langfield to thank for the police officer's willingness to drive out here to speak to me.

Either way, I tearfully walk through each detail of last night's altercation. Though I'm swamped with trepidation, I detail every incident I can think of, each time he hurt me. A broken ankle from being pushed down the stairs—he claimed I tripped while we were fighting, but I can still feel him leaning close, and I can still hear the hiss of his breath as he pressed a palm to my back and uttered the words "stupid bitch" as I was catapulted forward. Or the time he slammed me into the wall after one of my shows. For a week, there was this awful ringing in my ear that he blamed on my drinking. He couldn't explain away trying to rape me, though. By that point, I'd had writer's block for months. The stress of our toxic relationship made it impossible for any creativity to bloom. When he held me down and told me he'd give me something to write about, even as I begged him to stop, I knew there was no turning back. Our relationship was over. I kneed him in the balls and ran out of his apartment.

After hiding out at a hotel for two nights, I stupidly ran straight to my mother's house. I was desperate. Distraught. But Jason had already poisoned my family against me. He'd shown up with some sob story about how I'd had too much to drink and had accused him of awful things. He said he knew we needed a break and asked my mother to give me my things.

At the top of the box full of things, Jason had left my music journal. It was full of every song I'd ever written, lyrics and notes, my soul bled into every page. The relief I felt to hold it in my hands was short-lived, because when I opened it, I discovered he had taken a marker to every page. It was unreadable. Destroyed.

I left my mother's house even more broken than when I had come.

I don't say any of this to the detective, though. I keep it straightforward. Detailing the abuse. The attempted rape. Last night's events.

When the detective asks why I didn't report Jason's behavior before —yes, that's how he words it—Declan grips my knee beneath his desk and says, "I've got someone coming in for a meeting any minute. I assume that's enough information for now?"

As Declan walks the man out of the office, mortification eats at me, tearing me into pieces. I'm a twenty-eight-year-old woman with more than enough resources, and still, I was too afraid to go to the police. Too worried they'd believe Jason over me.

And why wouldn't they? My own family did.

Women who report their abusers are the strongest people in the world to me, but women who don't aren't coward. Why is it that a woman's character is questioned based upon her reaction to a man's bad behavior? Until you are in the situation, it's impossible to know what you'd do.

"You ready to go home?" Declan asks as he steps back into his office, hand gripped tight on the door handle.

Disappointment swells inside me. He has to work, and he can't babysit me all day. But I don't want to be alone in an empty house, and I don't think I can face Lake right now. I don't want to talk about last night, and I don't want to think about Jason or how close I came to being seriously hurt.

And what if Jason tries something again, and Declan isn't there? A shudder works its way down my spine at the idea.

"Would it be okay if I hung around the station for the afternoon? I promise I'll stay out of the way."

Declan loosens his hold on the door handle. "You sure? I don't mind taking you home."

I try to hide my wince. I'm being so damn needy. "Yup. You won't even know I'm here." I stand from his chair and walk toward the door, forcing a smile to my face.

For the next few hours, I leave Declan alone. He's clearly busy, because he doesn't come out of his office all afternoon. That doesn't mean I'm left alone, though.

While I'm pulling a bottle of water out of the fridge, Shawn Chase —the ex-baseball player turned firefighter, and Jules's boyfriend— appears and introduces me to all the guys on shift. Then he invites me to read along with their book club and helps me download their current read onto my phone so I can join their discussion later in the week.

I spend the next few hours reading about two hockey players who fall for the same girl. When one of them tells her he doesn't want to fight with his friend over her, my stomach tightens, and at the word *share*, I close the Kindle app and stand from the comfy couch in the lounge.

My imagination is running wild. Declan has been nothing but kind to me, and the last thing he deserves is to be the center of some taboo fantasy.

Cade is there, too, of course—how could he not be?—but he'd probably like the idea of it.

Needing a distraction, I step out into the bay. The guys are busy cleaning and organizing out here, so I stand off to one side and watch. I glance up at Declan's office, only to find him standing at the glass wall, arms crossed, wearing a frown. He's occupied with looking out over the bay, so I take a moment to study him unnoticed, relishing the freedom to take in all his rugged features. His cheeks are covered in a dark scruff, his jaw hard. Though his lips are almost always set in a straight line, his mouth is wide, and his lips are full. It's impossible not to imagine pressing mine against them. I don't see him being an aggressive kisser like Cade. Despite his gruff exterior, I think Cade is right. Declan would be gentle with me. The thought of Cade's aggressive lovemaking, his dirty, hot mouth on my neck, and Declan's soft tongue stroking against my lips has my cheeks burning.

Clearly, the book is getting to me.

I force my attention down to the floor in front of me, and an instant later, I feel Declan's gaze settle on me. I don't dare look up. Instead, I round a fire truck, my chest rising and falling with heavy breaths, and hide from his scrutiny.

An hour later, I'm playing cards with the guys who work for

Declan. Shawn seems like a genuinely nice guy. Colby is the obvious playboy of the group. I swear he winks more than he blinks, reminding me a hell of a lot of Cade. Mason wears a plaid button-down open over his BFD T-shirt and a scowl. I can imagine that he and Declan enjoy not talking to one another often. Dane is a single dad of twin boys he talks about practically nonstop. It's adorable.

But it's been hours since Declan has interacted with anyone. He just remains in his office, and I have absolutely no idea what the hell he does up there.

"Did you seriously just win another round?" Colby asks as I lay down my last match.

"It's Go Fish," Mason grumbles, shifting in his chair.

I laugh for what feels like the first time in days. It bubbles out of me, and when it hits, I can't stop it. Shawn and Colby are smiling, and Mason, of course, is still scowling when the door upstairs scrapes open.

On instinct, I search for the man I can't stop thinking about. He appears at the floor-to-ceiling window overlooking the bay again, zeroing in on me with a small frown.

I hold up a handful of cards and shriek, "I won!"

In response, his lips tug upward into a real smile.

My body is moving before I have the chance to overthink this. "Be right back, boys. I'm going to gloat."

"I'll start on dinner," Mason says, pushing from his chair.

As I scurry across the space, I keep my focus fixed on that smile waiting for me upstairs. I lose sight of him when I hit the stairwell, and by the time I make it up, he's moved back into his office. He probably expects to be left alone again, but my restraint is gone. I can't explain the way I'm constantly being pulled toward Declan, like he's the sun, and I'm caught in his orbit, but I can't deny the urge to seek him out, to demand his attention. Under his watchful gaze, I feel safer, more at ease, than I've ever experienced.

I tap on the door but don't wait for him to answer before I step into his office. When he looks up from his desk and zeroes in on me, my breathing stops. Why is it that when his brows pull together, almost like he's annoyed, my blood heats?

"You ready to go home?"

With my lip caught between my teeth, I wander toward him. "Are you?"

His forehead creases as he studies me. "I'm good with whatever you want to do."

I perch myself against his desk, right next to his chair. He has to tilt his head back to maintain eye contact.

"Are you done with work?"

"Melina—"

"Why do you always call me that?" I ask, frowning.

Declan doesn't make a smart-ass comment about how it *is* my name, after all. Instead, he regards me silently, his expression full of sincerity. "Because that's who you are to me."

My heart clenches. I'm certain he's the only person who can see through my façade to the real me. Sometimes not even Lake can tell when I'm wearing a mask. But Declan? It's like our souls connect on another level.

Cade may have my heart, but I think Declan has my soul.

Is it possible to fall for two people at the same time? To want them in different ways but also recognize that without one, the other couldn't make me whole?

I don't know how else to explain it. When I'm with Declan, I'm safer, more comfortable, than I've ever been. But thoughts of Cade give me butterflies. He's exciting, while Declan grounds me. But who am I to them? Based on the interactions I've observed between them, it's hard not to wonder whether they're the soulmates, and I'm the distraction.

I barely know them. They barely know me. But there is no denying that they are incredibly important to one another.

"Everyone else calls me Mel," I mumble, as if he doesn't know that.

He nods, his eyes swimming with confusion as they dart from my face to where I'm propped up on his desk and back again.

"What else am I to you?" Vulnerability leaches into my tone in a way I wish I had the ability to hide.

Declan doesn't shy away from the rawness of the question. He doesn't look away.

The tension between us grows as I wait for his response. Lips parted, he angles forward.

My heart rate ratchets up.

Is he going to pull me onto his lap? Kiss me?

I want him to. God, I want to feel his lips against mine. I want him to own me with his mouth. I'd give him everything.

At the shrill sound of my phone ringing, he lurches back, and his expression goes blank.

CHAPTER 16

Cade

"HEY, TROUBLE," I say into the phone, chest tight and overwhelmed with emotion. I'm so fucking pissed that I can't be with her right now.

"Hi, Coach." Though the nickname is sweet, she sounds distant, tired, upset.

Of course she's upset, asshole. She was attacked last night.

I settle against the headboard in my hotel room, hating the feel of the rough fabric and wishing more than anything I was cozying up to Mel's soft body. "I fucking miss you." The ache in my chest turns into a sharp pang. I've never legitimately missed a person like this. This is fucking insane. What is this girl doing to me?

"Declan mentioned that you came by last night." She clears her throat, and when she speaks again, she's even quieter. "Thank you for that. Means a lot."

I suck in a harsh breath. "If you think a world exists in which I wouldn't have come to you after what happened, you've lost your mind."

"We just met," she murmurs. "I'd understand—"

Teeth gritted, I let out a low growl. I don't care how long we've known each other. My feelings make no sense, and I don't have the first clue why she means so much to me, but my mother always said that when I met the right person, I'd know.

You'll stop fucking around, Cade. You'll just know.

I laughed every time she brought it up, because I'd already met that person. He just didn't feel the same.

And now? I don't know what the fuck to think. Is it possible to have that connection with two people? Because Mel has set my skin on fire. The pull I feel to her makes sitting here instead of hopping on a plane and heading home immediately almost unbearable.

"You understand nothing if you think I wouldn't be there right now if I could be. Hell, I probably would have been a no-show for the game if Dec hadn't practically kicked me out of the house."

She laughs, the sound a little lighter than her mood so far. "He can be a bit abrasive, huh?"

By the teasing tone, I have a feeling he's beside her. "He's all right," I admit.

"He certainly is." Her tone is full of genuine affection.

My stomach twists in response, though I don't think it's jealousy. It's an emotion I don't think I've ever really experienced. If I had to name it, I guess I'd call it longing. The two of them are together while I'm here. More than anything, I want to be sitting in that room with them. Not just her, but them.

I'm not sure what that even means.

"I'm just happy he was there to protect you," I admit.

"Yeah, it was lucky that he decided to come to the game after all."

And that's when it hits me. I'm not sure how I didn't realize sooner. Maybe because I'd been so worried about Mel, but I never even questioned why Declan was there.

I asked him to come.

Invited him into my bed.

Is it possible he actually considered it? That he got into his car and drove to Boston with the intention of spending the night with Mel and me?

No. That's ridiculous. He's just a control freak, and he knew Mel was in danger. He didn't want to let her out of his sight. And thank fuck for that.

Rather than dwelling on the confusing thoughts racing through me, I say, "So tell me about your day."

Somehow these phone calls are going to have to get me through to Friday. I should be used to it. I've survived on nothing but bits and pieces of the person I care about most for the last twenty years.

The Heart Wants What it Wants

CHAPTER 17

Declan

IT'S OFFICIAL. I need to leave town. Or work all weekend. Anything but spend another minute with my best friend's fake-slash-real girlfriend. I don't know what Melina is to Cade, but they speak every night, and he's texted her incessantly all week. Obviously, she's more than just a hookup to him.

And despite how hard I've fought it, she's more than just a house-guest to me.

I watch her sleeping form, chest aching. Fuck, I'm going to miss this tomorrow.

All week, she's asked me to lie beside her while she falls asleep. Inevitably, I nod off too, and in the morning, she's always curled around me.

"Shit, I fell asleep," I mutter every time, like I didn't mean to, only to do it again the next night.

It's sick how addicted I am to having her close. To her smell. To the soft sounds she makes while she sleeps.

I'm fucked.

I want to savor the last few minutes in bed with her, but I'm not doing either of us any favors by not getting up. And I'm definitely not doing right by Cade, so I extricate myself from her hold, gently slipping her soft hands from my chest. But I can't let go that easy. For a moment, I hold them, study them. Would it be so bad if I just kissed her fingers?

My stomach twists painfully. *Yes, Declan. It would be fucking bad. And asking yourself this shows just how totally fucked you are.*

Even so, I can't stop myself. I pull her hand closer and brush my lips over her knuckles. Her eyelids flutter in response, so I release her. The last thing I want is for her to catch me mauling it.

Without another second of hesitation, I jump out of bed and head straight for the kitchen. *Coffee. Go make coffee. And breakfast. Give yourself something to focus on.* Anything but the beautiful woman lying in the other room who has made it clear that she wants me to kiss her as badly as I want to kiss her.

It's a craving.

A sick craving.

As if my best friend can sense my fucked-up thoughts, he chooses this moment to text me.

> Cade: Headed to practice. Any suggestions on a nice place in Bristol we can take Mel tomorrow night? I'll make a reservation.

We? Why the fuck would I come with them to dinner?

With a grunt, I put the phone on the counter.

A nice restaurant? There are a couple in town, but fancy doesn't suit Melina. She enjoys burgers at Thames, like me. Or a donut from Jules' while we sit in the corner so she can watch the people coming and going and make up stories about their lives.

Yesterday she concocted an entire backstory for an older woman who was sitting by herself on the opposite side of the shop. Melina decided that she'd moved here from Ireland as a young girl. That she'd come with absolutely nothing and met the love of her life in Boston. The two of them had worked hard for years, scraping together every penny they could, and eventually bought a little cottage on the water here. The two of them, along with their children, spent their summers here, and once the kids were grown and gone, she and her husband retired and moved to Bristol permanently. She has a whole brood of grandkids who visit, and now even her great grandkids spend their summers on the beach here.

I didn't have the heart to tell her that the woman she created this rags-to-middle-class story about was none other than Mrs. Milsom, Jules's grandmother and the wealthiest woman in town. Her family has owned the majority of this town for generations. There was no trip to Ellis Island or working in a factory in Boston, and there are definitely no great grandkids. Not yet, at least.

The only time the woman smiled that day was when Jules delivered a donut and a cup of tea to her table. She has a soft spot for her grand-daughter, even though she's always been horrible to Jules's twin sister, Hailey.

Rather than burst Melina's bubble, I sat and listened, and when we bundled up and headed toward the door, she smiled at the old crone. Thank fuck the woman's lips lifted a fraction. If they hadn't, I'd have told her where she could stick her donut.

> Cade: Never mind. Daniel gave me the name of a place. I'll make a reservation for the three of us.

Clenching my fist, I drop my head and give it a shake. No, I'll work the whole weekend. It's safer. Smarter.

I'm so in my head that I don't notice that Melina has appeared until she wraps her arms around my waist and presses her cheek against my back. I'm so taken aback by the move that I don't pull away.

"You're up early," she says with a gentle squeeze.

I shouldn't wrap my arm behind me and hold her there, but I do. And with one hand on her to hold her steady, I turn and take in the woman who is slowly unraveling me. "Was just texting with Cade."

She smiles up at me without even an ounce of guilt or apprehension over the way she's touching me while talking about him. "You were texting with Cade, or Cade was texting you, and you were grunting at your phone?"

I will my face to remain impassive, but her teasing smile and the general joy she finds in my grumpiness make it hard not to smirk. With my hands laced behind her back, I heave out a breath. "He answered his own question before I could come up with a response."

Snorting, she pulls away. I'm not ready to let her go.

"Because you were really going to reply."

"I've replied to him all week," I argue, pulling two mugs from the cabinet.

She takes one and fills it, then doctors her coffee so it's just how she likes it—extra sweet. "What did he have to say this morning?"

"Just mentioned making plans for the weekend with you."

Smiling, she cups her mug with both hands. "That's thoughtful. So what are we doing?"

I turn away from her affection, tamping down on the effect her words have on me. "He wants to take you out to dinner. I'll be working all weekend, so you'll have the house to yourselves."

"*Declan*—" Her voice comes out soft, full of pity.

Irrational anger bubbles under my skin. There's no need to feel sorry for me. I've watched plenty of people fall in love over the years. My sister. The guys at the station. This is nothing different. I knew Cade would eventually meet someone.

Just never thought I'd have feelings for the woman too.

"I have to head to the station," I say without turning around. "Want me to drop you at Lake's on my way?"

She doesn't respond, and the silence bleeds for so long that I don't have a choice but to turn around and look at her.

She assesses me with those green eyes of hers, then shakes her head. "No. She's picking me up. We're getting our nails done."

I nod. That's good. Less time alone with Melina is good.

Then why do I feel like I've been kicked in the gut?

CHAPTER 18

Melina

YOU JUST HAVE *to lean into it.*
It don't have to mean nothing.
You're a fighting machine.
Oh my god. Could this get any worse? *Lean. Mean. A fighting machine.* Those are the best lyrics I can come up with?

It's about time I told Ford that I'm not going to make any of my deadlines this year or next. Hell, I should probably tell him to scrap the album. My music is gone.

I storm toward the door, desperate for fresh air.

In the past, when I've had difficulty with a song, I've taken to running. Sure, it's winter in New England—in other words, frigid—but something has got to give.

My emotions this week have been all over the place. Even so, I'm comfortable in Declan's house. Content in this town. I take a left out the door and follow the path toward the water. The same path Cade and I used to get here that first night.

It's odd thinking about it now. How comfortable I was with Cade. How naïve too. I thought he would be nothing more than a fling. Maybe that will still turn out to be true, but it doesn't feel that way. Cade is like a glorious sunrise, warming me from the outside in.

And then there's Declan.

I let out a sigh.

If Cade is the sun, Declan is like a sky full of stars. Hard to capture, sometimes hidden, but god, when they're visible on a clear night, they bring light to even the darkest of canvases. He's everywhere in this town. Everywhere I look.

Sky full of stars.

Midnight moments.

You and me...we'll never—

An animal bursts from the woods and onto the running path, charging right for me.

"Oh shit!" I shriek.

My heart pounds so wildly as the damn deer darts into the woods on the other side of the path and disappears into the bare trees. "Come on, Bambi. I had a song forming," I whine. I pull my phone out of the side pocket of my leggings, hoping I can remember the lyrics and type them out. But I come up blank. Was it about the constellations? Or the stars? Shootings stars? Hmm, I could work with that.

Frustrated, I stare up at the gray sky. There is no sun today. Fitting, since Cade isn't here.

With that thought, I dial the man who warms me even in frigid weather.

"Hey, Trouble," he says, picking up after just one ring.

I bite my lip, tempering my smile. Just his voice makes me giddy. "I was almost roadkill."

"What?" He makes a choking sound. "Are you okay? Did someone almost hit you? Is Dec there?" The sheer panic in his tone has me feeling a bit guilty, even as I practically float down the path toward the water, unable to wipe the smile off my face.

"I'm fine, babe. It was a deer."

"Babe?"

I hum, trying to play off what I just called him.

"Nuh-uh," he says. "You aren't getting off easy on that one, Trouble."

"*Fitz.*"

"Fine. Are you okay, or did Bambi take you out?" He chuckles as he says it, but I don't even care.

I don't want to get into a conversation about calling him babe. Not that I think he's averse to it. Because it definitely sounded like he liked it.

"I'm fine. He just scared me, is all. Now I'm heading toward the fire station."

"Oh yeah? Why's that?"

I roll my eyes, still irritated by the grumpy man who's doing his best to avoid talk of this weekend. "Because Declan is ignoring my texts. Claims he has to work all weekend, but I'm not buying it."

"I'm sorry about that. Dec is—" Cade huffs a breath, like he's not sure how to explain his best friend's behavior. I don't need him to explain Declan to me, though. I understand why he's hiding from me. Hell, I should probably let him. We've grown incredibly close this week, sharing the same bed, spending far too many hours just sharing one another's company.

But I'm sleeping with his best friend. And I really like Cade.

God, none of it makes sense.

"Dec feels like the third wheel," he finally says.

"Who's to say that's a bad thing? Semis need more than two wheels," I counter.

Cade chuckles. "Never said it was. Truckers are hot."

We both laugh, though it dies out quickly. The three of us would be hot. Cade knows it, I know it, and I think if Declan were honest with himself, with us, he'd agree.

"I'll talk to him," Cade murmurs. That simple sentence alone, the knowledge of what he wants to say, has chills running across my skin.

"No need. I'm going to convince him to join us for dinner."

Cade's laughter is low. "Okay, trouble. Can't wait to see you tomorrow."

"You too, *babe*."

His laughter rings out as I tap the End button, a grin splitting my face.

When the phone rings only seconds later, I assume it's him again and answer quickly. "Miss me already?"

The smile is wiped clear off my face when I hear the voice on the other end of the line.

CHAPTER 19

Declan

> Cade: Mel says you have to work all weekend?

> Cade: You don't have to disappear because of me. It's your house.

> Cade: It's fucking annoying how you never reply.

> Cade: Mel is coming to the station. She's going to ask you to go to dinner with her, and you're going to say yes. Be a dick to me, I don't care, but if you're a dick to her, we're going to have a problem.

WITH A GROAN, I pocket my phone and pop open the compartments on this side of the rig. We spent the afternoon dealing with a fire in another abandoned warehouse. We couldn't get close enough to put it out, so though it was controlled, it took all fucking day. The rig is a mess, and we're all worn the fuck out.

Every fire wears on a department, but here in Bristol, most of us suffer from some degree of PTSD after losing Chief Reilly, which makes it more of a challenge, naturally. Out of all of us, I'm probably the one who was hit the hardest by his death. Not only was he one of my best friends, but he was also my mentor. And to a lot of these guys, he was family.

All I want to do is sit next to Melina and listen to her chatter on about her day or tell me made-up stories about strangers. I want the soft cadence of her voice in my ear, her warm body pressed against mine, her smiles and laughter. Fuck, I just want *her*.

But I can't have her, and Cade needs to stop pushing her in my direction.

"Chief, we got this. Go home and rest," Shawn says.

I shake my head. "Dane should go home to the twins. I can help."

"The twins are with their mom this week," Dane says from the open roll-up door of the bay. "Besides, looks like you've got company." He thumbs over his shoulder.

Chest tightening, I step closer and peer up at the second floor. Sure enough, Melina is pacing along the floor-to-ceiling windows outside my office.

"Fuck," I mutter, scrubbing a hand over my face.

Shawn gives me a concerned frown. "What's going on?"

I keep my shit to myself, and even if I didn't, I wouldn't open up to the guys who work for me. I'm the one they come to when *they* need help. Though I normally tell them to get out of my office and take their girl talk elsewhere. But fuck, they're all good with the feelings and shit. Between their book club and all their talk about relationships while we eat dinner, they're practically experts. And I listen. It's virtually impossible to tune them out when Colby is as loud as he is. At least Mason is usually around to tell him to shut the hell up when my head starts pounding.

"Cade is coming for the weekend."

Shawn presses his lips together and nods, like he gets the issue.

With a long breath out, I lean against the building.

The whole crew is standing around, watching me.

Crossing my arms, I give them the glare they've probably come to expect. "Don't you have a job to do?"

Dane laughs and pulls on Colby's shoulder. "Help me grab the hose."

Mason's already disappeared. He never sticks around to gab. Now it's just Shawn and me.

I can't help but peer up at her again. She's stopped pacing. Now she's standing at the glass, watching me. When our eyes meet, the words tumble from my mouth. "She's his. I know that. But I can't help but feel like she should be mine."

Her brows furrow in concentration, like she's trying to read my lips.

"What about Cade?" Shawn asks, drawing my focus.

"What about him?"

He pins me with a knowing look.

I glare right back at him.

"Did you read this week's book?"

Fucking A. I'm trying to open up to the guy about my feelings, and he wants to talk about his romance book club? "Forget it," I say, striding toward the stairway.

"Ask Mel about it," he calls as I take the first step. "And Chief—"

I pause with my other foot on the second step, but I don't turn around.

"Talk to Cade."

Closing my eyes, I curse silently. The last thing I need is to open up to Cade about how I feel. About her. About him. Especially when the emotions are so convoluted. They're twisted and tangled.

All I know is that I can't get the two of them out of my head, and I'm jealous that their connection is so easy. That they can just fuck and not overthink it. Like it means nothing. If I touched either of them, it would mean everything.

Stopping outside my office, I steel my spine and fill my lungs, preparing to turn her down gently but firmly. I'll say I still have work to do. It's not a lie. There's always more to do around here. After she leaves, I'll breathe easier knowing I didn't make a move on my friend's girl.

With that resolution firmly in mind, I push the door open.

"Declan?" Melina all but gasps, like she's surprised to see me in my own office.

With a curt nod, I head to the locker in the corner where I keep a change of clothes. "Everything okay?"

I glance over my shoulder as I slide my suspenders down.

She nods, her focus lowered to the floor, so I pull my shirt off and quickly replace it with a clean one. I still need to shower, but I need her out of my space first. When I turn around to face her fully, her eyes are wide.

"I'm sorry," she whispers, worrying her bottom lip and wringing trembling hands. "I shouldn't have come here. You're busy."

My heart lodges itself in my throat at the fear radiating from her. "What's going on?" I ask, taking a step closer.

She shakes her head. "It's nothing. I was just in my head."

Eyes narrowed, I search her from head to toe for any indication that she's hurt. "It's not nothing. What happened?"

She sucks in a breath. "It's my brother." She looks toward the window. "He called from an unknown number, so I wasn't prepared when I picked up and—" A tear slides down her cheek, but she quickly wipes it away.

"You shouldn't have to be prepared to talk to family."

Her green eyes go misty, looking like polished sea glass. "With mine you do." Tears cascade down both cheeks with that simple sentence.

I want to pull her into my chest, hold her close, promise I'll protect her. And I will protect her the best I can. But there's no shielding her from her emotions, no matter how badly I want to. All I can do is be a safe place for her to express them.

She blows out a breath so tremulous, she shudders. That simple whoosh of air is uncontrollable and full of pain.

Fuck. How could a brother treat his sister in a way that would have this kind of effect? All my life, my only instinct when it's come to my baby sister is to protect her.

Melina sucks in a sharp breath, hiccuping. "Jason is going to sue you."

I shake my head, my shoulders tensing. Of course this is about Jason.

"What does that have to do with your brother?"

"Did you hear me? He's going to *sue* you. You stepped in and helped me, and look what happened—I'm not worth it; you should have—"

A flash fire of anger ignites in my veins. "Should have what? Let him hurt you?" I grit out, my words far too harsh for her fragile state. "Fuck that. Let him breathe another moment without knowing the kind of fear he instilled in you? Also wasn't happening. And if you hadn't been there, I'd have done a hell of a lot worse."

Disbelief flashes across her tear-streaked face. "Why? You barely know me. Why do you care so much?"

Fuck it. This time I don't hesitate to pull her against my chest. With one arm around her back and one hand tangled in her hair, I tug so she's forced to look up at me. "Stop with that. I cared the moment I met you. It's impossible not to care about you."

"Because I'm weak," she whispers. The devastation in her tone is what breaks me.

"You are not weak because someone took advantage of you." I lean my forehead against hers, inhaling her sweet scent. "You are not weak because you've been hurt."

"I wasn't strong enough to fight back," she mumbles.

Gut lurching, I confess, "Neither was I."

She pulls back a fraction, her misty green eyes growing wide.

I've never told a soul what happened all those years ago, and I had no intention of ever sharing, but we both need this. Tugging her back into my chest, I hold her tighter. Fuck. I won't be able to get it out if she's looking at me.

"My father left when my sister was still a baby, and for years, the only thing my mother worried about was working to put food on the table and keeping a roof over our heads. When I was old enough to help out, I did. I worked at the fire station, I bused tables, I delivered newspapers, I caddied at the golf club. Anything to make a buck." I cough out a laugh. Damn, some of those jobs were a blast. Others were hell. "Cade lived at the hockey arena. Back then, he was hoping to go pro. We were both insanely busy, and while all our friends—his friends, really—were out partying on the weekends, we were focused on our goals: For me, taking care of my family; him, hockey."

Melina pushes back, and I take the hint, releasing my hold on her, but I keep my attention averted as she settles beside me, propping herself up on the edge of my desk.

"My mother cleaned for a wealthy woman in town. She was kind to her, and over the years, they'd become friends. The woman was all alone, so my mom started including her in our Sunday dinners. The woman got sick, and during my senior year of high school, she passed away. It wasn't until my mom got a call a few weeks later that we discovered she'd left everything"—I peer down at Melina—"and I mean *everything*, to my mother. Suddenly, I had the means to go to college and I didn't have to work three or four jobs at a time. We had money for new clothes for my sister, and for the first time I could remember, my mother could breathe easy. We were all just...I don't know, lighter, I guess."

For as well as I've kept this story locked in a vault for all these years, the words are tumbling out easily now. Melina is the only person I've ever met who makes me want to bare my soul. "I went to college the following fall, and things were great. My mom even started dating, which was something she didn't have the time for or interest in before. She met a guy, and it got serious pretty quick. It was a relief, knowing she and Liv had a man around. Honestly, everything was so great that year."

My chest tightens, and my breaths get shallow here. Things were so good then. I don't even let myself think of that time anymore. It's too painful to reminisce about what I can never have again.

"Cade and I both moved home the summer after our freshman year of college, and for the first time in my life, I had the time to just hang out. We'd go to the beach and hit up the bars. We weren't old enough to drink, but even just sitting and having a burger and soda felt like a freedom I'd never known in this town."

Hands clenched, I will my heart to beat steadily as I dive into the worst part.

"That following spring, my mother and my sister were out of town to look at colleges, but I'd come home for some reason or another. My mom's boyfriend had stayed behind, and because I liked the guy, I hung around and had dinner with him one night. Everything was fine—" I swallow hard, forcing myself to lock eyes with her. Regardless of how painful the memory is, she needs to hear this. "Until it wasn't."

Mouth turned down, she clutches my hand. "What happened?"

I take as deep a breath as the anvil resting on my chest will let me and keep my eyes on her. "I was bigger than him. Stronger than him. And none of that mattered."

Melina's face crumples, and her shoulders sag. "What did he do?"

Eyes closed, I block out the images that still haunt me when I let my guard down. "Doesn't matter. The point is, I wasn't weak, but it happened anyway. I was caught off guard. There was no way to anticipate what he did. I was mortified, humiliated, and…I don't know." I grip my neck as the weight on my chest turns crushing. "Guilty, I guess. I didn't tell my mother. If I had, maybe we could have salvaged something. But I took off. He did too. He disappeared, but not before he wiped her bank accounts." I drop my head back and blink away the emotion building behind my eyes. "She still has no idea why he left."

My mother and sister came home to find both of us gone. I'd gone back to college like a coward and pushed everyone away, including Cade. Thought that if I ignored it, I'd forget the feel of that man's hands on me as he held me down.

But when my mother called me crying, saying he'd stolen everything, I knew I'd never move on. She blamed herself. Said she never should have trusted him.

"My mother didn't have money for groceries, let alone my college tuition. I came home and begged the chief for a job. I've been here ever since."

My confession leaves me raw. Exhausted and strung out. Yet for the first time, the guilt of it all doesn't feel so heavy. Like telling her that she's not to blame for Jason's attack, that she shouldn't feel weak for *allowing* it—as if that's a thing—has made me realize that I've been harboring the same kinds of thoughts.

"I haven't written a word since he touched me." Melina's confession brings me out of my own head, and I find myself studying her. Eyes worn, face etched with defeat. She's so broken. "It's been months since he first laid a hand on me, and—" Her voice cracks, and I swear I could kill the man. I should have squeezed tighter. Should never have let go. Her eyes meet mine. "I had this journal. It was so worn the leather felt like my favorite sweater. It would soothe me if I simply touched it." She offers me a sad smile. "It had every song I'd ever thought into existence in it. Ten years of doodles." She shakes her head and blinks away a few tears. "All of it gone because he didn't get his way."

My fingers clench into fists as I will myself to breathe.

"I don't know how to start over," she cries. "It's like he stole my music. *My soul*. It's so much more unbearable than if he'd only stolen years of my life. I can't write a song. Not even a line." The way she's looking at me, the desperation in her gaze, the heartbreak in her tone, eats at me.

Unable to stop myself, I grasp her hand, needing to touch her. Wishing I could do more. Wishing I could ease her suffering and help her find herself again. Give her back her music.

But I've barely built a life worth living. I simply put one foot in front of the other every day and try to do the right thing. I don't have anything to offer.

"How do you do it?" she whispers, clutching my hand to her chest and squeezing tight.

"Do what?" I ask, my voice hoarse.

"Move on. Trust again." Her words shake as she adds, "Feel safe."

I blink several times, processing the question. I'm not sure I did until I met her. I've never trusted anyone with my secrets. And I certainly haven't moved on. I've spent years atoning for an incident I had no control over. Making sure my sister went to college. Making sure my mother never had to stress about paying the bills. They wouldn't lose out because I had been too weak...

The thought startles me back to reality. Fuck. There I go, doing exactly what Melina is doing. Blaming myself.

"I'm working on it," I say gruffly, pushing to stand. Suddenly, the air has gotten too thick. My eyes itch, and my chest burns.

"How?"

Focusing on a blank spot on the wall, I settle my hands on my hips. If she were anyone else, I'd turn into the asshole I'm known to be and storm out. Or I'd growl and tell her to go home. When my chest gets this heavy, all I want is to be alone. I can't control this feeling, and the last thing I want is for others to see that weakness.

But I can't push Melina away. She needs me. She's been nothing but kind to me. Though no one deserves to be lashed out at the way I tend to do, it physically pains me to think of hurting her in that way.

I've gone this far, so I might as well go all the way and show her how I handle the pain and the anxiety and the intrusive thoughts. I stride back to my locker, yank out the coil of jute rope, stride back to Melina, and hold it out. It dangles between us like the tension in the air.

Her throat works as she swallows audibly, eyes wide and set intently on the jute.

I extend my arm farther, letting the rope sway. "You can touch it."

Slowly, she reaches out and runs a finger across it. Her eyes jump to mine. "It's prickly."

"I have softer ones at home."

Nibbling on her bottom lip, she surveys me, then the rope, then me again, as if she's trying to work out what I do with them.

I sit in my desk chair, keeping a couple of feet between myself and Melina. "Not long after I hired Shawn, he opened up to us about his anxiety. He's big on talking—and reading—and he has made it his mission to get the guys to open up more. As you can imagine, that's not my thing, but this?" I lift the rope. "After hearing how it helped him, I did a little research of my own. And surprisingly, it does help."

"How?" Excitement glints in her eyes. The sadness is still there, but it's lessened. It's accompanied now by an eagerness. Like maybe she wants to understand what kind of power it holds and whether it will cure her.

"It gives me somewhere to focus my energy when I feel out of control, when my emotions are too big for me to contain." I grasp the rope with my other hand and work at the knot that holds it together. "Just touching it soothes me. Working on different types of knots, creating designs. As I've gotten better with it..." I shrug. "I don't know why it works, but it does."

"Do you ever do anything else with it?" The way she asks it, tentatively, but also with a sexy rasp, has my lips twitching into a smile.

"Do you mean sexually?"

I swear the air crackles between us as her eyes flare. "Yes."

One brow arched, I nod. "I have. Yes."

She heaves in a deep breath, like she can't get enough oxygen. "Would you show me?"

I squeeze the jute in both fists. Fuck. There's nothing I'd like more. But... "That's not a good idea."

Melina scoots across the edge of my desk, ducking her head to catch my eye. "Why?"

Her question hangs between us, and I have to press my hands to my thighs to keep from reaching for her. Lowering my head, I say, "Because you're Cade's girlfriend."

"So?" There's a sexy lilt to her voice. She doesn't deny it. She's his. The reminder is a knife to the chest.

I knew his feelings had moved beyond just physical attraction when he drove through the night to make sure she was okay, but I didn't know precisely how she felt until now.

"So I don't think he'd like it if I touched his girlfriend like that," I say slowly, finally daring to look up into her eyes. It's a mistake of epic fucking proportions, because if I'm not careful, I could get lost in them.

She grabs her phone and hands it to me. "Why don't we ask him?"

CHAPTER 20

Melina

DECLAN STARES AT THE PHONE, brows furrowed in intense scrutiny. The expression isn't all that different from the one he usually wears when looking at a device. He hates phones. That much is clear. But with a heavy sigh, he takes it from my hand, and then, with a defeated huff, he turns his gaze to me again. "I don't even know what to say."

Hope does a jig through my veins. Holy shit. He isn't saying no. He could simply play things off and insist on showing me how to tie knots. But if his trepidation is any indication, he understood my meaning completely when I asked him to show me, and now he's considering how to ask Cade whether it's okay that he fucks me.

Maybe I should feel bad about initiating this without talking to Cade first, but even though we haven't known each other long, I'm certain he won't be upset by it. In fact, I think he'll be intrigued. Especially if Declan is the one asking. I wouldn't be surprised if Cade wants this even more than I do.

And that's saying a lot, because I really, really want this.

There's a ruggedness to Declan right now, an almost dangerous quality. His olive skin tone tinged in soot, his scruff somehow wilder, his dark hair tousled, the ridges on his hands dark. I want to watch the soot

118

and ash disappear down the drain as he stands beneath his shower head. I want him to put me on the counter and face me. And I want to see his cock jut out as he strokes himself.

My toes curl just thinking about it.

I don't want it to be a onetime thing. I want to be the woman he comes home to after every fire.

Want him to lay all his burdens at my feet.

I want to be the person he trusts and fucks and loves. I can already tell that if he lets me in, he'd easily become mine.

The comfort I feel in his presence, the ease that washes over me when I'm even in his vicinity, isn't a trauma response. I'm not latching on to the person who protected me. No, this desire is so much more than that.

But he's still figuring out what this all means. He doesn't know how Cade could have me and he could too. And he doesn't understand what's so perfectly clear to me. That these two men fit, with me and with each other. And none of us will be satisfied until we take this next step.

"Tell him exactly what you told me."

He scowls.

"Not all of it. I just mean about the rope tying. And how it helps. If you want, I can tell him about my freak-out and how you're trying to help me."

He shakes his head. "No." With a heavy breath, he studies the phone again. "I should do this."

Yes. Yes, he really should. And I need to hear what he'll say. Need to know what he's asking for.

As expected, Declan doesn't text Cade. He would never use such an impersonal source of communication to have this conversation. No, he pulls up Cade's number and taps Call without another second of hesitation. It rings twice before Cade picks up.

"Hey, Trouble. We just finished practice. Did Dec agree to dinner tomorrow night, or is he still being grumpy?"

Declan scowls. "No, I'm not being grumpy, although you are right about one thing—your girl is trouble." He glances up at me, and his scowl is replaced by something else.

His face softens. His eyes heat.

But at Cade's laughter, he swallows audibly, and his expression goes carefully blank.

"Well, hello, Dec. Glad to see Mel convinced you to hang out."

Declan clears his throat. "Not so sure you'll still feel that way after I tell you why I'm calling."

Tell, not ask. I love that.

"Oh yeah? Mel causing more trouble?" Cade teases.

Declan cocks a brow and holds my gaze. "So much fucking trouble." It's said with such heat, such grit, that my thighs clench of their own accord.

The jarring sound signaling a FaceTime request startles us both. I jump, and Declan grunts. His signature scowl returns as he eyes the device. Like he can't decide whether he wants to tap Accept. Despite how badly I want him to do this, to have control over this himself, I'm happy to give him a little push. I slide the bar, accepting the request, and then Cade's smile fills the screen.

I peer down at him, my face appearing upside down in the small window in the bottom left corner, my forehead kissing Declan's. Declan himself is still wearing a menacing look of surprise.

I give myself a second to appreciate the three of us on the screen. How good we look together. Cade's blond hair, bright blue eyes, and big smile. My dark hair, vibrant green eyes, and playful expression. Declan's dark gruffness. The beautiful sight makes butterflies flutter in my belly.

Cade coughs out a laugh. "Not gonna lie. With the way Dec was talking, I thought you'd be naked right now."

Declan grinds down on his molars. "And yet you're smiling."

I catch my lip between my teeth, but there's no fighting my massive grin.

Cade's eyes dance. He's just as entertained by Declan's surliness as I am. "A guy can dream, right?"

When Declan is quiet for a long moment, the humor dissipates, and tension thickens the air. His expression has turned more apprehensive than anything. Like he's been left tongue-tied by Cade's easy admission. This isn't hard for Cade. Though likely not because of the long-term implications that have run through my mind, but because sex isn't a big deal for him.

In contrast, it clearly is for Declan. And after his confession earlier, I understand why.

Compassion has me gently taking the phone from Declan and settling in his lap. As if his hands know what his mind hasn't quite figured out, one grips my thigh and holds me in place.

"Look what Declan just showed me." I pick the rope up off the desk and hold it in front of me.

Cade's pupils blow wide, making my stomach swoop. Good. He's already caught on to where I'm trying to go with this.

Quickly, though, he affects an impassive expression and eyes his friend. "And what do you do with that rope, Dec?"

From where I'm sitting, I have to study Declan's image on the phone screen for clues, though the way his body goes rigid beneath mine is much more telling. "I tie knots."

Cade's lip twitches. "Feel like expounding on that?"

"No."

Though a laugh escapes me, Cade keeps his cool and only offers Declan a shrug. "Okay."

Annoyance flashes through me. It's like pulling teeth. "Not okay," I say, spinning so I'm facing Declan.

When he gives me his full attention, our mouths are mere inches from one another, and the inclination to lean in and kiss him hits me like a wrecking ball.

His eyes drop to my lips, signaling that he's thinking the same thing.

We suck in a breath at the same moment, as if the realization has hit synchronously, and not just for the two of us, but Cade too. I turn to face him, hoping to find that he's just as turned on by this as I am. The blatant longing in his eyes confirms it, so with a relieved sigh, I turn back to Declan.

"Tell him what you want to do to me."

As the words hang between us, Declan pokes the tip of his tongue out and rolls it against his bottom lip. Back and forth, back and forth. Then, with a thick swallow, he turns his attention to Cade. "I'd like to tie her up."

Cade's eyes flare, and instantly, Declan backtracks.

"For therapy purposes," he sputters. "To help her."

I can't help but drop my head back and roll my eyes. That is so not why he wants to, but if he needs to tell himself it is, then I suppose I'll let that slide. This time.

"You going to do it right there at the station?" Cade asks, ignoring Declan's justification altogether.

The man holding me close scowls. "No. I need to shower, and I'd never—" His mouth forms a thin line as he chooses his words. "Melina deserves privacy."

Heat builds low in my belly, and I give him a devilish smirk. "But you know I love to be watched."

Declan shakes his head violently. "Not by my guys."

At the same time, Cade says, "No. Only by us."

Us.

God, why do I like that word so much? The warmth in my core goes hot, leaving me throbbing in anticipation.

Declan likes that word too, if the thick rod he's trying to hide by shifting me so I'm leaning forward is any indication. As if I wouldn't notice how turned on he is. His reaction only makes me more ravenous. He wants me. He wants *us.*

"Go home and shower," Cade instructs. "Then get set up in the living room and call me. On FaceTime."

My breath catches at the demand. Damn, I like bossy Cade.

And I like his instructions even more.

CHAPTER 21

Cade

I'M NOT EVEN REMOTELY surprised when the text comes in a half hour later. Declan probably started panicking about the time he hopped in the shower. He's no doubt trying to figure out what the fuck he agreed to. And how to get out of it.

I sure as fuck don't want him to back out, and I can guarantee Mel doesn't either. But he needs to want this just as badly as we do.

> Declan: I could just talk you through a demonstration, and you could do this with Melina tomorrow night instead. No need for me to be involved.

I scoff as I read his text, my grip on the phone tightening.

Maybe it's wrong that I want this so much. That I want my best friend to touch the woman I'm borderline obsessed with. And not only do I want him to touch her, but I want him to fuck her.

I've been involved in plenty of threesomes, and it's always been for the hell of it. To have a good time. Nothing more. Hell, even the one I had with Declan all those years ago didn't *mean* anything. The girl was a friend from school. Declan had been visiting, and we'd all been drinking. She and I started fooling around, and when Dec offered to go hang in the other room, she'd looked at me and said she didn't mind if he stayed. And then...

I shake my head. This is nothing like what happened back then.

Besides, after that night, he changed. It was spring break, and he went home. Despite how many times I texted and called, hoping we could hang out, he never replied. I didn't see him again until summer break, and even then, he was still *off*.

Instead of returning to college that fall—he started working at the fire department, and slowly, things got better between us.

Despite how hard I tried, though, it was never the same. And he was different. But maybe that's what growing up does to a person. He wasn't drinking and partying like I was. He was at home working and helping his mom with the bills.

Though things eventually got better between us, from then on, I watched my behavior toward him, convinced I'd taken things too far that night. I like men; he doesn't. I suppose I can understand his discomfort when I overstep. Even when I touch him innocently, he pulls away. There's a wall between us, and it's best that I remember it. Even so, I keep working on our friendship, keep reaching out, because it's the most important relationship in my life. The one constant.

So should I be worried about crossing a line again with him?

Maybe.

Probably.

But if I keep our focus fixed on Mel, give her what she wants, I think we'll be okay.

And he wouldn't be texting me if he didn't want to do this. He would just straight-up say he didn't. That's how he is.

Although he *has* spent his entire life putting the wants and needs of others before his own.

So it might be best to just come out and ask him. Make sure this is what he truly wants. Then assure him it's what I want too. Because it won't be meaningful if he does it *for* Mel and me only.

I'd never use him for my own pleasure.

> Me: I don't know how to tie the ropes. You do. And for what it's worth, I'd love to see you do it. But if you aren't comfortable, we don't have to do this.

His reply comes so quickly that the dots don't even dance.

> Declan: I'm not uncomfortable.

> Declan: But you need to tell me if you get uncomfortable.

I huff a laugh and rough a hand over my mouth. That won't happen.

There's nothing he could do to her that I wouldn't be totally on board with. Just the thought of him touching her has me so hard I can barely breathe.

> Me: FaceTime me when you guys are ready.

Come & Get It

CHAPTER 22

Melina

DECLAN TOLD me to get comfortable while he went to shower, so instead of watching the water sluice down his body like I envisioned, I'm in my room, slipping on a black cropped camisole and boy shorts. I put my hair up in a messy bun, pinch my cheeks, and stare at the girl in the mirror.

I barely recognize her. I was so naïve when I left for Nashville twelve years ago. Jason was my brother's best friend. Four years older than me. And as soon as I made it, he was there. Every step of the way.

What I once saw as support, I now realize, was control.

And I want the control back.

I want to feel comfortable in my body. Comfortable asking for the things that bring me pleasure.

A soft knock has me straightening and sucking in a breath. "Come in."

When Declan pushes open the door and hovers at the threshold, I practically choke on my tongue. He's wearing a black T-shirt that hugs his chest, highlighting the hills and valleys of muscle that lie beneath it. He's all man, far older than me, and so sexy it's sinful. With dark, conflicted eyes. "Still want me to show you how to use the rope?"

There's a hint of hopefulness in his question, like maybe he's hoping I say no. Or maybe he's just prepared himself for rejection in the event that I do.

I step up to him, and the smell of his shampoo—something with cedar in it—has me closing my eyes and inhaling. I can't help but splay a palm over his chest as I peer up at him. "God, you smell good."

His cheeks go pink under my praise.

Pressing up against him, I run my nose up the soft scruff of his chin. I brush my lips over his jaw, my mouth watering at the possibilities in front of us, and give him the tiniest of kisses. It's nowhere near what I really want, but it sends the message. "And yes, I still want you to teach me."

Declan remains rigid, lowering just his eyes to regard me. "You like playing games with me, Melina?"

There's a breathlessness to his tone. Or maybe it's just my breath he's stolen. Because yes, I really would like to play games with this man.

Rather than answer, I take a step back, giving him room to breathe. "Where to?"

Declan thumbs down the hall, toward the living room. "I already have the phone set up so Cade can watch."

A frisson of need fires through me so urgently that I have to bite down on my lip to keep a whimper from escaping.

"So he knows what to do next time," he clarifies.

With a smirk, I strut past him. "Sure," I call over my shoulder. "That's exactly what he's watching for."

"*Melina.*"

Dropping my chin to my chest, I fight back a laugh. Why is his aggravated growl so damn sexy?

"Should we have a drink?" A little alcohol would go a long way in settling my nerves.

I'm rounding the bar when Declan says, "Better if you're sober for this. But I'll grab a couple bottles of water. Go relax on the couch."

Butterflies dance in my stomach as he heads to the kitchen, all swagger. The impressive part? He's not trying. This isn't an act. He's the type of man who just exists in this world. Every move he makes is out of necessity. Simple. He doesn't put a single thought into what he looks like to others.

My every move is choreographed, planned. At least it feels that way. In the beginning, I suppose it was necessary. To attract an audience, to build a fanbase. Then, even in my personal life, each step was measured to ensure I wouldn't upset Jason. So that I'd be attractive enough for him. A sway of my hips, a flirty gesture. If he knew it was for him, I'd be rewarded, but god forbid he believe I'd done it when he wasn't around. If he caught wind of any moment that could be construed that way, he'd lose his mind and tell me that all I cared about was the fame. That I'd chase it at the cost of my own purity. I'd sexualize myself to sell music.

It was all bullshit, but he stuck to it, and after a while, my family joined in on the nonsense. First my brother, then my own mother.

Now I have no one. No family.

Though I do have Lake—and now Ford.

And this week, I've had Declan. A man I can't imagine losing.

I'm still lost in thought when I realize he's standing in front of me. Blinking back to reality, I take in his stoic expression.

Without a word, he hands me the water and nods, silently urging me to take a drink. Once I've recapped the bottle, he sets it on the table. Then he settles himself beside it, directly across from me. "I need to tell you something, and it may change your mind."

Despite his serious nature, I smile. "I highly doubt that."

Declan frowns. "Earlier, you asked me how I felt safe again. I don't mind sharing this with you, but you need to know you're safe."

His words sober me immediately, and I feel the claw of anxiety taking hold. "*Declan.*"

He holds up his hand, asking me to just listen. "I know the reason you snuck out of the house to go to the game without talking to me— and the reason you left to get snacks at the concession stand rather than just ordering them from the attendant."

I swallow, suddenly feeling far more on display than my tiny scraps of clothing leave me. "You do?"

Declan nods. "You felt caged. While we just wanted to protect you, I understand that it felt stifling to have your every move under scrutiny."

A whoosh of relief hits me. I've never felt so understood. I try not to get emotional, though, because that's not what I want to think about tonight. The Worst Human Alive doesn't deserve anymore of my thoughts.

"I want you to know that I want you here, and you are welcome to stay for as long as you want—" His words catch me off guard, and I brace for him to say something I won't like. "But you don't have to stay here to be safe. You aren't being watched. You are free to walk out that door, and you'd be safe. I promise."

How can anyone promise that? And why do I instinctually believe him? For so long, I've trusted no one. At least not completely. And yet I trust him.

"How?"

"He's under surveillance around the clock. Right now, he's in the hospital, but eventually he'll get better. I'm not going to sugarcoat it and tell you that the charges will stick. Things happen." Declan squeezes his fists. "But he will not take a step out of that hospital without being followed. His every move will be tracked. And they'll make it obvious. He'll be uncomfortable. He doesn't get to walk around free."

I'm not sure anyone has ever done something so kind, so selfless, and so monumental for me. Money isn't endless for firefighters—at least I don't get the impression it is—so I have no doubt this arrangement wasn't a simple matter for him. To hand over a bunch of cash to a security firm to make someone's life miserable? Ford could do that for Lake. Hell, I could do that for myself. But this is so much more than throwing money at a problem. This took effort on Declan's part. And if I had to bet, he had to swallow his pride and ask his brother-in-law for help.

It's the second time he's done it for me, and I don't take it lightly. But I also don't know how to express how much it means to me without breaking into tears. And I don't want to break tonight. So with my chin held high, I meet his eye, trying to tell him without words that his gift—one he keeps giving to me, the gift of feeling safe enough to walk out this door—is one I'm incredibly grateful for.

"Thank you." It's all I can get out.

Declan merely nods. "Like I said, you don't have to do this. If you change your mind—"

"I won't."

Jaw clenched, he gives a simple nod. Then he reaches behind him and produces three ropes. One is black, one is red, and one is a deep green.

He hands me the green one. As I really take it in, my stomach does a swoop. I swear it's the color of my eyes.

"It's softer than the one in your office," I say as I run my hand against the silky material. "And god, it smells good." I lift it to my nose and inhale to get a better hit of the scent.

"It's the oils. To soften and prep it."

"I'd love to watch you do that one day."

Declan nods. "Does it feel okay? I'd like to use that one, as long as you're good with it."

Warmth spreads through me, the sensation full of genuine affection for this man. "It's perfect."

He flushes again, this time the color creeping up his throat, along his Adam's apple. The sight is so damn sexy.

"I'll get Cade on the phone." Abruptly, he stands and unlocks the device.

This is it. He's dialing his best friend. The man I'm dating is about to watch Declan tie me up.

Nerves skitter down my spine. What must Cade be thinking?

Maybe it's odd that I didn't immediately go to the bedroom and call him when we got home. But for some reason, that felt like betraying Declan. I want this to be about the three of us. Not Cade and me plotting to get Declan to do what we want.

The FaceTime call connects, and Cade's image fills the screen. My entire body heats instantly. God, it's ridiculous how much I like this guy. How one smile from him lights me up inside. His existence alone makes me happy in a way that can't be explained.

"Hey, Trouble," he drawls as he settles against a headboard in what I imagine is his bedroom.

"Hey, Coach."

With a lift of his chin, he chuckles. "Tonight, our coach is there with you." He eyes Declan. "You all set?"

The stoic man standing only a few feet away turns to me. The weight of his attention is heavy, intense. Like he can see into my soul.

He has a way of always knowing what I need, and so far, he's been more than willing to give it to me.

Many people can read cues and infer a person's needs, see when they're hurting or helpless. But most turn away from that uncomfortable moment, either too in their own heads to take the time to help or just uninterested in doing so.

Declan doesn't possess the ability to not care. Regardless of his mood, I can all but guarantee if he comes across someone in need, he'll do what he can to help.

And if he can do it without recognition? Even better.

Because that's who he is.

And somehow, I'm lucky enough to revel in it. I get to witness him in action. My heart clenches each time I look at this strong, silent man. He opened up to me, shared his burdens and his traumas. I don't take any of this lightly.

"Before we get started," he says, "I need to know that you trust me, and I need to trust you to tell me if the rope gets too tight, if your arms or legs start to tingle, if you get dizzy. If you notice anything that is out of sorts at all, Melina, you *need* to tell me."

Chest aching at his sincerity, I nod. "I trust you, and you can trust me. I won't lie to you. *Ever.*"

Sinking his teeth into his bottom lip, he nods. "Good."

"What about a safe word?" I say, my words infused with humor, in hopes of lightening the mood.

Cade chuckles. "Always the troublemaker."

"Your safe word is stop," Declan says coolly. "I won't do anything that hurts you. You tell me you want me to stop, and everything ceases."

When Cade and I are silent in response, Declan drapes the rope over both palms and holds it in front of him. "This isn't about a kink. It's not a game." He pauses, zeroing in on me. "Doesn't mean it can't be enjoyable. That I can't find ways to make it"—he darts a look at Cade, then focuses on me again—"pleasurable. So long as we maintain a healthy respect for limits. You could get very hurt if we're not careful. It's simpler than safe words. You say stop, and I stop. We'll use colors for everything else."

"Colors?" Cade asks, his voice tinny through the phone.

Declan keeps his attention fixed on me. "Green means you like what I'm doing," he says, his deep timbre rolling through me, causing the hairs on my arms to stand on end. "Yellow if you're too close to the edge."

What edge? I want to ask, but I'm afraid to speak. I'm locked in his spell, and I don't want to be freed. If my assumption is correct, the edge he's referring to is the one I'm desperate to be hurtling toward.

"What about red?" Cade asks.

This time Declan does glance at the phone, but an instant later, he's got me caught in his snare again. "If she says red, we stop everything. Good or bad, you say red, we end it."

Good or bad what? Once again, I'm too eager to get started to bother asking for clarification. I know to say stop, and that's enough for me. Everything else? I'm elated at the knowledge that any of it is even on the table.

"Most basic designs use a simple knot called the single column tie." Declan uncoils the rope and lets it dangle in front of him so we can watch as he slowly demonstrates the steps and then ties it off, creating what quite literally looks like a column.

Sinking my teeth into my bottom lip, I angle forward, studying each step as he does it again. With each knot he makes with the rope, his breathing eases, and the tension in his posture and in his expression dissipates.

"How did you learn this?" I ask, watching him work.

His cheeks are pink above his scruff as he peers over at me. "YouTube videos, books. There's a lot of information out there. If you can sort out the more kink-based things and narrow it down to technique, there's not a ton, but Shawn helped me find stuff to help with my anxiety."

On the phone screen, Cade is wearing a perplexed frown. It's clearly all new information for him. Now is not the time to get Declan to open up to Cade, but eventually—

"Would you like me to try it on you?" Declan asks, cutting off my thoughts.

"Yes, sir."

He lets out a low, pleased hum in response. He's focused on

undoing the knots he's created, but there's no denying someone is watching me. I turn to Cade and find him leaning forward, looking from me to Declan and back again. As if my answer pleases him even more than it pleases Declan. He's fixated on me now, his gaze intoxicating.

The heat in my core simmers on low, bolstering my courage. "Should I remove my clothing?"

It's a mechanical way to ask, but I can't help but wonder if it'll make things easier for Declan.

He peers at me through his lashes again, as if I surprised him. Then his lips twitch and tip up in a cocky smirk. "No."

"No?" Disappointment washes over me. The hunger I feel for this man is unreal.

He kneels in front of me, pushing my knees wide with his sturdy body, and brushes back a lock of hair that has fallen out of my messy bun. With each long, steady exhale, his minty breath skates across my skin, sending goose bumps prickling over my chest and down my spine. From this close, I can count his black lashes as they flutter. Feel the rapid beat of his pulse. When he swallows, I'm fixated on the way his throat works. Blinking, I drag my gaze up to his face and settle on his lips.

He's mesmerizing.

A tantalizing dichotomy of a man. To the world at large, he's hard, rough. Yet with me, he's soft. Kneeling at *my* feet.

"Only *I* undress you." His fingers dance across my jaw and down my neck, sending sparks flying in their wake. "*I* take care of you." He slips a thumb beneath the strap of my camisole and tugs. "*I* please you."

Dipping my chin, I watch as he slips the strap down my arm.

It's barely a touch, barely a caress, and yet the gratification it gives me is enough to have me sucking in a breath like he just sank inside me.

He does the same thing on the other side, his tongue swiping at his lip as if he's trying not to dip down and lick me. God, do I want him to.

"Fuck, that's hot." That simple, strained phrase reminds me that we're not alone. Cade is watching the way he touches me too. He's moved even closer to his screen, as if he's desperate to dive through it. His pupils are blown out, and by the way he shifts, it's clear he's adjusting himself. He's turned on.

I understand it, because I feel it too. I'm so wet I'm going to embarrass myself if Declan truly does undress me. He'll see the evidence of what he does to me.

I think I want him to.

Ghosting his fingers over my forearms, Declan garners my attention again. "Give me a color."

"Green."

Lips curling up, he slips his hands down my arms and over the fabric that covers my belly. "Lift your arms."

I obey, and he gently pulls the camisole over my head. He doesn't throw it like I imagine Cade would, desperate to focus on my breasts, which are now practically in his face. No, Declan folds the shirt and then places it on the cushion next to me. His movements are slow and deliberate. It feels like a lifetime has passed before he returns his focus to me, his eyes locked with mine, and pushes back so he's balancing on his toes, his knees no longer on the ground. He brings his right hand to my ankle and squeezes, then slips it up my inner calf. "Still green?"

"Yes," I whisper, though it comes out more like a plea.

The smile Declan gives me isn't big, but it's full of satisfaction.

My stomach whooshes spectacularly at the knowledge that I've pleased him again. When both of his hands have reached my inner thighs, I tremble. Before he can be concerned about me, though, I breathe out, "Still green."

Humming, he skates his fingertips against my boy shorts. Then he leans in close, flattening his palms on my thighs and inhales deeply.

"Fuck," Cade whispers.

Declan looks over his shoulder. "She smells delicious."

"I know." Cade's response is smug. "She tastes even better."

I'm going out of my mind with want. It takes all I have not to squirm, not to clutch his hair and bring him closer. Will he taste me? Lick me? Make me come?

Declan sets those warm brown eyes on me, his expression heated and his breathing a little quicker. "Can I take these off?"

"Yes." The sound is more like a moan than a word.

When he finds my waistband and pulls them off, he does it with a gentle ease, sliding them down my legs and off one foot, then the other.

Rather than fold them neatly and set them aside like he did with the shirt, he fists the fabric roughly and brings it to his nose.

"Fuck." It's a low growl. With my wet panties still in his hand, he locks eyes with me. "This because of me, Melina?"

The simmering heat in my belly ignites, creating a flame that heats my skin. Why do I like my name so much better when it comes from his lips?

"You know it is."

Eyes closed now, he inhales once more. Then he turns jerkily and drops them onto the coffee table behind him. He's so turned on that, for a moment, he's lost his sense of patience. His meticulous need to have everything in order.

Turning back, he rakes his gaze over me, taking in my spread legs and my breasts as they rise and fall with every rough breath I take. The oxygen burns in my lungs. As I wait for what's next. As I'm frozen in place, worried that if I move, I'll break the spell and discover this was all a dream. Or that I'll shift, and he'll realize I'm dripping on his couch. That he'll see disorder and be unable to help but put things to rights rather than continue this game.

Instead, he licks his lips and shakes his head. "By the time I'm finished with you, there'll be a puddle."

His eyes flutter shut, and he takes a steadying breath. After he's let it out in a slow stream, he regards me again, his eyes clearer, more focused. "Still green?"

I nod.

"Okay, I'm going to tie you up now."

The smile that splits my face is uncontrollable. It's all I want. To be under his control. In his care. With him, I'm safe, and I hope that by giving him that power, I'll find that I can let go of my fear.

It's almost contradictory, yet I believe with my whole being that his care and comfort will allow me to shed the unease and anxiety that have become my constant companions.

Declan slides the smooth green rope across my thighs first, the sensation sending a shiver through me. "Just getting you used to the feel of it," he says, his tone low but smooth.

He does it once more, then he begins to work. He's quiet, his focus set completely on the rope as he snakes it around my thigh. It's not what I expected at all. From the moment he showed me that jute in his office, I've envisioned him tying my hands behind my back or above my head. I suppose that misconception goes along with what he mentioned about kinks.

As he works, the design becomes clearer: one rope, then another, woven in and out; the columns he creates; the gorgeous contrast of the dark green rope against my skin. When he reaches my waist, he looks up at me. "Do you trust me?"

I nod. "Completely."

He asks that same question every few minutes as he continues to work. He reminds me I'm safe with him. Tests the pressure of each knot. Asks for my color. It's always green. The sensation of the rope against my skin is decadent, comforting, tightening around me like one of his hugs. Especially when he leans over me, his breath against my neck, as he continues to create new designs. Connecting one rope to the next until I'm a kaleidoscope of colors and designs. Tied up and bound like an offering for him.

When he's finished, he assesses me, his eyes swimming with pride and pleasure. The ever-present tension in his jaw and shoulders has subsided. It's clear to me now, what he meant when he said this helps him focus and eases his anxiety. Helps him find his own control.

He holds out his hand. "Come with me."

I slip my palm against his, surprised that I can move so easily, and stand. The ropes confine my body, not my movement. The restraint lends comfort without taking away any of my abilities.

Silently, he picks up the phone. Cade is quiet too. Both men are focused on me. On the way Declan is choreographing the interaction. He guides me to a mirror hanging on the wall near the dining room table and places the phone on the mantel so Cade still has a full view.

Stepping behind me, he cups my shoulders and meets my gaze in the mirror. "Do you see how beautiful you are?"

Try as I might to focus on his work—that's what he wants, and he deserves my obedience—I can't. Though I'm naked, he's still in his black T-shirt and boxer briefs. I'm desperate to please him, so I try again, but it's no use. Then his words from earlier hit me.

I need to know that you trust me, and I need to trust you.

I promised then that I'd never lie to him.

I'm in charge. He's made that abundantly clear. He wants to bring me pleasure.

"I need you to take your shirt off," I say, meeting his gaze in the mirror.

Declan's lips curve into a slow smile, the slight move causing my world to tilt. My axis shifts, but only for a moment before resetting itself.

When he grasps his collar at the back of his neck and tears his shirt off with one hand, Cade sucks in a breath. His attention is heady, heavy, weighted. He likes what he sees.

Now that Declan's chest is bare, I focus on our reflection. This time, I see nothing but perfection. His dark skin, dusted with even darker hair, my smooth skin, striped with green and black rope. The design weaves across my chest, under my breasts, over my shoulders, and down to my toes. I'm completely bound, and yet I feel like I've got his heart in my hand. Like if I told him to get down and kiss my feet, he would.

The man watches me with reverence and longing. When I check on Cade, his expression is just as devout. Though his reaction is to more than just me.

With a hand on my shoulder, Declan brushes his lips against my ear. "Now you're in control. Tell me what you want, and I'll show you that even when you're bound by me, you call the shots."

The words slide out like silk against my lips. "I want you to fuck me."

With a sharp intake of breath, he zeroes in on Cade.

Straightening, I say, "You said I'm in control." My tone is full of confidence, authority.

Slowly, he drags his attention back to me. Lips pressed together, he regards me in the mirror. As if he finally sees his beautiful work. How he's tied the knots, how the ropes press into my skin. How my chest heaves with desire.

Desire for him.

God, I want him so badly.

"You are in control," he says. The words are clear, but his voice is pained, like he's admitting to so much more.

And god, why does that thrill me?

Filling my lungs, I turn to Cade. I care for him, and I need to make sure we're all on the same page.

His grin is wide, his eyes bright. "I want him to fuck you too."

Molten lava travels through my veins at his words.

"Put her up on the table," Cade instructs. His involvement instantly turns that fire blazing in my core into a full-on inferno.

Declan lifts me easily, then places me on his dining room table. It's a deep, dark wood surrounded by chairs in the same shade. He moves the one at the head of the table to the side and then pulls my legs so they hang off the edge.

When he steps between my thighs, he slides his tongue along his lower lip. But when he drags his focus to my face, his expression is nothing but earnest. In this moment, the world disappears, and it's just the two of us.

"I really need to kiss you."

"Please," I murmur.

Without a moment of hesitation, he slips one hand behind my neck and pulls me close. At first, our lips brush gently. But it doesn't remain that way for long. Declan nips at my bottom lip and swipes his tongue along it. Pulling me so close that my entire body is pressed up against his, he delves into my mouth, exploring. His hard chest, the rough scrape of his chest hair against my skin, are nothing short of ecstasy. The rope tugs on my legs as I writhe against him, seeking pressure and pleasure.

Declan shifts, and his length, though confined to his boxer briefs, rocks against my clit. "You're soaking my dining room table," he says between kisses.

"I'd lick it up," Cade says, that simple phrase sending heat searing up my spine. He's watching. He's rapt. And soon enough, he'll be here with us.

"Let me grab a condom," Declan says, releasing me. He strides away quickly, leaving me alone with the other man I'm involved with.

"Hi," I say to Cade, my tone timid. "You sure you're okay with this?"

His blue eyes dance. "Trouble, this is the hottest fucking thing I've ever seen. I'm more than okay with it."

Relief washes through me. "Good."

Declan reappears an instant later, completely naked now. His hard cock bobs with his every step across the living room.

At the sight of him, I practically choke on my own saliva. He's all man, dark hair covering his thick thighs, a hard, rugged chest that hints to how he spends his days, working hard and taking care of this town and the people in it.

Tonight I want to take care of him.

Bring him pleasure.

Watch him fall apart.

He gives Cade a meaningful look as he steps up to me. No words are spoken, but he nods once, and then he's staring down at me again.

"Color?"

"Green," I say easily.

He holds a condom out between two fingers. "Good. Put this on me."

It's already open, but I give myself a moment to grip his hard length without it. I slide up and down, reveling in the feel of him beneath my fingertips. When I brush my thumb over his tip, he grunts.

I smile, batting my lashes at him. "You're huge."

"You'll take me beautifully," he rumbles.

I sigh, soaking in the moment. He's right. Everything about us is right. After one more tug, I slide the condom down his shaft. When he's fully sheathed, he presses forward, kissing me again, coaxing me into submission, his tongue warming me up. Then, gripping my thighs, he drags me closer and doesn't stop until I'm teetering on the edge of the table.

When he grasps my hips, his fingers digging into the flesh, and holds me still, I can't help the moan that slips past my lips.

"Barely touched her, and she's already purring for you," Cade murmurs. It's like he's in the room. Like he's right here with us, involved in every step.

Declan notches his cock at my entrance but only slips in far enough for his swollen head to disappear. He takes a breath, and I do the same. Then, while we're both fixated on where we're joined, he thrusts in, disappearing completely. I whimper as he fills me, stretches me, with his fat cock. It's so much thicker than any I've ever taken. The feel of him, the way I break for him, is unlike anything I've ever experienced.

"Oh my god," I whisper as he lets out a muffled "fuck."

"She's so fucking tight." He clutches my hips and holds himself deep inside me, eyes locked on mine. "You're so fucking perfect, Melina. Beautiful, kind"—his throat bobs—"and so fucking tight."

He pulls out and then thrusts back in again, making my tits bounce and my breath hitch. His gaze falls to them then, and he looks at me. "I want to suck on your nipple."

Liquid heat rushes through me at the request. I've never had a man ask for approval like this. Before each step. And before this moment, I would have claimed I wanted a man who knows what he's doing, takes what he wants.

Declan *is* that kind of man, yet he's giving me that power. I've never experienced anything hotter.

"I'd love that too."

Dipping his head, he presses a kiss to one, then the other. He stops there, focusing on licking, then flicking my nipple with his tongue, making the peak impossibly hard and sending sparks firing through my body.

"Fuck, that feels good."

He continues, all the while thrusting slowly, still firmly holding my hips in place.

On the phone screen, Cade is breathing heavy.

"Are you stroking yourself?" I rasp out between ragged breaths.

Declan pulls back and peers over his shoulder.

Teeth gritted, Cade gives us a silent nod.

"Show us," Declan demands.

"Yes, please," I whimper, practically melting in response to his rough tone.

As Cade lowers the phone and his hard cock comes into view, Declan swells inside me.

The sensations are overwhelming. The hard surface beneath me. The sight of both men. Declan's rough calluses and thick length. It's almost too much, yet I want so much more.

"Spit on your hand," Declan commands.

Without taking his focus off us, Cade obeys.

"Now fuck your hand and imagine it's Melina's hot mouth. You can't have her pussy because it's mine for tonight."

Cade's lips tip up like he loves Declan's dirty mouth. I mean, what is there not to love? Then he works himself, and god, the way his huge hand grips his shaft as he tugs on it adds a healthy dose of gasoline to the fire already blazing here.

Declan thrusts faster, still watching Cade, his breathing getting shallower, and when he turns back to me, he asks, "Can I play with your clit?"

"Please," I beg, splaying my hands on the table and arching into him. I'm so damn close.

With a hand between us, he rubs small circles against my clit with his thumb, never changing the pace of his thrusts.

His grunts twine with Cade's, creating a harmony that sends me hurtling toward release.

"Are you going to come for us?" Declan asks.

"Yes," I pant, forcing myself to keep my eyes open. To watch both of my men.

He gives Cade a look. On the screen, Cade has slowed his jacking and is massaging the head, rolling his thumb over his slit, then following the move up with gentle tugs.

"How about you?" Declan asks. "Will you come for us?"

"I need a better angle," Cade grunts.

Declan releases my hip and grabs for the phone. "Where do you want it?"

"I need to see you both."

Fuck. Cade wants to watch Declan's cock pumping into me.

Without needing clarification, Declan lifts me, gripping my ass with one hand and juggling the phone, and shuffles to the couch. He sets the phone on the side table and adjusts its angle. From this position, Cade can see our faces and our bodies as we come together.

"Just like that," Cade rasps, jacking himself steadily again.

Declan rolls his hips in time with Cade's movements, watching him watch us. When he zeroes in on me again, the desire emanating from him is so potent I think I may choke on it.

"Need your lips," he says. This time he doesn't wait for me to say yes before he presses his mouth to mine, his tongue teasing, our moans mixing.

When he arches back and lets out a guttural cry, I chant his name.

"Declan, yes, I'm coming."

He thickens inside me and pulses, his jaw unhinged and a rumble low in his throat. His eyes flutter to the screen as Cade comes along with us.

But it's not my name on Cade's lips.

"Fuck, Dec," he groans, his focus locked on his best friend as he fills his hand.

Declan tenses above me. Breathing through his nose like this, he's more bull than human. Trying to make sense of what just happened. Unsure of how to feel about Cade's reaction. Trying not to *feel*.

Thought after thought flutters through his mind in a matter of seconds.

Desperate for him to hold tight to the peace he possessed after tying me up, I press my palm flat against his pounding heart. The tension in his jaw relaxes, and he shifts so that he's focusing solely on me.

"Are you okay?" he murmurs.

I smile up at him, flooded with warmth. "I'm perfect."

Every second of the last hour has been exquisite. From the way he tied me up to the moment he finally pressed his lips to mine to the sex and the fucking and the orgasm. Every moment is imprinted on my skin like the marks this rope is sure to leave.

And all I can think is "When can we do it again?"

CHAPTER 23

Declan

"PLEASE," *I beg, my voice raspy, my heart beating wildly.*

Cade's grin is devious as he drags his attention down from my face to my dick. "I like when you beg. Tell me, Dec. What do you want me to do to you?"

My hips buck of their own accord. My cock is so hard it's painful. We both watch as arousal drips from me.

Cade licks his lips. He's hungry for me, and fuck if I don't want to know what it feels like when he runs that tongue around my tip. I watch him, taking in his blue eyes and the thick black lashes that make them seem impossibly bright.

"Come on, Dec. Just say it, and I'll give you exactly what we both want." He grins so wide that his dimple pops.

A groan rumbles from deep in my chest as I buck my hips again. He pulls back slightly and flattens his palms on my thighs, holding me still.

"Tell me. Tell me you want this as much as I do. Tell me you want me to suck your cock."

"Now who's the one begging?" I grumble. The words are rough, raw, as I force them past the fire burning me alive from the inside out.

"Is that what you need, Dec? You need me to beg?" He swipes his tongue along his lips again. Then, squeezing my thighs, his grip almost brutal, he

tugs me closer. When he looks up at me again, the air between us sparks with electricity. "I've dreamed of sucking this cock for far too long. Please, Dec. Let me make you feel good."

Catching my lip between my teeth, I cuff the back of his neck and tug him down. "Open," I growl.

Without hesitation, he obeys, and I thrust into his mouth. The moment his hot tongue touches the underside of my shaft, we groan in unison, in desperation. I fuck his mouth with abandon. I've never been so hungry for another person. Never been so unhinged. I buck and grind against his face and—

At the sound of a feminine whimper, my heart lurches, and my eyes fly open. It takes several seconds to register the sight before me. Her dark hair is fisted in my hand. Her body is fitted between my legs. And it's her lips that are suctioned around my cock.

My lungs seize. *Shit.* I've been brutally fucking her throat. *Not* Cade's.

"Fuck," I mumble, releasing her hair. "Fuck, Melina, I'm so sorry."

She rolls her neck and smiles at me. "Don't apologize. I liked it."

I gasp for air, my heart pounding and my cock impossibly hard and wet. *From her,* not him.

What the fuck is wrong with me?

I can't wrap my head around the dream I was having. Cade.

What. The. Fuck?

"Cade," I rasp. Not an admission, but a warning. He's not here. We shouldn't be doing this.

Melina wraps her fingers around me and rolls her thumb over the head, eliciting a groan from me. "What about him?"

I close my eyes, forcing air in through my nose and back out again, willing my heartbeat to steady. Willing my mind to focus on the woman between my thighs and not how my best friend is the reason for my raging erection.

Though if she was giving me head, then she caused this, right?

Even as I rationalize my hard cock, I know this is a stupid game.

"We can't," I grit out.

"Can't what?" she asks, the words a throaty rasp I'm sure has little to do with sleep and everything to do with the way I was just aggressively fucking her mouth.

I swell in her hand at just the thought. There we go. All about her. I imagine the way she must have climbed over me and positioned herself between my legs. Was I already hard? Did she lick her lips in anticipation?

My heart rate quickens again. Okay, definitely still attracted to Melina.

The dream must have been caused by the games we're playing. The fucking around on the phone last night. The way Cade uttered my name. It's all in my head. Anyone would be confused. Even turned on.

Right?

"You're his," I reply weakly, my resolve weakening with every roll of her thumb across my swollen tip.

She dips down and licks up the salty mess I'm making, moaning and bucking against the bed. "Then call him and tell him that his girlfriend is about to suck his best friend's cock."

Heat flares inside me, hotter than the fire my crew put out yesterday. Holy fuck.

Without waiting for me to pick up the phone, she circles my cock and sucks, moaning in a way that almost steals all rational thought. How the fuck am I supposed to think, let alone talk, when she does that?

I grab the phone beside my bed, hit Cade's name, and put the call on speaker. It rings once, and then he picks up.

"You're up early," he says, his tone chipper.

"Uh, yeah." I fumble for words as I study Melina, who sits up and pulls off her shirt.

Her perky breasts bounce as she crawls up my body, a hand and a knee on either side of the mattress, until she straddles my hips, her pussy hot against my hard cock.

And wet. She's so goddamn wet.

When she rolls her hips, her clit teasing the tip of my cock and her pussy opening for me, the silky feel of her exposed heat pulls another groan from my chest.

"Hey, Cade," she says as she grinds against me again, her tone deceptively light.

"Hey, Trouble. I should be there in twenty."

"Great. I'm naked and straddling Declan, but he wanted to make sure you were okay with us getting started without you."

Cade groans. "Is he hard?" That sound, those words, send a bolt of desire shooting up my spine.

She hums, the sound deep and sultry. "So hard. I had my lips wrapped around his cock, but he made me stop."

"God, Dec," he practically curses. "How'd you stop that? Her lips are magic."

Grunting, I drop the phone to the mattress and throw an arm over my eyes. These two are going to be the death of me. "So is that a yes or no?"

Cade laughs at my misery. I can picture the mirth in his eyes, the dimple coming out to play. "Yeah, make her scream for me. If I can't be there, I want to hear every sound. She tastes delicious when she comes."

I still haven't tasted her, but instantly, it's the only thing I want to do. Without warning, I grab her hips and pull her up my body. "Grab the headboard, sweetheart."

"Oh, fuck," Cade mutters. "Is he going to eat that perfect pussy?"

"God, I hope so," she says as she settles with her thighs on either side of my head and clutches the headboard.

Digging my fingers into the soft flesh of her hips, I pull her down and lick up the mess she made while she ground against me. The taste of her, sweet and tinged with arousal, has me lapping and licking and grunting.

With her head thrown back, she moans and bucks against my face.

Okay, definitely more than attracted to Melina. Her whimpers, the taste of her against my tongue, her scent, every detail, every part of her, is magic. I'm obsessed. The ache building inside me as I continue working her over isn't from my need to fuck her. No, it's from this desperate need to keep her. For this to be more.

Whatever the fuck that looks like when she's dating my best friend.

"You enjoy his tongue, Trouble? Like knowing that I won't make you choose? That the idea of you riding my best friend's face has me rock hard?" he taunts her.

She eats up every word, her clit pulsing. When I guide her hips a little higher and slide two fingers inside her, bending them until they're at just the right angle, she shatters around me, squeezing my fingers tight as her warmth drips down my hand and coats my tongue.

"I need your cock, Dec. Need it so bad."

Cade laughs. "Hear that, Dec? She needs *your* cock. Your cum. She needs you to fill her up."

Cheeks burning, I slide her down my body. I will myself to ignore the way my every cell heats when Cade talks to me. Not just *talks*. Dirty talks. Filthy.

He's such a filthy boy.

And I fucking love it.

Melina peers down at me, green eyes dark and needy, and for a moment, everything else fades away. My thoughts. My confusion. My stress.

Silence blankets us. Even Cade, who isn't here to feel the palpable connection tethering us.

Lips tilted slightly, she presses her mouth to mine. It's a soft kiss. Gentle. We remain like that, our breath one shared, singular thing. Finally, she slides her tongue between our lips and licks at mine, tasting herself on me.

I bite down gently, holding her tongue there. Her green eyes widen and ignite. Still holding her tongue in place, I give it a lick. She wiggles her hips, trying to roll herself in a way that'll force me to slide inside her, each move more desperate than the last.

She's certainly wet enough for it to happen. And I'm definitely hard enough.

"Holy fuck, what's happening over there?" Cade pleads, like he can feel the tension growing thick in this bedroom.

Before she can respond, I press my lips against hers hard, keeping this moment between the two of us, and buck up into her heat. She grinds down, taking me inch by desperate inch until I hit the most inner part of her.

Her.

Melina.

My best friend's girl.

The woman I intend to make mine.

Releasing her hips, I still, waiting for her to fill him in.

Tell him that I've taken her bare. Or maybe that she's taken me bare.

Either way, I'm inside her, thrusting up slowly, every inch of my cock surrounded in her warmth.

Her pussy flutters, and her eyes gleam.

She loves this silent game too.

"You guys are killing me. I'm taking the turn now."

The image of him walking in and finding her riding me almost sends me over the edge. Fuck, it's impossible not to create visions of the three of us. Him in the doorway, her coming with my cock deep inside her.

What will he do when he realizes just how fucking gone I am for her?

Will he pull his own cock out and thrust into his hand as he watches? Will he rush in here and rip her off me, then fuck her too? Will he allow her to keep riding me and grip her hair like I did earlier, forcing her mouth around his cock, so we can all find release together?

Bliss blurs the lines in my head, and I swell at the memory of the way he thrust into his hand last night. At the way his voice broke as he came calling *my* name. That single image has me growling out a curse and fucking her brutally, gripping her hips hard, my cock swelling and jerking until I paint her insides. Melina rolls her hips while I hold her tight against me, her tits bouncing, and then she's arching back and crying out with her own release.

"Holy fuck," she murmurs as she falls against my chest, panting just as violently as I am.

I'm not even remotely satisfied. Not because it wasn't the best sex of my life, but because I want more.

Like Melina last night, I want to know when we can do this again.

The front door slams, causing the house to shake and my eyes to fly open.

With a kiss to Melina's forehead, I slip out of her. "Let me get you something to clean up." Fuck, I need to get out of this room. I can't be lying here a puddle of want and need when my best friend walks in.

It was one thing to imagine Melina as mine—as ours—last night. Even in the sleepy haze this morning.

But in the light of day, I know that can't be a reality.

I roll her onto the mattress and head for the bathroom, disappearing before he opens the door. Their conversation is muffled, but if I focused, I could make out their words. I don't want to make out their words, so I turn on the tap to drown out all sound. Palms on the counter, I hang my head and close my eyes, trying to wrap my mind around what the hell we're doing.

I should go to work.

I should make myself scarce, like I originally planned.

Nothing good can come from spending time with the two of them in this bedroom.

Forcing myself to straighten, I glare at my reflection in the mirror. My cheeks are flushed, and my eyes bright, the typical stressed-out bags under them missing.

It's Melina.

I know it's Melina.

I sleep like the dead when I'm with her.

Cocooned in her warmth. Pressed against her back. Surrounded by the sweet smell of her coconut lotion.

I cup my hands under the faucet and splash cool water on my face. Then I set it to warm and grab a washcloth. Once it's soaked, I wring it so it won't drip, steel myself, and leave the bathroom.

"I got a towel for—" I stop abruptly when I find Cade between Melina's legs, lapping at her.

He pauses his work and gives me a lazy smile. "I'm taking care of the mess." His words are like expensive whiskey, husky and smooth. The smile he's directing at me is the one he gave me in my dream. Lazy and sinful, his dimple popping. With a quick lift of his chin, he turns back to Melina and slides his tongue through her drenched lips.

The lips drenched with my cum.

Hers too.

Instantly, I'm painfully hard. The sight of him sucking my cum from her body while moaning in pleasure is too much of a turn-on to ignore.

And I don't know what the fuck to think of that.

CHAPTER 24

Cade

I WASN'T the least bit surprised when Declan saw me between Mel's thighs, grew about ten inches, and then disappeared, claiming he had to get to work.

He wasn't ready. Maybe he never will be.

I can't deny, though, that I'd hoped he'd at least be open to fooling around with us. Because watching him and Mel last night? It was so fucking hot.

But a small part of me—the part that spent decades fighting this unreasonable crush—knew that I couldn't handle it if we took things too far, only for Declan to pull back and decide he didn't want it. Didn't want me.

And really, why would he?

He's never given me any reason to hope. Any reason to believe that he would ever want me that way.

Mel herself is truly enough. The taste of them together, though? The sounds they made while he fucked her? It was otherworldly.

A vision I dream about but will never truly have.

I make peace with that.

Eventually.

Right now, I'm balls deep in Mel, thrusting and cursing as she squeezes around me every time I remind her of what I heard this morning.

"Bet you were a fucking dream, riding him like that." Thrust. "Your tits bouncing." Squeeze. "Your pussy clenched him so tight he saw stars, didn't it?" Roll.

With a flick to her clit, I drag one of her legs up so her calf is resting on my shoulder. Fuck, the deeper angle is almost enough to send me over the edge. "And you let him have you bare."

She's panting, biting down on her swollen lip as she rolls her hips against me, seeking more.

I'm in a condom. I was too impatient to have the safe-sex talk first thing, though I intend to fuck her bare once I've confirmed we're all good with it.

Declan was reckless this morning. Though I know he's been safe, he has no idea what the fuck I've done.

Who I've done.

Even if it's only been Mel since I met her.

If I have my way, it'll only be her for a long fucking time.

And the last person to have her before Declan was me.

The image of him thrusting into her has me teetering on the edge of losing control.

"Come for me, Trouble. Squeeze my cock just like you did his, and then I'm going to come across these hot tits."

The color in her cheeks deepens. She arches her back, head tilted up, and screams out my name, coming apart at the seams. I grit my teeth, working her through her orgasm until she's finished pulsing around me. Then I pull out of her, toss the condom to the floor, and jack myself over her. Images of the two of them flit through my mind as my impending orgasm looms. And as I realize that Declan's and Mel's moans filled this room only a little while earlier, I come across her chest in spurts, painting her with my pleasure.

"Holy. Fucking. Shit," Mel chants, her chest rising and falling rapidly.

Chuckling, I slump onto my side next to her.

"Is there such a thing as too much pleasure?" she huffs, though she's smiling. "Because shit...you boys are killing me."

With a laugh, I bite down on my lip. She's so goddamn beautiful. So perfect. I blow out a breath and jump out of bed. Fuck, I'm at a loss for what to do with this feeling in my chest, the way my ribcage is strangling my heart. If I lie beside her any longer, I may blurt out something I can't take back.

Still reeling, I grab a washcloth—the one Dec brought out, only to find me cleaning Mel up myself—and run my tongue along my lips, savoring that taste.

Declan. Melina. Them.

I wet the cloth again, warming it, then stride back to the bed. Kneeling on the mattress beside this beautiful woman, I delicately swipe at her skin.

When her green eyes flutter and she smiles that knowing smile of hers, my cheeks heat.

"Fuck," I curse out through clenched teeth. "You're so perfect. So much trouble, but so fucking perfect." Dipping low, I swipe my tongue across her lips, then dip into her mouth.

I can't just kiss this girl. A press of our lips would never be enough. When I kiss her, the need to devour her overwhelms me. Her moans, her whimpers, her thoughts. I want them all.

"Did you enjoy yourself?" I pull back, giving myself space to breathe. As much as I'm willing to risk my heart, I'm not willing to risk hers. If she's catching feelings for Declan, we may have a problem, because Declan doesn't do feelings.

Then again, who the fuck am I to talk? He'd probably be better at the whole relationship thing than me. Not that either of us has ever been in one.

God, we're a mess.

"Let's see," she teases, tapping her finger against her chin. "I got fucked by not one, but two hot men, and I've come four times already this morning. Yeah," she says, "I'd say I enjoyed myself."

Despite the lightness her snark always brings, there's still a niggle of doubt in my mind. "You know what I mean."

I settle beside her again and pull her to my chest, hoping she can sense how much this means to me. That it's so much more than just sex. Silently urging her to understand that I can be the person she talks to, the person she feels comfortable enough with to share more than just her bed.

"Did you enjoy yourself?" she asks, hitting the real issue here. Declan. Me. Declan and me. Whatever the fuck that is.

I lace our fingers and pull them to my lips, keeping my gaze on her. "I loved watching him fuck you, if that's what you're asking."

She smiles. "I loved it too."

Heat builds inside me at the satisfied look on her face. "He stretch you differently?"

Blushing, she sinks her teeth into her lip.

I loom over her, tickling her side. "He did, didn't he?"

She giggles, her cheeks darkening further. "He's got a really thick cock."

I groan, awash in heady desire at the memory of exactly how that thick cock looked when he fisted it last night.

"And yours? It's so fucking big it hits me in just the right place," she rasps.

Balls aching, I claim her mouth. Damn. The more she talks about my best friend, the harder I get. Pretty sure I could fuck this woman all day.

"So you're saying you need two cocks?" I bite down on her lip and suck it into my mouth.

"No," she moans when I release her, rolling her hips against me. "I'm saying I need *your* two cocks."

That's all it takes to destroy all sense of control. With a grunt, I rut against her, sliding my cock through her wet heat.

"You want his, don't you?" she whispers as she grabs ahold of my cock and squeezes, holding me in place.

I shake my head, a confusing mix of disappointment and desire swirling inside me. "Dec's not like that."

Mel smiles. "And if he was?"

"Trouble, Mel. You are so much trouble."

"Tell me your fantasy, Cade, and I'll put you inside me bare too." She runs the tip of my cock along her slit, then holds me at her entrance, squeezing tight.

"I'm safe," I tell her.

She smiles, her eyes warm and soft. "I know."

My heart pangs. *Fuck*. I really like this girl.

With a brow arched, she licks her lips. "Now tell me."

Whimpering, I let my mind go wild, sorting through all the things I'd do if the feelings were reciprocated.

My mouth waters as I imagine settling my hands on his thighs. The hair on his legs coarse against my palms, his cock jutting out.

"I'd tell you to sit on his face, and I'd watch as he ate you."

Her grin widens, her breaths picking up just a little. "What else?"

"I'd slide down his shorts to see how hard he was from your taste."

She pushes me inside her, just an inch.

"He'd be rock hard," she whispers. "Just like you are right now."

My tongue tingles. "There'd be a bead of precum on the tip of his cock because he's so turned on by you," I tell her.

Moaning, she slides me in another inch.

"I'd stick out my tongue and taste it."

"He'd whimper between my legs." Digging her fingers into my ass, she pulls me into her with more force than I thought she was capable of, taking my entire length in one move.

A zap of electricity shoots up my spine. "I'd suck him to the back of my throat."

"He'd thrust up into your mouth. He tastes so good, Cade, and he loves it rough."

We're fucking with abandon now. Rutting against one another as we dream about the man who's already left. The man who's too scared to let any of this happen.

The man we both want.

CHAPTER 25

Melina

Lake: Hi! It's me. Your best friend. You ever leaving that sex dungeon?

Me: LOL. It's not a sex dungeon. Cade just got here this a.m.

Lake: Are you telling me nothing's happened with the chief?

Me: I'm not not telling you that.

Lake: Okay, I read that like six times, and this momma brain isn't sure if you're confirming or denying that something is going on with Declan.

Lake: Hello?

Lake: Melina?

WITH A GIGGLE, I pocket my phone, ignoring my best friend. Making her suffer gives me a sick satisfaction, I guess. It's midmorning, and if we don't get out of this house, I'm pretty sure we'll just continue fucking. The idea is beyond tempting, but I'd like to save a little energy for Declan tonight.

If he actually comes home.

Cade pulls me against his chest, the small act of affection warming my body. He's so good at this—showing me exactly how he feels; kisses, cuddles, catching me in front of his team and spinning me around like I'm all he sees.

"Where are we headed?" he asks as I lead him through town toward the bakery. It's become my addiction since Declan took me last week.

It's wild to think it's only been two weeks since my life turned upside down. Three weeks since I met Declan and Cade. With Christmas around the corner and Jason in the hospital and under surveillance, apparently, I don't really need to stay at Declan's anymore.

I shove that thought down. Hopefully, I can enjoy this last weekend with the two of them, in this little haven of a town I've found, then figure out my next steps.

Going back to my apartment in New York feels too daunting. But maybe I could get a place in Boston. That way I'd only be an hour from Lake. And I'd still have Cade. If he still wants to hang out, that is. And I could come visit Declan...

God, get out of your head, Mel.

"Donuts, then shopping."

Cade smiles. "Jules'?"

"You know it?"

He laughs, a white cloud forming in the air in front of him. "I grew up here, remember? I visit pretty often, and since Declan's only indulgence is food, yeah, I know it."

Stomach swooping, I bite my lip. "That's not his *only* indulgence."

With a squeeze to my shoulder, he hums but doesn't say anything.

"Does he know how you feel?" I ask.

From what I've seen, Cade's interest in Declan is so much more than sexual. The way he talked about his fantasies while we were in bed blew my mind, but at the memory of the pain in his eyes, the longing when Declan disappeared, my chest aches.

Oddly, I don't feel threatened by Cade's feelings for his best friend.

I've been known to be a jealous person, and I thrive on attention—of course I do; I love the spotlight, being on stage, having all eyes on me—but I don't mind sharing that spotlight with Declan. It doesn't feel like Cade wants him more than he wants me. He wants us both. Together. Like the three of us together would be his ultimate dream.

And though this kind of thing never crossed my mind before I met these men, I can say with certainty that it's now my dream too.

The question is, where does Declan fit into all of this? There is a longing there, I have no doubt, but I'm not sure he'll ever allow himself to act on it.

"About you?"

Oh, he's being cute, trying to evade my question by focusing on me.

Ahead of us, two women walk out of Jules' with coffees in their hands, bundled up and talking loudly.

I can't see their faces, but one has blond hair sticking out below her black beanie. Her friend has caramel-colored hair, and when she practically trips down the steps, her friend grabs her, keeping her from falling.

"We need to wrap you in bubble wrap so that my niece survives this pregnancy without too many bruises."

The woman who tripped splays her hand over her stomach and smiles brightly. "You sound like your brother."

The girl scoffs. "Please, if I were Jack, I'd say, 'Sassy, you have to be more careful. I love you too much to see you hurt.'"

My chest fills with warmth at their banter, and as the blonde looks up and spots us, I recognize her immediately. "Amelia Pearson?"

"Mel?" She lunges forward and scoops me into a hug. "Lake told me you were in town. Chief must be keeping you on some serious lockdown. I haven't seen you at all."

Amelia and her husband Nate lived in Nashville when Lake and I were there. Though Lake was the first to get her big break, Nate also found fame. Amelia, his girlfriend at the time, has an incredible voice too. They released their first album together a few years ago and are pretty well-known around the country, but they spend the majority of their time here, in the town where they grew up.

Amelia steps back and yanks Cade into a hug as well. "Visiting for the weekend?"

"Yeah." He steps back and sticks his hands into his pockets. "We don't have another game until Tuesday."

Just the idea of Cade leaving on Monday morning has dread sinking in my stomach.

"Staying at Declan's?"

"Yeah, I'll have dinner at my mom's tomorrow."

Breath catching, I blink at him. How did I not know that his mom lives in Bristol too?

The answer blares loudly in my head, making my gut churn. I didn't know because we're only fooling around. This isn't a date. I'd somehow begun to think the little game we'd been playing of being boyfriend and girlfriend had turned real.

We're having sex.

Mind-blowing sex. But that's all we're really doing.

Amelia steps back and pulls her friend to her side. "This is Charlotte, my sister-in-law. Charlotte, this is Cade Fitzgerald. He was a few years ahead of Jack in school, and this is—"

"Melina Rodriguez," Charlotte says, nudging her friend in the side. "This woman does not need an introduction. I'm a huge fan." Her cheeks go rosy as she smiles at me.

I laugh. "Well, thank you. But here, I'm just Mel."

She blinks several times. Then, out the side of her mouth, she mumbles, "Did you hear that? Melina Rodriguez said I can call her Mel."

We all laugh again, the simple action relieving the ball of dread sinking in my stomach.

"You going into Jules'?" Amelia asks.

"Yeah." Cade thumbs over at me. "This one has become obsessed with their donuts. Then we're going shopping and who knows what else."

"Make sure you come by the flower shop. I'll set a bouquet aside for you to take to your mother," Amelia says with a wink. "And maybe we'll see you both at the Christmas festival tonight?"

Cade dips his chin. "Thank you."

"It was good to see you," I say to Amelia, then turn to Charlotte. "And so nice to meet you."

Charlotte gives me an awkward wave and giggles—she's adorable, with her tiny pregnant belly and her fan-girl moment—and then they're gone.

Cade pulls the door open, and the smell of sugar and espresso almost bowls me over. "Come on, let's get you your sugar fix."

The shop is small, but there is a single empty table available. Cade kisses my temple and points to it. "Go save a seat, and I'll order. What do you want?"

A kaleidoscope of donut options filters through my head, making my mouth water. "What do I want? What do I want?" I hum, scanning the choices behind the glass. When I discover that the special is cinnamon streusel, the choice is an easy one.

Once I'm seated, I allow myself a moment to watch Cade. The young woman behind the counter blushes as she rings him up. How could she not? He is stupidly good-looking. He's pretty. Blue eyes, dirty-blond hair peeking out of his backward Bolts hat, broad shoulders, thick thighs, a bubble butt, and god, when he turns and smiles at me, laughing at something the girl must have said, my heart flips over.

I like this man.

A lot.

The sound of a chair scraping against the floor breaks the Cade trance I'm in. The woman at the table beside me has pushed her chair so close it's almost kissing mine. "Is that Cade Fitzgerald?"

She's got to be in her eighties, with white hair, round cheeks, and a knowing glint in her eye. Her bright blue muumuu is similar to the kind my Vovo wears around the house, though I don't think she'd be caught dead wearing it in public like this.

Beside her, a gorgeous woman with long jet-black hair leans over and pulls on the woman's chair, bringing her back to her table. "Leave them be, Carmella."

I bite my lip on a smile as the older woman—Carmella—swats at her younger friend. "She's staying with our broody chief. Just trying to figure out the story."

"Gossip," the woman chides. She angles forward and gives me an apologetic smile. "She loves to gossip."

I chuckle. "I am staying with the broody chief. And that is Cade."

Carmella wiggles in her seat, brows dancing. "Oh, I can't wait to see how this plays out."

And I've got to be honest, I can't either.

CHAPTER 26

Declan

WORKING side by side with Colby, the rookie, I run the cloth over the truck until it shines. I never do this. Washing our fire engine is a job reserved for the new guys. My job is to be in my office. To talk to the mayor. To attend functions. To delegate.

But today I need to work off my stress. My usual method, with rope, is out of the question. Just the idea is steeped in thoughts and visions of the two people I'm currently trying *not* to think about.

What the hell was I thinking, using my escape with them?

"I don't know if I could share like that, Cap," Colby says to Dane.

On my other side, Dane grunts. "I'll give my wife to anyone who will take her."

Colby laughs, but the comment leaves a bad taste in my mouth. Dane and his wife have been having troubles, and I can't say I like the woman even a little, but that isn't what has my stomach souring.

Shawn appears out of nowhere and slaps me on the back. "They're talking about our book for book club."

I roll my eyes. *That's* what has me squirming. "Is there nowhere safe?"

"Nope," Mason grumbles.

Mason may be the one person here who talks less than I do. Though

164

I've heard rumors that he has no trouble rambling to the reindeer on his farm and the kittens that never seem to age.

"But we promised Mel we wouldn't talk about it until tomorrow," Shawn adds, cocking a brow and pinning Colby with a look.

This is the book Melina is reading along with them?

Turning, I take a step closer to Dane. If Colby heard me, he wouldn't know how to stay quiet. Everything about the kid is loud. "Sharing?"

Shawn leans in—apparently that single word wasn't quiet enough. "I told you to ask Mel about it."

I affect the impassive expression I perfected years ago and look between the two of them, waiting for an explanation.

Dane chuckles. "Two best friends fall for the same woman."

Despite my flat look, heat creeps up my neck, so I turn, hoping like hell they don't notice. "So they share her?" I ask in what I hope is an even tone, keeping my attention focused on the truck.

Shawn chuckles. "I don't give spoilers. Ya gotta read the book. But..."

His pause has me turning to face him.

Fucker is smiling that damn knowing smile. "Mel already asked if she could pick the next one and told me in it, the guys don't *just* share her."

I scowl. "What the hell does that mean?"

He shrugs. "Ask Mel."

CHAPTER 27

Cade

WITH HER LIP pulled between her teeth, Mel studies her phone, then taps the screen like she's sending a text. All afternoon, we've strolled down Hope Street, perusing the shops and admiring the Christmas decorations in each one. Mel has purchased at least one thing from every store, like she wants to support the shop owners, and she's only too happy to talk to each one of them, taking her time to smile for pictures when they ask and asking questions about the history of each place.

Between shops, she creates stories about each couple we pass. Made-up tidbits that are so detailed, I'd swear they were true if I didn't actually know most of the people she's spinning complex stories about.

"Something making you smile?" *Or someone?* That's what I really want to ask. I'm greedy. I'd rather not share those smiles with anyone but Dec.

She turns the phone to face me, showing me the message thread.

> Declan: Can't Keep Our Hands to Ourselves?

"Declan texts you?" I say, chest tightening.

166

She shrugs like it's no big deal.

Fuck, he really likes her.

Emotions war in my head, and my gut cramps at the realization. He's treating her like she deserves to be treated, and fuck if I don't love and appreciate that. But those feelings are mixed with an unease I can't name. Am I jealous that he texts her and not me? Am I envious of the bond they share that doesn't involve me?

I don't truly think it's that.

With a deep breath in, I decide to worry about it later and continue on, reading her response.

> Mel: You reading it?

"Reading what?" I ask.

Mel presses her lips together, fighting a smile, but her eyes dance, nonetheless. She nods toward the corner of the shop we're in and leads me over.

Once we're out of earshot of the shopkeeper, standing between a clock that looks like a chicken screaming cock-a-doodle-doo and a Christmas tree with legs, she leans in close. "It's this week's book club read. It's about two best friends who fall for the same woman."

A horde of thoughts flutter through my mind at that statement, but only one makes its way to the forefront. "Declan is part of a book club?"

The pang in my chest is all the evidence I need to understand that this feeling really is jealousy. Mel is getting glimpses of him that I've never seen, and it fucking hurts.

With a laugh, she splays a hand over my chest. "No. The guys in the department. Shawn says Declan never participates."

A wave of relief hits me then. Thank fuck. My best friend hasn't completely hidden a side of himself. Though I am intrigued by the idea that he's reading this book. Did he know what it was about before he picked it up? Is he interested in exploring what a real relationship would look like between the three of us?

Am I?

What does any of this mean, and what the hell am I doing diving so deeply into my psyche while standing beside a dancing Santa toy?

Mel watches me closely, reading my every thought as if it's flitting across my face.

She licks her lips, her expression soft. "You didn't answer my question earlier. Does he know how you feel?"

Heart in my throat, I shrug. "I think I've done a decent job of hiding it." I blow out a breath. "Or I did. Until you."

"Why me?" she whispers, her eyes searching mine.

"I don't know. When it was just Dec, I could hold back these feelings. But the idea of you and him together? It does something to my brain chemistry—"

"Alchemy," Mel says so quickly it's almost like it's part of her breath. Like she's been holding the word back. Like she's been waiting for this moment. "There's no other way to describe this feeling between the three of us."

"Alchemy," I repeat, my heart beating just a little faster. Outside of the Taylor Swift song, I've never heard the word. "Means chemistry?"

Melina shakes her head. "It's so much more than that. It's freeing yourself from fears, altering and transforming, refusing to limit yourself to what the world at large may believe is right or proper. It's the art of transformation, inner liberation, and change."

"Alchemy." Wonder and hope course through me at that single word. She's right. That's exactly what transpired between the three of us in the pub weeks ago. Declan's eyes on her? That simple act ignited a need inside me like the flame of an old kerosene lamp that had lain dormant and dredged in water for years. When the fire sparked, it burned dark at first, the soot transforming as the years burned away until it was just a bright, beautiful dancing flame. One I'm not sure can ever be extinguished.

Will I get burned if I get too close? There's a good chance. Regardless, I've been cold for too long. I could use a little warmth.

Her phone buzzes in my hand, and without looking, I hold it out to her. Whether it's Declan or not, it's none of my business.

With a smile, Mel looks up from the device. "Declan wants to know what we're doing."

My heart skips a damn beat at the affection mixed with need in her tone. "What do you want to tell him?"

Eyes sparkling with the same kind of heat that's growing in my chest, she says, "That we'll do whatever he wants."

Fetish

CHAPTER 28

Melina

I'M PRACTICALLY VIBRATING as we approach the station. Tamping down the excitement around the guys is going to be a challenge. Being summoned by Declan like this? It lights up all my nerve endings.

As it turns out, I don't have to swallow back my glee and play it cool around the guys, because the garage bay is quiet, and one truck is gone.

"They go to a fire?" Cade asks as he scans the open space and the second truck that's polished to perfection.

Disappointment clangs loudly in my chest at the possibility that there was an emergency and Declan isn't even here.

At the sound of a throat clearing above us, I snap my head back. Instantly, I break out in goose bumps. Outside the wall of windows on one side of his office, Declan is standing, watching. He looks like an imposing god, gripping the metal frame tightly, his eyes a storm of emotions so violent they're palpable even from here.

"Where is everyone?" Cade breaks the silence.

Thank god. I can barely get air past the lump in my throat, let alone speak.

Tension settles around us. Reality circles. My world tilts on its axis again. The universe is changing, shifting for a second time.

"Christmas festival." The low rumble of words both soothes my nerves and stokes the fire burning within me. "Come on up."

Clutching my hand, Cade eyes me and gives it a squeeze. This is it. I can feel the change in the air. Can he? Are we ready for this?

Yes. There's no question. I want to have both of these men. Together. Separately. Any way they'll allow me into their lives. But this moment is so much bigger for the two of them. Their lifelong friendship is on the line here. The longing on Cade's face is all the evidence needed to know that he wants this. He wants his best friend. But he's afraid. I wish I could tell him that his heart is safe in Declan's hands, but I'm not sure that's true. And I'm not sure mine is safe either.

What's certain is that I'd break my own heart for a chance to experience this with them. For a chance at the alchemy that exists between the three of us. And it's clear Cade feels the same way.

It's worth it.

It has to be.

Without a doubt, I believe Declan wants it too. And if he's calling us here, I have to assume he thinks he's ready. Damn, do I hope that's the case.

When we reach the stairs, I release Cade's hand and hold the railing. Cade stays close, his proximity keeping me moving forward. At the top, he settles his palm on the small of my back, comforting me again. Declan disappears into his office, and once again Cade and I glance at one another. His expression is as uncertain as mine, but after only a moment of hesitation, we move.

I suck in a rough breath as I step inside the office and find Declan seated behind his desk, his expression unreadable. I stop short, waiting for a signal as to how he wants this to play out. If giving him control will help him feel more comfortable, then I'll gladly give it all to him.

Not surprisingly, Cade acts unfazed. Stepping up beside me, he lifts his chin. "All the guys went to the festival?"

Declan nods once. "Dispatch is covering the phones. I told the crew I'd join them in a few hours."

We're all silent, watching one another, waiting for someone to speak up or make a move.

Declan is the first to break. He snags a paperback from a drawer and tosses it on the desk, face down, with a loud *thwack*. I don't need to ask the title. It's the book I picked for next month's book club. Although I'll be reading mine on my Kindle app, Shawn already brought a few copies to the station because some of the guys prefer reading physical books.

"You picked this." It's not a question.

My eyes travel from the book on his desk, up his thick chest covered by a simple black shirt, to his neck. As I take him in, he swallows thickly, his Adam's apple working. His face is covered in dark scruff even though he shaved this morning. His strong jaw is hardened, the angles aggressive despite how soft he is for me. Those brown eyes are practically black, the storm inside him a physical presence.

Shoulders pulled back and chin raised, I smile. "Yes."

"Is there a reason you picked this one in particular?"

Oh god. His tone is a little mean and a whole lot cold, but it sends a thrill through me.

He's goading me. He wants me to admit to my fantasy. Little does he know that I'm not the least bit ashamed to admit I want both him and his best friend.

"Because the idea of the two of you fucking me makes me want to strip my clothes off right here."

Beside me, Cade mutters a quiet "fuck."

I glance at him, offering him a grin, my heart rate taking off at the fire ignited in his eyes.

"And that's what you want?" Declan asks the grinning man next to me.

Cade takes a single step forward. "Fuck yeah."

"Lock the door," Declan grits out. "And shut the shades."

The whimper that slips up my throat can't be stopped.

"And you—" Declan's tone is deep, his eyes eating up every inch of me. "Do you remember your colors?"

I nod jerkily, heat pooling in my core.

The sound of the shades sliding shut behind me is like a starting bell.

"I want to watch you undress her." Declan relaxes back in his chair, his arms behind his head, as if he's unaffected.

I, on the other hand, am so keyed up I can barely catch my breath.

Cade steps up behind me and gently brushes my hair off one shoulder, then presses his lips to my neck, sending goose bumps skittering down my arms. "You ready for this, Trouble?"

"Yes." It's a whimpering breath of a word.

I keep my attention fixed on Declan as Cade slips his hands beneath my sweater. He fondles my breasts, squeezing each one, then follows Declan's order.

"Bra too," Declan says, his voice thicker now. I can only imagine how hard he is beneath his pants.

Cade unhooks my bra, and I relax my arms, letting it fall to the floor. Then he's pulling at my pants, sliding them down my legs, and removing my shoes. Crouched in front of me, he lifts his head, his expression hungry, and rakes his gaze over me, before licking his lips.

The attention makes my core pulse in anticipation. I want his lips on me. His tongue. His fingers—

"Bring her to me."

Apparently, Declan has other plans.

It wouldn't surprise me if Cade ignored the order and dove in. Instead, he doesn't so much as flinch at Declan's command. He lifts me into his arms, wrapping my legs around his waist. With his hands settled beneath my ass, he crosses the room and gently lowers me to the desk.

For a moment, no one speaks. No one moves. Cade and I are both transfixed, waiting for Declan's next directive.

"Fuck, Melina. I've been thinking about eating you on my desk since the first time you visited me in here."

Heart stumbling, I suck in a breath. "Me too."

"Spread those beautiful legs for me, sweetheart. Let me see how pretty you are when you're wet for both of us."

Without a single ounce of modesty, I swing my legs wide. Both men have licked me, fucked me, and watched one another pleasure me.

Finally, *finally*, if I'm lucky, I'll get them both at the same time.

Declan leans in close and slides his thumb between my lips. "Look at that," he says to Cade. "Look how fucking wet she is."

Cade steps closer, right into Declan's space, and leans down until they're shoulder to shoulder. "Bet ya she tastes really sweet right now."

"Why don't you test it for me?" Declan suggests, his voice wavering just a little.

The little slip makes my stomach flip. Despite the stern tone and stoic expression, he's nervous. Just like I am. Just like Cade.

He holds me open and shifts to one side. At the same time, Cade presses a hand to my thigh and angles in. With a groan, he licks me from my opening to my clit, brushing Declan's thumb along the way. Declan's responding hiss has me gushing, and when Cade turns, tongue still touching me, and holds Declan's gaze, my core pulses.

Cade laps at my clit, grazing Declan's thumb again.

Grunting, Declan adjusts himself and gives his length a tight squeeze through his pants. "Again," he rasps.

This time Cade sucks my clit into his mouth, taking Declan's thumb with it, and when Declan hisses even louder, I'm certain I'll combust.

"Your turn," Cade says, pulling back.

Without hesitation, Declan clutches my thighs and brings me to the edge of his desk. Then, with his head between my thighs, he eats me like he's trying to lick Cade's taste from me.

"Holy fuck," I cry, slapping my hands to the cool, smooth surface of the desk.

Declan glares up from between my thighs. "She needs something to shut her up, or the dispatchers will think we've got an emergency up here."

With a lick of his lips, Cade straightens and undoes his belt with a flourish. He pulls his hard cock out in one quick motion, then rounds the desk. "Lean back, Trouble. We need you quiet."

Chest heaving, I ease back and smile up at him.

He rolls the head along my lips and chuckles. "I think she planned it this way. You're absolutely dying for my cock, aren't you?"

Pussy pulsing, I glide my tongue over his head, relishing the salty taste of his arousal.

He slides himself past my lips and boldly fucks my mouth without waiting for me to ready myself. Moaning, I suck him hard. Fuck, I love the way he fills me.

"Green?" Declan asks.

Without stopping my work, I nod.

"I think she needs two cocks." Grunting, Cade thrusts to the back of my throat.

Declan chuckles, his warm breath tickling me. "She gushed the second you said that. I think you're right."

He presses the softest of kisses against my clit and exhales, his breath ghosting over my overly sensitive skin.

I give Cade a deep suck, and above me, his jaw goes slack.

"Yes, Trouble, just like that. This fucking mouth. It's perfect." Slipping a hand beneath my head, he fists my hair. "Are you ready for both of us?"

I nod eagerly, taking in shallow breaths through my nose.

Cade looks up. Though he doesn't stop moving, he's now focused on Declan as he undresses. His expression is painted with desire. Cheeks flushed, lips parted, eyes blazing.

Spine tingling, I drink him in. If I could, I'd make it happen for him. I'd wrap Declan up and hand him over.

As much as I want them for myself, I want them to have one another even more. As devastatingly hot as I know it'll be to have them both at the same time, I won't be satisfied until they fuck one another just as hard as they fuck me.

That thought alone has me pulsing around nothing, desperate to be filled.

"Still green?" Declan asks softly. Slotted between my legs and hovering above me, he lowers until his head is bent low so that he can make eye contact with me.

In this position, his face is incredibly close to Cade's cock. Cade has stopped all movement, waiting for what comes next, panting above me.

I roll my tongue beneath his shaft and pull back slightly, letting him slip from between my lips. As his length bobs between us, Declan sucks in a heady breath.

"Still green," I say.

Though he asked the question, he's no longer focused on me. Instead, he's distracted by Cade. A frisson of elation courses through me as I take them both in. "Color, Declan?"

Blinking, he forces his attention back to me. "Green, sweetheart. When I'm with you, it's always green."

My chest swells in the best way. This man, from what I can tell, lives his life in yellow, perpetually prepared to be hurt and so cautious he forgets to move forward. Yet with me, he's comfortable enough to relax.

The feeling is mutual. When we're together, my worries fade.

It's incredible, knowing I have the ability to bring him this level of comfort.

Some people wield that power, knowing the opposite is just as true. If they can bring someone comfort, then they also have the power to hurt that person. Jason lived for that.

None of us in this room are like that. It's what allows me to do this. To be this open with not just one, but two people.

"And you?" I tip my head back and peer up at Cade.

His smile is easy. "I live in the green, Trouble."

"Great. Since we're all on the same page," I say with a long breath in and back out. "I want you both to fuck me, knowing that I also live in the green. In fact..." I eye Declan. "I dare you to try to get me to say yellow."

He chuffs, his eyes glittering with amusement. I'll take the reaction, though I long for a real laugh. A deep belly laugh and a wide smile. One that makes lines form on his face. I want to witness the way each one settles into his skin over the years.

I want him.

And I want his best friend.

With a smile up at Cade, I lick my lips and use a hand to guide him back into my mouth.

When Declan leans closer, his hand pulling me apart as he pushes into me slowly, I arch my back and moan around his best friend's dick.

In sync, they thrust slowly, causing tension to build in my core. With my head tipped back to take Cade's length, I can't see them, but I can imagine the way they're watching one another. How they communicate silently to time their thrusts, working together to please me. The desire swirling in this room is more intense than I've ever experienced. And when Cade angles over me, his dick slipping farther down my throat, and runs his fingers against my clit, the man inside me swells.

Fuck. Did Cade just stroke Declan's dick?

The mental image sends me diving off the cliff into what I'm certain is the first orgasm of many tonight.

CHAPTER 29

Cade

I NEVER COULD HAVE IMAGINED that watching Dec fuck Mel would be more of a turn-on than the perfect way she's sucking my dick right now. But watching my best friend sink inside my girl has my blood heating in a way that is permanently altering my body chemistry.

And then he has to go and moan when I accidentally slide my fingers against his dick.

It honestly was not intentional.

I touched Mel in an effort to ground myself to this moment. I felt as though I was floating away, lost to the thrill of witnessing his powerful thrusts jolt her tits in a way that had me halfway to orgasm. But when he thrust as I was teasing her clit, causing my fingers to graze across his hard, wet cock, and a deep growl rumbled through his chest? I about lost it.

Teeth gritted, I rein myself in. Once I know I won't lose control, I'm feeling all sorts of brave.

Mel convulses around his cock in response to his reaction, a long, low, muffled sound escaping her as she clenches around him.

As she rides out her orgasm, I do the most ridiculously brazen thing.

I grip his cock and squeeze. Jaw locked tight, I grit out, "Don't come."

Declan's eyes widen, then zero in on me.

Fuck. Did I go too far? Is he about to tell me to back up?

To my fucking delighted surprise, rather than losing his shit, he pants through the moment, his chest heaving as his hungry gaze holds mine.

I've stopped thrusting, allowing Mel time to come down from her first orgasm. "Give me a color," I say to Declan.

Eyes flaring, he swallows audibly. He's going to say red. He's going to admit this is too much.

But fuck if I'm not wrong again. Instead of backing off, he thrusts into Mel, into my hand, his face giving nothing away. "Green."

I inhale, unable to breathe through this lust-filled haze.

I'm touching Declan's dick, and he's not stopping me. In fact, if the way he's slowly thrusting is any indication, he doesn't want to push too hard into her for fear that I'll release him. Maybe he likes my touch.

Maybe he wants more.

That hope has me growing even more curious. Even more daring.

I live for risks. For the thrill of the moment before I take one. When possibility looms large, and the potential for failure is a thought I put aside to deal with later.

But this is Declan.

Not a game of hockey.

Not a one-night stand.

Our relationship is the most important I've ever had, and one wrong move could ruin it all.

But with the way he looks from my face to my hand to Mel, and with the way he's inching closer, it doesn't feel like such a risk at all.

So, holding my breath, I twist my hand around his shaft and cup his balls.

In response, his eyes widen, and he lets out a guttural moan.

Spurred on by his reaction, I squeeze lightly and tug just a little.

"Just like that," he whispers.

With excitement zipping up my spine, I do it again.

Mel, who released me when I stopped fucking her mouth, angles up and watches the way he sinks inside her slowly while I touch him.

"Like that?" I ask, directing the question to her. I want her to be okay with this, because god, I'm not sure I can stop.

"Oh, yes," she murmurs wickedly, her tits rising and falling with her harsh breaths.

In one quick movement, she's flat on her back, and her mouth is around my dick again, like the idea of my hands on Declan just ramped up her desire. She's swirling her tongue, working her hand up and down my cock, squeezing me, cupping my balls, just like I'm doing to Dec, all while he watches us, never slowing his movements.

This moment is so much better than even my wildest fantasies.

Mel whimpers, catching my attention. As I focus on her, a niggle of worry worms its way into me. Am I being too rough, too aggressive?

Declan brings his hand to her clit and massages her slowly. "Need more, Melina?"

She nods around me, closing her eyes in ecstasy.

He thrusts deeper this time, hitting her where I know she needs it.

She moans around me, the vibration making my balls tingle and tighten. I squeeze Declan's, and they do the same. I give them a tug, and he curses.

"Fuck, I'm going to come, sweetheart. Where do you want it?"

I want to beg for him to empty into my mouth. I want to feel the swell of his cock on my tongue. Hear his guttural groan as he comes down my throat.

But I stay silent.

Melina wraps her legs around his hips, pulling him closer, making it obvious she wants him to unload inside her. Fuck, that's even hotter than my instinctual need. Just the image of him swelling and coming in thick spurts as she pulses around him has me losing control.

"Fuck," I groan, lost to the sensation. Overwhelmed with bliss, I'm blinded by white spots in the darkness. "I'm so sorry, Trouble," I mutter, palming her cheek and rubbing my thumb against her soft skin as she swallows me down.

With a lick of her lips, she smiles up at me, her eyes watering but bright.

"Let me get a towel, and we'll get you cleaned up."

Once again, Declan shocks the hell out of me when he slips out of her and waltzes over to the couch in his office. He settles down with an ease I don't think I could muster right now and says, "No. Clean her up with your tongue."

CHAPTER 30

Declan

MY BEST FRIEND touched my dick, and I had the best orgasm of my life.

Those words flash through my mind on repeat while I watch him lick my cum from Melina's cunt like he can't get enough of our taste.

How I can sit here, palms pressed flat against my thighs, rather than storming over to the two of them for another round, is beyond me.

It's probably shock.

Because another round of what?

What do I even want to happen? What does *Cade* want to happen?

I've never cared so much about what another person is thinking than I do in this moment.

There's no lying about how good it felt to have his hand wrapped around me while I was buried inside Melina. Is it only a physical thing? That's possible, right? How could I not enjoy being touched while I thrust into her warmth?

There was no pretending that he wasn't the one touching me. That it wasn't his fist, his fingers, *him*. I looked him right in the eye as he did it. He was testing me, I'm sure. Probably expecting me to pull back so he could gauge my boundaries. The problem is, I'm not sure a boundary exists when it comes to Cade.

I've never wanted another man. Never been turned on by the idea of another man's hands. Lips. Tongue.

Yet I'm practically salivating over the way Cade's tongue moves languidly over Melina.

It's undeniable: I'm turned on.

Hard.

I unloaded inside her minutes ago, yet I've got a full-on chub just watching them.

And I have no idea what any of it fucking means.

Maybe it's because I'm so comfortable with him.

My most trusted friend.

He's a good-looking guy. Anyone with eyes would have a hard time disagreeing with that. But would they look as closely as I am right now? Would another straight man look at Cade and focus on the way his forearm flexes as he holds himself up? Would they be focusing on the way he's stroking her pussy with his tongue? Or would they be solely focused on her?

Don't get me wrong—she's the fucking sexiest woman I've ever seen. She's my obsession. I'm crazy about her.

And by the way she's writhing, she's about to come.

I'm transfixed by the way her breasts swell and her nipples harden. By the way her thighs are stretched wide and she's digging her feet into Cade's sides as she screams through another orgasm.

Fuck. I shoot to my feet and stride to her side. With a hand over her mouth, I muffle her screams. Ignoring the man between her thighs, I lean down and whisper, "Shh, these sounds are only for us, sweetheart."

"It's so nice of you to come to the festival, Chief," Carmella says in a singsong voice.

As if I had a choice in the matter. Hope Street is decked out with stalls upon stalls for this German market–inspired festival. Residents display their homemade goods up and down the street, hocking artwork, crocheted blankets and hats and mittens, spiked apple cider, and Bristol-themed clothes.

Carmella and her grandson's wife Belle are selling homemade limoncello that they brew at the winery Belle co-owns. It's incredible, but I don't give it a second thought today. I'm too focused on finding the two people who left my office a half hour ago.

A phone call came in as we were all cleaning up, and—thank fuck— I had to stay behind while Cade and Melina headed out. I needed the time to myself to wrap my head around what the fuck we did and work through how I want to proceed.

I've yet to figure that out, because I don't know what the fuck to make of my physical attraction to Cade.

It was probably the heat of the moment.

That thought makes my stomach twist. It doesn't explain the thoughts that have plagued me every other time I've seen him since Melina moved into my home. Still, I'll go with that. Now that we're in town, dressed, and he's not fucking the woman I'm obsessed with, I'm certain this feeling that I'm going to crawl out of my skin if I don't touch him will go away.

It has to.

"They're over there." Carmella points, wearing a knowing smirk.

Fuck. It can't be that obvious, can it?

"I'm here by myself." I lift my chin and focus on Belle, patently avoiding looking in Cade and Melina's direction. "Can you wrap one of those bottles up for me? I think my sister will love it."

The raven-haired woman smiles, and I find myself noticing the exact color of her eyes for the first time. They're a deep blue close to the shade of Cade's, though his irises have an almost turquoise ring around the pupil that makes the blue lighten when he smiles.

I run my hand through my hair. *Lighten when he smiles. Turquoise.* What the *hell* is wrong with me?

In the thirty-plus years I've known Cade, I've never thought about his eye color. What the fuck has changed?

And do I want it to stop?

"Why don't I wrap it up, and you can pick it up when you're done with the festival? That way you don't have to walk around with the bottle," she suggests.

"Actually, that'd be great." I pull out my wallet and pay, then head in the direction I pretended I had no intention of going.

But as I scan the crowd and don't spot the two people who have me all tangled up inside, my irritation grows.

Did they go home?

Or head to dinner without me?

"Dec." The voice has my heart leaping.

The way my stomach swoops in excitement when I lock eyes with Cade is embarrassing. And the fluttering in my chest is so intense, I rub at the space above my heart to ease it.

"Thought that was you," Melina says as she releases Cade's hand and slips her arms around my midsection. No hesitation. No consideration for what the people around us might think. She does what she wants, and though I don't normally enjoy public displays of affection, I don't exactly hate it when she squeezes me tighter and tilts her chin up, smile blazing, waiting for me to kiss her hello.

But I do hate the way I taste Cade on her lips. Not because the flavor is a turn-off, but because I can't reach for him and do the same.

Fuck.

And when I look over her head and lock eyes with my best friend, the hungry expression on his face tells me that the feeling is not one-sided. The need I saw in his eyes as he watched Melina undress is now aimed at me.

Once again I don't know what the fuck to make of any of it. But my dick sure knows how it feels. This is going to get uncomfortable quick if I don't get my head in the game. So I pull my gaze from his and wrap my arm around Melina instead. Pointing at the limoncello stall, I say, "I was grabbing a gift for my sister. Cade, you should get a bottle for your mom. I bet she'd love the stuff."

Beyond Cade, Carmella and Belle are surreptitiously watching. Dammit. What are they thinking? Are they judging? With a sharp breath in and back out, I push the intrusive thoughts away.

"She loves it," Carmella says, not even trying to act like she wasn't eavesdropping.

Cade grins and has Belle wrap up a bottle for him. "I'll take it over tomorrow, along with the flowers Amelia set aside. Looks like I'm a shoo-in for favorite son."

I snort. "You're her only son."

"Always good to put in the effort, though," Carmella chimes in. "Now go on, you three. The night is young. Enjoy the festival."

With Melina between us, we wander the street, stopping as she peruses the goods and makes a purchase at almost every stall. Conversation is easy between Cade and me as she chats with everyone she meets.

My body is finally beginning to relax, and I'm realizing that things haven't changed that much since before I knew what Cade's touch felt like. Maybe it really is just a sexual thing. It doesn't have to *mean* anything more than that. He's my best friend, and we enjoyed sharing a woman. Sure, it may be hot when the three of us are together and body parts brush against one another, but—

"I'm officially starving," Melina says, pointing at Thames. The sky has gone from burgundy to black, and the bar on the water looks cozy, all aglow the way it is. The stars twinkle above it, and beyond, the dark water appears almost angry as it thrashes against the docks.

Cade wraps one arm around Melina's waist and kisses her neck. His other arm is loaded down with her purchases. "Our girl did get quite the workout this afternoon."

Our girl.

My heart thumps wildly against my sternum. I love the sound of it. Love the idea that she's ours.

That the woman I'm obsessed with isn't just his. She's mine too.

Feeling bold, I step in close on her other side. "Eat up, sweetheart. You've got more work to do tonight."

She inhales sharply, and all I can do is imagine that her nipples are poking against the green sweater beneath her winter jacket.

Melina wraps a hand around my neck, pulling me even closer, and kisses me. Her tongue is sweet from the cider she picked up at one of the booths, the flavor intoxicating. I moan against her, surprised by the easy affection.

My surprise turns into a strange heat I've never experienced when she turns, wraps her other arm around Cade's neck and she repeats the move with him.

I watch on, studying the way he dips his tongue into her mouth, how he bites down on her bottom lip and gently tugs, like he's relishing not only her taste, but mine.

"Come on, you two," I grunt. "I'm not going to make it through dinner if we keep this up."

Melina laughs against Cade's mouth, and when she pulls away, they turn in unison, both smiling. They're so similar in so many ways. Happy. Light.

Their smiles are enough to ease the constant weight pressing down on my shoulders.

I take off toward the restaurant. If my mind keeps running in this direction, I'll be tempted to force them back to my house now, but we need sustenance first.

Thames is loud and crowded with townspeople seeking refuge from the chilly night. But when Hailey spots us, she motions to the hostess to set up a booth for us by the fireplace. Like all small towns, Bristol has its share of problems, but good service is not one of them. I hold a hand up to Hailey in thanks as we're led toward the table. Halfway there, Cade splits off and disappears to the bathroom.

Melina slides into the booth, and I settle on the other side. "God, I love this place," she says as she removes her jacket.

I roll my neck from one side to the other, working out a kink. "Don't miss the city?"

She bites her lip. A nervous tic, I've come to realize.

What does she have to be nervous about now? Jason should no longer be an issue. And if he is, she's got Cade and me to keep her safe.

"Not really," she says, focusing on the table between us.

Cade reappears, and though I expect him to slip in on Melina's other side so she's between us in the round booth, he pushes into mine so I'm in the middle.

With a steady breath, I will myself to act normally. I've sat next to Cade in this bar plenty of times. Though I've never been so focused on the way his knee brushes up against mine as he spreads his legs wide and turns his body toward us. "You know, I'm pretty sure you've bought a gift from every person in this town," he says over me, his focus entirely on her.

Her responding laugh is raspy, pulling my attention from Cade for a moment. As I'm watching her, he rests his arm on the back of the booth behind me.

"I've always loved Christmas," Melina says. "I love watching people open gifts, and I love spoiling my family." Her voice trails off at the end, and pain flashes across her face. "If I can't spoil my family this Christmas, then at least I can support the shopkeepers here."

I reach beneath the table and squeeze her knee, hoping the gesture is reassuring.

The server appears then, focus set on her order pad. "What can I get you to drink?"

When she looks up and scans us, her eyes widen, and I swear she takes a step back. Is she cataloging every point of contact? My hand on Melina's knee, Cade's arm around me, his knee touching mine. Or am I being paranoid? Can she even see anything but Cade's arm slung casually over the back of the bench?

Either way, my cheeks flame, and I shift away from Cade a bit, spreading my knees wide so he can't move any closer.

With a quirk of a brow at me, he orders his standard vodka tonic. Mel asks for a wine list, while I pull on the front of my shirt, suddenly feeling as though I can't get enough air.

"You hot?" Cade murmurs, leaning in so close that his body heat only adds to the problem, his lips at my ear, his warm breath ghosting over my cheek.

Holding my breath, I peer over at the waitress. She's watching me, pen still poised over her pad.

Behind her, a group of older men who hang out on the corner of Hope Street, drinking their coffees most mornings, are also staring.

As a bead of sweat trickles down my spine, I elbow Cade, forcing him to give me space, and order a beer on tap.

Melina takes her time picking out a wine, and while we wait, Cade's gaze burns a hole in the side of my head.

The second the server is gone, he pounces. "Something wrong?"

Stomach sinking, I keep my expression neutral. "Nothing's wrong."

Melina watches on, seemingly having missed the interaction now causing this tension.

"You worried about what people will think of how close we're sitting?"

I grind my teeth, a knot of dread sinking in my stomach. "Of course not."

Cade's chuckle lacks any kind of humor. "Worried they'll think you're dating the gay boy?"

"Oh my god," Melina mutters, grabbing my thigh. "Tell him you don't give a fuck what other people think."

I sigh. She's right—I don't. But I am the local fire chief, and sitting this close to another person, regardless of gender, draws attention. That attention makes me itchy. And sitting between the two of them? The scrutiny is multiplied by ten. Doesn't he feel any sort of way about that? People will judge her. Us.

"It's fine." Cade shoves out of the booth and points to the bar. "I'll hang with Hailey. Let me know when you're ready to go home."

He doesn't even give me a second to speak. To correct his ridiculous assertion that I give two fucks about his sexual orientation. When have I ever given him any inclination that I do? I've watched him flirt with both men and women for years. Witnessed him walk out of many bars with them. Heard the play-by-plays after the fact.

I never batted an eye.

He should know me well enough to know I'm not a bigot who would view him through a lens colored by his sexual orientation. He's so much more than that. We all are.

I grind my teeth, shoulders tensing in annoyance.

"You have to go talk to him," Melina says quietly, squeezing my thigh.

Tucking my chin to my chest, I blow out a breath. "I will."

I'm not about to let his overreaction or my stupid inability to speak up quickly enough ruin what is obviously a good thing.

And I sure as fuck won't let it screw up our friendship.

We're both stubborn assholes most of the time, but for Cade, I'll make an exception. As I'm sliding to the end of the booth, his loud laugh echoes through the entire space.

Hailey is leaning over the lacquered bar top, and Cade is angling in closer, with his mouth to her ear.

My stomach drops to the floor.

Is he fucking *flirting* with her?

Right in front of Melina?

What. The. Fuck?

Who Gays

CHAPTER 31

Melina

"I THOUGHT you were going over there," I say, worry rolling through me.

If the guys don't talk now, things will only fester and get worse. Neither handled that little hiccup well at all, but it's plain as day that it's only because they both care so damn much. These men who have come to mean more to me than I thought possible are struggling to come to terms with the way their relationship is changing. I'm spoiled, I suppose, because I'm part of it while also being an observer. I'm experiencing it for myself, but at the same time, I'll never truly understand what they're working through. They've got a decades-long history. Eons of shared experiences that affect the way they are both—so badly—handling this new development.

I've never known either of them without the other. I've never not wanted both of them. So while, in that respect, I'm on the outside looking in, I also have the advantage of not having nearly so much to work through.

Not only are these men settling into something new with me, but they're coming to terms with how their relationship is changing.

Declan wants Cade, although he may not fully know that yet, and Cade has always wanted Declan. Now they need to find their rhythm together. Once they do—and if they still want me then—I truly believe our relationship would be incredible.

Declan growls under his breath, pulling me from my musings and fantasies about happily ever afters with my boyfriends and sending me straight back to being concerned.

With a deep breath in, I slump. "What now?"

"He's fucking flirting right in front of you," he grits out.

Chin lifted, I find Cade at the bar. He's smiling and chatting with the bartender in what looks like a pretty typical way. "He's talking."

"She was basically in his lap." Declan practically breathes fire as he glares in their direction.

I can't help the snort that slips out. "He's being Cade."

Going rigid, he turns his full body my way. "Doesn't it bother you? That he can't go anywhere without flirting with every person he sees? That you're sitting right here, and he's over there laughing with another woman like she has a shot at getting him in her bed tonight?"

My heart pangs, but not for the reason Declan would think. He's worried about my feelings, when in reality, his are the ones being hurt right now. "I like that other women are attracted to the men I'm sleeping with." I nod at two women across the room who've checked Declan out several times already tonight.

Cade is hot. There's no doubt. But Declan is ruggedly handsome. Everywhere we go, people stare, but Declan is oblivious to how many of those looks are directed at him. He's mysterious. He's gruff, and his smiles don't come easy. That only makes the people around him more eager to earn them. Or maybe that's just me. Because damn if it doesn't create an ache deep in my chest every time one finally breaks through.

Declan looks at the two women and grunts. "Not interested."

"Right, because you know that when we get home, I'm going to fuck you while I suck his cock."

He chokes, eyes bulging, but rights himself quickly.

"Or vice versa. Or..." I leave it at that, worried I'll scare him off if I delve into my desires.

Declan presses closer, hands fisted on the table. "Or what?"

Lips pressed together, I inhale deeply, working up the nerve to be completely honest. "Or you two could—"

He shakes his head, his movements harsh. "No."

"Why not? You're obviously jealous of the way you think he's flirting with her." Is he really so obtuse that he doesn't recognize the emotion for what it is?

Declan runs a hand through his hair, his face flushed. "I'm not jealous. It's just... Fuck, this is such a weird situation."

I scoot closer and press my hand to his heated cheek. "It's not. You want him over here with us because you like when he's around."

Holding my gaze, he leans into my palm, the scruff on his face rough against my skin. For a moment, he just breathes. Then, straightening, he clutches my hand and brings it to his lips. "Of course I want him here. He's my best friend."

"I think it's more than that," I say softly.

"I don't know how to feel about all of this," he admits, his eyes darting back and forth, like he's hoping he'll find the answers written on my face.

I suck in a breath. "Can you do something for me?"

He sighs heavily, his shoulders slumping. "You know I can't say no to you."

There's no fighting my smile. "I'm counting on that."

Even as he shakes his head like I'm exasperating, his lips tilt up, and I'm graced with that beautiful smile of his. Even if it's a half smile, a rush of adrenaline courses through me.

"Tonight," I urge, "just let things go where they go. Stop worrying about the world out here." I lean in close and ghost my lips across his. "Just worry about us."

Our breaths mingle as he lets my words settle between us.

"It doesn't bother you?" he rasps.

The fear in his tone makes me want to wrap my arms around him and hold him tight, but I resist.

"What?" I play dumb. He needs to come to terms with this attraction, the ache he has for the man he's known his whole life. If he doesn't, then we're doomed right from the start.

"The idea of Cade and me..." He lowers his head, likely hoping I'll let him get away with not finishing his sentence.

He's wrong. So, lips pressed together, I arch a brow and zero in on him.

Beside me, he twitches, his leg bouncing. "The way I..."

Holding on to my patience, I give him a sweet smile. He'll get there.

He lets out another breath, as if he's expelling all his worries, and then he blinks at me. "I want him. That doesn't bother you?"

The smile that splits my face is so wide it hurts. "It gives me butter-flies, Declan." I grasp his hand and press it to my pounding heart. "And it makes me unbelievably wet."

"We should take our food to go," he mumbles.

With a laugh, I bring my lips to his again.

When we pull apart, we're both smiling. "You going to get Cade?"

Declan nods, his eyes swimming with apprehension but also excite-ment. "Yeah, I think it's time."

CHAPTER 32

Cade

"HOW GOES THE HUSBAND SEARCH?"

Declan mentioned that Hailey is in a tough spot because of her controlling grandmother.

Her red hair, pulled into a messy ponytail, swishes as she angles closer and places her hand on my forearm. "Why? You offering to be my hockey coach in shining armor?" She bats her hazel eyes flirtatiously and gives me her biggest smile.

Hailey is gorgeous. She's all curves and sex appeal. Only a few weeks ago, I was looking at her like I wouldn't mind spending a few hours getting to know her body. Bet she'd be fun. We'd probably laugh and fuck the night away.

Now, though? I don't feel an ounce of attraction. I can flirt and smile no matter my mood, of course, but in this moment, my mood is piss-poor, and there's nothing she can do to change that. Not that I'll ever let her or anyone else know that.

"You really can't take ownership of the bar unless you're married?"

Hailey deflates, shrinking a good couple of inches in front of my eyes. "Yeah, Grandmama is a bit controlling."

"Grandmama?" A chuckle escapes me.

Throwing a rag over her shoulder, she shoots me a wink and walks away. "She hates that nickname."

I can't help but laugh again, despite my sour mood. Shaking my head, I pick up my drink and watch her disappear into the kitchen.

The weight of Declan's and Melina's stares is heavy, making it almost impossible not to turn around. My position puts me directly in their view. I chose this seat on purpose. They can see me, but I can't see them. I'm regretting that decision immensely now as I wonder what they're doing.

Is Melina talking Declan down? Urging him not to storm out of the restaurant in anger?

Is he stewing quietly, refusing to speak?

Is she cursing me for leaving her to deal with him?

Or are they too busy flirting to even notice I'm gone?

The last one hurts the most, if I'm being honest. My entire life, I've been the guy who leaves because I don't want to be the one left behind.

And despite popular belief, I'm sure, I'm not too emotionally stunted to be oblivious to it. I am, however, too stunted to do anything to change it.

My dad died when I was twelve, leaving me with a hole in my heart so big, there's no way it can ever fully heal. He was my biggest supporter. Both of my parents, really. While I wasn't out as bisexual at that age, I have no doubt that my dad would have been just as supportive as my mother is. When we lost him, I threw myself into hockey. It was the only thing that eased the pain.

Several years later, when Declan and I had a threesome with a girl from college and Dec practically ghosted me, I poured all my energy into figuring out why he didn't want me and how to right our friend-ship again.

Shortly thereafter, it became obvious that I'd never make it to the NHL, so I walked away from the dream before it could be taken from me.

There's no sob story there. I just wasn't good enough. Even in my early twenties, I was self-aware enough to see it. To spot my own weak-nesses. It's why I'm a good coach. With only thirty-two teams in the

NHL and only two goalies on each team, it takes a lot more than a strong work ethic and decent talent to play.

I never had anywhere near the raw talent that Brooks Langfield does, but it's a fucking honor to be his coach.

The point is, I walked away from the competition before I got rejected.

Before I lost yet another precious part of my life, like I lost my dad and then Declan.

In all the years since, I've made sure to never put myself in a position where I can be hurt like that again.

Until now.

And what I've found myself entangled in? It's so much worse than just about any other scenario I can come up with. Because I haven't gotten too close to just one person, but two. And I've stupidly allowed a dream I've had for decades to play out. I've begun to envision a future I so desperately want but had resigned myself to never having. A future that includes Declan.

How is it that a man who barely strings three words together at a time, who's got the personality of a cactus, has me so bent out of shape that I'd take this damn risk again?

Hope. It's the biggest risk of them all.

I promised myself I'd skate backward down a mountain before I'd fall for this again.

And yet here I am.

"You going to drink that or just glare at it all night?" Declan asks, his tone deep and rough.

My heart lurches, but I hide the reaction. Instead, I take a page out of his book and grunt, forcing myself not to look at him as he settles on the barstool beside me. I've got one leg propped up on my stool and my hat turned forward and dipped down low.

Once he's settled, I remain silent. If I speak, then I can guarantee I'll turn to him and ask why the fuck he has to be so difficult. Why he had to go and ruin a perfectly good day.

Why I'm not good enough.

"I'm not good at this," he says, angling toward me, his voice low.

When I don't reply, he hooks his fingers under the seat of my stool and drags it until I'm positioned between his thighs. Fuck. He's so close, I can't breathe.

"I'd really rather not do this in a bar, but if you need me to prove to you that I don't give a fuck about your sexual orientation, then I'll gladly make it obvious to everyone in this room that the last thing I am is turned off by your touch."

Lungs seizing, I snap my gaze up to his face.

He runs his tongue over his bottom lip, keeping his focus fixed on me. For the space of half a dozen heartbeats, he doesn't move, and when he finally does, it's only to glance at my mouth. Then he's back to locking eyes with me, his irises dark and swimming with a myriad of emotions.

"So what'll it be?" he murmurs. His thighs bracket my chair, our bodies so close, the intimacy has to be obvious to anyone who can see us. He slides a hand—the one closest to the bar—from his thigh to mine and drags his thumb back and forth along the denim there. Fuck. The move is simple, discreet, but I feel like he's stripped me naked and asked me to detail my every desire.

My throat is dry, my tongue too big for my mouth, but I force myself to speak. "What'll *what* be?"

He leans in close, so close I can smell the clean scent of him, his voice a raspy whisper. "Is this about us or them? Because if you need me to show you that I don't give a fuck about them, I will. But I'd rather keep this moment just for us."

Tamping down on the hope bubbling up inside me, I lift my chin. "And what would this moment you keep referring to be?"

Declan's lip lifts on one side, and he gives me the sexiest smirk I've ever seen, all ease and confidence and control. "The moment I first kiss you. I'd rather it be just for *us*. You, me, and Melina," he says.

Fuck. The way he's including her? And how he's spelling it all out for me? I focus on his lips again, stomach flipping, and replay his words. Could it really be that simple? We just...kiss? And then what?

Fuck, the warning bells are all there: He doesn't like men. He's never shown an ounce of interest in me like that. I've had this massive crush on him since I was sixteen.

Maybe I should shy away, but there's not a chance in hell I'll miss out on this opportunity. Standing quickly, I clear my throat. "What are we waiting for? Let's grab Mel and get the fuck out of here."

Good For You

CHAPTER 33

Declan

DESPITE MY BRAVADO at the restaurant, the moment we step inside my house, nerves riot inside me. Cade drove Melina back while I waited for the food and then walked back to where I left my truck at the station. As I enter the dining room where I fucked Melina only last night, their low voices go silent.

My stomach lurches, and insecurity grips me. What if Cade has changed his mind? What if he's not actually attracted to me that way? Being bisexual doesn't mean he's attracted to every man he meets.

And I'm his best friend. Maybe he feels like he has to do this because I'm interested and he doesn't want to turn me down.

Or maybe Melina is uncomfortable. Maybe she was just pretending to find my interest in Cade hot.

In the span of a couple of heartbeats, I spiral. Fuck. I need to get a handle on these thoughts and trust that they'd tell me the truth.

It's just...I've never done this.

And I don't just mean fooling around with a man. I've never done the whole dating thing, period.

My relationships with both Melina and Cade, separate and together, are firsts for me. From what I know about them, neither has ever had a real, healthy relationship either. There's a good chance that none of us has the experience necessary to guide us through this.

"Your parents loved each other," I say to Cade.

Fuck. I shouldn't be surprised that I'm spouting nonsense. This happens every time I get nervous. And when Melina is around, I just start fucking talking.

They blink at me like I'm an idiot. They're not wrong.

I set the food on the table and fold my arms across my chest. Might as well own my statement. "Well, didn't they?"

Cade glances at Melina and then looks back to me. "Yeah. They loved each other a lot."

I nod and take a deep breath. "Okay."

"Okay?" Melina is facing me, but she furrows her brow and side-eyes Cade.

"He knows what a healthy relationship looks like," I explain, heading toward the kitchen to grab cutlery.

When I return, they're both still quiet.

Annoyed, I huff. Why must I explain myself to everyone? Why can't they just get it without so many goddamn words?

"Do the rules from last night still apply?" I ask.

Their looks are dubious. Okay, then. Looks like I'll have to spell it all out.

"The honesty. The trust. You'll tell me if you're uncomfortable. If you don't want to do something. Stop means stop. I can handle it if this is all too much for you." I look from Melina to Cade. "Or if you've changed your minds."

Melina's shoulders relax, and she breaks into a wide smile. "Oh, he thought you'd forgotten about his promise to kiss you in the time between when we left him at the bar and when he got here."

I roll my eyes. She's teasing me. But I'm grateful she dumbed it down and laid it out in plain language. Because sometime in the thirty minutes we were apart, my mind spun out, and I began questioning everything that happened while we were in that bar.

Though I'm not questioning whether I want to do it.

I know exactly what I want. That hasn't changed since I opened up to Melina about it.

But am I ready for what this all means?

Are they ready? Are we ready?

My heart pounds loudly in my ears. Crossing this line with Melina is one thing, but crossing it with Cade? We've got to be damn sure we're ready for the fallout.

I'm not willing to risk our friendship.

"I promise I'll tell you how I feel." Cade's eyes are bright with intensity. I find myself stepping closer to him, and he lifts his chin up, holding my gaze before adding, "And there is *nothing* you could do that would make me say stop."

My cock jumps at the confidence in his tone and the implication in his words.

Any doubt I may have harbored about my attraction to my best friend goes out the window in that moment, leaving room for thoughts about all the very filthy things I'd like to do to him. The way I want to use his body. I could never treat Melina like that, but Cade—fuck, Cade is so filthy, he would probably love it.

"Good." I pull out the chair and settle in for dinner.

"Good?" Melina questions, her eyes dancing and a smile playing at her lips.

"Eat. Both of you." I look from her to Cade. "You'll need your energy for what I've got planned."

CHAPTER 34

Cade

DESPITE OUR DECADES-LONG FRIENDSHIP, I still don't know how to read Declan. Not in certain situations. But our girl can. Thank fuck, because the two of us are pretty terrible at this whole communication thing.

I never would have guessed Declan was nervous. Or insecure.

But as we finish dinner, I can't help but replay a comment Melina made about Declan using the ropes to ease his anxiety.

He's always been quiet, and the broodiness set in when we were in college. So I've always just accepted that it's who he is. Is it possible that he's broody and quiet because he's anxious? Because he doesn't always know what to say?

I guess I've noticed that when he's in control, when he's comfortable, he's more open. At least with me.

Mel seems to know what he needs without words, though.

Surprisingly, their connection doesn't make me jealous. I'm thankful for it. Because around her, he's comfortable enough to accept the man he truly is, and apparently that man wants to kiss me.

So yeah, I'm not jealous at all. I'm fucking ecstatic about the possibility of learning more about my best friend.

"I'll clean up. You two go get in my shower."

I startle at Declan's command, even as Mel laces her fingers with mine and guides me toward his room.

"He needs a few minutes to himself," she tells me as we approach Dec's bedroom, once again proving my theory.

"Oh yeah? And what are we going to do while he does that?" I tease, trying to relax.

Mel glances back at me with a wicked smile. "Whatever we want."

I pause at the threshold. I've never been inside his bedroom before. Walking into his personal space now feels like a monumental feat.

Mel doesn't stop. She doesn't even slow. Of course, she's probably already been in here.

Has she slept beside him in this bed?

I take in the king-size bed. Is it possible that it's bigger than a king? I swear it's larger than my bed at home. The dark navy comforter is folded down and made as if a drill sergeant inspected the room this morning.

A gray lamp sits on each dark-wood nightstand flanking the mattress. The ornate headboard is a dark wood as well. Above it, a large picture of the Mount Hope Bridge at night, lit up in red, white, and blue—as it always is on the Fourth of July in Bristol—hangs.

Finally stepping into the room, I head straight for the picture window. Outside, the yard is well-manicured, with a large arborvitae separating it from the water, allowing for complete privacy.

As I take in the scene, one Declan must see every night, I take a long breath in and let it out, feeling my nerves settling.

My mind turns to the many nights we've sat in that backyard at the teak table, or around the fire pit, beers in hand, bullshitting. I guess I'm the one typically doing the bullshitting. Declan's additions to the conversations typically involve grunting in acknowledgment of something I've said.

What is it about him that made me fall so hard?

There's no explanation for the way my heart picks up the minute he walks into a room. The way my eyes search for him when I know he's near. How I breathe easier when I'm in this town, in this house, in his proximity.

But that's not giving him enough credit.

Declan showed up at my house the night my dad died and never left.

Physically, he went home, of course—though he often stayed all night. But even then, I knew he was only a phone call away. That he'd show up in a heartbeat if I needed him.

That's always been Declan.

He's the steady one. The strong one. My rock.

I startle when slender arms wrap around my waist and squeeze.

"Shower is warm." Mel presses a kiss to the space between my shoulder blades.

I spin and take her cheeks in my hands. "You are perfect, you know that?"

Head tipped back, she gives me a knowing smile. "No one's perfect, Cade."

Angling closer, I press my lips to hers. When I pull back, I keep my focus locked on her eyes. "You are. For us. You always know what we need. Space for Declan, time for me. Your hugs. You just..." My throat goes thick with emotion, making it nearly impossible to get the words out.

She blinks up at me, patient, not rushing me or filling the silence.

"You complete us," I breathe out. "Tonight wouldn't be happening if not for you."

Mel slides her teeth over her bottom lip. "I've never felt more like myself than when I'm with the two of you. Maybe it's selfish, wanting you both—"

Shaking my head, I slide a thumb along her cheek, relishing the smoothness of her skin. "No more selfish than me wanting you both. Can you feel the way I'm shaking? My body is vibrating with want, knowing he's on the other side of that wall. We need him. And I'm okay with admitting that."

"Just remember, this is a big step for him," she reminds me. "He cares so deeply for you, but he's going to get things wrong."

Like earlier. That's what she's referring to. How we handled the fight in the bar. How I lashed out at him for not being ready.

My insecurities got the best of me, and I projected. It was unfair of me, but the idea that he was embarrassed by us hurt.

"I'm going to get things wrong too," I admit.

She pops up on her toes and brushes her mouth over mine. "We'll go slow, then. No rules, no expectations."

I smile against her lips. "You never did like rules, Trouble."

"True." With a wicked chuckle, she slips her tongue into my mouth. She undoes my pants and slowly undresses me. All the while, we're a mess of hands and teeth and tongues, dropping clothes throughout Declan's neat room as we kiss.

"He's going to lose his mind when he comes in here," I say, pushing her into the now steamy bathroom. Grabbing her by the thighs, I lift her into my arms and step into the oversized shower.

She grinds against me with every step I take. *Fuck.* It takes everything in me to not push inside her. To not take her against the wall of his shower, fucking her roughly until she cries out on my cock, loud enough that Declan can't help but come watch us dismantle his carefully crafted plans.

Though Mel did say no rules, so keeping ourselves entertained while we wait for him isn't out of the question. I'm squeezing her ass, rubbing her over my cock, ready to thrust into her, when the bedroom door bangs against the wall, startling us.

"Don't worry, I'll clean up in here," Declan hollers.

Mel buries her face in my chest, laughing.

Need courses through me, heavy and all-consuming. "Think I can get you off before he finishes putting away our clothes?"

Eyes flaring, she rotates her hips against me, moaning as the head of my cock slides against her clit. "Bet you we both can."

Bucking against her, I press her against the wall. Then I use my grip on her hips to slide her up and down my shaft, watching as she massages me with her clit.

"Yes, Cade, right there."

Maybe it's the unknown, all the possibilities, the way my mind is running rampant, but we've barely fooled around, and already, I'm close to losing it.

The sound of Declan opening and closing drawers and walking around his room only adds to the excitement. A thrill shoots down my spine at the idea that he could catch us at any moment. My body buzzes as I consider what type of punishment he'd dole out.

Would he spank Mel?

Would he spank me?

My cock swells at the thought of Declan forcing me to turn around. My breath hitches when I imagine the moments of anticipation while I wait for his hand to meet my ass.

Biting down on my shoulder, Mel grinds against me. Then she's crying out and coming apart in my arms.

"You're going to pay for that orgasm, sweetheart," Declan says as he steps into the shower behind me. His tone is all stern daddy, the sound of it, along with his proximity, making my ass clench. "And you—" He grips my shoulder, and then he's close, the heat of him radiating, his presence overwhelming me when I'm already so close to coming all over Mel's stomach.

Heaving in a harsh breath, I peer over my shoulder. *Fuck*, he's close, his mouth mere centimeters from mine. Water from the rain shower above us streams from his dark hair, dripping across his eyebrows and past his rugged nose, landing on his parted lips as he runs his tongue across his teeth.

"You're going to pay for making me want you. Making it impossible to think about anyone but the two of you since the minute you brought Melina into my home, gave her my tequila, and then let her sit on *my* cock."

My knees wobble, and my heart stumbles, but somehow, I manage to tease him. "Your cock?"

The way Declan arches his brow, as if he's unimpressed by my denial, has me ready to blow. In bed, I typically prefer to be in charge. In control. But there isn't a world in which Declan will allow that, and fuck if that thought doesn't make my insides molten.

"Pretty sure she was riding *my* cock, Dec. Like she did just now when she came all over it."

Mel whimpers against me, pulling Declan's attention to her.

Glaring, he grunts. "Then she has a mess to clean up, don't you, sweetheart?"

Heart pounding, I survey Mel, searching for signs of how she's feeling.

Her pupils all but eclipse her irises, and her chest is heaving, like this is her greatest dream. "My pleasure," she purrs as she uses her hold on my neck to pull herself closer so our chests are flush.

Then, over my shoulder, they're kissing, and he's pressing against me from behind, wrapping his arm around my side and pulling her in tighter. Like this, I can feel every ridge of his body. From his muscular chest to his firm abs to the thick cock Mel loves so fucking much.

There's no stopping my body's instinct to roll my ass against his length. He groans against Mel's lips, and then he's pulling his mouth from hers, cuffing my neck, and pressing his lips to mine.

I'm so stunned, it takes me a few seconds to do anything but stand there and keep Mel pressed against the wall. I'm still holding her up, but he's cocooning the both of us with his strong arms.

And holy fuck, Declan is kissing me.

His lips are rougher than Mel's, but his movements are gentle to start. But when I run my tongue against the seam of his lips, he ruts against my ass, making it clear that he likes what's happening. He opens for me, and as we explore one another's mouths, Mel wiggles free from my arms. Once she's steady, I release her and allow Declan to spin me and press me against the wall—which is cold as fuck compared to his warm body—and then he's diving in for another kiss.

It's rough, the way we're going at it, rubbing against one another while we war for control. His fingers tug on my hair, my hands find his hips and we grind against one another. It feels so fucking good. His lips on mine, his breath, his pounding heart. Declan yanks back, and for a second, my heart sinks. But then he's pulling Mel toward us and grabbing her chin, his eyes blazing.

"Clean him up for me, sweetheart." He presses his lips to hers and wraps his fingers around my cock.

The groan that slips from my throat is nothing short of animalistic. "Fuck, Dec."

We're all transfixed on the way he strokes me. He thumbs my head, then releases me and holds his thumb up to Mel's lips. Without hesitation, she sucks him clean.

He cups her shoulder and urges her to her knees. With his other hand, he squeezes my cock. Then he's guiding it into her warm mouth.

I stare, slack jawed, in ecstasy.

"You are such a good girl," he murmurs as he strokes her cheek. "Sucking *my* cock like that." He turns to me, wearing a challenging frown, daring me to defy him. "Tell her, baby. Tell her how good she's doing."

Jaw clenched, I focus on breathing through my nose and holding myself back from exploding. This moment is perfect. Declan is fisting my cock while Mel sucks me down. The way he watches me like he can't wait to send me over the edge, like my pleasure *is* his pleasure, is the hottest thing I've ever witnessed.

And fuck, he called me *baby*.

It's nearly impossible to speak, but I manage to force the stilted words out. "Y-you're perfect. Like always, Trouble."

Mel looks up at me, eyes full of liquid heat. She's loving this just as much as I am.

"And whose cock is she sucking?" Dec's tone is condescending. Why the fuck is it so hot? If this is how it feels when he owns me, I'll give him the reins from here on out.

I drop my head back against the tile, my body racked with tension as I stave off my orgasm. "Yours."

The smile that lances his face is exquisite. Angling in, he presses his mouth to mine again. He forces his tongue between my lips, and as I reciprocate, licking into his mouth, he sucks hard. And, *holy fuck*, I come without warning. Declan inhales my cries while Mel swallows me down. Neither relents until I'm spent. Until my legs shake and Dec is holding me up against the shower wall.

Once he's sure I'll remain upright, he scoops Mel into his arms and murmurs in her ear, telling her how good she did, how proud he is of her. He pulls her in and kisses her, instantly whimpering. Tingles creep up my spine as he dives in for another taste of her. Because it's not just her he's tasting. It's me, and he fucking loves it.

CHAPTER 35

Melina

"DRY OFF AND then meet us in the bedroom," Declan growls over his shoulder as he carries me out of the bathroom. I'm so wound up, I'm pretty sure I'm leaving a trail of my desire behind as we go. Watching Declan kiss Cade was like nothing I've ever seen. The dominance, the sheer power they fought over, and the lust—*god,* that is what songs are written about.

Pure want, need, and love.

At dinner, Declan asked Cade if he'd known real love. What he doesn't realize is he knows it too. He and Cade have been showing it to one another in small ways for years. But tonight—*tonight*—they finally unleashed it all.

And I got to witness it. Hell, I got to be a part of it.

I'm forever changed. No matter what happens, I'll never accept anything less than what I saw transpire between them tonight. I'll never settle for anyone who doesn't need me so badly they practically combust at my touch.

Declan runs a hand through my damp hair, pushing it off my face. "You okay, sweetheart?"

I let out a shaky breath. "That was just..." Words are almost impossible right now. I'm still in such awe.

As he waits for me to explain, his brow dips low with concern.

Not wanting him to get the wrong idea, I suck in a breath and focus. "It was beautiful."

His lips cant up, and his eyes light up like a kid on Christmas morning. "Yeah?"

Sinking my teeth into my lip, I nod. "If I forget to say this later, thank you."

Declan's smile grows. "For what?"

"For letting me be here for this." My throat tightens with emotion. "For taking a chance. I'm so proud of you."

Rather than respond with words, he presses his lips to mine. Our tongues play and our hands wander, and just when my heart starts to pound and my body wants nothing more than to continue this until we're fucking, Declan drops me onto the bed and pushes himself back. "I think you'll reconsider that thank-you when you hear what I have planned."

Cade walks out of the bathroom behind him, a towel wrapped around his waist.

Cocking a brow, I spread my legs, certain that one of them will take the hint and give me what I need.

With a smirk, Cade makes a beeline for me.

Declan turns and throws an arm out, smacking a palm to his chest and stopping him. For a moment, I don't breathe, transfixed by the way the two of them watch one another. Cade's chest rises and falls as his lips part, and Declan's back ripples with tension. He's standing in the middle of the room, naked, and for a moment, I think he might demand Cade drop to his knees and suck him off.

My blood ignites at the thought. I'm not sure anything could be more beautiful than watching Declan accept who he is while, at the same time, Cade getting everything he's ever wanted. *Declan.* He is clearly the love of Cade's life. For the moment, I won't allow myself to worry about what that means for me.

When Declan finally speaks, I have to actively focus on breathing. "Last night, Melina helped me with my anxiety, and this morning, I woke up calm and feeling grounded." He gives Cade a once-over, then slips the hand from Cade's chest down his abdomen until it hovers just above the knot in his towel. "But then you went and got me all worked up again by flirting with someone else at the bar."

I smile at the memory of how jealous Declan got watching his best friend talking to another woman.

Cade licks his lips, his blue eyes wide. "I'm sorry," he says, his tone sincere.

Declan lets out a caustic laugh, clearly not appeased by the simple apology. "You telling me you won't do it again?"

I hold back a chuckle. We all know that asking Cade to stop flirting is like asking a snake to not shed its skin.

Cade shrugs.

"That's what I thought." Declan turns to me. "And *you*—I promised you that you would pay for that orgasm in the shower, didn't I?"

Heart beating wildly at the prospect, I shift to my knees and nod eagerly.

He chuckles darkly. "So excited to be punished."

"Are you going to tie me up?" I whisper as heat pools in my core.

Turning back to Cade, he replies, "No. I'm going to tie him up."

With that simple phrase, all the air is sucked from the room. The image of the dark, broody man working meticulously with his rope while the lighter, brighter man is bound to his bed makes me dizzy with desire.

Declan tugs on the knot of Cade's towel and lets it fall to the floor. "Does that work for you, baby? Can I tie you up?"

Cade stands before him, hard and breathing heavy. "Yes."

Declan nods. "Lay next to Melina while I get the rope." He looks at me, chin lifted high. "You. Stay just like you are, but face Cade. I want your hands on your thighs. No touching. Cade or yourself."

I press my lips into a flat line to hold back a whimper. I have a feeling I know where this is going, and though I have no doubt that it will all be worth it, watching Declan tie Cade up—*while they're both naked*—without at least touching myself is going to be incredibly difficult.

Sauntering to the bed, Cade mouths, "No tempting me, Trouble."

He climbs onto the mattress, keeping plenty of space between us. Smart man. If he were any closer, I'd break the rule and kiss him.

Even if I can resist, I still long to check in with him. To splay my hands over his chest and feel his pounding heart, to press my lips to his and let him know that we're in this together. We're getting everything we want right now, and the experience is so much sweeter because Cade is at my side. He makes everything better with his smiles and laughter and his easy-going nature. Already, he owns my heart. Simply watching him get what he wants is enough to bring me a joy I've never known.

Despite those desires, it's hard not to want to obey Declan. I want to give him the control he craves. The control he needs. I trust that he knows what we need and that he'll give it to us. I have faith that he'll figure out what it'll take so we can all move forward together.

As Cade settles himself on the mattress beside me, I realize that Declan has stripped the bed of nothing but one pillow and the fitted sheet. The rest of the bedding has been folded carefully and placed on the chair in the corner. My chest warms at the thought of him preparing for this while we were making out in the shower. He knew he'd have to punish us before he stepped into the bathroom, because he knew what we'd do if he sent us into the shower alone.

This devious planning gives me yet another glimpse into who Declan is. With each facet of him I discover, I find myself falling harder.

"Do you remember your colors, Cade?" he asks in that tone that makes my blood heat. It's gruff and slightly condescending.

The cocky bastard smirks, unbothered that Declan always seems to be calling the shots. Leading us. If I had to guess, Declan needs it like that. And since neither Cade nor I hold any reservations about what happens next, it's not hard for us to relent.

"Green: good. Yellow: slow down. Red: stop." He's so cocksure as he holds his arms out wide, taunting Declan, all but begging him to tie him up.

"And why would you ask me to slow down?" The heat behind Declan's words spreads through me, reigniting the need Cade incited in the shower.

Cade cocks his head and studies his friend. After a moment, as though the answer has hit him, his smile grows. "Because I'm close."

Brow furrowed, I worry my lip. Close to what? Maybe I should ask, but I leave it alone. The guys are on the same page, and that's all I care about.

The dark man looming over us shifts his focus to me. "Would you like to learn, or would you prefer to watch?"

God, I can't imagine I could concentrate with how keyed up they've got me, but if I let him teach me, I could get closer. And more than anything, I want to be closer to him in this moment. In every moment. I want him just as fiercely as Cade wants him. I know I've said Cade is like my sun, but in this moment, it becomes clear that Declan's *our* sun. Holding us in his orbit and providing everything we need. But god, when he's far away, when his focus is elsewhere, the chill goes straight to my bones.

"Yes, please."

Declan tilts his head, one brow arched, as if he's waiting.

For a moment, I study him, at a loss for what he's silently communicating.

Cade is the one who clues me in. "Yes, sir," he says, smirking at me.

A flush works its way up my chest and neck. That single word, *sir*, in reference to Declan is hotter than seems possible.

A mixture of pleasure and need flit over Declan's face. "Good boy," he mumbles. The words escape him harshly, in the same way he'd curse if my lips were wrapped around his cock. Like he can't believe how good it feels. Like it slipped out, surprising us all.

Cade shifts his hips, his cock thickening as they assess each other.

"Where do you want me, sir?" I breathe out, my words cutting through the thick tension in the air.

Declan strides to my side of the bed and presses a kiss to my neck. "The things I want to do to you both."

His words ignite a wildfire beneath my skin, setting forth a course of shivers.

"Are you ready, sweetheart?" he asks, raking my hair away from my face, then fussing with it.

"Are you braiding my hair?"

I tip my head slightly, but Declan cuffs my neck, stopping the movement. He doesn't respond, and he doesn't go back to toying with my hair. When the silent seconds bleed together, I look to Cade for a clue.

He arches a brow, silently reminding me of how we're playing this.

With a smirk, I tack on the magical word. "Sir."

Declan leans down and nips on my earlobe. "Figured he'd be the brat, but he's much better behaved than you are."

"It's because she loves her punishments," Cade says with a grin.

"And you don't?" Declan's tone is full of amusement rather than reproach.

Cade swallows thickly, his focus moving from the man commanding us to me and back again, like he's searching for an answer.

He doesn't need to speak. The way his cock bobs makes it clear that once again, the thought of Declan touching him—whether it's for pain or pleasure—is everything.

"I'll take whatever you give me, sir," he finally says, his tone low and his voice full of heat.

Holy fuck.

Please, *please*, if I die, let this be my heaven. These two men. This night. Those words.

"Yes you will," Declan says, tugging on my hair like he's tying off the braid. With his mouth next to my ear again, he adds, "Safer with the ropes."

My heart sinks in disappointment. "You've done this before." It shouldn't bother me. Of course I wasn't his first. He was open about his experience with Shibari. But somehow, this braid, his tone, his confidence, confirm that this is a lifestyle he's comfortable with.

"Yes."

He steps back from me and then kneels on the bed. His cock hangs close to Cade's head, and when Cade turns, his mouth is only inches from its tip. But he keeps his eyes on Declan's face, as if he's more interested in what he's doing than what he's packing.

Newsflash, he's way better at this than I am. I'd have already slid my tongue out for a taste. It's impossible not to taunt Declan into being reckless with me.

"She really is trouble," Declan mutters as he catches me staring at the two of them.

Chest heaving, I drag my attention back to his dick. How the hell is he not rock hard right now? It's as if he's completely immune to us. As if the way the two of us are practically salivating over him doesn't affect him even slightly. God, why is his self-control so hot?

"You gave her the nickname," Cade teases.

With a smirk, Declan grunts. "And then you used it to taunt me."

"Just offering a little push."

"That's all you ever do. Push and push. Right, baby?"

Oh, fuck. My core tightens at that term of endearment. He called Cade *baby* in the shower, but I assumed it was a slip of the tongue or a throwaway word. But now, when Declan is exercising so much control, it's clear that it was no accident.

Holy hell. If he's this comfortable already, then I can't imagine that his feelings for Cade are as new as he would have us believe.

I'd bet they've been simmering for years.

Cade swallows thickly and nods. "You know me better than anyone else."

"I do." Declan grips his hand, ready to get started with the rope, but pauses there and squeezes. "Trust me to know what you need?"

Cade regards him, eyes wide, as if no one on earth exists but the two of them. And there isn't an ounce of jealousy in my heart. Cade, the man I fell hard for the day I met him, is getting everything he's ever wanted with Declan, the man who's come to own my body and my soul just as equally. There's no threat here. It may be the most beautiful moment I've ever witnessed.

"I do," Cade whispers, his eyes glassy. "Just don't break me."

Declan leans down without hesitation and presses his lips to Cade's. "I'm going to try really hard to get this right."

A tear slides down my cheek at the admission, at Cade's plea, and I don't swipe it away.

"Ready, baby?" Declan asks. He kisses Cade gently one more time.

"I'm ready."

Declan meticulously winds the black rope around Cade's arm, explaining each step and the reason behind it. As he works his way across Cade's chest and to his other arm, he straddles him, completely oblivious to how we're tracking his every move. His hands work the rope. His tongue peeks out as he checks the tightness. His dick slides across Cade's chest as he moves from one side to the other. All the while, he's completely unaffected.

Me? I'm sitting in a literal puddle of desire. Poor Cade is so hard he's leaking down his shaft.

When he's finished tying the rope around Cade's hands, he surveys his work, his lip between his teeth. "You look so fucking sexy tied up with my rope."

Cade's eyes swim with longing. "Yeah?"

"Yeah, baby. But you'll look even better tied to my bed while our girl rides your cock."

Pushing up on his knees, he flicks the top of one bedpost, exposing an open ring.

"What is that?" I hiss, my already overworked heart pumping faster.

Declan turns to me with a smirk. "Specially made bed."

He lifts Cade's hand and kisses his wrist, then attaches the rope there to the ring.

On Cade's other side, he does the same.

Without a word, he stands, gives us one more perusal, then strides to the chair in the corner. "Ride him, sweetheart," he commands. "But be ready with your colors."

I almost tumble off the bed as I scramble to sit on Cade's impossibly hard cock. Once I'm straddling him, I splay a hand over his abdomen and slide down his length. "Oh god," I cry, shivers coasting down my body. "That's too good."

The way he fills me is incredible. The sounds of his groans, the feel of each vein as I work my way down his shaft. Holy shit. I'm already close. Anxious to come, I roll my clit against him, and colors dance behind my eyes.

"Yellow," Cade grits out.

I'm rocking against him, lost in my head, desperate for release, when Declan grasps my hips.

"Hold still, sweetheart," he says into the crook of my neck. Shifting so he's focused on Cade over my shoulder, he grunts. "She feels too good?"

My pussy clenches at the sound of Declan's voice. At the way it rumbles through me.

Cade grits his teeth. "Feels like heaven."

"Sinful, really," Declan muses. "She's got us both hard as a rock, and she's completely oblivious while she grinds on your dick and taunts me with this perfect ass."

Cade hisses, throwing his head back, his neck straining. "Exactly."

"It's like she needs to be punished."

A shiver runs through me in response to Declan's words, and I roll my hips.

He presses a hand between my shoulder blades and pushes until I'm flat against Cade's chest and burying my face in his neck.

"How many?" Declan asks Cade.

Though I have no idea what he's talking about, my heart flutters.

"Three on each cheek."

They're in sync, carrying on a conversation with few words. Damn, is it a turn-on.

"You're going to spank me?" I ask, pushing up so I can see Declan over my shoulder.

Licking his lips, he smooths a palm over my left cheek. "Yes, sweetheart. I'm going to spank you, and when I do, you're going to squirt all over Cade's cock."

I flex, tamping down on the need to ride Cade until I come.

Beneath me, he groans. "Still fucking yellow."

Declan's dark chuckle vibrates through me. "And that's where you'll stay."

Then, without warning, his hand lands on my ass. The sting is so shocking, I lose my breath.

"Holy fuck," Cade cries as he tenses beneath me.

I zero in on him, forgetting the flash of pain. "What?"

"You squeezed me so tight I almost came."

"Red, baby?" Declan asks, soothing the ache with a soft caress over the globe of my ass.

Cade takes a deep, stuttering breath. "Green."

"Good boy," he rumbles as he smacks the opposite cheek.

Holy. Shit. My chest tightens, and my body convulses. My orgasm builds, making it hard to breathe. Seeking friction, I wiggle on top of the man who's still impaling me, but with the way he's tied to the bed and how the man behind me is holding me down, it's not going to happen.

I whimper. "I need—"

Declan covers me with his body, sandwiching me between two hard chests, and brings his lips to my ear, whispering, "What I give you. You need *only* what I give you."

Yes. Okay. Right. Despite the way I'm flooded with desire, my body knows that it must obey. My nerve endings bleed into one another, and an electric current takes hold of me, keeping me at the ready.

"Yes, sir—" The last word leaves me in a rush as he slaps me again.

"Color?" he rumbles.

"Green." So fucking green. I've never spiraled so out of control.

As he smacks me again, Cade grits, "That's four."

I suck in a breath at the knowledge. Two more. I can do this.

This time, when Declan makes contact, it's with both hands. As both cheeks sting, my orgasm begins to crest like a wave.

"Holy shit. I'm going to—"

Declan clutches my waist and yanks me off Cade.

Heart stopping, I let out a cry. I try to turn, ready to smack him for depriving me of my release, but he holds me in place.

"You didn't say yellow," he practically growls in my ear.

Oh. *Oh.* Yellow doesn't mean I can't handle what we're doing. It means I'm close to coming. I'm only now understanding the rule, I suppose. And red means stop because I'm going to come.

He's restricting our orgasms.

Shit. My pussy clenches around nothing, still seeking that release.

Cade is glowering at his cock, probably because he can't even squeeze it to relieve the pressure. "Please," he whines, lifting his hips.

"Please what?" Declan's tone is gruff as he breathes through his teeth.

Cade meets Declan's eyes, his own so full of need and love and hope that I swear I lose my breath. "Make me come."

Grasping my hips again, Declan thrusts me onto Cade so fast that I don't have time to prepare. I'm impaled on his cock, still adjusting to the full sensation, when Declan works me over him, lifting me like I'm a doll whose purpose is to pleasure the man beneath me. Like he's a dildo meant to give me mine.

Declan moves me up and down until Cade is hissing out, "Yellow—please—fuck—yellow." Releasing me, Declan jacks himself. "Ride him, sweetheart. I want you to come all over his cock, then I'll do the same."

If there was even a chance I could hold out, it goes up in flames right then and there. I come so hard I almost black out, barely registering the way Cade thickens or the groan he releases. All I know is that one second, I'm impaled on him, and the next, I'm being yanked away again.

Declan drops me onto the bed beside them as he settles a knee on either side of Cade, straddling him. Then Cade thrusts upward while Declan grinds their cocks together and leans down, taking Cade's mouth roughly. They're fucking one another, rutting and groaning until Cade cries out that he's coming.

Declan pulls back, his gaze transfixed on Cade's pulsing cock, and fists his, jacking himself until he comes in hot waves all over his best friend's dick.

Euphoric, I stare at the two of them, still panting, knowing that from this moment forward, nothing will ever be the same.

Hands to Myself

CHAPTER 36

Declan

I WAKE up with Melina wrapped around me. I give myself ten minutes to hold her, and when I force myself to get up, I roll her into Cade's arms and drop a kiss to her shoulder.

This is easily the most insane morning of my life, because I'm not freaking out in the least. After tying my best friend up, edging him for almost an hour, then coming all over his cock, I'm completely calm and can admit that it was the goddamn hottest night of my life.

After we finished, I untied him and kissed each indentation left behind. By the time I'd gotten to them all, he and Melina were asleep. Only then did I close my eyes and drift off too.

For as outrageous as the whole scenario was, it couldn't have been more perfect.

I'm half hard just thinking about the marks he wears on his body. The evidence of what we did.

Despite how turned on I am, apprehension slithers through me as I pour myself a cup of coffee. I don't have the first clue what to expect today. Will we fuck again? Will it get awkward? Will Cade leave?

My chest pinches at the mere thought of him going.

"Making breakfast?" he asks, his voice scratchy. As he steps into the kitchen naked, he yawns, arms outstretched and dick bobbing between his legs. No fucking shame.

"Didn't want to put on clothes?" I tease as I turn and prop myself up against the counter.

Grinning, he circles his hips, making his cock swing ridiculously. "Couldn't find clothes. Besides, this thing is beautiful."

Heat licks up my spine as I allow myself to take him in. He's long and thick, even when he's not aroused. I've never been turned on by the thought of another man's dick, but Cade's? Fuck, I can't take my eyes off it.

Chuckling, I walk past him, determined to find a pair of shorts he can slip on so I'm not so distracted.

He stops me with a hand to my waist. "I was thinking," he mumbles, stepping up closer. "You should be naked too."

When I meet his eyes, he's smirking. "Oh yeah? And why is that?"

"It'll be easier for me to suck your cock that way."

My body heats, but I hold steady. "Melina's still sleeping." Not sure why, but it feels relevant.

"She is," Cade says with a smirk. "Think you can be loud enough to wake her up?"

Without waiting for a response, he tugs my shorts down and drops to his knees.

Blood rushes to my cock so quickly, I sway on my feet, lightheaded.

From the floor, he peers up at me and takes me in his hand. "Do you remember your colors?"

"Fuck you," I laugh as tingles course down my spine and into my balls.

"I'm serious, baby," he says, stroking my shaft. "Tell me green, and I'll swallow this fat cock right now."

Dropping my head back, I groan. "Oh, fuck."

"Say it, Dec. Say please, and I'll make you see stars."

His hooded blue eyes are my undoing. My body heats as I stare down into them. Are we really doing this? Fucking the same girl is one thing. Touching one another with her in the room takes it a little farther, but still, it's about her.

Kissing him certainly crossed a thousand lines, but still, she was there.

Right now, it's just the two of us.

Am I ready for this?

Even as I ask the question, I know the answer.

I'm ready for this. *We're* ready for this.

"Please, baby." I stroke his cheek as I slide my dick across his lips, painting them with precum. "Let me fuck your mouth."

His tongue darts out, licking up my arousal. "My pleasure." He slides his lips over my crown, and I get lost in the wet heat of his mouth.

Pleasure washes over me, and my eyes roll back. It's not just the feel. It's the vision. The truth and the history behind all of this. The man I've been captivated by for far too long is sucking me down. He takes me deeper, using more suction than I've ever experienced.

Grasping his hair, I pull him closer and fuck his face. I'm rough, and he's gagging, but I don't stop. If anyone can take it, it's him.

I don't slow when Melina appears, wearing nothing but my shirt. Arm outstretched, I beckon her, needing her close. Our girl doesn't hesitate. If anything, her expression is full of intrigue. As she steps up beside us, I stop thrusting for a moment so I can set her on the counter.

"This okay?" I need to know she's on board with my feelings for my best friend. I need *her*, but now that I've opened the door, there's no stopping my need for him too. He's in my blood, and now that I've tasted his lips, felt his heart beat, and rubbed my cock against his, there is no going back.

Melina's smile is warm and full of affection. "Best way to wake up."

A laugh rumbles from my chest. "Tell me about it."

Cade sucks me deep again, and like he promised, stars dance in my vision. With a hand on the counter for balance, I rest my head against hers and watch Cade work, licking and swallowing and jacking me with his hand.

With a pop, he releases me and shoots me a taunting grin. "Color?"

"Green, baby," I say as he circles his thumb over my head. "So fucking green."

"I can't wait to make you scream yellow," he warns, his voice rough.

My balls tighten and my spine tingles. Me fucking too.

As Cade swallows me down again, I devour Melina's mouth. This is audacious. My best friend is sucking my cock while the woman of my dreams tangles her tongue with mine. There isn't a luckier bastard in the world.

"Fuck, this is so hot," Melina whimpers, squirming on the countertop.

"Get down, sweetheart." I loop an arm around her waist and slide her to the edge. "Let Cade fuck you while you finish me off."

Eyes on me, she drops to her hands and knees, ass out, and waits for Cade to fill her.

With a kiss to the head of my cock, he backs up. "She gets to drink you down today, but next time, your cum is mine."

While I'm doing everything I can to rein in the orgasm threatening to overtake me, he lines himself up and thrusts deep. In unison, they groan. He weaves a hand through her hair and tugs so her mouth meets my dick. With all she has, she takes me into her mouth and sucks me good.

It's filthy and hot, and we come within seconds of one another.

Fuck, I never want this weekend to end.

CHAPTER 37

Melina

"YOU'RE AWFULLY QUIET," Cade says as he settles beside me on the couch. I'm curled up with a cup of coffee, and he's right. I'm a bit lost in my thoughts, I guess.

The last forty-eight hours have been life-altering.

It's a reminder that life can change on a dime. A car crash, a birth, the right producer liking a song, *a slap across the face*. It's just that this one feels so monumental and *not* like it happened out of the blue. It feels like my life has been building to this moment. Like everything that has happened up until today has led me to these two men, has led me to being open and ready and willing to start this next chapter...

And yet I still can't find the words to describe how I feel, and *that* is leaving me quiet.

There's no melody guiding me into this phase of my life, and that void feels loud, like a wind tunnel I can't escape.

The words, the notes, the chorus and the bridge, they're all there. That's how I live my life, in song. And yet I can't *hear* it.

"Just relaxing," I say simply. Because how would I even explain all the thoughts plaguing me?

Cade pulls me onto his lap and snuggles me close, burying his face in my neck. "You smell so good."

I laugh. "We all smell like sex."

He nips at my shoulder. "Fucking delicious." Pulling back, he hits me with that boyish grin I love so damn much. "Sure you're okay? I don't want to do anything you aren't comfortable with."

Warmth flows through me, and that noise in my head dims slightly. "It all seems too good, if I'm being honest."

With a shake of his head, he bites down on his lip. "There's no such thing as too good, Trouble. I'm going to go shower." He raises his brows in suggestion, then lifts me off his lap and sets me on the couch again. "Feel free to join me, and I'll get you all cleaned up."

With a roll of my eyes, I laugh, watching him stroll down the hall toward the guest bathroom, whistling, then stop when he gets to the door so he can turn around and wink at me.

It is too good. Every single minute of it.

A moment after he disappears, the door to the master bedroom swings open, and Declan, fresh from his shower, walks toward me, his gait determined, with a small package in his hand. "Want more coffee?"

With a shake of my head, I set my cup on the table. "No. I'll be a jittery mess at high tea if I do. As it is, I'm nervous that if Carmella even looks at me, I'll blurt out that I fucked the chief and his best friend."

Declan barks out a surprised laugh, the sound making my insides warm and gooey. God, it feels good to know I can make him truly smile. These moments are so rare and beautiful, so I soak up every single ounce of his joy. "Yeah, maybe don't lead with that story," he says. "You have nothing to be nervous about, though. The girls are all great, and they'll all love you."

I shrug as Declan eases onto the couch beside me. "I know it's silly, but I like to be liked." Swallowing hard, I turn and give him my full attention. "And these are Lake's friends. So they're important to me."

With a hand on my thigh, Declan squeezes gently. "You're a sweetheart. There's no way they won't love you."

The way he says it, not just the words or the tone, but also the way he's looking at me, like I hung the moon and the sun and the stars in the sky, makes me believe that maybe he finds it impossible not to love me too.

A girl can dream, right?

"What do you have there?" I ask, ready to change the subject before I spill all my silly hopes.

He grips the package in his lap tightly, like he's worried I'll swipe it from him. "Just a little something I picked up for you at the festival last night."

There goes that hope again. It floats up, making my heart bob like a buoy in my chest. "You bought me a present?" I ask, squealing with a little too much excitement.

Declan shakes his head slightly, trying to downplay the beautifully wrapped gift. "It's just a little something." He presses it into my chest, assessing me.

Nervous, I can't help but worry my lip, though my smile doesn't leave my face. "Thank you."

"You don't even know what you're thanking me for."

I do. I really, really do. For thinking of me. For putting me first, time and again. For being here. "It's the thought I'm thanking you for. Once I open the gift, I'm sure I'll have more to say."

I slide my hand under the tape, trying hard to not tear the thick purple paper. The package has weight to it, and when I fold back the wrapping paper, I discover it's because it's a leather-bound book.

A deep navy blue journal with a gold compass on it. The sight of it, the soft feel of the leather, are a comfort.

"Sorry, everything in this town is either nautical or red, white, and blue." He shrugs like this gift needs an apology. "Thought maybe you could use it to write down the stories that pop into your head." He lifts one shoulder again. "Or ya know, maybe music."

He bought me a new journal.

My throat grows incredibly tight.

"It's got a compass," I say stupidly, as if he doesn't already know that. I brush the pads of my fingers over the surface, noting how the gold is raised, making it slightly rugged, just like the man in front of me. I close my eyes, savoring this moment. "Maybe it will help me find my way," I whisper.

When I open my eyes, Declan is closer. I immediately reach for him, crawling into his lap, the journal still in my hand, and press it against his chest.

"This was—"

Once again, I'm at a loss for words, but right now, it doesn't feel debilitating. Words don't feel necessary. A kiss is all the moment needs. Like our lips know exactly what we both need.

Just like Declan always knows what I need.

CHAPTER 38

Declan

"YOU SURE YOU HAVE TO GO?" Cade asks as Melina heads for the door, his lips turned down.

Although Cade wants her to stay, she really should head out. She and Lake have plans with a few other girls in town, and I'm fucking elated about it. She's making friends in Bristol. Forming attachments outside of us.

It's hard not to hope that maybe she'll want to stay. That one day, she might see a life for herself here. With me. With Cade. With us.

I've gotten way too ahead of myself. I realize this. I have no idea what my best friend thinks of that idea. In all the years we've known each other, he's never once suggested that he's interested in settling down.

Even if she wanted to stay, and he wanted to settle down, I can't even begin to imagine what a relationship would look like. Would our family and friends accept us? It's one thing for me to come out as bi and dating my best friend. It's another entirely to show up at my sister's house with not one but two people. I don't even want to think about what Beckett would have to say about that.

Is Cade worried about any of this? Or is he only thinking with his dick? Is this really only sex to him?

I watch him as he watches her leave. He's finally dressed—thank fuck—wearing his signature backward Bolts hat, a long-sleeve Bolts shirt, and black athletic pants. She leans in and whispers, and with a growl, he pulls her in, planting his mouth on hers.

"Really?" he mumbles, releasing her.

Once she's gone, he finally turns around. When he finds me staring at him, he smirks. "Did you really stick a plug in her ass when I was in the shower?"

Chuckling, I head for the kitchen to grab a water. Only after I ate her out and made her come twice. Giving her the journal felt monumental somehow. I freaked out that she'd freak out and decided to go for what works for us: sex.

She definitely didn't complain.

"She'll be ready for you tonight."

With water bottles in hand, I close the fridge, only to find Cade standing beside me.

"You're gonna let me have her ass?"

I lift a shoulder. "Figure we can break her in with yours."

Eyes wide, he scoffs. "You trying to say your cock is bigger than mine?"

A lightness I haven't felt in a while washes through me as we banter. "You had it in your mouth. You tell me."

The way he laughs, his head falling back, shocked, probably, at my candor, has me smiling and relaxing.

"You know, you're actually fucking hilarious when you talk." With a flick of his wrist, he uncaps his bottle. Then he holds it up between us. "You should do it more."

I take a sip of my water and wipe my mouth with the back of my hand. "I talk."

Cade leans against the counter and lifts his chin, assessing me. "To someone other than Liv or Mel."

I scoff. "I talk to you."

Lowering his head, he gives it a shake. "Not really." He roughs a hand over his mouth, thoughtful. "Not for years."

My stomach twists at the sadness in his tone. "We hang out when you're in town."

"Exactly. I come to you, and I talk. You just grunt."

I twist the cap back onto my bottle, then untwist it and do it again. "Fine," I say, forcing myself to lock eyes with him. "What do you want to know?"

Cade blinks like he's confused by the question. "What?"

I open my arms wide. "Floor's yours. I'm an open book. Ask me whatever you want."

For a moment, he only surveys me silently. Then his eyes flash. "Mel said something the other day when you were tying her up. About you needing it..."

I should have known he'd have cataloged that, even while turned-on. He swallows thickly. "Why do you need it?"

Once again, my inclination is to keep this light. To tell him it's all about sex. Or to growl and tell him I don't want to talk about it. Or that he misunderstood. Vulnerability is hard for me. Especially with men.

But this is Cade. And just like I can't imagine ever hurting Melina, the idea of treating Cade like he's just another friend doesn't sit well anymore. He deserves more. He deserves the truth.

"Anxiety."

He watches me, questions swimming in his eyes. He wants a deeper explanation. As much as I don't want to, as much as I'd like to avoid talking about the past, there's no way we can move forward together if I don't. And the idea of going back to just being friends again? It's untenable.

"It started when I dropped out of college."

Cade's jaw ticks. He tries to hide it by scratching at his scruff, but he does a piss-poor job.

"It wasn't because of that night," I assure him. Maybe I should have told him that a long time ago, but then I would have had to get into things I wasn't equipped to talk about.

I can't blame him if he thought I pulled away because of our encounter all those years ago. But if anything, this weekend should show him that it was never about my feelings for him. That I was never uncomfortable around him. I've always had some kind of feelings for him. I'm not sure I could have ever put them into words, or that we would have gotten here if not for Melina, but it's always been there. An undercurrent, a pull, a need to be near him.

Cade nods, accepting my statement at face value. "Then what was it?"

Though I'm racked with nerves and breaking into a cold sweat, I lay it all out there. He deserves to know about it. From the minute I walked into dinner that night at my mom's house to the moment her boyfriend put his hands on me, I detail every excruciating moment and the extreme shame that came after.

How my life felt out of control until Chief Reilly offered me a job. And friendship.

It didn't come easy, trusting another man in power. But he was patient and kind. He gave me something else to focus on—this job that I've come to love.

"And then he died," Cade says slowly, like he's putting all the pieces together.

"Once again, I spiraled. I'd taken a risk, opened myself up, and lost another person I cared about. At his funeral, I couldn't help but watch Lily, Ben, and Michaela—fuck." I shake my head, wishing their tears didn't haunt me. "I'm chief *because* he died."

"You're chief because you're damn good at your job. And loving people doesn't always end in devastation, Dec."

Pain lances my chest. "You don't know that. We almost lost Melina when that psycho came after her."

Cade's jaw goes hard, as if the idea of losing her is just now crossing his mind.

"See?" I say, feeling vindicated.

"I know you've lost a lot. And if I ever see the men who hurt you or her, I will likely kill them." He clenches his fist and takes a deep breath. "You have to know, you're safe with me. You don't have to do every-thing, Dec. You don't have to be everything for everyone. I've got you, and together, we'll protect Mel."

My eyes get hot and my nose stings. "I can't lose our friendship," I say, rubbing a hand over my face. That fear has plagued me all weekend, even if I don't regret a thing that's happened between us.

"You won't," Cade promises, his tone fierce.

A small wave of relief hits me, easing my anxiety. I leave it at that, even if more questions swirl in my mind. What if I don't only want his friendship? What if I want more? Would he be open to it? Because while it may be easy for him to go back to being just friends after this weekend, it would be hell for me.

Look At Her Now

CHAPTER 39

Melina

"THIS IS THE TEA SOCIETY?" I whisper to Lake as we settle around the hair salon with Long Island iced teas in hand.

She grins. "Isn't it great?"

Carmella, the older woman I met at the bakery, is wearing a muumuu that reads *I'll jingle your balls*. She leans over, and in a loud whisper, asks, "Want to add a shot of limoncello to your Long Island? I find it's not sweet enough."

Her granddaughter-in-law Belle shakes her head. "Ignore her, or you'll be carried out of here by the firefighters."

Jules raises her hand, her eyes dancing. "Been there, done that."

"Only that was intentional, darling," Carmella croons. "Shawn would carry you everywhere if he could."

The door opens with a jingle, and Lake squeals. "Ames!"

A whoosh of cold air hits us as Amelia and Charlotte appear. Both women greet us with hugs, then pull off their heavy winter coats.

"*Oh*, you've been invited to tea time. It's like you're a real Bristolian now," Amelia says with a grin.

"I'm so confused," I say, peering into my drink. "You all just hang out at the hair salon and drink Long Islands?"

Charlotte pours herself a glass from the pitcher by the register. "Just tea for me. But yeah, Lily"—she nods at two blond women chatting in the corner—"owns the salon. Her husband was the fire chief until he passed away a few years ago. We come here weekly for blowouts and to have a drink. It's the perfect way to catch up."

Throat going tight, I look back at the woman who can't be much older than me. "He died?"

She nods. "He was older than her, but they hadn't been married long. Their son was so young when they lost him."

"Chief was the nicest guy," Amelia says, her eyes glassy. "His daughter was twenty when he died, and Benji was just a baby. Breaks my heart, because he's only a year older than my Paulie." It's still wild to me that Amelia and Nate have a little girl who is three.

With my heart in my throat, I ask, "How did he die?"

Lake grasps my hand and shakes her head.

Amelia presses her lips together, lowering her voice. "Fire."

My stomach sours, and a cold sweat breaks out on the back of my neck.

The idea of Declan being in real danger never occurred to me. But he's a firefighter. His job is dangerous by design.

"He and Declan were really close," Charlotte adds, as if she can read my mind.

It's yet another tidbit of information that paints a clearer picture of the man I've fallen for. He lost a friend, then had to step into the man's shoes. I can only imagine how difficult that was for a man like Declan, who feels so deeply.

"So we get blowouts," Belle explains. "It's about the only way Lily will let us help."

"And we get to have cocktails while we do it." Carmella holds her glass up and winks.

"Honestly, it's my favorite hour of the week," Lake says with a sweet smile.

Scoffing, I eye her.

She covers her mouth and lets out a giggle. "Don't tell Ford."

"He'd be sad if he knew *hot tub time* after Nash goes to bed isn't your favorite."

Lake's cheeks go pink, and she shushes me, though she can't help but laugh. She's genuinely happy, and it's a beautiful thing to see. She found her person. A man who loves her more than anything. She settled here, and she clearly fits in well. Before Ford, Lake was lost. Quiet. The only time she came out of her shell was on stage, but that was a persona. Here, though, with these women, in this town, she's so free and easy.

I long for even a modicum of those feelings. Is it possible that Bristol could offer me the same refuge? Could these women be my safe place too? And could Cade and Declan see themselves sharing a life with me?

Lake leans closer, her voice low. "So how are things with the guys?"

I try hard to remain aloof, but just the thought of the two men I left to come here has my cheeks heating. Lake scoots her chair closer. "Oh my god, something happened!"

"Shh." I look around the room but notice the only person who is paying us any attention is Carmella. A saccharine smile tugs at her lips, and she turns her head, pretending she's not eavesdropping. "I honestly don't even know what to say."

She blinks slowly. "Melina Rodriguez at a loss for words? Never thought I'd see the day."

I laugh, even though her joke hits a little too close to home. I still haven't written a single lyric. It's been months since I left Jason, and still, he's got some type of hold on me. I don't want to focus on him, though. I want to focus on the good in my life. The hope I'm clinging to since Declan first lay down in my bed and didn't leave. The joy that radiates through me every time Cade even looks in my direction. The two men who are piecing me back together. The music will come. No man will be responsible for taking my words or giving them to me. I'll do that work myself.

"Yes, something happened," I finally say.

Lake's eyes bulge. "Don't leave me hanging. What happened? Did the chief finally give in and admit he wants you?"

"And Cade."

"Right. Cade and Declan want you. God, what will you do? How do you choose? On the one hand, Cade is fun, and I really think you could use some fun—"

"He's not just fun. He's sweet and vulnerable. I love how I never have to wonder what he's thinking or what he wants. He shows me with his constant affection. Talks to me." I'm slightly defensive of Cade, because I don't think anyone sees what a beautiful person he truly is. He's always been a playboy, yes, but I can see now that he was like that because he didn't want to settle down with anyone but Declan.

"So it's Cade, then." Lake nods. "Makes sense. While the whole broody hero thing is hot, having a man who speaks in more than grunts is probably more your style. Besides, Declan is the chief here. How would you make that work?"

"Declan is so much more than broody." I sigh. "He makes me feel safe. He's thoughtful. You know he surprised me with a new journal today because I told him that Jason destroyed my old one?"

Lake pushes forward in her seat, her anger palpable. "*He what?*"

Ignoring her blazing stare, I twirl my straw, then take a sip of my drink. "For so long, I dated someone who tried to control me. Who hurt me. Who gaslit me into believing that if I disagreed with him—or anyone, for that matter—I was a bitch. And I let him because I wanted to be loved so badly. And now I have these two men who just—" I try to find the words as emotion gets the best of me. "They just want me to be happy. They listen when I talk. Check in with me constantly to make sure I'm okay with whatever we're doing. They find joy in my pleasure, whether they're involved or not. Declan bought me a freaking journal," I say again, still feeling ripped open at the seams when I so much as think about it.

Lake inhales deeply, her eyes growing wide. "So how will you choose?"

I smile, not the least bit concerned, because I don't have to choose, and neither do they. Though I'm unsure of whether not choosing means they actually are choosing us. Choosing this connection, this bond, even after this weekend.

"Right now, all I'm choosing is this Long Island. I'll figure out the rest later."

I'm two drinks deep when my phone rings. Lily hasn't gotten to me yet, so I step outside to take the call. The cold air feels good on my heated cheeks as I slip the device from my pocket.

My heart stutters a little at the name on the screen. My mother.

"Hi, Mom—"

She doesn't let me finish the greeting before she launches into her native Portuguese.

It's the only clue I need to know she's upset. Her voice is high-pitched and angry. "Did you know that Jason was arrested?"

It takes me a minute to respond. A moment to come to terms with this new information. For the first time in who knows how long, I've made it a solid twenty-four hours without thinking of that man. Which means I spent twenty-four hours without the fear-inducing anxiety that cripples me so often.

"Arrested." The word is said reverently. Someone believed me. My truth held meaning to enough people to make a difference, to ensure he was brought into custody and charged him with a crime. It's...liberating.

"Yes. And after your brother drove up to Boston to bail him out, they got into a car accident." My mother is hysterical now. Her words make little sense as she continues to wail about how my brother's leg is broken and Jason is in a coma. "You must come home. It's time to be with family. Your family needs you. Come home."

I try to keep up. Truly. But I'm stuck on one detail. I can't seem to care about the rest. "Manny bailed him out?"

Anger burns, running wild through my veins.

Any words my mother speaks are lost to me in that moment. Strangers believed me, yet my own family didn't.

My brother bailed out the man who abused me. Who threatened me, slapped me, hurt me, and tried to rape me.

"You need to come home," my mother wails.

I truly feel sorry for her. But not enough to ever go home.

I end the call without saying a word. My voice would be wasted on her. She doesn't get any more of my words. None of them do.

On the sidewalk outside the salon, I survey Hope Street. From Jules', where I've gone daily for donuts and coffee, to the bar I spent my first night in, down at the bottom of the road, over to the fire station, where I have book club and play poker with the guys when I drop in to visit Declan.

And if I follow the path to the water, I can walk the boardwalk to get back to his place.

Home.

The word has so many meanings, but in this moment, where I stand, it means Bristol. It means Declan and Cade. It means Lake and Ford and Nash. And maybe even the women in this salon. It means the safety and acceptance and comfort I never experienced until I came here. And just like that, the lyrics start spinning.

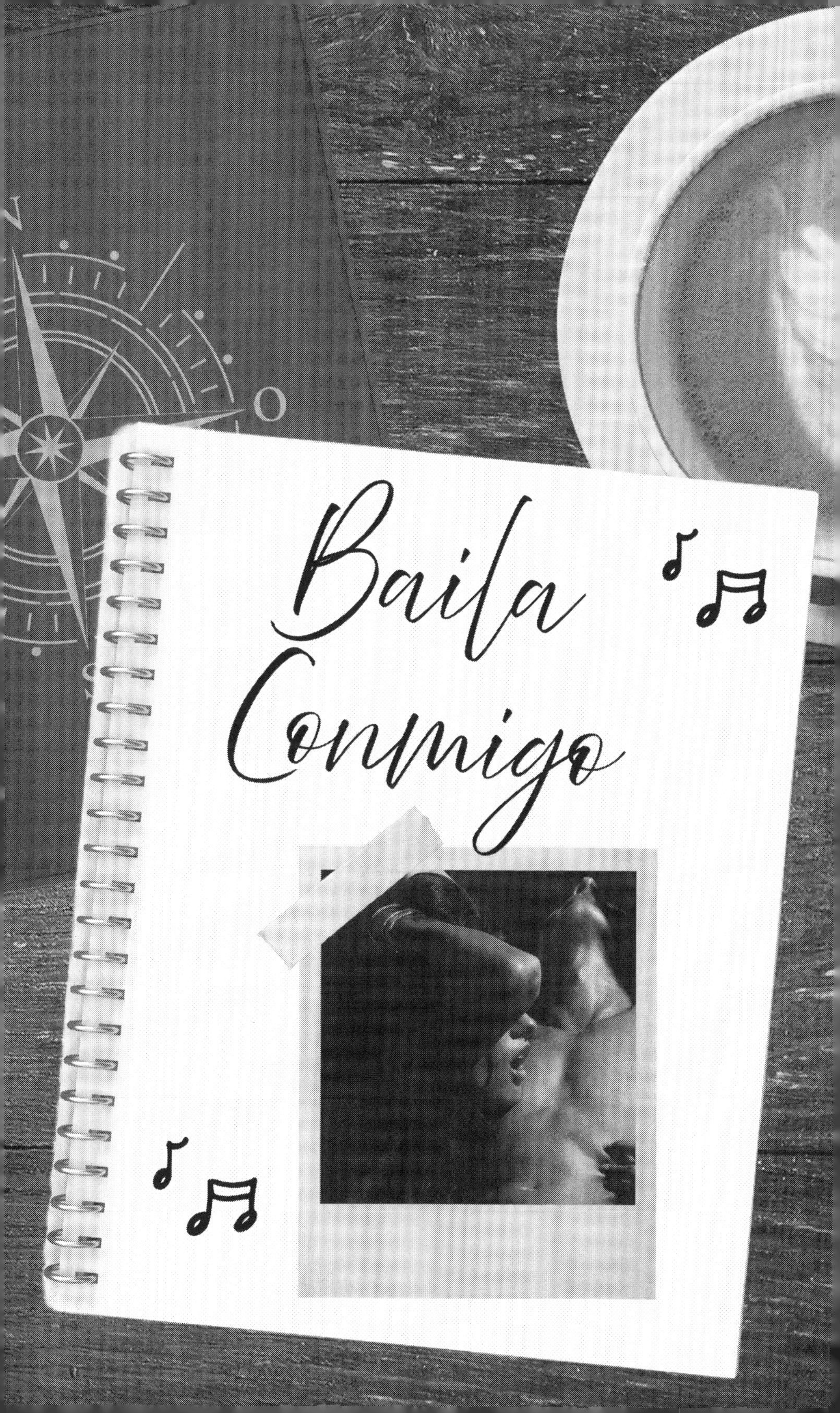
Baila
Conmigo

CHAPTER 40

Cade

AIDEN HAS CREATED A CHAT.

Brooks, War, Gavin, Beckett.

Aiden: Lex and I are having drinks at the Port. Who's around?

Brooks: Lennox mentioned it to Sar. We're in. Should we make a reservation?

Gavin: Mills and I are out. We're taking Vivi to see Santa with Beckett and co.

Me: thanks for the invite, guys, but I'm in Bristol.

Aiden: Say hi to Mel for us!

Aiden: That was from Lex, but I second it.

Brooks: And Declan!

Gavin: Clearly, that was Sara.

Brooks: Hey, Brooks is nice. He'd say that.

Gavin: Hi, Sara.

Me: Sara, I'll tell them you said hi.

Aiden: War, you in?

War: Sorry, can't. Have fun.

Aiden: What are you doing?

TEN MINUTES LATER:

Aiden: War, why haven't you responded? The text says read...

Aiden: Hello?

Brooks: Not everyone is attached to their phone.

Aiden: It says read!

BECKETT HAS LEFT THE CHAT.

With a laugh, I shake my head and navigate out of the thread to pull up a new one so I can shoot our right winger a text separately.

Me: Everything okay?

War: Went from a single guy with no family to responsible for three kids. How do you think I'm doing?

My chest tightens. The rest of the guys don't know yet, but War's life has gone through an enormous change over the last few months, and it all took a dramatic turn two weeks ago. It's not my story to tell, but he could use a friend. As much as I don't want to leave Dec's, I may need to head back to Boston to see if I can help him.

So many of our friends and colleagues have settled down recently, leaving only a handful of single guys who still go out after games. Daniel

249

and Camden, the young fucks, scour the bar for their nightly conquests pretty quickly, then disappear. War seems to have lost interest in the meaningless hookups, and I have too, choosing instead to be War's sounding board. Guy needs it, and to be honest, it's felt good to be needed.

The more we talked, the more I realized that maybe I could see myself settling down with someone.

> **Me:** want me to head your way? Happy to hang with you and the kids or watch them for a bit so you can get out.

> **War:** Nah. I'm good.

> **Me:** promise?

> **War:** yeah, I've got a plan. I'll fill you in next week.

"What should we do until Melina gets home?" Dec asks, instantly garnering my attention like he does every time he walks into a room.

When I take him in, my heart trips over itself. Will I ever look at this man and not feel this way? God, I hope not. He makes me feel alive. Like I have a purpose. Even if it's merely to entertain him. The things I would do to make him smile...

I pocket my phone and focus on the man in front of me. War would tell me if he needed me.

Declan's fresh from the shower, his dark hair damp and his scruff neatly trimmed, wearing a pair of black athletic shorts and a long-sleeve Bolts T. I like seeing him in my team's colors way too fucking much.

"Want to watch football?" I ask. "Notre Dame plays at one."

It's just another normal Saturday. That's what I tell myself, anyway. So what if I was on my knees for him a couple of hours ago? So what if I know what his lips taste like? He's still Declan, my best friend, and on Saturdays, we watch college football.

If I don't focus on keeping things normal, I'm liable to beg him to join me in the bedroom. Now that I know how he feels rutting against me, I could spend hours doing nothing but fucking around.

We have a ton of shit to figure out first. Namely, how to be the people we were this morning while still being who we've always been, because I can't lose us.

He grunts. "That works. Should I order food?"

I give him a simple nod, and he's off to order. We don't have to discuss what we want, because we always order the same thing when we watch football. Overloaded nachos, wings, and beer. These are the only cheat meals I allow myself.

Declan may be disciplined in most things, but food ain't one of them. Ironic, since my food plans are about the only rules I do follow.

I pull two beers from the fridge and am popping the caps when he ends the call.

"Food will be here in about forty-five minutes," he says, taking a bottle from me.

"Fine by me. I feel like we just ate."

"I know I did."

Head thrown back, I bark out a laugh. Fuck, it feels good joking around with Dec. About sex, no less.

"You think she's having a good time?" I ask as I settle at my usual spot on the couch.

He's frozen in the middle of the room, surveying me, his expression unreadable. Damn, what I'd give for the ability to read him like Mel can.

With a sigh, he settles into his normal chair. "Yeah. I think spending time with the girls is good for her," he says. "She tell you how things are going with her family?"

"Not really," I admit, trying not to feel defeated. "Think she talks more freely with you."

"I've just been around more since she came to Bristol," he says, obviously trying to make me feel better by downplaying their connection.

"No. I think she feels safe with you."

I may wish she felt as safe with me as she does with him, but I can't fault him for that. And I get it. Declan's the protector. He makes me feel safe too. Always has.

"The night she came to see you at the game, her cousin tried to warn her about her ex. But she'd turned off the phone because her family was doing some annual Christmas thing. She was disappointed she couldn't be there."

My chest tightens with sadness. Fuck. I'd do anything to keep her from being disappointed or sad. "Any idea what kind of Christmas thing?"

He shrugs. "No."

For a moment, he's silent, and I figure that one-word response is all I'll get.

As I'm filing away the mention of the family Christmas activity, figuring I'll ask Mel later, Declan says, "You think she's happy?"

There's no fighting my smile. My best friend is a fool for her. I'm enthralled by Mel, yeah, but I've never seen Declan like this with anyone. "Yeah, I think she's happy."

"You don't think she—" He rakes a hand through his hair, grimacing.

I stay quiet, allowing him time to put his thoughts into words.

"You think she's okay with—" He points between us.

My smile turns into a grin so big, my cheeks ache. "I think she's more than satisfied."

He nods slowly, his expression guarded. "And are you...satisfied?"

With my elbows on my knees and my hands clasped between them, I lick my lips and nod. Damn. This man, who was always so confident, so put together, so *straight,* is being vulnerable with me, and it thrills me in the best way.

"Yeah, Dec, I'm satisfied."

He lets out a slow breath and settles deeper into his chair. I figure he's done talking. We've talked more today than we normally do in a month, but he surprises me with yet another question.

"Are we supposed to be, like, holding hands or talking about our feelings?"

I cough out a laugh. He's just as bad at this as I am. "I mean, I was really hoping to watch football, but if you want, we can."

He shakes his head and rolls his eyes. "Fuck, I'm awkward. Just ignore me."

"The last thing you are is awkward, Dec. And it would be impossible to ignore you."

His eyes light up. "Yeah?"

I laugh. "Yeah. But seriously, we can just be us. On Saturdays, we eat an absurd amount of food and watch football. That doesn't have to change."

He brings his beer to his lips and takes a long sip, studying me the whole time. "So," he says, setting the bottle down, "just when Melina's around?"

Does he think I'm setting boundaries? I don't mean to be setting boundaries. I just want him to be comfortable, but fuck, if he wants to hold my hand or talk, then what the hell am I doing all the way over here?

I set my beer down on the coaster on the end table and lean forward, elbows on my knees. "If Mel were here, I'd probably have pulled her onto my lap already and slipped my hand down her pants."

Declan nods like that makes total sense.

"And you'd be hard as a rock watching us, wouldn't you?"

With a heavy swallow, he nods.

"I'd get her off while I watched the game. Maybe you'd come over here, kiss her neck."

Declan adjusts himself.

Fuck.

He's hard, just like I am. I lean back and slide my hand beneath the waistband of my sweats. When I adjust my own dick, I position it so that the tip just barely peeks out. I'm that fucking turned on.

Declan's watching, his beer bottle dangling from his fingers and his lips parted. "You're hard." The way he says it, the deep rumble of his voice, the wonder in it, makes me want to stroke myself, but I don't know that he's ready for a move like that.

My heart thunders in my ears. "Fucking steel."

"If Melina were here, she'd already be on her knees." He says it so matter-of-factly, his focus fixed intently on me.

If I was any good at reading him, I'd think he's contemplating what it'd be like to do that himself.

"She would."

He zeroes in on the bulge in my pants like he's picturing it. Working through something. Then he meets my eye, his expression full of determination. "I'd like to try that."

Holy fuck. My cock pulses at the thought of Declan's mouth coming anywhere near it. At the image of the man I've been obsessed with for literal decades crawling over to me, settling between my legs, and taking me into his mouth.

I've dreamed of fucking those lips for years. Punishing them for their lack of words, the lack of emotion they show, their infrequent smiles.

I want him to smile at me more than goddamn anything.

"Okay." I blow out a breath and settle my hands on my thighs, taking a back seat, desperate for him to lead.

With a nod, Declan sets his beer down on his coaster. Then he's walking toward me. The sound of the coffee table scraping across the floor as he pushes it back is jarring.

He lowers himself to his knees at my feet. The sight is a complete mindfuck and has me weeping in my pants.

"You're going to have to talk me through this," he says quietly, his dark eyes locked on mine. "I've never done this before."

"Right. Yes," I hiss.

Fuck, this is good. We're communicating. While I assumed he'd never been with another man, I couldn't be totally sure. Not after the way he controlled every move in the bedroom last night.

Now, having the powerful man who tied me up at my feet, ready and willing to learn how to suck *my* cock, has me swelling with pride.

"You know what feels good, so I'm sure you'll do just fine," I say.

Declan smirks at that. "I like it rough. I like when Melina swallows me down, but damn, I loved fucking your throat today."

Heat creeps into my cheeks, and I have to look away as I smile, a low chuckle breaking free. "I liked that too."

Declan settles a palm on my knee, pulling my attention back to him.

"I like it rough too," I grit out.

Declan merely nods. "I kind of assumed that." Then, between one blink and the next, he morphs from the unsure man who's asked one clarifying question after another to the confident, dominant man from last night. His eyes have gone a little harder, his jaw set, as he considers me. Like he's determining exactly what I need, even as I'm stumbling through how to do this with him. How to teach him. What to do if he changes his mind after he starts.

"Take out your cock." His tone is so rough, so assertive, it banishes the racing thoughts in my mind. I pull my swollen dick from my pants, then cant up a little and slide my shorts and boxers down.

As I slip them over my ass, he takes over and drags them to my feet. Once he's removed them completely, he tosses them over his shoulder. Jaw working, he glances at my face, then back down to my groin. He takes a deep breath, readying himself, but before he can lean down, I cuff his neck and pull him close, kissing away my nerves and hopefully his too.

His tongue tangles with mine immediately, and for a moment, I'm lost to this connection. To his mouth, his lips, his tongue, his taste, and the sounds he makes as we war for control. He pushes up farther, wrapping one hand around my neck and trailing the other down my chest, toward my stomach. When he reaches my cock where it stands tall between us, he squeezes and rolls his thumb over the head.

I whimper into his mouth. Fuck. I'm done for. He's won. And all it took was one damn touch.

"Please," I beg, thrusting into his hand.

Nipping at my lip, he splays a hand over my pecs and pushes me into the leather cushion. His eyes remain locked on mine as he works his fist up and down my shaft. "That's right, baby. Beg for it," he demands. "Tell me how much you want me to suck this cock."

With my hands on either side of me, nails biting into the leather, I grind against his hand, desperate to get closer to his mouth.

He hits me with a fierce look and shakes his head, as stubborn as ever. "I need to hear it."

"I do. Please. Fuck, Dec, this feels—" My mind is a jumbled mess, and I'm coming apart at the seams. I'm so fucking gone for this man.

I want him in any way I can have him. Stolen moments on his couch, early mornings in his kitchen, late nights with Mel between us. I want all of him, but I'll take any pieces he's willing to give. If he wants me to beg, I'll gladly do it. "Please, Dec. Let me fuck your throat. Let me fill your mouth. Let me *in*."

Breaking out in a sinful smile, he angles low. And when he guides me into his mouth, I see stars. He's warm and wet, and the way he suctions is just how I like it. Instinct has me reaching for his hair and pulling him closer. He gags in response, so I loosen my grip and back out slowly. His eyes are closed, and the muscles in his face are lax, like he's content to continue. My lack of movement hasn't stopped him from running his tongue along the bottom of my shaft, exploring me. Memorizing me. Learning me.

"That's it, baby. You're doing so good," I encourage.

The words settle him further. He takes me deeper and rolls my balls tightly, just the way I like.

Probably the way he likes too. I make a mental note to try it next time.

"Fuck, you have no idea how many times I've thought of this." I suck in a harsh breath, losing myself in the moment, watching him take me, watching him enjoy himself. Witnessing the way he comes into himself, studying clues to determine what he likes.

And if I'm not mistaken, Declan Everhart, my grumpy asshole of a best friend, really likes to suck my cock.

"Yes, right there. Shit, I'm close." I can't imagine he's ready to dive in so thoroughly that he wants me to come in his mouth, so I flex my abs and pull back.

He doesn't let me go far. He grasps my hip with a controlled hand and holds me in place while he strokes me from root to tip and then hollows his cheeks and sucks hard.

There's no holding back. The violence with which he drags my orgasm from me is impossible to contend with. I pulse in his mouth, and he moans, deep and low, in response. God dammit. The idea that this man wants to taste me as much as I want to fill him has me exploding. With a hand in his hair again, tugging hard, I curse and demand he drink every last drop.

I'm still panting, and dots still dance in my vision, when he rolls his tongue across my sensitive crown and hums in satisfaction. "Yeah, I like that," he mumbles, settling back on his toes and looking up at me.

I can't help the laugh that escapes. "Fuck. Yeah. I liked that too."

CHAPTER 41

Melina

"HONEYS, I'M HOME!" I push open the door, a rush of excitement hitting me at that word again.

I truly feel like I'm home.

Searching the space for my boys, I find them on the couch, cuddled up. The sight has me grinning. Declan's arms are crossed, his lips turned down in a frown, as he leans against Cade, sleeping.

"Aw, he even looks grumpy when he naps," I mumble as I slip off my jacket and place it on the hook by the door.

Cade lowers the phone he was scrolling on and puts a finger to his lips. Then he shifts Declan off his shoulder, dropping a kiss to his forehead. My stomach somersaults at the simple act. At Cade feeling comfortable enough to do that. Once he's settled Declan, he saunters toward me where I'm lingering by the front door. Wearing a big grin, he picks me up and pulls me in for the biggest hug I've ever received.

"Fuck, pretty girl. I missed you something fierce today." He nuzzles my neck like he's trying to burrow inside me. Like he can't get enough of me.

I don't know if I've ever felt so cherished. So wanted. So loved.

It's too soon for that, right?

It doesn't feel too soon, though. No, Cade looks at me, reaches for me, *kisses me*, like I'm his lifeline.

The same way he does with Declan.

He carries me into the kitchen and deposits me on the counter, his palms resting on my thighs as if he needs to keep a point of contact at all times. "How was your afternoon?" He lifts his hand and brushes my hair behind my ear, then steals another kiss before I can answer.

It's needy and sweet, nips and tugs and tongue. When he finally pulls back, his eyes are dancing.

"Mine was good, though based on how I found the two of you, yours seems to have been even better."

Cade licks his lips. "It was..." He blows out a breath. "Perfect."

"Ah, your favorite word."

"Only when it comes to the two of you. Fuck, Mel, I'm so fucking happy. I can't believe it's all real."

I couldn't agree more. It all feels so good. Too good. Even after my horrible phone call with my mother, just walking in the door and knowing my men were here was comforting. Forget being welcomed in Cade's arms like this. I'm almost afraid to jinx it by admitting how happy these two make me. I wrap my ankles around the backs of his thighs and pull him closer. "What did you guys do?"

Cade runs his hands down my shoulders, massaging them as he speaks. "We watched football, ordered a ton of food like we normally do." He bites his lip, eyes flashing, and adds, "and then we fucked around a little bit."

I let my mouth fall open, feigning shock. "You played without me?"

Those blue irises dull just a little as Cade assesses me nervously. "Are you mad?"

With my heels, I dig into the backs of his legs and pull him closer. "No. I want to hear more. What did you do?"

He sucks on his bottom lip, and when he speaks, his tone is full of disbelief. "He gave me a blow job."

"Shut up," I hiss, peering back toward the room where Declan is sleeping. I'm honestly shocked. And a tad upset that I wasn't here to watch. "How was it?"

An uncharacteristically shy smile spreads across his face, making my stomach swoosh wildly. This man is sexiest when he's like this. Unguarded. Excited. A complete golden retriever. "His mouth is unreal."

My core clenches. "Tell me about it." I study Cade for a moment. "And did he handle it okay? No freaking out or anything?"

He shakes his head. "We talked. He shared stuff with me I never knew. Told me his fears..." He lifts the hat off his head and runs his hand through his hair before setting it back in place. "Fuck, Mel. I think he may just be ready for this. It feels like we may get what we both want."

Nervously, I ask what I've been worried about for the past few hours. "And what is it you want?"

Cade leans in close, his hand going to my face again, his lips so close I can taste him. "You. Him. Us."

Hope does a desperate jig in my heart. "Yeah?"

"Fuck yeah," he says before kissing me. It's a kiss I get lost in. One that feels as though it has no beginning and no end. We're pressed close, lips tangled, moans colliding, but all I want is to be closer. This isn't about sex, it's about acceptance.

Accepting the change in our relationship. A change that will hopefully lend itself to a future.

"Now tell me about your day," he says once we've pulled apart.

"My day seems boring now."

"Boring how?" The question comes from behind us.

Together, we turn toward our favorite grump. His hair's disheveled, his eyes are still heavy with sleep, and he looks so damn cozy I want to crawl into his lap and never leave.

I hold out a hand to him, beckoning him closer. "Have a good nap?"

Cade shifts to one side of my thighs, making room for Declan. And when the still sleepy man is within reach, I pull him to me and lay my head against his chest, finally relaxing completely. With Cade's arm still wrapped around my waist and Declan now between my legs, I settle into the feeling of home.

"Nap was fine," he says, his voice thick with sleep. "Now, what was wrong with your day? Someone do something wrong? Do I need to talk to Carmella?"

Laughing, I push him back and focus on his warm brown eyes. How is it possible that so few people see what a gentle giant this man really is? He's so kind and so damn caring when it comes to the people he loves. Chin on his chest, I shake my head. "Everyone was perfectly wonderful. Carmella, especially."

Lowering, he presses a kiss to my lips. "Then why did you have a bad day?"

"I didn't have a bad day. My day was just boring compared to yours." I bite my lip, brows lifted, waiting for him to catch on to my meaning.

A flush works up his chest and then colors his cheeks in the most glorious red, leaving even the tips of his ears rosy.

He turns to Cade, who is wearing a cocky-ass grin.

"Well, I—" Declan sputters.

I smooth my fingers down his cheek and press my fingers to his lips. "Heard it was the best blow job of Cade's life."

Cade didn't say it in so many words, but he didn't have to. My guys look at one another, lingering that way. The heat and awe radiating from them confirm my suspicions.

Ready to put Declan out of his misery, I say, "All I did was write a song."

He zeroes in on me, his expression severe. "You wrote a song?"

A laugh bubbles out of me. It feels so damn euphoric to finally have my music back. And that's what I'm focusing on. Not the shitty conversation I had with my mother. Not even the knowledge that Jason was arrested. Nope. I'm focusing on the good that came out of today—I got my damn voice back.

"Yes. I was standing outside the salon, looking out at all my favorite places on Hope Street, and the words just started tumbling out. I ran inside and got my new journal, and I didn't stop writing until I had a whole damn song."

"Mel, that's incredible," Cade says, squeezing my hip tight.

"I went back to Lake's so I could get the track down in their studio. It's not perfect, but god, it felt so good to get back to the music."

"I'm so proud of you, sweetheart," Declan says, his expression one of pride. "In fact, this calls for a celebration."

"More of a celebration than what you already had planned

tonight?" I tease, already keyed up and ready for what Declan promised me hours earlier. Him inside me while Cade takes me from behind.

I can't wait for the three of us to be one again. To have them both at the same time. I shift, and instantly, the anal plug settles deeper, adding to the ache that's been slowly building all day.

Declan grips my jaw and tips it so that he can take my lips. "Oh, Cade's still going to fuck your ass while you ride my cock." He sucks on my tongue until I'm burning with need. "But first we gotta run to the grocery store. You're going to pick out your favorite food, and I'm going to cook a celebratory dinner."

He pulls back, leaving me breathless, then nods to Cade. Our other partner leans in and he kisses me too.

Declan presses his lips to my neck while Cade's tongue tangles with mine.

With a sigh, I sink into this feeling. Onto this beautiful moment with both of my men.

"This is just cruel," I whine as Declan carries me out of his bedroom and into the kitchen. I was on my back, with Cade's head between my legs, and on the precipice of an orgasm, when Declan appeared in the doorway to his bedroom to announce that dinner was ready.

"You need to eat, sweetheart. You're going to need the sustenance for what I have planned."

Cade swipes at his mouth as he follows us into the kitchen. "Food smells amazing," he says as he drops into a chair at the table, "but I agree with Mel: you should have let me finish my appetizer."

Declan tosses me onto Cade's lap, the move making the plug in my ass shift, pulling a whimper from me and forcing me to jolt upward.

"I'll serve the food, and then Cade can feed you while I keep you on edge."

Oh shit. I can't help but smile at the prospect. Thank fuck the fun isn't ending yet. Not that it ever seems to when I'm with them.

Declan plates the shrimp Mozambique, which is my grandmother's recipe and one of my favorite meals of all times. I helped him make the sauce, but when he told Cade to warm me up while the food simmered and he cleaned up the kitchen, I certainly didn't complain.

With rolls to dip and shrimp and rice on the plates in front of each guy, Declan finally takes a seat and pats his knee for me to join him. Unlike my position on Cade, where my weight is evenly distributed—leaving the plug in my ass to just relax—this new position has his knee pushing it in farther. I shift, seeking relief, but Declan splays a hand over my stomach, holding me in place, then slides his fingers between my legs and slowly strums my clit. I'm only wearing a T-shirt because Cade was between my thighs when Declan so rudely interrupted us. Not that I'm sad about it anymore.

What's odd—and maybe hotter than I'd like to admit—is the way Declan starts up a conversation with Cade, as if I'm not even there.

"How do you feel about the games coming up this week?"

Cade dips a piece of shrimp into the sauce, and with one finger, he pulls my bottom lip down. Then he feeds it into my mouth. As the spicy garlic sauce explodes on my tongue, I lick at my lips to get every last drop, moaning as I do.

"Good," he says. "It's taken some time to adjust to all the changes since McGreevey retired, but I like the look of the rookies."

Declan continues to roll circles on my clit, edging me while he eats and sips wine and talks to Cade.

For every bite Cade takes, he feeds me as well, though he ignores the way I thrash on Declan's leg, desperate for him to slip a finger inside me. I pulse with the need to be filled, and while I know there's a method to Declan's madness, I'm practically delirious with the need to come.

When Cade tries to stick another piece of shrimp into my mouth, I fold my lips and shake my head. "Enough," I cry. "Please, I need to come. One of you, please." My need leaves me begging and whiney, and I don't even care. "Give me your cock. Hell, I'll take your fingers or your mouths."

Declan laughs, making my body shake, which only shifts the plug further, making a shudder run through me. Dammit, I hate him so much in this moment. He's holding me hostage with his hand across my body. "You just want one cock, sweetheart? We were going to give you two." His words are a rasp against my ear, and even though he's taunting me, he slides a single digit inside me, offering a little relief. "But if you only want one—"

He lets the words hang even as I thrash and beg.

"No," I breathe, arching back against his shoulder. "I want you both. I need you both."

"Hear that, baby? She wants you to fill her ass." He sucks on my earlobe while Cade pushes his chair closer and pulls my legs onto his lap. "Not going to lie, sweetheart. I'm a little jealous you get to feel him inside you like that."

Cade and I make strangled noises at that. Cade's is full of shock, while mine is a guttural need.

When Declan snags the hem of my shirt, I lift my arms to make it easier. As it flutters to the floor beside us, I realize that Cade is still staring like he's lost in the idea that Declan has painted. A dream moment, where Declan lets him fuck his ass. Or maybe being fucked by Declan. All of us fucking one another.

The possibilities are endless, but if one of them doesn't happen now, I'm going to combust. No more teasing, no more edging. *I need to come.*

"Give her a finger," Declan commands. "I want her first orgasm to be *ours*. Just like she is."

Cade smirks. "Hear that, pretty girl? You're ours." He leans forward and works his finger in next to Declan's, then takes my mouth.

Their fingers work in tandem, pulling moans and incoherent chants from me. I've never experienced anything so hot. That is, until Declan grabs Cade's neck and pulls him in for a bruising kiss. Chest to chest with Cade, his heart pounds against my sternum.

The two of them are licking and grunting in my ear, all the while fucking me with their fingers. I'm pancaked between them, unable to move, engulfed in their heat and loving every minute of it.

Cade pulls back, gasping.

"Play with her tits. She loves that," Declan mumbles.

An instant later, Cade's hot mouth is there, his teeth sinking into my flesh, and I'm seeing stars. As an orgasm washes over me, Declan talks me through it, his voice a deep rumble. "That's right sweetheart, give it to us. Soak our fingers. We need you to be a needy mess so that you can take our cocks in all your holes."

Screaming, I come so hard I swear I wet the floor, stars dancing in my vision.

"Oh fuck, she squirted everywhere," Cade mumbles, dropping to his knees. "God, Dec—" He laps at me, desperate. "She tastes so good. You need to try."

He hauls himself back into his chair and pulls me onto his lap. I'm as limp as a rag doll, unable to control my limbs. Then Declan's leaning forward and sucking me dry. Cade's hands roam over my body, tweaking my nipples, fondling me.

I swear I'm in some sort of love-drugged haze, so I have no sense of time. Declan eats me for what could be seconds or maybe hours, and then I'm coming again. As I come down from the high, still shaking, I'm certain I won't be able to make it through the night.

Declan leans back on his haunches, wiping his mouth, staring up at us both. "Fuck, I don't think this will ever get old. You in his arms. Watching the two of you together. Kissing you. *Pleasuring*"—A slow, sexy smile pulls at his lips—"both of you."

Cade's heart pounds against my back. It's what we both want. For Declan to want us. For Declan to want *this*. And god, based upon the hearts in his eyes, I'd say we might just get our wish.

"It's time," I say, holding my hand out to the dark, serious man in front of me. He takes it and stands, then pulls me from Cade's arms and carries me toward the bedroom. Finally, we're all going to be one.

CHAPTER 42

Cade

"PRETTY SURE SHE'S WET ENOUGH," Declan says with a chuckle as he eases Mel onto the bed. Fuck, is she gorgeous, with her skin flushed pink from all the edging and two orgasms.

"Still needs lube," I say as I head for the drawer where I spotted the supplies last night.

When I come back around the bed, he's got her settled on a pillow, ass up for the taking. *Fuck*, am I ready to take it. I glance over at Dec, who's standing still as a statue, watching me. "You just gonna watch, or you gonna get naked for me?"

Laughing, he tugs his shirt over his head. As I drink in his bare torso, I'm hit with a niggle of guilt. At this point, he's the only one who hasn't come yet, since I came down his throat only a few hours ago. But if I know this man at all, I know that he loves holding himself back. If he enjoys edging us, he enjoys edging himself ten times more. He's a giver, a pleaser. The man lives to watch others enjoy themselves, so I'll give him something to watch.

Leaning over, I place my hand on Mel's back, my lips close to her ear. "I'm going to play with your ass a little bit. Get you nice and warmed up. And if you're a good girl, I'll even let you suck Dec's cock after, okay?"

She turns her head completely and leans in, lips pursed. I meet her, diving in for a kiss. I like this girl something fierce. She's intoxicating, and I'm quickly falling harder than I thought possible. I set the lube on the bed and undress, then motion for Declan to come closer. As he steps beside me, I can't keep my eyes off his cock. It's heavy against his stomach and standing up, angry and practically purple.

His comment about being jealous that Mel would get to have me inside her flashes at the sight. Does that mean he's thought about letting me fuck him? About what it'd feel like if I did? I'm doing my best to take things slow with him, but when he says things like that? Fuck, it makes it hard to breathe. And it makes it hard not to bend him over and push inside him. Show him what he's been missing out on. The orgasm I could give him, the way I could manipulate his prostate to make him black out—fuck, he'd love it.

Many men don't realize just how good it feels to be fucked in the ass, but Declan will get the best of both worlds: His cock inside Melina, and my dick inside his ass.

But not tonight.

I have to slow down. We have time.

I hope.

There are so many things I want to try with him. So many things I want him to experience.

This is just the beginning.

But first I want to show him how to make it good for her. And hopefully teach him what to do when he's prepping me. Fuck, I can't wait for the day he's ready for that.

"Hey, Trouble, can you play with your pussy for me? I'm going to take the plug out."

Our girl doesn't hesitate to lift up and stroke herself. With lube softening my hands, I grasp the plug and ease it out. Then I drop it on the bed beside me and replace it with my thumb. "You want to stretch her good before fucking her," I tell Declan, who's watching the scene with an eager, earnest expression.

"Is it the same for a man?" he asks, his attention still focused on the way my thumb stretches her.

I suck in a breath to temper the wave of lust that engulfs me. "Yeah, baby, it's the same."

He shifts, his focus now fixed on my face, then licks his lips. "How does that feel, sweetheart? You like being stuffed with Cade's thumb, or do you need more?"

"More," she moans, backing up and taking more of my thumb. She's so needy and still dripping. Her ass feels like heaven. So smooth and tight. It's going to grip me phenomenally.

"Want my cock, sweetheart?" Declan taunts as he crawls up the bed, leaving me to work, and angles so his cock is near her mouth.

When she nods, he lifts her chin, holding her in place, and slowly slides his tip against her tongue. "Keep that mouth open. Stick out that tongue for me."

She does as she's told because she's an obedient thing, desperate for us to give her what she's been dying to have for hours. "That's right, slurp it up. Get me nice and wet so I can stuff that pussy while Cade stuffs your ass."

My dick bounces, and lightning zips up my spine.

Fuck, I need to be inside her.

"C'mere for a sec," I say to Dec.

The man stops his thrusting and stares at me.

"I want you to spit on it." I grip my cock in my other hand.

Dec's eyes flare, and without hesitation, he drops to the bed and crawls over to me.

Declan Everhart fucking *crawls* to me.

And then he smiles as he leans close and spits on my dick.

"Get inside her before I blow right here," I warn him as I pull my thumb out of her ass, ready to replace it with my cock.

Chuckling, Declan crawls back up the bed and guides Mel until she's straddling him, pulling her right onto his dick in one swift motion. He's fucking huge, so she whimpers, a sound of pleasure mixed with pain, and adjusts herself. I don't dare get into position until she peers over her shoulder, letting me know she's ready.

Once I'm given the all-clear, I crawl between Declan's thighs. As I move, the coarse hair on his legs scrapes against my skin, sending shivers through me. *Fuck*. With a sharp inhale, I press my lips to Mel's back. "Lean down, Trouble. It's about to get really tight."

Declan grasps Melina's neck and pulls her to him, taking her mouth with his. While she's distracted and languid, I slide my crown inside her tight hole. I stay shallow for a moment, thrusting an inch, then back, slowly, gently, letting her get used to the size. When she cries out, I freeze. Dammit. I don't want to hurt her. Heart in my throat. I squeeze the base of my dick, ready to pull out, but before I can, she pushes back into me, forcing me deeper.

"Go quick," she mumbles. "It will only burn for a second."

I should have known she'd respond this way. Mel is stronger than anyone I've ever met. My heart swells as I watch Declan push her hair back and kiss her, murmuring encouragements.

Holding my breath, I do as she's asked and thrust all the way in. When my hips hit her ass and my cock slides against Declan's, with only a thin barrier between us, I nearly lose my mind. And I swear, the three of us let out desperate sighs as one.

"She's strangling me," Dec says over her shoulder, his brown eyes fixed on me. They swim with so much raw emotion. Gripping one of my thighs, he squeezes. "And I can feel you inside her. Fuck, you feel good."

He presses another kiss to her shoulder and squeezes her thigh with his other hand. "You okay, sweetheart?"

Mel swivels her hips, pulling matching groans from us. "Yes, I need you to move. Both of you. Fuck me. *Please.*"

We start slow, partially because pulling out of her leaves me bereft. The feel of them both is just too good.

"Does his cock feel good, sweetheart?" Dec asks in that smooth way that has tingles going down my spine.

"So good," she murmurs.

He plucks one of her nipples, and she arches up for a moment, though quickly slams back down on him, pulling a grunt from us both.

"Shit, shit. Yellow. I'm going to come." She whines the words, knowing, like I do, that Dec is going to stop her.

"Not yet. Hold it. Be our good girl and squeeze down. Don't let yourself come yet."

Sweat coats her skin from her efforts to keep herself still as he gives tiny little thrusts, teasing my cock from the inside.

"Still yellow?" he rasps.

She lets out a sigh. "I think I'm okay."

"We should try to get Declan to say *red*. What do you say, Trouble?"

The man beneath us zeroes in on me over her shoulder. But he doesn't look mad. No, he looks intrigued. He knows what I want. We both know what he needs.

"Can I play with your ass, baby?" I ask gently. "I want to make you feel better than you've ever felt while she fucks you and I fuck her."

Dec spreads his legs, giving me all the invitation I need. Careful to remain seated deeply inside Mel, I reach back for the lube and pour a generous amount. Then I work to find the spot that's going to make my man spiral. For a moment, I only drag my fingers down his perineum, massaging softly while he fucks slowly up into Mel.

He lets out the lowest growl. It's sexy and filled with need. "Oh, fuck, baby. Why does that feel so good?"

"Because it's us. Because you were meant for this. You were meant to be owned by us. Give it to me, Dec. Give me this ass and let me show you what you've been missing." I push into his asshole, pulling a grunt from him. His muscles tighten automatically, trying to keep me out. But I'm dedicated to making this good for him, so I keep playing, every move smooth, gentle. "Come on, Trouble. Keep our man happy. Rub that hot pussy all over his cock."

"Yes." Declan hisses air through his teeth. "You're so filthy, and I fucking love it. My filthy boy."

At his praise, my dick goes impossibly hard. Mel tightens, too, strangling it. Any second now, we're all going over the edge. But he needs to be the one to topple first. We're holding out. We're winning this round.

"Come on, baby. Give us your cum. Fill our girl up." I pulse my thumb in and out, and when he's loosened a bit, I switch to two fingers, stretching him until I hit his prostate.

Finally, fucking *finally*, he goes over the edge. He throws his head back against the pillow, cursing and groaning, with my fingers in his ass and my girlfriend on his dick. It's not a romantic moment. No, we're fucking filthy right now. But in this moment, it's clear that I'm in love with them. That I'll never be the same again.

As Declan sputters out breaths as he comes down from his high, I'm fucking ecstatic that Mel and I have held on this long. We're going another round, and Dec will just have to survive it.

"That was—" His chest heaves as he stares up at us both. "So *fucking* good."

I push Melina down so that she's flat against him, and she goes easily, resting her cheek against his collarbone, a smile on her face. I kiss her first and then turn to him, a growl slipping from me, my lips to his. "I may have to share your cock, baby, but your ass is mine."

Round & Round

CHAPTER 43

Declan

YESTERDAY WAS PERFECT. Even though Melina was out with the girls for most of the afternoon, nothing between Cade and me got awkward. Like any other Saturday when he's in town, we grabbed beers and watched college football.

First, though, I gave him the best blow job of his life—his words, not mine—and I loved every fucking second of it. The feel of him, the control I wielded, every single aspect. And fuck, was it easy to settle into our regular Saturday routine afterward.

It's a huge weight off my shoulders to know for certain that despite how much has changed between us, so much is still the same.

It was nice.

Easy.

Once Melina returned, the air shifted, and the temperature bumped up a few degrees. After her news that she'd finally gotten rid of her writer's block, we went to the grocery store, and while I pushed the cart up and down the aisles, Cade held her hand and let her drag him from shelf to shelf, grabbing far too many ingredients that we'd never use. But despite that, I felt a happiness I've never known. I smiled more just doing a mundane thing like grocery shopping with them than I have on any other day with anyone else.

When we returned home, he poured her a glass of wine, and she snuggled up against my back and told us more about her afternoon. I set her on the counter so I could have her close while I cooked and they talked.

A sense of peace I've never experienced took over the moment the three of us were together. There are no words to describe the sensation, but it was so innate, so right, and I knew I wasn't ready to give up.

After dinner, we teased orgasm after orgasm out of our girl, ending the night with her riding me and Cade fucking her ass.

And then Cade sank his fingers into my ass, and I knew in that moment that I could never go back to being just friends. I saw fucking stars. With her on top of me and him inside me. I don't ever want to live any other way.

It was perfection.

This morning, that perfection appears to be continuing. The moment I open my eyes, I catch sight of my best friend settling between my legs. He peers up at me, a brow lifted in question.

"Please," I rasp, bucking up into his waiting mouth.

Why is he so good at this? Why do I love it so much?

Fuck only knows.

With his lips around my dick, he sucks hard and runs his fingers against my balls. Groaning, I tangle my hand in his golden hair and thrust up.

Beside me, a naked Melina blinks her eyes open.

My heart stumbles, even as a wave of need courses through me. Will she freak out about how much I like this? About how much I want them both?

The sleepy smile that takes over her face douses all my fears. She's not bothered in the least. I hold my free hand out to her, and she curls into me, bringing her mouth to mine. "Morning, Chief."

I kiss her slowly, losing myself in this moment. In the euphoria infused in my blood. Cade continues to suck, his mouth hot and so damn perfect. Melina tangles her tongue with mine, moving in lazy circles.

She gasps into my mouth, then lets out a low moan. The sound sends a zap of electricity straight to my balls. Catching her lip with my teeth, I tug, and when I release her, I drop my gaze down to Cade. He's still sucking me off, but now he's also spearing her with two fingers.

"C'mere, sweetheart," I grit out. "He shouldn't have to do all the work." Though I don't want to release my hold on Cade, I need both hands to pull Melina onto my chest. Gripping her thighs, I force her onto my face. "Ride me till you come," I say, my lips brushing her pussy. "Then I want to watch Cade fuck you until he does."

The man between my thighs moans in response.

She's so sweet, soaking my face almost instantly. I lick and suck and finger her until she's thrashing above me and crying out. As she does, Cade grasps my shaft and jacks me while continuing to work me over with his mouth. In seconds, I'm coming in hot, uncontrollable spurts.

When I come back down to earth, Cade wipes his lips and smiles. "Hold her for me."

Clutching Melina's sides, I flip her so her back is pressed to my chest. Cade settles between her thighs and slips in with a groan. With each thrust, her body rocks into mine, pushing me into the mattress. Fuck, it's like he's fucking us both. I love it.

I play with her tits while he's deep inside her and watch as pleasure sweeps across his face. I'm hard again before either of them orgasms.

When she shudders on top of me while he comes with a roar, there's no doubt that I love more than just the sex.

And I need to tell them.

"Holy fuck, Trouble. You are incredible." Cade hovers close and kisses her. Dammit. If I don't stop them, things are going to heat up again, and we'll never stop fucking.

I slide her onto the mattress next to me and press a kiss to her neck. "I'll go get something to clean you up. Be right back."

Cade eyes me, his eyes flashing with desire. "Or you could clean her up with your mouth."

Heat rushes through me at the suggestion. The idea of his cum inside her is hot. Cleaning her up? Even hotter.

But whether they like it or not, we need a minute. "If I lick her right now, I'll end up fucking her again." With a chuckle, I stride to the bathroom.

"I'm not hearing a problem," Melina calls as I close the door behind me.

Planting my hands on the counter, I bow my head and let out a breath. I don't see a problem either. I could keep doing this with them forever. And I'm tempted to walk back into that room and start it all again.

Instead, I run my hands under the faucet and splash warm water on my face. As I towel it off, I meet my own eyes in the mirror and smile. I'm happy.

Really fucking happy.

And so light I feel like I'm floating an inch off the ground. It's a sensation I've never experienced, and it's one I don't want to lose. I pull a washcloth out of the drawer and get it wet, then head for the bedroom. I need to tell them. I need to know we're on the same page.

The two most beautiful people I know are still lying together on my bed. Melina's dark hair is spread across Cade's strong chest. Fuck. The sight of the two of them has my heart pounding.

"So you'll be in New York at the end of the week?" Melina asks.

"Yeah. You're heading there tomorrow? Want to meet for dinner?"

Melina bites her lips and nods.

Wait, she's leaving?

They're both just *leaving?*

Devastation sweeps through me so quickly I have to clutch the doorknob to steady myself. In doing so, I accidentally send the door slamming against the wall.

They startle, both jolting and zeroing in on me where I'm standing like a creep, listening in on their conversation.

Their conversation about spending time together without me.

Away from here.

Back to their normal lives, where they both belong.

I hold up the cloth but lower my focus to the floor between me and the bed. "Why don't you get cleaned up? I'll make breakfast." I shuffle closer and drop the washcloth into Cade's hand. Then I spin on my heel and hurry out.

I need out of this room. Right this fucking minute.

CHAPTER 44

Melina

I CAN'T HELP but gape at Declan's back as he hightails it out of the room. "You think he's okay?"

"He's big on Sunday breakfast." Cade shrugs, running a hand through my hair. "Anyway, are you sure you're ready to go back to New York?"

A heavy weight settles in my chest. That question has been flitting through my head on and off since I got into the studio yesterday.

Especially after the incredible night with the guys. God, my mind is running wild with melodies and music I want to create.

But the idea of leaving my guys, of not waking up in Declan's bed every morning, guts me.

With a sigh, I shrug. "I don't know. I owe quite a few songs to the label."

I should lay it all out. Tell Cade what's really eating at me is the uncertainty of what happens next for us, especially if I leave. But that's a conversation all three of us should be involved in.

If I want this—a relationship with both of them—keeping everyone in the loop needs to be a priority.

The last thing I want is for Declan to think we're strategizing about how to deal with him. He's done so well the last few days. If I'm honest

276

with them both over breakfast, maybe we can figure out how to make this work.

God, just the thought of it has my nerves twisting, but excitement is there too.

"You know you can talk to me," Cade says gently, his mouth fixed in a straight line.

Shit. I've probably been silent for quite some time.

"I know," I say, running a hand over his jaw. "And I will. I'd like to talk to both of you, actually."

With a smile, he stands and pulls me to my feet. "All right Trouble, I have a feeling I'll like whatever you have to say." He kisses me and leads me toward the shower. "But first, I promised Dec I would clean you up."

By the time we make it out of the bedroom, the house smells like the most incredible combination of bacon, pancakes, and coffee.

In the kitchen, Declan is setting plates on the table.

As I step closer and notice there are only two, I frown. "This looks amazing," I say, though my tone is slightly guarded.

He nods, but he doesn't meet my eye. "I have to get ready for work. Enjoy breakfast."

"You're working today?" Cade asks, brows pulling together.

"Yeah, I took off yesterday, but today's my day on."

Disappointment rolls through me like a wave. Cade is leaving tomorrow morning, and if Declan is working, that means we won't get more time together until Cade visits again.

"You can't stay for breakfast so we can talk? I wanted to discuss something."

"I'll be home later tonight," Declan says, finally looking at me, his expression shuttered. "Unless you don't plan on being here?"

What? Why wouldn't I be here? And why is he acting so strange? What happened between the moment he climbed out of bed and now?

"I'm having dinner with our moms tonight," Cade says. "They want to meet Mel. I was hoping the three of us could go."

Declan scowls. Actually scowls. My heart sinks. Is the idea of introducing me to his mom that awful?

"I wish you would have mentioned it earlier. I would have told you tonight doesn't work for me."

"Guess I thought we had more time," Cade says, his tone full of defeat.

The words are like a punch to the gut. They hold so much more meaning. More time today. More time after. To talk about where we go from here. How we can make this work.

"Yeah, well, I don't," Declan says. Though his tone is brusque, it's laced with hurt.

Confusion engulfs me, and pain lances my heart. How the hell did we go from being so in tune with one another's needs to *this*?

I stare at Cade, silently urging him to push Declan to stay. Then I turn back to Declan, wishing like hell he'd stop closing himself up. Neither understands my unspoken pleas, and I'm too scared to voice them. Too scared I'll say the wrong thing and lose them both.

Back To You

CHAPTER 45

Cade

"I'M SO glad you could make time for me before heading back to Boston," my mother says as she pulls me in for a hug. She's good like that, chiding me gently while wiping away my annoyance by hugging me. My mom gives the best hugs, and I'm most certainly in need of one after the way I left Declan's house.

"Of course, Ma, and I brought gifts." I rest a hand on the small of Mel's back.

Beside me, she's wearing a coy smile and holding the gifts I bought in town, including the bouquet Amelia set aside.

"Oh, a girl? This really is a good gift," my mother says with far too much delight.

I chuckle, ignoring her teasing. "I mean the flowers and the limoncello. Brought one for Andrea too. She here?" I crane my neck to look past her, but she's not having any of it.

"Introduce me to the girl," she hisses, side-stepping to remain in my field of vision. Her glare quickly turns into a smile, and then she's focused on Mel. "I'm Cade's mother, and you are—"

"Is that Melina Rodriguez?" Declan's mom asks as she materializes in the dining room behind my mother. My parents built this home when I was a kid, and I've helped Ma keep it up over the years.

"It is," I say, pulling Mel closer. "Mel, this is my mother, Janine Fitzgerald, and this is Declan's mom, Andrea Everhart. Moms," I say, not bothering to fight my smile, "this is Mel."

"It's so nice to meet you both," Mel says, holding out the bouquet to my mother.

Mom takes it, but with a shake of her head, she stuffs it into my arms. Then she pulls Mel in for a hug.

"Never thought I'd see the day that my son brought home a girl."

I cough out a laugh as they embrace.

Andrea steps up and wraps her arms around Mel too. When they pull apart, she frowns at me. "No Declan?"

"He had to work," I say, swallowing back my annoyance.

"The boy works too much," his mother replies, though she seems to take the news in stride as she and my mom usher us into my childhood home.

"He's got an important job," Mel says, as if she feels the need to remind us.

I brush a kiss to her temple. "He's right. You are a sweetheart," I mutter. With a small smile, I step away, taking the flowers and bottle of limoncello to the kitchen.

"Has my son been a good host?" Andrea asks Mel as we settle around the kitchen island, where appetizers have been laid out. "He can be pretty reserved."

My mother laughs. "That's her nice way of saying that Declan talks in grunts."

Mel's responding smile is tight. "He talks to me."

I bristle with annoyance. If Declan had come to dinner, our mothers wouldn't be peppering Mel with all these questions.

Though it would have been a big step to show up together now that we're—

Fuck, what the hell *are* we?

My irritation melts into concern, and I find myself reaching for my phone and texting Declan.

> Me: You should see our mothers with Mel.

I stare at the screen, heart beating quickly, waiting to see that little *delivered* message turn to *read*. When I've watched far longer than is polite while in the presence of other people, I give up and stuff the device into my pocket.

Declan doesn't text.

With the exception of Olivia and Mel.

Even after all this time, even after all that's transpired over the last few days, I'm not one of his exceptions.

Why the fuck does that bother me so much?

The moms and Mel have moved on to a new topic when I finally force myself to remain in the present. Unsurprisingly, both women are enthralled by my girl. She entertains them with stories about music tours and other musicians.

By the time we say goodnight and my mom pulls me in for an extra tight hug, the older women have exchanged numbers with Mel and have planned a trip to Boston to watch a game and meet the two of us for dinner.

Tonight was exactly the type of night I'd have wished for if I'd ever thought of being in a committed relationship. Before Mel, I'd never seen myself as the committed type.

Now, though?

Now the idea of hanging out with her and our moms is easy. Incredible. It would have been perfect had my phone not remained dreadfully silent all evening.

I had to hold myself back from checking my messages at least a dozen times.

And when we get in the car and I finally pull it out, only to find Declan still hasn't responded, anger takes over. For thirty-five years, we've been friends. Sure, he had to work today, and maybe disappearing the way he did had nothing to do with Mel and me. But he could have fucking responded to my text. Could have—fuck, I don't even know. Declan's never been one to talk. It shouldn't bother me so much, but the difference between the way he communicates with me and the way he communicates with Mel is hard to ignore. The lack of contact is like a punch to the gut.

Despite how much he does talk to Mel, she didn't seem upset when he said he was busy today. She didn't check her phone all night long like I wanted to. She always knows exactly what he needs.

And I don't.

"Cade," she says, her tone concerned, like maybe it's not the first time she's said my name.

I look over at her, our surroundings coming into focus. Shit. I'm parked in Declan's driveway, and I don't recall a single moment of the drive.

She nods toward the door. "We going in?"

I shake my head. No. I have zero interest in hurting myself by walking in there and exposing my raw heart to my best friend. "I think I'll just head back to Boston so I can get some rest before the team flies out tomorrow."

Mel's green eyes widen, and she settles back in her seat. "Cade."

"It's fine."

"We should talk to—"

"We've talked enough this weekend. He's done a lot. Maybe too much," I add bitterly.

It's all too much too soon. For him, at least. Me? I've wanted Declan for more than twenty years. What I've gotten so far is nowhere near enough. We're moving at a snail's pace in my mind, but for him...

I drag my hand through my hair. "He kissed me today. Then I asked him to come to my mom's for dinner, and he said no." Swallowing past the lump in my throat, I blink at her, willing her to understand what a big deal tonight could have been for us. And how disappointed I am that he wasn't ready. That he was okay touching me, but that he wasn't ready for anything more than that. "I need a little space."

Shoulders falling, Mel squeezes my hand. Though her posture is one of defeat, her expression is understanding. She gets it, and she knows precisely what I need, so she won't argue. "Okay. I'll miss you, though."

I angle over the center console. Fuck, I hate that I have to leave her already. "This changes nothing for me. I'm happy you met my mom. She loved you."

Mel's lips curve. "Yeah? I liked her a lot. Both of them. They're wonderful."

Cupping her jaw, I brush my thumb against her cheek. "You're wonderful."

She closes her eyes and presses her lips to mine. They're warm and soft and exactly what I need.

Cursing myself and my stupid feelings, the need to leave, I press my thumb to her lip and pull back. "Don't think you need to keep yourself from him because I'm not there." I turn and survey the front of the house. "You don't have to call me to ask for permission."

She bites down on my finger, the move meant to draw my attention back to her face. "Call me when you get home?"

Nodding, I press my lips to hers, hoping like hell this isn't the last time I get to taste her.

Vulnerable

CHAPTER 46

Melina

I SWALLOW the lump in my throat as I climb the porch steps. I never thought I was a jealous person, but I'm beginning to think I've been wrong all this time. Cade is leaving before we've defined what this relationship is. Without a label, I can't expect him to twiddle his thumbs while he travels with his team.

And I won't ask him to commit himself to us. He has to want us. Choose us. Decide that Declan and I are enough. But for that to happen, Declan needs to fucking show up, and today, he didn't.

For as much as I defended him tonight, Cade had every right to be upset. Declan should have been there, and if he absolutely couldn't, then he should have given us a real explanation.

He had to have seen the hurt on Cade's face when he shrugged him off, saying that tonight just wasn't good for him. He had to know he was crushing the person he so obviously loves.

And people say women cause unnecessary drama. God, these men are infuriating.

Declan's car is in the driveway, but I'm still startled when I find him sitting in the darkened living room.

Just the sight of him boils my blood, though my tone is cold as I ask, "What are you doing here?"

Declan eyes me warily, jaw tight. Like he expects my anger, even welcomes it. And he says absolutely nothing.

My frustration ignites, turning into blazing anger.

"Infuriatingly stupid man," I mutter, striding past him, heading straight for my bedroom.

I slam the door, giving in to the urge to make a show of my anger. But as I fall against the cool, solid wood and tip my head back, my breaths coming out unevenly, my anger bubbles over.

I fling the door open and storm back into the living room. "You know what? I'm not doing this," I say, propping my hands on my hips and glaring down at the man on the couch.

He looks up at me wearing an expression that almost looks like relief. Like he wants me to yell. Like he'd rather I curse him out than walk away.

And god if that doesn't break me.

My heart cracks in two, and I deflate. My anger remains, but it's turned down to a simmer.

This man has been patient with me since the moment I met him. He's protected me and gone out of his comfort zone *for me*. The least I can do is give him my words.

"With Jason—"

"Don't compare what we have to what you had with him." His jaw is rigid, and gone is the softness in his eyes from only seconds ago.

I square my shoulders and heave a deep breath, centering myself. "Then let me talk. Because he didn't."

Nostrils flaring, he fists his hands in his lap, focus fixed on me, waiting.

I round the coffee table and drop one knee to the cushion beside him. With my hands on his chest, I straddle him. Then I pull him in close and hold him tight. "I want to start this conversation as your safe place," I say, my lips brushing his ear, "Because you've become mine."

Shuddering, he loops his arms around me and squeezes.

For several long moments, we stay like that. Silent. Holding one another. Our hearts beating wildly but in sync.

Finally, he breaks the silence. "I'm scared."

My battered heart pinches at the vulnerability in his tone. "I know."

With a heavy sigh, he pulls back and regards me, pushing a strand of hair behind my ear. "I'm falling for both of you, and you're leaving."

Tears prick my eyes as I run my fingers through his messy hair. "I'm not going anywhere. I'm right here."

Brows pulled low, he dips his chin and focuses on a spot somewhere around my throat rather than holding eye contact. "But you have a life —and you don't need to stay here anymore."

I swallow past the lump in my throat. Tamp down on the trepidation that has kept me from opening up completely to both men. "What if I want to stay? What if I want you? You and Cade and us and this." My voice wobbles.

Honestly, what I hope for is probably too good to be true. But I have to say this. He needs to know the depth of my feelings. And it's hard to deny that sometimes, especially when this hard man is so soft beneath my fingers, what I long for feels so real and tangible.

I rest my palm against his pounding heart. "I want this, but you need to want it too. I can't fall for another person who's going to break me."

He brushes a thumb over my lips, the move sending a shiver down my spine. "I would never hurt you."

Head tilted, I give him a sad smile. "Not opening your heart to Cade and me *is* hurting me."

Declan takes a few steadying breaths. "I'm in love with my best friend."

My heart floats at the admission, and my smile turns easy. This all feels so delicate and new. "I know."

"And I'm fucking gone for you, Melina." His eyes dart furtively between mine, as if he's dissecting my reaction. "You own me, sweetheart."

His voice is tortured. Like he doesn't know how to convey what he's feeling. Like he's desperate for me to believe him, and he's not quite sure I do.

Holding myself still, I assess him. My body is taut with tension, because honestly, I am questioning it. "Maybe it's meant to be just you and Cade. Maybe—" My heart sinks, and I worry my bottom lip, knowing that what I say next will likely bring on the tears. "Maybe I was the glue that brought you two together." I sniffle. "But I don't have to be involved forever."

Declan shakes his head, the movement so violent it jostles me on his lap. "No, sweetheart. We've had decades to figure it out, yet it only works because of you. You're what makes us *us*. I'm awkward as fuck when I'm alone with him now. Hell, I gave him what was probably a mediocre blow job yesterday, because when we're alone, I can't help but fuck around with him."

I laugh and smack his chest, feigning offense. "Excuse me, are you saying that doesn't happen with me?"

The laugh that rumbles out of him sends waves of delight through me. God, is it a beautiful sound. Deep and gritty and full of affection. He smiles, suddenly cocksure. "Sweetheart, if I could live inside you, I would." He sweeps a thumb across my cheek, strumming it reverently. "But I can also sit with you for an entire night and not feel the least bit compelled to force conversation. Just being in your presence puts me at ease. That's special." He angles in close, tightening his arm around my middle. "That's love."

He brushes his lips against mine, and my heart stumbles and falls over itself.

"You are my soulmate, Melina, mine and Cade's. We wouldn't be us without you. But with you," his voice grows smooth, confident. "With you, I think we could really make it."

Warring between smiling and bursting into tears, I bite my lip. "Cade was really upset."

Eyes downcast, Declan frowns. "I hate that I hurt him. I just—I was so afraid to lose you, to lose him, and I didn't know how to ask him to stay. I should have asked him to stay."

"Why didn't you? What happened this morning between the time you left our bed and the time we found you in the kitchen?"

His frown deepens. "I heard the two of you making plans to leave. You said you were going back to New York, and Cade was leaving—"

God, the way all of this could have been avoided if I'd just spoken up earlier. If I'd said something last night.

With my finger, I tip Declan's chin up and meet his sad eyes. "I was considering it, yes. My mother called and told me that Jason was arrested and that my brother bailed him out."

Declan's jaw locks. "I'll kill them both."

I press my fingers to his lips. "They got into a car accident on the way home. Jason's in a coma. Or he was as of yesterday." I shrug. "I don't know his current status, and I honestly don't care. When my mother called and asked me to come home, it was like a switch flipped inside me. I realized there was nothing I could say to them—no words I could conjure—that would ever get her to be on my side." I sigh. "And I don't know. I guess recognizing that freed me from trying so hard. From thinking too long on it. And I think that's how I got my voice back. I'm not trying to be the person someone else thinks I should be." I rub my thumb against the frown lines beside his eyes. "*You* and Cade helped me find my voice. Helped free me by just loving me for me. And now I can't stop the lyrics from flowing. So I wanted to get into the studio and get them all down before I lost this creativity streak. And my studio is in New York."

"Do you want to leave?"

My answer is far easier than it should be. "No. But I don't want to hide away either. It's been so long since I've written music, and yesterday, it felt good to do it again. I felt like I was finally reclaiming a piece of myself."

Declan watches me as if he's deep in thought. Then he seems to accept what I've said and nods, his hands settling on my hips and squeezing. "Can I show you something?"

I don't hesitate, knowing I want him to show me everything he's got. "Okay."

He doesn't let me go as he lifts me, and I squeal as he heads toward the basement door. "You going to put me down?"

In answer, he holds me tighter, with one hand on my ass, then opens the door. "I won't drop you."

"I know."

As he climbs down the steps, I don't even consider worrying that he might drop me. Declan has brought me an innate sense of safety since the moment I met him. Even when I'm unsure about every other aspect of my life, I'm comfortable with this man.

"It's not done yet, but the guys are coming over in the morning to finish it up." He turns on the light, and as the space is illuminated, I suck in a breath. "This has been down here since Liv left for college, so it probably needs to be tuned," he mumbles, setting me on the edge of a worn piano. It's a dark brown wood and nothing fancy, but...

"And Shawn knew a guy who had a guitar." He points to the instrument settled on a stand in the corner. Then he scans the walls, which are only half covered. "We got a good portion of it done today, but by Tuesday, this space is yours. If you want it."

"Declan," I whisper, though once again, I don't have the words to convey the depth of my emotions.

"It's not a fancy music studio like what you probably have in New York, but it will be soundproofed, and..." He sighs again. "Please, Melina. There's nothing I won't do to keep you. I know I don't deserve you. You probably want a nicer studio, a bigger house. And if that's what you really want, I can look into—"

I cover his lips with my fingers. "What I want is you and Cade. My home is with you. Wherever the two of you are. I can't believe you—" I shake my head, blinking back tears. This is unbelievable. He built a soundproof music studio. *For me.* Sure, it isn't extravagant, but it's the thought, the action, that shows me that he's all-in.

"I don't need a fancy studio, and if I want to make upgrades, I'll pay for it. I'm not with you for your money."

Declan chuckles, the lines around his eyes crinkling, making me fall more in love with him. "That's good. I love what I do, but I'll never compete with you or Cade when it comes to that stuff."

I hook my feet around the back of his hips and pull him close, settling my arms on his shoulders and my chin on his chest. "I love you, Declan. Just you as you are. No bells or whistles needed."

He presses his lips to mine, and when he pulls back, he rasps, "I love you so damn much, sweetheart."

Everything about this moment is perfect except... "I wish Cade were here."

Declan brushes my hair back. "Me too."

"You know what that means?" I ask as I regard one half of my happiness.

"Hmm?" he murmurs, dipping low and pressing a kiss to my collarbone.

"It's time to grovel."

Eyes flashing, he pulls back and gives me that devious smirk. "You trying to tell me you want me on my knees, sweetheart?"

His teasing tone instantly banishes the weight that's been holding me down all day.

"No. Though that wouldn't hurt."

A Year Without Rain

CHAPTER 47

Cade

"YOU KNOW it's not the greatest idea to tire me out before the game, right, Coach?" Brooks groans as I force him through another set.

I'm struggling just as much, going full-out to keep up, when he falls to his ass on the ice.

Chest heaving and lungs burning, I hold up my hands. "You're right. Sorry, I just..."

Brooks shakes his head. "I get it. When Sara drives me nuts, I tend to work it off this way too. Mel coming to visit soon?"

Lips pressed together, I shake my head. Mel is so not the problem. I've been traveling all week, so I haven't seen her, but we've talked every day.

It's the person I haven't heard from that's causing all this frustration.

Brooks, who's on his skates again and stopping at the edge of the ice, picks up his towel and drags it across his sweaty face. "Come on, tell me what's going on. If getting it off your chest will keep you from forcing me into these extra practices, I'll even grab Aiden and listen to him give you relationship advice."

I chuckle as I skate to his side. "It's just..." I rough a hand over my face. "You and Sara were friends first, right?"

Brooks nods. "She was my best friend."

"Weren't you nervous that you could ruin what you had if your relationship didn't work out? How did you know that you wanted the same things? That one of you wasn't more invested than the other?"

"Sara is honest to a fault. We talked about everything," Brooks laughs, "and I mean *everything*, before we jumped into a real relationship. She made sure to tell me what she was feeling, and that freed me to do the same."

My chest tightens further, making it hard to breathe. "So talking? That's your big advice?"

Brooks grins. "Yup."

I'm falling for a person who says about three words a year, so basically, I'm fucked.

It takes me hours to decide what I want to say to Declan, but even after I've finally typed out the message, I chicken out before hitting Send.

As I head into the arena, having resigned myself to trying again later, my phone pings. I slip it from the pocket of my suit pants, assuming it's Mel. She said she'd be in Boston this weekend. Hopefully she wants to make concrete plans.

But it's not her name on the screen.

It's Declan.

> Declan: I've been told I need to grovel, but I have no fucking idea what that means. Even so, I didn't want to let another day go by without saying I miss you.

My heart beats out a tattoo as I reread the message.

Declan *texted* me.

It's such a simple move, and it's stupid for me to let hope take flight the way it is.

But there's no stopping the flurry of butterflies in my stomach. I'm still smiling when I walk into the arena.

"Isn't that Melina?" Aiden points to a section where his wife normally sits with the rest of the team members' significant others.

We're in the second period, and they've just come in for a trade with the next line.

As I scan the faces in the crowd, War nudges me. "And Declan."

Instantly, I find them, and the air whooshes from my lungs.

Groveling. That's what he said.

Is that what this is?

Declan has never come to a Bolts game. The year I came on staff for the Bolts, I asked him over and over if he wanted tickets. He turned me down every time, so when the next season started, I didn't bother. I haven't offered since.

Fuck, I've never considered what it would be like to look up and see him here.

Seems irrational to be filled with such an inexorable sense of pride. I'm not the one playing.

But my chest is tight and my cheeks are aching as I take them in. Fuck. Yeah, it feels a hell of a lot like pride.

"Yeah, I think it is."

Gavin sidles up to me, tablet in hand, asking for an opinion on a play. I let my focus drift back up to the stands one more time. And when Declan smirks at me, I know that I'll like whatever the man has planned.

Groveling.

Is that a kink? Because if so, it's one of mine.

I slap my goalie's back. "Guess our practice wasn't too rough on ya, huh?"

The game was a shutout. Three to nothing.

He laughs. "Heard Mel is here. That the reason for the big-ass smile?"

Aiden and War are standing at their lockers, each working on their ties before they head out for postgame interviews.

I shake my head and keep my mouth shut. They know why, but I'm not ready for the rest of the team to be privy to the details. Until Declan is on board with it, I'll keep them to myself.

Doesn't stop me from wanting to tell them that my boyfriend and girlfriend are here, though. Doesn't stop me from hoping it's true.

But that's ridiculous, right?

Me? The permanent bachelor, dating not one, but two people. Declan Everhart and Melina Rodriguez. It's too fucking good to be true.

And yet when we walk out of the tunnel after interviews are over, they're both waiting for me. Lennox is there too. When she sees Aiden, she takes off and jumps into his arms.

Mel is worrying her lip, shifting from foot to foot as I make my way over. Declan is, unsurprisingly, wearing an expression I can't read. It's one I've never seen before. He doesn't look angry, but his mouth is turned down. He tracks my every move, my every breath, his look growing more intense the closer I get. Until I'm right there, a step away from them, and Mel is launching herself into my arms and squeezing me tight.

"I missed you," she breathes.

Fuck, she feels good. I wrap my arm around her, burying my nose in her neck and inhaling.

Declan is still silent, still wearing that unreadable expression.

"I heard there'd be groveling." I pull Mel into my side and meet Declan's brown eyes.

He rears back in surprise and coughs out a laugh. "You want me to grovel here?" Swallowing audibly, he scans the space where my coworkers and hockey players and their spouses and children, some of whom are part of his extended family, are mingling.

Mel digs her fingers into my hip and squeezes. "Don't tease him. He's got a plan."

I drag my attention back to her. Fuck, she's pretty.

Her green eyes swim with delight. "It's a really good plan," she adds.

Declan clears his throat, garnering our attention. "I could grovel here." He rolls his shoulders back and moves closer, like he's working up the courage to do whatever he was going to do in private, right here, right now.

I hold my breath and then let it out in one big whoosh.

Before either of us can speak, Gavin appears with his daughter in his arms and his wife by his side. "Great game tonight, Fitz." He nods. "Dec, Mel, glad you could make it." He holds out his hand to Declan. "You coming to Beckett's tomorrow for Christmas Eve?"

With a nod, Dec shakes his hand. "Yeah, I'll be there."

"Great." Gavin hikes Vivi up a little higher. "Have a good holiday, Fitz. See you next week."

Millie gives Mel a quick hug, and then the little family is gone.

Heart thumping, I turn back to Declan. "Not here." I don't want to share this moment with anyone but the two of them. "My place."

Declan's lips tilt up, and his eyes brighten a little. That small response speaks volumes. Knowing I've pleased him is enough to send a spark of excitement through me.

With my arm around Mel and with Declan by my side, I usher them to the garage where the players and coaching staff park. It isn't until Dec steps in front of me to open Mel's door that I catch sight of the back of his Bolts jersey.

The sight of *Fitz* emblazoned on the Bolts blue fabric takes my goddamn breath away. Swallowing hard, I angle back without letting Mel go. Sure enough, hers says Fitz too. But they're wearing different numbers. On her back, under my name, is a 1. Declan's sporting the number 5. I shake my head, lips pursed, confused.

"That's another part of his grovel," Mel whispers.

Declan's watching me, holding his breath. Like he's waiting for me to put the pieces together. After a solid thirty seconds, he pulls Mel to his side, and they turn their backs to me.

It hits me then, like a punch to the solar plexus.

"Get it now?" he mumbles, turning back, hiding the number 15. Fifteen. My number through high school and college.

I still don't quite get it, though. Why didn't they put 15 on each of their backs?

Declan, obviously sensing my confusion, takes Mel's hand. "Separately, our jerseys were meaningless, right? But put us together, Cade, and we're perfect for you."

I rear back, so bowled over by the admission that I almost lose my balance. "That's really fucking good."

Mel breaks out in a bright smile. "I told you it was a really good grovel."

Declan steps closer and runs his thumb across my bottom lip. "Will you forgive me for taking so long?"

"It's only been a few days. I can't imagine you could have custom jerseys made and shipped overnight," I sputter. My mind is jumbled, and my heart gallops at his proximity.

Declan shakes his head. "That took a few days, but that's not what I mean."

I swallow. I know what he means. It took him a while to be ready for this. For us. Nose stinging, I pull in a breath to rein in my emotions and pull Mel in close. "Like you said, it's perfect like this. We wouldn't work if we weren't all together."

Mel bites her lip and blinks. "And that's what you want?"

I guess we are doing this in public. "Yes, Mel. You and Dec. If that's what the two of you want, then that's what I want."

Declan's relieved breath fans against my cheek as I kiss our girlfriend. When I pull back, he's watching me, his focus intent. Then, jaw working, he scans our surroundings. Guys are still trickling out to their cars, hollering *goodbye* and *merry Christmas* to one another.

Despite my concerns about how he's handled things, I don't need him to do this here. It doesn't need to be public to count.

Before I can tell him that, he cups my face, his thumb pulling on my lips.

"Fuck it," he mumbles. Then he's pressing his lips to mine.

For an instant, I'm stunned, rigid. But his warm lips and rough calluses brushing against my jaw soothe me, and I kiss him back.

Between us, Mel squeals.

I melt against her, craving Declan's firm embrace. These two, this moment, are everything.

He pulls away, but not before sinking his teeth into my lip and tugging. "Take us home."

Love On

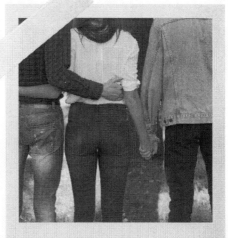

CHAPTER 48

Melina

THE RIDE to Cade's apartment is quiet, but it's comfortable. There's so much to say, but after five days apart, it's incredible to be this unit of three again. To soak in every detail of one another. The guys are in the front, and I'm in the back, taking in the city as it flies by. It's charming, though now that I've been to Bristol, there's no doubt that small towns are more my vibe.

"Hungry?" Cade asks, his blue eyes meeting mine in the rearview mirror.

Declan chuckles from the front seat.

The sound instantly warms my chest, and it brings a smile to Cade's face. Our stoic guy doesn't laugh much, so pulling one from him is a rare feat.

"She tried just about every item in the suite," Declan explains, peering over his shoulder at me. "I thought I might have to roll her out of there."

"Listen—" I swat at him playfully. "Beckett said the sausages at the arena couldn't compare to the ones at Lang Field, so I had to try them."

Declan drops his chin and shakes his head. "That man is such an idiot."

Cade's laugh is light. "Eh, he's not so bad." With another glance in the rearview mirror, he lifts his brows. "So were they?"

I shrug. "Never tried the ones at Lang Field, so I can't really say. But I told him the arena's were better."

Declan folds his arms over his chest proudly. "That's my girl."

Cade barks out a laugh. "How did he react?"

"Told me I have to try them one after the other before I can make that decision. Then he disappeared with his phone to his ear, working to make it happen."

I smile the whole way to Cade's building, though a thread of trepidation worms its way through me. I've never been to his apartment, but that alone doesn't worry me. No, I can't stop thinking about what to expect now that things are more out in the open between us.

It's been a week since I've had them. Declan didn't even try to touch me while Cade was gone. Not after how they left things. So I'm ravenous, but it's not for food. I'm hungry for their hands, for their attention, and I'm salivating at the thought of watching the two of them together.

But sex isn't always the answer, regardless of how incredible it is with them.

"Could we walk for a bit?" Declan asks when we get out of the car. He helped me out of the back seat and kept hold of my hand, but his attention is fixed on Cade. "I've always loved this area at Christmas."

Cade nods and stuffs his hands into his pockets.

With a grunt, Declan squeezes my hand. "That all right with you, sweetheart? You warm enough."

I reach for Cade, who pulls his hands back out of his pockets and yanks me into his side. Then I squeeze Declan's palm. "I've got my two guys to keep me warm. Of course I'm good."

The warmth in his brown eyes melts me. With a kiss to my forehead, he takes off, and the two of them guide me down the street. It's late, after ten, but the sidewalks are busy. Couples walk by, bundled up and cozy, holding hands, and groups of friends chatter loudly, likely heading home after a night of drinking.

The crisp air is renewing, the bright lights warming.

We stumble upon Quincy Market, where shops and restaurants

line the cobblestone street. A content sigh escapes me as we pass under a string of twinkling lights. The strands are attached to the buildings on either side and crisscross above our heads, creating a sparkling ceiling. As music filters through the air, I can't help but hum along. For the first time this season, I'm hit with just a hint of Christmas spirit.

"This reminds me of the festival my family goes to at home."

Declan stops walking, his hand still gripping mine. "Is that a good thing?"

I turn back, bringing Cade with me, and smile up at him. This stoic man cares so deeply about his loved ones. "It's a great thing." For a moment, I watch a man playing the saxophone nearby, taking a moment to enjoy it before admitting the truth to even myself. "But I doubt it will ever feel like home again."

Cade loops an arm around my waist, frowning. "I hate that."

I shrug. "Even if I was able to forgive them, they'll never understand this." I point at both men, then myself.

If I thought Declan was stiff before, it's nothing compared to how he goes rigid now.

I immediately reassure him. "They don't need to understand it, though. Because the two of you make me happy."

Cade drops a kiss to the crown of my head. "I happen to know my mother loves you. Dec's too."

"I love them both too." My stomach knots a little, though, as I prepare to ask a question I'm not sure I want to know the answer to. "But aren't you worried that they won't accept us?"

Cade laughs. "Please, our mothers have been hoping we'd settle down for decades. They'll be thrilled."

Declan's demeanor is much more reserved. He scratches his chin. "Not sure they expected us to settle down together."

The smile that splits Cade's face is so big it makes him squint. "No. I think you surprised all of us with that."

Without a thought of how the three of us might look to passersby, Declan steps closer and splays a rough hand over Cade's cheek. He cups mine with his other hand and gently strokes us both. "The two of you surprised the hell out of me too. I'm sorry I didn't handle it well. Sorry I didn't express myself better." He sighs. He's clearly still beating himself up.

But I certainly understand that coming to terms with who he is and who he loves didn't come easy. That when the world is sure to judge us, it would obviously make it less than easy to be honest about how he was feeling.

Communicating can be a challenge, even when a person's only concern is whether someone feels the same. Throw in fear of judgment and ridicule, and the challenge multiplies. It took incredible courage for Declan to come to terms with all that he has in such a short period of time. I'm proud of him.

"You owe me no apologies," I tell him, cupping my hand over his. "And in case I haven't said it today, I love you, and I'm proud to be yours."

Lips curving into a delicious smile, he dips down and kisses me. When he pulls away, he turns to Cade, his hand still on his cheek. "And you. Can you forgive me for getting it so wrong?"

"I forgave you when you texted me."

Declan scowls. "What?"

Cade's easy smile falls into place. "You never text anyone but Mel and Liv. It took a lot for you to send that message."

"That's ridiculous." Declan huffs.

"What is?" Cade frowns, looking from Declan to me.

"That your standards are so low," Declan grits out. "Baby, you need to demand more from me. You deserve more."

Cade chuckles, but Declan's expression remains serious.

"Well," Cade says, "you did mention groveling."

Declan steps up to him and murmurs against his lips. "I'm going to grovel so good." The kiss he lays on Cade is completely different from the one he shared with me. Where ours was sweet, theirs is aggressive. Nips and growls, tongue and teeth.

Cade's fingers dig into my sides as he pulls away, panting.

"Okay, you need to take me home before I start stripping right here," I tease, my breaths coming quicker now too.

With a laugh—that rare, beautiful laugh—Declan drapes an arm over me and turns. "For what it's worth," he says, guiding us back toward Cade's building, "I have no idea how my family is going to react either."

From my other side, Cade replies, "I think you'll be pleasantly surprised. Liv is your biggest fan—besides us, of course—and the Langfields are the least judgmental people I know."

Declan lifts his chin and assesses Cade over the top of my head. "Beckett is the most annoying person I know, but the rest of them are fine, I guess."

Despite the goose bumps over every inch of my body, Declan's humor has a way of warming me from the inside out. He's so serious, so gruff, and that makes moments like this so special.

Declan scans the buildings as we pass, so his face is turned away when he says, "I guess we'll find out tomorrow."

Cade and I blink at each other before we turn in unison to Declan.

"What's tomorrow?" I ask.

"Oh," Cade says, "the whole family goes to Beckett's for Christmas Eve." He doesn't elaborate, as if that should make sense to me, before he lifts his chin, eyeing Declan again. "And you want us to be there?"

With a sigh, Declan drops his head back. "Do I have to *say* everything?"

I laugh. "Yes, Declan. Use your words."

He huffs, his breath clouding in front of him. "Fine. I'd really like it if my boyfriend and my girlfriend would spend Christmas Eve with me and my family. Does that work?"

Stopping in the middle of the sidewalk, I cup his face and rub my thumb against his lip like he always does to me. "Yeah, Chief. That works."

"You two go get in the shower. I'll get things ready," Declan says the moment the door is shut behind us.

A thrill zips up my spine. He's as anxious to be together as I am, and

I'm 100 percent on board with his command. We can play it slow another night.

It's ridiculous how much it turns me on to see him so comfortable taking the lead even in Cade's space. I shouldn't be surprised. This is our dynamic. It feels like we're all settling into who we were meant to be. With one another and on our own.

"You don't want to join us?" Cade asks, though he's already tugging me toward his bedroom.

"Just tell me where the lube and toys are, baby. I'll meet you in there once I've got everything set up."

With a shake of his head, Cade chuckles. "You just assume I've got it all."

Declan strides across the room and cuffs his neck. "You're my filthy boy," he says, bringing their faces close together. "Of course you do."

Cade's breath hitches. "Top drawer. Left-hand side."

With an arch of a brow, Declan drops a quick kiss to his lips. Then he gently pushes us toward the bedroom.

Cade's apartment is sterile in comparison to Declan's home. No wonder he spends his free weekends in Bristol. Though I'm sure Declan has more to do with that than how empty this place feels.

Cade's shower isn't quite as big as Declan's, but there will still be plenty of space. Once he's got the water going, he turns, his eyes warm as he studies me. "How are you feeling?"

My heart flips at the genuine affection in his tone. "I'm good. Really, really good."

With a hand on my cheek, he pulls me in for a long kiss. It's sweet, like coming home. "You know how much I missed you?" he murmurs, his lips brushing against mine.

"If it's anything close to how much I missed you, then it had to be a whole lot."

He smiles that easy smile of his, one dimple popping. "Oh yeah?"

"Yeah," I murmur, nuzzling into his neck.

"Do you know that I love you?" His words are so soft, I almost miss them.

Butterflies swarm my belly as his truth registers, their wings fluttering so violently I think they could carry me away. "I love you too."

His eyes light up. "Yeah?"

"Yes, Cade. I'm in love with you."

"I still can't believe you're both here." He nips at my lip, his tone light. "Can't believe we're doing this. You're the first person I've ever said that to, ya know? That I love you."

Chest to chest, I tip my head back and study his face. "Really?"

He nods, eyes never leaving mine.

"But I'm not the first person you've ever loved."

He averts his gaze, one side of his lips ticking up in a shy smile, and shakes his head. "No, I suppose that's true. Though the feeling is different now."

"It is different." I lace my hands behind his neck. "You shouldn't be afraid to tell him, though. He loves you too."

Cade looks away, his breath stuttering. "Isn't it too soon?"

"To tell the man you've always loved how you feel about him? Was it too soon for us?"

"Fuck no," he says on a laugh.

I tilt my head, waiting for him to really look at me. "Then why would it be for him?"

He rubs a thumb gently over my cheek. "I don't want to rush him."

"He kissed you in front of your team. He's taking you to family Christmas tomorrow." I give him a sharp look. "He loves you."

With his forehead pressed to mine, he closes his eyes. "Maybe."

Before I can rebut, his lips are on mine again. It's the kind of kiss a person can get lost in. One of those that begins softly but then grows until waves of heat emanate between us.

We're groping one another, moaning, nipping, and licking, when Declan's voice startles us apart.

"Why are you two still dressed?"

With my lip caught between my teeth, I smile up at the bossy man I'm so in love with. "We didn't want to start without you."

Declan grunts. "Seems like you were doing just that."

Steam billows around us, and the mirror is nothing but a white fog.

Cade spins me toward Declan and grasps the bottom of my jersey. "Maybe I just wasn't ready to peel her out of this."

Declan smirks, lifting his chin. "The jersey was a nice touch, huh?"

Cade ducks down and laughs into my neck. "It was perfect."

Declan crowds us. He's so close that all I can see is his matching blue jersey. With one hand on my hip, he uses the other to pull Cade's mouth off my neck and toward his own. They're kissing with me sandwiched between them again. Fuck. Being in the middle of their embrace, with Declan's heat at my front and Cade's at my back, has me squirming, losing my mind with lust.

Declan pulls back with a curse, his focus lowering to me. "Sorry, sweetheart."

"Never apologize for going after what you want." I pat his chest. "It's incredibly hot."

There's that delicious smirk again. "Good. Right now, what I want is you naked and in the shower."

I point at Cade, arching a brow. "First I want to watch him take off your jersey."

"I like the way she thinks," Cade grumbles. He grasps my sides and lifts me onto the bathroom counter. "Think you can be a good girl and sit here for a minute?"

I nod as warmth pools between my thighs. I'm so fucking wet, the idea of a shower is comical.

Cade spins around and takes a step toward Declan. "I swear you've never looked better than you do in my jersey."

"I'll wear it again when you fuck me one day, but right now, I need us both naked."

Holy shit. Cade's jaw drops, and mine does too. The ease with which Declan mentioned being fucked by his best friend? The heat simmering low in my belly kicks up a notch. That scenario just jumped to the top of my list of fantasies. If I have my way, it's something we'll experience soon and often. I've got a lifetime to have it all. Them. Us. It's what dreams are made of.

Cade runs a hand through his blond hair. "I gotta fuck you because your cock's too big for me to take?"

Declan shakes his head. "You'll take my cock just fine. I was made for you."

Cade undoes his best friend's belt, the metal clanking, then moves on to his zipper. As he tears his pants down his legs, he takes his boxers with them. The shirt is next. Cade is so tall that he tugs the jersey over his head with ease. As it flutters to the floor, Declan fists his thick cock, and my mouth waters at the sight. I'm tempted to hop off this counter and drag him to the ground so I can ride him here.

Amused brown eyes find mine. "Like what you see, sweetheart?" He strokes his shaft, moving down, then back up, flicking his wrist at the tip.

I squirm on the counter.

"I'm not enough for her on my own, though." He's talking to Cade, though he's got me locked in his gaze. Taunting me.

Cade chuckles. "Nope, our girl needs two cocks. Isn't that right, Trouble?"

He shucks his Oxford and dress pants quickly. Then, facing Declan, he strokes himself, mirroring his best friend's movements.

"She may need two cocks, but you only get one. Right, baby?" Despite Declan's hard tone, there's a layer of vulnerability just beneath the surface of the question. He needs reassurance that he's enough. That *we'll* be enough.

"Damn right." Cade bats Declan's hand away from his own cock and strokes him.

My stoic grump of a man lifts his chin, his neck muscles straining, and grunts. Cade pulls him closer, jacking them both simultaneously.

"Fuck, that feels good." Declan stretches an arm out to me. "I need your lips, sweetheart."

I scramble off the counter and fall into his arms. His chest heaves as he slips his tongue into my mouth. We only stay like this for a moment before he pulls away and pushes Cade toward the shower. "I need you both now."

As Cade steps beneath the stream of water, Declan turns and tugs my jersey over my head.

"I love you," I remind him.

With a smile, he pushes my hair behind my ear. "I love you so much."

Once I'm naked, he carries me into the shower, where both men take their time washing every inch of my body. It's decadent and beautiful, being with these men. *My men.*

The air, already heavy with moisture, thickens as we dry off quietly. The three of us have been together more than once. But that felt like fooling around. Like sex.

Tonight, our emotions are running high, and there are still unspoken confessions hanging between us. This is so much more than anything I've ever experienced.

Several toys are set up on Cade's nightstand. As I peruse them, I squirm, wondering which are for me and which are for Cade.

"Lie down on your stomach, baby," Declan says.

With a kiss to my mouth, Cade obeys, draping himself over the towel Declan laid out on the bed.

The man in charge tonight eyes me, one brow lifted. "You going to help me prep him?"

And I'm done for. For a man who's never fucked another man, he sure is taking to this quickly, and I am here for it.

I bite my lip, excited at the prospect. Thrilled that I get to be here for this. It's an honor to experience this first with them.

Declan rounds the bed and picks up a bottle of lube and a silicone anal plug. He coats the plug, then drizzles a healthy amount of lube between Cade's cheeks.

With one hand fisted on the mattress, he looms over Cade and whispers in his ear. Cade nods in response, then Declan slowly begins to work the plug into his ass.

Cade grunts, but he follows the sound with a "green." He's handling the sensation just as well as I did. Although when Declan did this to me, he ate me out until I was so wet, I didn't know what was happening. Feeling like Cade's been cheated, I step forward, taking control for once.

"My turn," I say. "Cade has forgiven you, and so have I, but you promised you'd grovel."

Declan arches a brow. "And what is it you'd like me to do for you, sweetheart?"

"Lie down."

Declan can't hide his smile in response to my bossy tone. He settles on his back next to Cade and laces his fingers behind his head as he waits for my next instruction.

"I didn't get to see the way Cade fucked your throat last week. I want to watch it while I ride you."

Declan's chuckle is dark. "Sweetheart, you and Cade are terrible at demanding apologies. It would be my fucking pleasure."

Cade props himself up on an elbow and kisses him. "Maybe we just like to see you happy."

Cupping Cade's neck, Declan gazes at him lovingly. "Then give me your cock."

Eagerly, Cade shifts into position on his knees. The way Declan licks his lips as he takes in the sight has heat racing up my spine.

"Don't go easy on him," I tell Cade as he feeds his length into his mouth. Fuck, I want to watch every second. See just how much they want one another.

I climb on top of Declan and slide up and down over his dick, coating him with my arousal. A moan slips out as I use him like a toy, rolling my clit until I'm edging us both beyond reason.

"Color?" I tease as I sink onto his length.

Cade has a firm grip on Declan's head and his dick shoved so far down his throat there's no way he can answer. "He's fucking green. Don't you worry."

Declan smiles around Cade and takes him impossibly deep.

"Stay that way. No one comes until I say so," I remind them.

He swells inside me, clearly liking this game.

Still fucking Declan's mouth, Cade leans forward and kisses me, sharing ragged breaths and tangling his tongue with mine.

"Fuck. Yellow," he groans after a moment, reeling back and pulling his cock out of Declan's mouth. Glaring at his best friend, he practically strangles his erection in his fist. "What the hell were you doing with your tongue?"

"Like that, baby?" Declan taunts.

With a deep breath in, Cade shakes his head, but then he's smiling. "Okay, green." He slips between Declan's lips again, this time moving slower, sliding himself in and out until he's once again pulling back. I can barely focus on my own orgasm when I watch them. They're so fucking beautiful like this.

Declan is thrusting up. Little teasing movements that have me grinding down in need of more. "Holy shit," he groans. "I need to fuck."

I peer up at Cade, scrutinizing his expression. Is he ready for this? He's focused on the two of us, just as lost in us as I was in him and Declan.

The hunger in his eyes is all the answer I need. I know what he wants. What the two of them need. And I intend to give it to them. Pressing my breasts against Declan's chest, I bring my mouth to his ear. "He's ready for you."

He stills beneath me and darts a look at his best friend. Above him, Cade worries his bottom lip. But he nods, his focus never leaving Declan's face.

"Thank fuck." Declan pulls me in for a deep kiss, then rolls so that I'm beneath him. He fucks into me, hitting me in a way that has my muscles spasming, before he pulls out. "I want to see you when I—" His voice catches.

With a grin, Cade nods. He understands what Declan wants, and he knows how to give it to him. He grabs a pillow from the head of the bed and settles himself on top of it, canting his hips just a bit. Then he holds out his arms and waves me to him. "C'mere, Trouble. You're going to ride me while Declan fucks me."

"Holy shit," Declan and I say in unison.

Cade grabs my leg and pulls me on top, not giving any of us a moment to overthink it. Then he slides himself inside me and pulls me close.

"I love you," I whisper, my body shuddering. Pressing a hand to Cade's chest, I arch back and peer at Declan, holding out a hand. "And I love you."

Declan, who's wearing his patented unreadable expression, visibly relaxes as he slips his hand into mine. "I love you so much, Melina. We wouldn't be here without you. We wouldn't be us without you." With his other hand, he squeezes Cade's thigh. "And I love you," he says to the man beneath me. "I love you so fucking much. I'm so sorry it took me so long to get here, but I'm damn happy to call you both mine."

Cade's heart beats rapidly beneath my palm, his eyes wide and his lips parted. "I love you too."

"Lean forward, sweetheart." Declan pushes gently between my shoulder blades until my breasts are pressed to Cade's chest. "I'll go as slow as I can," he adds. For a moment, he's quiet, working the plug out. Then there's a click—the cap to the lube bottle, I assume.

Cade is breathing through his teeth. Maybe in apprehension over Declan's big dick, or maybe he's still in shock after his best friend's declaration.

I strum my fingers across the side of his face. "You okay?"

He nods, the tension in his body melting. "He loves me," he whispers.

"Told you," I mumble.

With a smile so big both dimples pop, he pulls my mouth to his. As he swipes his tongue against mine, he groans.

Behind me, Declan shifts forward, working himself inside him.

"Holy fuck," he mutters. "You feel—"

"Perfect," I supply. "He feels absolutely perfect."

Everything about this moment is perfect. Because the three of us are joined. We're one, and these two deliciously wonderful men are all mine.

CHAPTER 49

Cade

FOR A MOMENT, I feel like I may actually black out. Like this entire night has been nothing but a crazy dream. These last few weeks, really. Because it can't be real—the woman of my dreams grinding on me like this while the man I've been in love with for more than half my life is burrowing inside me like he never wants to leave, like if he was given a choice between breathing or never feeling the inside of me again, he'd stay right where he was.

Declan's face as he finally works his huge cock into my ass, the pleasure that tinges his cheeks pink, that pulls a "fuck" from his lips and another heavy breath as he tries like hell to get used to this new sensation, is nothing short of beautiful. And despite the fact that he's filling me in a way I've never experienced—because like Mel and I lament constantly, the man is huge—I refuse to so much as blink for fear of missing a second of it.

"That feel okay, baby?" he asks in that soft rumble that makes my toes tingle. He's such a gruff man—one of so few words—so when he uses them, especially in that tone that is apparently reserved for only the ones he truly loves—I fucking melt.

"Nothing, and I mean nothing, has ever felt better than my girl on my cock and my man in my ass," I tease, trying to bring some levity to the moment.

If I don't—if I think about all we've gone through to get here—I may sob.

Every nerve ending in my body feels like a live wire, flying free and sparking each time one of them moves. Declan leans his forehead against Mel's back and sucks in a heavy breath. "Give me a color, sweetheart."

With her eyes on mine, she mumbles, "Green."

"What do you say we get him to yellow?" I grit out.

She leans down and presses her lips to mine. "That's your job tonight. Squeeze those cheeks. Give him a taste of his own medicine."

Declan groans, but I think he knows there's no way in hell I'm in control tonight. Especially when he finally moves, one of his hands landing on Mel's hip while the other grips mine. When he begins sliding out, it hits me that there's no way I'll be able to speak, let alone taunt him. Then when he slams back in, it's the greatest feeling I've ever experienced. That is, until I feel the hot gush that comes from Mel as she clenches around me. "Oh shit. You fucked up into me when he fucked you." Her eyes are wild, and they only grow more so as Declan fucks us both with abandon, using my cock and his own to pleasure us. It's insane how good he is at this. The way he knows what we both need. But it's not long before our girl is crying out, her pussy pulsing around me, and I'm seeing stars and panting "yellow. So fucking yellow."

Declan stops all movement, and I know what's coming before he speaks. "Hold it, baby. I want you to stay right there on the edge. Can you do that for me?"

Sweat coats my forehead, and a full-body shiver rolls down my spine as the aftershocks of Mel's orgasm pulse across my already sensitive dick. But I suck in buckets full of air until I'm able to nod.

Mel collapses on my chest, and I rub a hand over her back, soothing her through the intense emotions we're all feeling.

"What are you thinking?" I ask Dec over her shoulder.

He leans down and peppers kisses to her back, then meets my eye. "I want you to fuck me."

All the air in the room evaporates then, and I grow dizzy. Is there such a thing as too happy? As too perfect? Because having him suck my dick and then sink inside me has been a dream come true. But fucking him? Holy shit...

"Oh, I like that idea," Mel murmurs, even as her voice sounds sleepy.

"After Mel comes again," I say.

Chuckling, Declan leans over her and kisses me. The moment is filthy, full of tongues and teeth and dirty words. "I love that you love to make her come as much as I do."

Fuck, do I.

"Trouble, can I eat your pussy while Declan fucks me for a little longer?"

Mel practically scrambles off me. "Only if I can face forward and watch."

For a moment, Dec catches my eye, and when he thrusts up into me, I lose myself.

"This doesn't feel real," I whisper.

Declan leans forward, and with his chest to mine, I can feel the unsteady pounding of his heart. "It's real, baby. And it's forever. You, me, and Mel. This is it."

Mel is cuddled up next to me, her head kissing my own. She looks sated and happy and oh so in love. Without hesitating, I kiss her, getting lost when she whimpers in surprise. When we pull apart, Dec is watching us, expression hungry and full of lust, just like the first time he watched us kiss.

"Holy shit." I huff out a breath.

Dec gives me that dangerous smirk of his. The kind that makes me do crazy things like throw my heart at him for years when he barely blinked in my direction. He grinds up into me, and my cock pulses as he rolls his body against it. "If you want me to fuck you, you're going to have to give our girl her orgasm. I'm never going to last with your dick working its magic like it is right now."

Declan takes my mouth in a rough kiss. "Come, baby. We can clean up and go again. Let me see you come with my cock in your ass. Show me how good I make you feel."

Mel leans in and kisses my neck. Then she reaches between us and rolls gentle fingers against my weeping cock, squeezing and then fisting it, working me until I'm delirious.

We stare down at where our bodies are joined. The place where Declan fucks me ferociously. Like he's been doing it for years. Like this is how we were always meant to be. And with her hand wrapped around me and him deep inside me, I unravel completely.

"That's it, baby," Dec says as his thrusts grow slower, as if he's relishing the final moments of being inside me before he cries out. "Holy fuck, give me your mouth."

I obey, and then he kisses me while he pulses wickedly inside me, filling me with his hot cum.

Panting, he pulls back and takes Mel's mouth, murmuring *thank yous* and *I love yous* and reminding her that she's our everything. It's beautiful, despite our mess, because, like Dec said, we'll just clean up and start all over again.

Magic

CHAPTER 50

Declan

"YOU NERVOUS?" Melina asks as the three of us climb the porch steps of my sister's brownstone.

Last night, when Cade and Melina agreed to join me for Christmas Eve, I thought my heart might burst. Tomorrow, we'll have Christmas dinner at Cade's mom's house. She'll be here tonight, too. My mom didn't want her to be alone, and the Langfields are always happy to include the people we care about.

While I'm nervous about how my family will react to the three of us, I think Cade was probably right when he said to give them more credit. My sisters-in-laws are some of the most open-minded people I know. Though I am nervous about how my sister and her kids will react. They've never seen me with a significant other, let alone two.

Honestly, Cade could have asked for anything last night, and I would have given it to him. Likely still would. I'm head-over-heels in love with him and Mel, and the fact that he forgave me and gave us another chance is not something I take lightly. I'm deliciously sore, and I know they are too. I had no idea what I was missing all these years, but apparently, I really like ass play, and more than anything, I really love fucking Melina and looking down into her eyes while Cade fucks me.

Giving up control, allowing them to care for me, to know what I need, is indescribable.

But I also really fucking loved fucking Cade too.

And when he plays with my prostate? Yeah, I really fucking like that.

Truth be told, I just love the two of them. Doesn't matter whether we're having sex, just lying in bed together, or doing everyday things, like walking into my pain-in-the-ass brother-in-law's house like we are now. It's all better because I'm with them.

"It'll be fine," Cade says from my other side.

Shrugging, I step up to the door.

Before I can knock, it swings open, and an oversized dog rushes past us.

"Deogi!" Beckett shouts as he flies down the steps and chases after the dog.

I guide Melina and Cade inside with a roll of my eyes. "Pain in the ass."

Cade nudges me. "Watch out, or Finn will get ya with the swear jar."

I run a hand over my face. Yeah, I can't afford that. Unlike the guys here, I don't make millions playing hockey or coaching the sport, and I don't perform for sold-out stadiums. And unlike my idiot brother-in-law, who's guiding the pony-sized dog back into the house, I don't make millions by simply existing.

"Sorry about that," Beckett says as he waves us into the living room. "Make yourselves comfortable. I'll take your coats and put Deogi in the kitchen."

"Did he just call his dog D-O-G?" Melina whispers, eyes wide. She's probably regretting dating me already.

As Beckett disappears with our coats and his pony-dog, I roll my eyes at him and grip Mel tighter. Less chance she can leave me. "Try to remember that you love me today."

My girl giggles beside me, while Cade shakes his head, hiding his chuckle in his shoulder.

Beckett may drive me nuts, but a warmth settles over me as I step into the room and spot my sister with one of her twins in her arms. He did that. He gave her this. A beautiful home. Twin daughters. A safe place for her and for her other children when their own father was nothing but a disappointment. For all the shit I give the man, Beckett Langfield is a good one. He didn't hesitate when I asked for help after Melina was attacked. Not only with the police and the assault footage, but with the around-the-clock detail he had on Jason.

That's the reason I know that the asshole remains in a coma today. All is right in the world.

Beside my sister, Brooks Langfield's fiancée holds the other twin. Both women are laughing at Gavin as he yammers on, swinging his arms wildly.

"Must be talking about Aiden," Cade says to Melina.

Her smile is bright as she surveys the room. Yeah, I think this was a great idea. Seeing Melina happy, seeing her relaxed and glowing, makes all my apprehension worth it.

"Uncle Dec!" Finn flies down the steps and rushes me. Before he can bowl Melina over, I grab him and pull him into a hug.

"Jeez, what has Beckett been feeding you? You're getting huge."

Behind me, Beckett barks out a laugh.

"Who are you?" Finn asks Melina, his head tilted as he stares her down.

I eye Cade and set Finn back on the ground. My sister is headed our way, and my mother is talking to Cade's mom and Beckett's. When she spots me, she excuses herself and shuffles over.

"Guess now is as good of a time as any." I look from Cade to Melina.

Both are wearing calm expressions, while I'm sweating like I'm decked out in my turnout gear and headed into an inferno. I take Melina's hand and drape an arm around her shoulders. "This is Melina, my girlfriend."

My sister's jaw drops. *Okay.* Guess I was wrong about how obvious the three of us are. Apparently walking in with Cade and Melina and the palpable tension that exists between us wasn't enough of a sign. Looks like I'm actually going to have to spell this out. Like always.

Swallowing past the boulder in my throat, I scan the sea of people watching me and point to Cade. "And Cade is my—" I eye my sister. Fuck. Will she be upset that I'm telling her kid about this?

She gives me a sweet smile and nods, easing a fraction of my fears.

"Cade is my boyfriend."

I hold my breath, spine rigid, while I wait for the fallout.

Finn is the first to speak. "So should I call him Uncle Cade and her Auntie Melina like I do with Auntie Sar, Auntie Lex, Auntie Millie, and all the moms?"

I side-eye Cade, my heart stopping. Shit. Will he freak out at the insinuation of marriage? I'm pretty sure we're his first relationship ever.

To my absolute fucking relief, he's just shaking his head and fighting a laugh, one brow cocked like he's enjoying watching me squirm.

Beckett squeezes Finn's shoulder. "Wouldn't that be exciting? More people to love, Huck."

I try not to let my mouth fall open in shock, but I can't hide the way his genuine tone makes my eyes bulge.

Finn nods. "Yeah, and he's a hockey coach like Uncle Gav."

Cade grins. "Sure am. I'm in charge of your Uncle Brooks."

Over near the bar setup, Brooks laughs. "I'm not sure that's how I'd put it."

Sara nudges him. "Right. That's me." She grins at Cade. "But you can be second-in-command."

Melina bats her eyes at Cade. "Don't worry, you can be in charge of me any day of the week."

The room erupts with laughter, but Finn frowns. "So is that a yes?"

I pull Melina's hand up to my lips and kiss it. "That's a yes."

"You know," Beckett starts, "some would say this is my best match yet."

"Oh god," Gavin groans, dragging a hand down his face.

"Please stop," Liv begs as she bounces the baby in her arms.

Beckett scoffs. "What? I'm an even better matchmaker than I thought. I only meant to set him up with one person, and I got two people to fall in love with your grumpy brother."

"Hey," I growl.

Beside me, Cade chuckles and pokes my ribs with an elbow.

I turn my glare on him. "I'm not grumpy."

"Oh, you are, Dec," my sister says. "But we all love you anyway."

Melina pops up on her toes and kisses my cheek. "We really do."

CHAPTER 51

Cade

"NOT GOING TO LIE, Fitz. I didn't see this coming," Brooks mumbles. We're seated by the fire. Beckett, Liv, and Declan disappeared into the kitchen with our moms a few minutes ago, and Mel is busy talking music with Millie. The rest of us are hanging out in the living room, drinks in hand, relaxing.

Sara giggles. "Lennox called it."

The pink-haired beauty shimmies her shoulders. "What can I say? It's my special power."

"Not even I expected it, so I'd say you've got a real talent." I actually can't believe I'm sitting here right now with my guys and their significant others, discussing my relationship status. Never in a million years did I see things turning out the way they have. Declan and Mel telling me they love me last night is a fucking dream come true. A dream I never want to wake up from.

"You're happy, though?" Brooks prods.

I grin. I can't help it. Whenever I think of the two people who have stolen my heart, I can do nothing but smile. "I'm living my literal dream." I catch Mel's attention across the room, and my heart sputters. "Love you," I mouth.

She bites her lip, catching her smile between her teeth.

Today feels easy. I'm not surprised, if I'm honest. The guys in this room—and the women who have stolen their hearts—are some of the best people I've ever known. Judgment isn't something that concerned me when it came to them. But I know life won't always be like this. That we'll encounter people who won't understand how it's possible to have two soulmates. Who will not only find our love improbable, but will be ugly toward us because of it. I know that's why Declan struggled with coming to terms with it as well. I'll do my damndest to protect him, and her, from the ugly. I'll remember these moments, seated with my best friends, my girl within view, my boyfriend close by.

"I'm going to see if they need help in the kitchen," I say, standing, itching to get my eyes on Declan.

From beside me, Gavin chuckles. He's got a squirming Vivi in his arms. She's dying to get down and run around with all her cousins. "Can never be close enough, right?"

He says it knowingly, his eyes drifting to Millie. I always thought it was a little over the top, how his gaze never strayed too far from his wife. Now I get it. If they're within reach, I want to be near them. If they're a phone call away, I want to be on that phone. For a man who never allowed himself to grow attached to anyone for fear of losing another important person, I'm all-in now. Gavin is on my heels as I pass Millie and Mel, dropping a kiss to Mel's neck, interrupting her conversation. "I'm going to see if I can help in the kitchen. Need anything before I disappear for a few?"

Mel spins in my arms, wrapping hers around my neck, and tips her face up. "Just a kiss."

I grant her wish, pressing my lips to hers. "You having a good time?"

Mel bites down on her plump lip. "The best."

I nuzzle into her neck and squeeze her tight. "Good. I'll be back." I nip her lips once more before leaving her with Millie and Gavin, who now has one arm around his wife as Vivi has catapulted herself into Millie's arms.

In the kitchen, I find Declan standing over Beckett. And I mean literally standing over him, arms folded across his chest, a haughty look on his face. "You ready to give up?"

Beckett is holding a cutting fork in one hand and an electric carving knife in the other, and when I round the island, I see he's got a turkey laid out in front of him. He revs the cutter and shakes his head. "I've got this."

"You have to cut it at an angle," Dec growls.

Beckett's jaw ticks, and he glares over his shoulder. "I said I've got this."

"Beckett," Liv says softly. "Why don't you let my brother cut the turkey? You can help me get the kids settled."

Declan's lips pull up in a sinister smile. "Yeah, Becks. Why don't you do that?"

I fail at holding in my snort. These two men are exactly the same person. Controlling assholes one minute, then throwing their heart around to make their loved ones happy in the next. There's literally not a thing either one of these guys wouldn't do for any of the people in this house. And yet they don't see how similar they are.

As soon as Liv sees me, she deflates in relief. *Help me,* she mouths.

"Actually," I say, finally making my presence known, "I need Dec for a second."

My boyfriend's eyes snare me. He's not happy that he's being dragged away from his dick-measuring contest with his favorite brother-in-law. When I hold out my hand, though, his eyes soften, and he sighs. "Make sure he cuts it at an angle," he grumbles before heading in my direction.

My mom intercepts me before he can make it to my side, and Declan stops short of taking my hand. "Ah, it's so good to see both my boys for Christmas," she says, taking my outstretched hand and then reaching for Dec's.

"I honestly never thought I'd see the day," Declan's mother says, joining us at the edge of the kitchen.

Dec's gaze bounces back toward where Beckett is carving the turkey. It's taking everything in him not to tell him he's doing it wrong. Or maybe he's just trying to avoid this conversation.

"We spend every Christmas with you," I remind them. Since before my dad died, actually. I don't remember a holiday without the Everharts.

"You know that's not what we mean," my mother chides with a smile.

I pull her into my chest and kiss her forehead. "Yeah, Ma, I know what you mean. But it's new, so let's not get ahead of ourselves."

Declan pulls his focus from the turkey and zeroes in on me, his brows pulled together and his lips turned down. For once, I can read every emotion on his face. He's not hiding anything.

And he's not happy that I told them not to get ahead of themselves.

I'm not even sure why I said it. I guess because this is all too perfect. It's hard not to hold my breath and wait for Declan to pull back. To pull away. To tell me he's not actually ready.

Instead, the man steps closer. "Get ahead of yourselves, because we're not going anywhere. Cade, Melina, and me. Enjoy it. I know I am."

"Oh, Declan," his mom says, grasping his upper arms and pulling him into her chest. "It's so good to see you so happy. So open."

My mother looks up at me, but I can't seem to look away from Declan. He's hugging his mother, a warmth about him that I've rarely seen. They talk in low voices, but I can tell it's all good things. That it's a healing moment for them both. That Declan's acceptance of who he is has also opened him up to love in general, to accepting it and showing it more freely.

Could it really be this easy? He's making it so easy. My heart practically sits in a puddle on the floor for him.

Conversation continues around us, and I watch, quietly enjoying this moment. When Liv tells us dinner's ready, I hang back, still kind of struck by the beauty that I just witnessed. I take a few beats and then head out, ready to enjoy dinner with my family. But I'm stopped by Declan's back. He's leaning against the wall, his gaze forward, blocking my path. I step up behind him, trying to figure out what he's looking at, when I realize that Mel is holding Vivi, feeding her with a bottle.

"She's beautiful, huh?" I murmur, dropping my chin to his shoulder.

Dec's breath comes out in a whoosh. "Most beautiful woman I've ever seen. I'm so in love with her."

I smile and give his hip a gentle squeeze. "Me too."

He spins in my arms and meets my gaze. "I'm so in love with you," he says softly, like he's being gentle with his admission, even though it's not the first time he's told me this. Though somehow, this seems like more. Like he's trying to say something else. "Is this too much for you?"

Now it's my turn to frown. "Why would this be too much? This is literally my dream, Dec. You have been my dream for longer than I can even say. And Mel? Hell, I feel like I'm walking around in a fog because I'm so damn happy."

Declan's lips pull up in a delicious grin. "Good. I just—" He reaches for my face, but before he makes contact, he stops, his hand hovering in the air. Like he's second-guessing the idea of kissing in front of our families.

I wish he would, though. I hate that it feels so easy to kiss Mel and not as simple to kiss Dec. "I wasn't sure how you felt about the long-term implications of what my mother said."

Ah, so that's what this is about. He thinks I'm going to run.

With one hand, I grip his hip, and with my other, I caress his cheek. And then I get closer. "I want all the long term. I want every holiday, every weekend, every moment I can get with you and Mel by my side. I want messy and imperfect. I want this." I press my lips to his, not giving him a moment to overthink it. Declan doesn't pull back. He doesn't take it further either. He just allows our lips to connect softly. And then he pulls back a bit, wearing a rare smile.

"What about marriage? And kids?" Dec asks, one brow arching in challenge.

I clutch his arms and spin him so we can both stare at our girl again. "What do you think, Dec? I think she'd look beautiful pregnant." I lean in close to his ear, adding in a whisper, "And you as a daddy? Sign me up."

CHAPTER 52

Melina

IT'S impossible to get a word in during dinner. The Langfield brothers are all loud. Their women are equally so. And there are more kids in this single room than I've been near in years. Yet sandwiched between Cade and Declan at the table, I don't feel even slightly invisible. Declan has his arm draped over the back of my chair, his fingers randomly teasing the ends of my hair. Cade holds my hand while he eats with his other. He jokes around with the guys and stays overly involved in the conversations, while Declan and I are more subdued.

I fit with these two in a way that I've never fit with anyone else.

Until the doorbell rings, and in walks my best friend with her little boy in her arms, and suddenly, she's the loudest person in the room. "Oh my god. I can't believe you're here!"

My smile is wide as her gaze swings from Declan to Cade back to Declan again, before her attention fully settles on me. "And you have been holding out on me, woman."

I laugh as I get up so I can hug her. "No, I haven't. I just didn't have anything to tell you this week."

While Declan worked on his plan to get Cade to forgive him, I spent my week working on music with Lake. I even recorded a few songs just before my deadline with the label.

"What are you guys doing here, though?"

As if answering my question, Ford makes a beeline for Millie, who's already getting up to welcome him, with Vivi in her arms. "Couldn't miss Vivi girl's first Christmas," he says as he reaches for his granddaughter. The one-year-old I got to spend some time with tonight is now all smiles as she grabs Ford's cheeks and pinches, then slobbers all over one in what some might call a kiss.

"We had a meeting at the label, and I wanted to see you before we left Boston," Ford says, turning his attention to me.

I swear that comment has the eyes of every person in the room turning in my direction.

Apprehension courses through me at the scrutiny. Enough to make it hard to breathe.

"What's he talking about?" Cade rumbles, stepping closer.

Declan, who's appeared at my side, arches a brow as he stares down, imploring me to tell everyone.

I drop my head to his chest, pulling strength from him. His proximity is enough to allow me to get the words out. "While you were traveling this week," I say to Cade, "Declan finished the music studio in his basement, and I finished three songs."

Cade steps closer, his lips parted. "Music studio?"

"So she doesn't have to go back to New York if she doesn't want to," Declan explains. His eyes are soft as he takes me in. Then he drops a kiss to my forehead. "But it's nothing special."

"That's not true," I tell everyone. "It has a piano and a guitar. It's soundproofed too. And the best part is that it's in Bristol. *My home.*"

Declan grasps my hip and squeezes. This isn't a surprise to him. He knows how I feel. Where I want to live. And who I want to live with.

But Cade is looking at us like we're offering him every wish he's ever had. "Really? You built a studio for her, Dec?"

"I don't want either of you to ever have a reason to leave," Declan says quietly. "My home is your home."

Cade's easy grin goes wide, both of his dimples popping. The reaction makes the man behind me suck in a breath. The way these two love one another, the way they love me, is beyond special. It's rare. And I'm going to hold on to it. Because it's a once-in-a-lifetime love.

"Ah, I love this!" Lake's declaration breaks our little spell.

I blink back to the moment, only then realizing that everyone is watching us.

"You're really moving to Bristol?" she asks, her hands clutched at her chest.

I glance at my two guys, then nod. "Yeah. I'm sure we'll be in Boston so we can attend Bolts games, but Bristol is where I'd like to create a life."

"Hope I don't burst your bubble when I say this," Ford says, "but you'll have to spend some of your time touring, because this new sound is going to sell out arenas."

"Bolts Arena being the first," Gavin adds at the same time Beckett says, "Lang Field should be the first stop."

Liv rolls her eyes. "Do you guys need to make everything about the Langfields?"

"Yes," all four brothers holler, making the room break out in a round of laughter.

"New sound?" Declan asks, his focus, as always, remaining on the three of us.

"Yes. It's less pop; more emotional. The guitar addition on the last one was perfect," Lake says.

I can't help but fill with pride. The songs I created are 100 percent my own. For so long, I've followed my best friend's lead. And even now, I'm moving to her town, settling down and starting what I hope is a family right beside her. But this—my music, my sound—it's all me.

Okay, maybe not all me. It's the three of us. It's this feeling of safety and joy, of being comfortable in my own skin for the first time in my life because these two men have given me the space to feel that way.

It's not conforming to what's expected of me, or aligning myself to what I think I should be doing to sell myself. It's alchemy. A complete transformation of my brand, of myself.

And I'm in love with it.

I can honestly say that not only do I love the men flanking me, but I finally love myself.

Perhaps that's why I can accept their love. Because I can see what they see in me. I can see how I fit them just as much as they fit me. How I need them just as much as they need me.

"Can we hear it?" Millie asks.

Everyone is in the room nodding, but I'm shaking my head. "Let's just listen to some Christmas carols. Tonight shouldn't be about me."

"Every night should be about you, sweetheart," Declan says, dropping a kiss to my neck. "But in case we weren't clear, we want to hear your music."

Everyone around us seems to talk at once, begging for me to share my new sound.

Lake is the loudest. "Please. I think this is your best song yet. I'm obsessed."

Emotion makes it hard to swallow. Tears blur my vision. For so long, I was told to sit in the corner. To hide behind others. To dim my light so others could shine.

But no one here wants that from me.

Not only have Declan and Cade shown me love, and shared each other's hearts with me, they've shared their family.

It's so different from past Christmases. Where I faded into the background. Made-up stories to keep myself company. For so long, my music was comprised of nothing but stories of other people's lives. Romances I created because I had no real experience to work with. But now, in this room, I feel that love I only ever tried to write about until now.

So, wrapped in Declan's arms, while holding Cade's hand, I allow Ford to pull out his phone and play them my newest song.

The rest of the group settles in, finding their loved ones, and we listen to my song. A song about love, about finding oneself. And both my guys smile at me when they realize it's the story of us.

Acknowledgments

With every book I write, I like to challenge myself in a different way. Flip tropes, make a reader like an unlikeable character, figure out how to make someone smile through my words. This book was no different. The idea for Declan's story came quick and shifted multiple times as I sat with how this relationship would work. Because that's always important to me. Just like you as the reader question motives and realities of our fictional characters choices, I agonize over these decisions. Because most importantly, I want their story to remain true to them. I don't write stories for shock value or to make you all throw your kindle, I write them because these stories vividly exist in my head and I can't not tell you their truths.

And as soon as Declan and Cade existed on the page, I knew this would not be an MFM. I knew that it would be a story about two people who have loved one another for years but didn't make sense until they met *her*. Melina was important. She was integral to their story. And they were integral to hers. The three of them belonged to one another, but they had to work to get there. And boy did I enjoy the ride of getting them there. I hope you did too. So thank you for allowing me to share every story as it exists in my head. My truth for the characters, even if it's messy and somewhat unconventional at times.

As always, this story wouldn't exist without some incredible people. My amazing work wives and besties, Sara and Jenni. My fantastic editor Beth. My beta readers Becca, Ari and Emily. The amazing people who help with my social media and marketing, Andi, Glav, Anna, Jess, Mackenzie and Courtney and my amazing street team who are always shouting from the rooftop about my books. Thank you! This year has been incredible because of all of you.

And to my amazing readers, thank you. Thank you for reading my words, for all of your edits and your reviews and your support for these last three years. You have changed my life more than you know.

If you want to follow along on my writing journey and have sneak peeks into all the characters in Bristol, follow me on Instagram, join my awesome Facebook group, sign-up for my newsletter and follow me on TikTok.

Also by Brittanée Nicole

Bristol Bay Rom Coms
She Likes Piña Coladas
Kisses Sweet Like Wine
Over the Rainbow

Bristol Bay Romance
Love and Tequila Make Her Crazy
A Very Merry Margarita Mix-Up

Boston Billionaires
Whiskey Lies
Loving Whiskey
Wishing for Champagne Kisses
Dirty Truths
Extra Dirty

Mother Faker
(Mother Faker is Book 1 of the Mom Com Series, but is also a lead in to the
Revenge Games alongside Revenge Era. This book can be read as a Standalone,
or after Revenge Era and before Pucking Revenge)

Revenge Games
Revenge Era
Pucking Revenge
A Major Puck Up

Boston Bolts Hockey
Hockey Boy

Trouble

Standalone Romantic Suspense

Deadly Gossip

Irish

Made in the USA
Columbia, SC
31 March 2025

55976455R00191